MURDER
Simply Brewed

Center Point
Large Print

Also by Vannetta Chapman and available from
Center Point Large Print:

A Perfect Square
Material Witness

AN AMISH VILLAGE MYSTERY
BOOK 1

MURDER
Simply Brewed

Vannetta
Chapman

CENTER POINT LARGE PRINT
THORNDIKE, MAINE

This Center Point Large Print edition is published in the year 2014 by arrangement with Zondervan.

All Scripture quotations, unless otherwise indicated, are taken from the Holy Bible, *New International Version®*, *NIV®*. Copyright © 1973, 1978, 1984 by Biblica, Inc.™ Used by permission. All rights reserved worldwide.

The text of this Large Print edition is unabridged. In other aspects, this book may vary from the original edition. Printed in the United States of America on permanent paper. Set in 16-point Times New Roman type.

ISBN: 978-1-62899-081-2

Library of Congress Cataloging-in-Publication Data

Chapman, Vannetta.
  Murder simply brewed : an Amish village mystery Vannetta Chapman. — Center Point Large Print edition.
pages ; cm
  ISBN 978-1-62899-081-2 (library binding : alk. paper)
  1. Amish—Fiction. 2. Murder—Investigation—Fiction.
  3. Large type books. I. Title.
PS3603.H3744M87 2014b
813′.6—dc23
                                                2014004011

⋙ About the Author ⋘

Vannetta Chapman is author of the bestselling novel *A Simple Amish Christmas*. She has published over one hundred articles in Christian family magazines, receiving over two dozen awards from Romance Writers of America chapter groups. In 2012 she was awarded a Carol Award for *Falling to Pieces*. She discovered her love for the Amish while researching her grandfather's birthplace of Albion, Pennsylvania. Chapman lives in the Texas hill country with her husband.

Center Point Large Print
600 Brooks Road / PO Box 1
Thorndike ME 04986-0001 USA

(207) 568-3717

US & Canada:
1 800 929-9108
www.centerpointlargeprint.com

For my friend, Kristy Kreymer

I call to the LORD, who is worthy of praise,
and I am saved from my enemies.
—2 Samuel 22:4

This is the inscription that was written:
MENE, MENE, TEKEL, PARSIN

Here is what these words mean:
God has numbered the days of your reign
and brought it to an end.
—Daniel 5:25–26

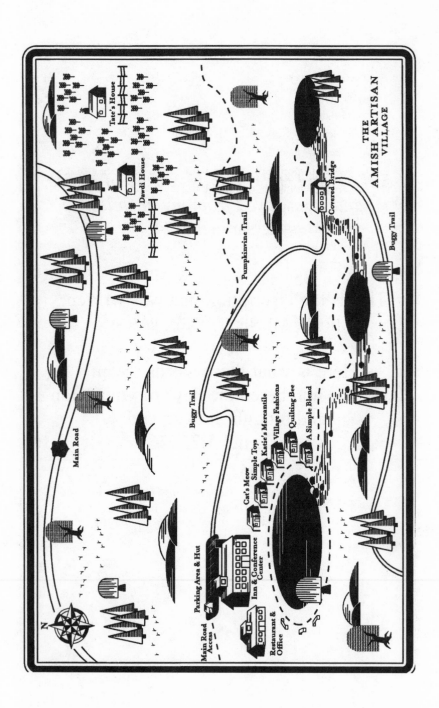

⇥ Author's Note ⇤

While this novel is set against the real back-drop of Middlebury, Indiana, the characters are fictional. There is no intended resemblance between the characters in this book and any real members of the Amish and Mennonite communities. As with any work of fiction, I've taken license in some areas of research as a means of creating the necessary circumstances for my characters. My research was thorough; however, it would be impossible to be completely accurate in details and descriptions, since each and every community differs. Therefore, any inaccuracies in the Amish and Mennonite life-styles portrayed in this book are completely due to fictional license.

Glossary

boppli—baby
bruder—brother
Dawdy Haus—grandfather's home
dat—father
danki—thank you
dochder—daughter
dochdern—daughters
Englischer—non-Amish person
freinden—friends
gern gschehne—you're welcome
Gotte's wille—God's will
grandkinner—grandchildren
grossdaddi—grandfather
gudemariye—good morning
gut—good
in lieb—in love
kaffi—coffee
kapp—prayer covering
kind—child
kinner—children
Loblied—praise song
mamm—mom
narrisch—crazy
nein—no
onkel—uncle
Ordnung—set of rules for Amish living

rumspringa—running around; time before an Amish young person has officially joined the church, provides a bridge between childhood and adulthood

schweschder—sister

wunderbaar—wonderful

ya—yes

MURDER
Simply Brewed

⇌ Prologue ⇌

Middlebury, Indiana
April 14

Amber Wright had the perfect job.

Five minutes after leaving work, she walked into her home, set her purse and keys on a small table by the front door, and proceeded to walk across the living room. Leo rubbed against her long denim skirt, meowing and generally kicking up quite a fuss. She squatted and scratched the yellow cat behind his ears, but he pulled away and strutted off to the kitchen, his tail high and his meows beckoning her.

"You cannot be starving."

Leo blinked at her, then wound a figure eight around her legs.

"Spoiled. That's what you are." She opened a can of cat food and dumped it into his bowl.

His purring increased until it resembled an idling engine.

"Your manners are deteriorating. You didn't even ask me about my day!" Amber moved to the refrigerator and peered inside, but she found nothing she could rustle up for dinner. Eggs maybe, except she'd had eggs the night before.

The doorbell rang before she could fall into

despair over her lack of cooking skills. Cooking? She didn't even bother to grocery shop. The Village kept her busy—the Amish Artisan Village. Set on seventy acres, it included an inn with one hundred rooms, a small conference center, a restaurant, a bakery, and six artisan shops. She loved her job as its general manager, even after twenty-two years. If working full days meant her diet suffered a bit, it was a price she was willing to pay. Besides, she could always order from their restaurant, which served tasty Amish dishes.

She looked through the front-door glass out at the beautiful Indiana afternoon and saw Larry Sharp, her assistant manager. He was holding a large bouquet of flowers. Larry was short, chubby, and had shockingly red hair. His skin was a pasty white—where it wasn't freckled. He certainly wouldn't win any beauty awards, but he was a top-notch assistant manager. Amber was happy to have him working at the Village.

She opened the inside door, then the storm door, and motioned him inside.

"For me?"

"Sorry to bother you. The florist delivered them at four thirty, not realizing you'd be gone."

"You mean they don't know that I arrive at work at seven in the morning? Service is slipping in this town." Amber carried the flowers—six yellow roses surrounded by daisies and baby's breath—into her dining room and set them on the table, with Larry following.

"Strange container." Larry eyeballed the pig-shaped vase that held the bouquet.

"Last time it was a boot, complete with spurs." Amber pointed to the corner bookcase near the dining room window. Every shelf was covered with an odd assortment of vases. "My sister has an interesting sense of humor. Miranda lives in Biloxi, Mississippi, and I have no idea where she finds such unusual vases."

Larry's gaze shifted from the newest bouquet, raked over the large, purple pig container, then flitted to the bookcase and back again. Finally he shook his head and muttered something that sounded like, "Women."

"Do you have time for a soda or some tea?"

"No. I need to get back. My boss likes super-vision on the property at all times."

"Indeed I do," Amber agreed as she walked him back out to the front porch.

"You haven't outgrown this house yet?" Larry stared at the tiny yard, the one-car detached garage, and the porch that was barely big enough for the two rockers she'd placed on it.

"Outgrow the *Dawdy Haus*? Never!" Amber loved her home. She thanked God for it every night. It was exactly the right size for her and Leo. The home was part of her salary package, provided by the owners of the Village, and it was

17

situated close enough to the offices that she could walk to work when the weather was pleasant.

Larry shrugged as he stepped off her porch and made his way down her front walk. He'd driven the golf cart over, a vehicle available to both of them though mostly Larry used it. He checked each store after closing, and the golf cart allowed him to move more quickly around the Village property. Amber followed him to the cart and was about to wave good-bye when a vintage blue-and-white pickup truck squealed out of the Village parking lot and down the road.

They both turned to stare after Ethan Gray. He was the manager of A Simple Blend, one of the shops that circled the small pond at the Village. Ethan accelerated the truck down the road, switching into the oncoming lane to pass a slow-moving sedan.

"Something wrong with Ethan?" Amber turned back toward Larry as she asked the question. For a brief moment, she caught his unguarded expression—what looked to be a combination of distaste, resentment, and an odd sort of satis-faction. Could those things be contained in one look? Yet Amber was certain those were the emotions playing out across his face.

"Larry?"

Her assistant manager blinked and then plastered a smile on his face. Starting up the golf cart, he muttered, "Best get back." He ignored her first question completely, and he acted as if he hadn't seen Ethan's mad race out of the Village parking lot.

Larry gave her a friendly wave and backed carefully out of her driveway. The *Dawdy Haus* was located on a small rise a short distance from the main Village property, so she was able to watch the progress of the cart as Larry made his way out onto the road and then back onto the Village property. He stopped and spoke with the parking attendant, though she couldn't see who this was, and then continued up to the main building in the Village, which housed the inn and the conference center.

Amber tucked her shoulder-length brown hair behind her ears.

Perhaps she'd imagined the expression on Larry's face, but she certainly had not dreamed up Ethan's strange exit. What was going on?

Leo had followed them out onto the porch. The lanky cat stretched and then sat on the welcome mat, his paws tucked beneath him.

Amber settled beside him on the porch steps and tried to figure out what had just happened. The last thing she needed at the Village was for two of her employees to be engaged in some sort of battle.

⇜ *One* ⇝

April 21, one week later

Hannah Troyer's Monday morning was off to a wonderful start.

She'd turned twenty-two the day before and was still feeling the joy of a new year. Nothing had gone wrong so far—no fights with her siblings, no disagreements with her parents, and no disastrous discussions with the two boys who seemed interested in courting her.

Everything was perfect.

She'd ridden her bicycle from her parents' home to the Amish Artisan Village, pedaling through the April morning along the Pumpkinvine Trail. The trail had been under construction by the town of Middlebury for some time. The portion that passed near her parents' home had been completed the previous year. She'd heard it would soon run from Elkhart all the way to Shipshewana. Although horses weren't allowed, it offered a wonderful path to travel while walking or biking.

The weather was cool but not cold. The green ash, American holly, and crab apple trees had all leafed out nicely into a dazzling display of green. She'd passed a few neighbors while riding—a few, but not too many. And she did feel pretty in her new lilac-colored dress and white prayer *kapp*.

Not that she was going to focus on her looks this year.

Vanity was a sin—one she struggled with of late, perhaps because of her age, or maybe because it seemed that boys suddenly acted differently around her. It wasn't so much that she thought she was beautiful. With her plain-colored brown hair, plain brown eyes, glasses, and too-thin build, she could best be described as average. She was fine with both being plain and being average, but she did realize that too often she focused on how she looked. It had been six months since she'd joined the church. That was an important day in her life. She'd confessed her faith in Christ before their congregation and vowed to follow the rules of their *Ordnung*.

So why did she struggle with vanity? She liked new dresses and pinning her *kapp* where a bit of her hair peeked through. Even the new glasses weren't bad. They were small brown frames with flecks of blue that made her eyes pop. She'd wanted the bright blue glasses but hadn't dared to buy them. They weren't *simple* at all.

As she pedaled into the Village parking lot, she tried to puzzle out her feelings. She loved their plain style of clothing, because it was how she'd always dressed. Wearing *Englisch* clothes had not been part of her *rumspringa*, though she had once tried to drive a car. That had been disastrous when she'd backed it into the tree near her friend's front porch.

No automobiles? No problem.

Plain clothing? Fine.

Hers was more a problem of attitude—braiding her hair different ways to see which was most attractive, choosing fabric with colors that accented her eyes, wondering if a small touch of blush and powder on her cheeks might help her look a tad bit older. She hadn't actually worn makeup, but she'd thought about it. The new glasses were something she needed because her prescription had changed. But the new frames? Those were a luxury that she'd paid for with the money she'd saved from her job.

Yesterday had been her birthday, and today was a new beginning. She did not want a guilty conscience worrying her as she began her twenty-second year. Or was it twenty-third? Birthdays always confused her. Was she ending a year or beginning one?

Her youngest sibling, Mattie, had turned two after Christmas. She had celebrated the end of her second year, which meant yesterday Hannah had celebrated the end of her twenty-second year. She was beginning her twenty-third year. The thought brought a huge smile to her face. Twenty-three had a nice ring to it.

She stored her bicycle in the shed behind the inn and set off on the path that circled the pond.

Most of the buildings that made up the Village had been added on to the property as the business grew. The original buildings, the restaurant and inn, were located with easy access to the parking lot. The inn was the largest structure with the conference center addition attached to it. This building stretched across the entire northern end of the pond. Branching away and to the south was a concrete path that led around the tranquil water.

She'd seen pictures from years ago, pictures that were framed and hanging on the wall in the inn's lobby. Back then the pond had looked like something in a farmer's pasture. Weeds grew high around it and cows grazed nearby.

Now there was the path circling the pond with trees that provided shade, and the grounds crew kept the bushes trimmed and the grass cut. The six shops began at the inn and stretched halfway around the pond. The other half of the walk had benches where guests could rest. If you walked the entire thing, which only took ten minutes at the most, you ended up right back at the center of the complex, near the inn and the restaurant.

She could have taken a shortcut from the parking lot, through the lobby of the inn, and back out the far door. But the April sunshine beckoned her outside. She enjoyed working in the quilt shop on the far side of the pond. Carol Jennings managed the Quilting Bee. She was a fair boss, if a bit strict.

Hannah was used to strict, so she had no problem with her boss's rules. One rule was that the shop must be opened by eight a.m. on the dot, which meant Hannah had to arrive at seven thirty. There was the display board to set out on the walk. The music needed to be turned on, filling the shop with the tunes Carol insisted had been proven to soothe shoppers and put them in a buying mood. Any dusting had to be done before the door was opened because Carol wanted her clerks to give complete attention to customers.

The concrete path that skirted the pond was completely empty. Several of the stores did not open until eight thirty or even nine. Hannah had the morning walk to herself. She enjoyed the sweet moments of solitude. Occasionally she peeked at her reflection in the shop windows. When she did, she would smooth down her apron or adjust her *kapp* slightly. She rather liked being the one to open the shop. She enjoyed the moments of quiet before the day began.

No one else bothered to come so early.

No one except old Ethan Gray, who would have arrived ahead of her. His shop, A Simple Blend, was the last in the line that circled the northern and eastern sides of the pond. The shop practically adjoined theirs. Only a small grassy area separated the two buildings. All day, Hannah smelled *kaffi* and lattes and espresso. All day, *Englischers* strolled to the end of the line of shops to purchase

Ethan's drinks. Once they had their first quota of caffeine firmly grasped in their hands, some of those customers would blink twice, notice the Quilting Bee was open, and walk inside.

Hannah unlocked the front door of their shop and hurried to the back room. She still had twenty minutes to prepare for opening, but she would rather be ready a minute early than a minute late. Mrs. Jennings had told her more than once, "Hannah, you do everything I ask and you complete the task early. You're a *gut* girl."

Her boss wasn't Amish, but sometimes the Pennsylvania Dutch words they used slipped into her vocabulary. Perhaps she'd lived among the Amish for so long, she was almost Amish.

The next twenty minutes passed quickly. She made sure there was plenty of change in the cash register. Checked the roll of register tape and checked that there was an extra under the counter. Turned on the music and dusted the shelves of their bookcase, which held quilting books. Where did so much dust come from? Hadn't she done the same thing two days ago?

Satisfied that everything was ready, she walked to the front door and turned the sign to "Open." The temperature was supposed to rise to the low sixties, so she propped the door open with a life-size iron cat. Then she moved their Daily Specials board out in front of their display window. It was a chalkboard, like the ones in her old schoolhouse, but built on an A-frame. Each day Carol had different items on sale so that customers staying several nights at the inn would return. The board currently declared, "Fat Squares for Spring—Starting at $1.29."

She pushed up her glasses and pivoted in a circle, studying the walk, the pond, and then their shop. Something was wrong.

Hannah reached for the strings of her prayer *kapp* and ran her fingers from the tops to the bottoms. She again checked the sign. It looked fine to her. She glanced left and then behind her, but saw nothing out of place. Ducks were floating on the pond. A few customers had stepped out of the inn and were walking down to the water's edge. The Quilting Bee's display window sparkled —sunny and inviting, showcasing a pretty variety of spring fabrics.

So what was amiss?

Why was there a niggling doubt at the back of her prayer *kapp*?

Kaffi!

She didn't smell Ethan's *kaffi*, which he always had brewing well before she arrived.

Stepping to her right and moving into A Simple Blend's front flower bed, which was a little muddy from the sprinklers, she pushed up on her glasses again and tried to peer through the front window. When she did, her mind had trouble piecing together what she saw.

There were several holes in the bottom left corner of the store's window, and cracks in the glass had webbed out in every direction.

What could have caused such a thing?

When could it have happened?

Her heart beat in a triple rhythm and her hands slicked with sweat as she moved closer. She again attempted to peer through the window, but it was like trying to look through broken eyeglasses.

Slowly, she continued past the window to the door and tried the handle.

It was unlocked!

Where was Ethan?

A dozen tiny spiders slipped down Hannah's spine. She slapped at her neck, then chided herself. There were no spiders. She was acting like a silly child.

Still, she whispered a prayer.

Of course the door was unlocked. It was nearly eight o'clock. It was time for them to begin their day, a perfect day up until this moment. Hannah chided herself again for hesitating. The shop was no longer locked because old Ethan was inside making *kaffi*, and soon she would smell its rich aroma drifting outside and down the sidewalk.

But the window . . .

She pulled the door open, intending to step inside and call out to Ethan.

Which was when she saw him.

Her heart slammed against her chest and she stumbled backward.

Ethan lay slumped sideways over the front counter, one hand at his heart and the other resting on top of a spilled pile of dark *kaffi* beans. He'd never placed the beans into the grinder, and Hannah realized as she rushed to his side that he never would.

Ethan Gray was dead.

She stopped short of the body, stopped and prayed that he had found favor in God's eyes and that even now he was standing with the angels.

Amber Wright had been at her desk in her office on the second floor above the Village restaurant for nearly an hour when her cell phone rang. The switchboard didn't open until eight, but a recording directed visitors to dial nine for an emergency and she had any such calls forwarded straight to her cell. No doubt this was not an emergency, but whoever was calling probably thought it was, thought whatever it was couldn't wait until eight a.m. when the offices opened. Ninety-nine times out of a hundred, it could.

Years ago, when she'd first started the job as general manager of Amish Artisan Village, she'd learned that her only moments of uninterrupted quiet were from seven to eight in the morning. So when her phone rang at seven fifty-five, she was not happy. She'd been counting on that additional five minutes.

"Amber Wright." She aimed for a pleasant but busy tone.

"It's Ethan. Ethan is . . . what I mean to say is he's . . ."

"Slow down."

The young girl on the other end of the line sounded frantic. Her voice trembled and her Pennsylvania Dutch accent was strong. So strong Amber had trouble making out what she was saying. The girl sounded as if she had been running. Amber could hear her panic loud and clear—more clearly than the words she was stumbling over.

"Who is this?"

"Hannah, but that doesn't matter. What matters is Ethan, and he's . . ."

Amber's mind combed over the nearly five hundred employees and landed on a young Amish girl. "Hannah. You work at the quilt shop, correct?"

"*Ya*, but it's Ethan I'm calling about. He's—"

"Ethan Gray." Ethan had been at the Village longer than Amber had, and she'd been there more than two decades. She'd taken the job straight out of college. In all those years, she'd never heard anyone sound so desperate.

Now the girl's story came out in a rush, like a storm blowing down from Lake Michigan. "Ethan from the *kaffi* shop, *ya*. I noticed I couldn't smell *kaffi* yet, and I stepped over to check on him, and that was when I saw the glass. The glass was all cracked and I couldn't see through it. I opened the door, and I found him. He's . . . he's dead."

"Hannah, I want you to take a deep breath." Amber was already logging off her computer and grabbing her tablet and ring of keys—the keys she never left her office without. There was no telling what room or closet she might need access to. They'd been meaning to master key the entire Village, so a single key would open any door, but it kept being pushed down her to-do list. Until then, she and Larry each carried a large ring of keys. The tablet she took with her out of pure habit. She typed all her notes on the tablet.

Amber pressed her cell phone tightly against her ear as she rushed out of her office. She wanted to keep the girl talking.

Her office assistant, Elizabeth, was at her desk in the reception area outside Amber's office. She was bent over, storing her purse in her bottom desk drawer, and all Amber could see as she rushed out was the top of the woman's gray head.

Elizabeth called out, "Something wrong?"

But Amber slowed for only a few seconds as she started down the stairs and then hollered up, "Call 9-1-1. Have them meet me at A Simple Blend. We need an ambulance." Then she fled down the remaining stairs and out the door into the hall of the restaurant.

Maybe Ethan had passed out.

Maybe he merely looked dead.

She prayed the girl was mistaken.

"Are you still on the line, Hannah?"

"*Ya.* I'm here."

"Where are you now?"

"In the quilt shop. I ran back to use our phone. I left him there. He's alone. Shouldn't I—"

"Hannah, you're doing great. You did the right thing. I want you to go next door and make sure his sign is turned to 'Closed.' Make sure no customers go into that shop. Do you understand?"

"No customers."

"Right. I'm on my way now. I can be there—"

It sounded like Hannah dropped the phone. Amber heard it clatter and could make out the sound of shoes slapping against the floor. She had intended to keep the conversation going in the hopes she could calm the girl down. But Hannah had done exactly as directed. No doubt she was headed next door to close the shop and stand guard at the door.

There was a moderate crowd in the restaurant, but few seemed to pay attention to her. One older Hispanic man held the outside door open as she rushed through it. The shops fanned out around the pond from the central point of the inn and

31

restaurant. They made a nice little village—and the name Amish Artisan Village fit what she was staring at perfectly. The shops offered products made by local Amish men and women. Amber considered them all to be artists, whether they sewed quilts or made wooden toys or baked. She was proud of the fact that their stores offered original Amish goods and in the process helped to provide income for local families.

Inn with a conference center. Restaurant. Shops.

The Village had expanded over the years until now it circled halfway around the pond. Ethan had always worked at a coffee booth, which had originally sat next to the restaurant. A year ago, they'd moved him to a shop on the far side of the other shops, hoping the desire for a strong cup of coffee would lure shoppers as they strolled down the walk, which circled the pond. It had worked. Sales had been up 12 percent since they'd made the move. Some customers even skipped morning coffee at the restaurant and went straight to A Simple Blend.

But now something had happened, and she knew deep down that today she would have more to worry about than sales.

⇒ *Two* ⇐

Tate Bowman stood in the middle of his field at the fence gate separating his two western pastures. He stood there and stared after the ambulance and police car speeding past his farm. Their declaration of emergency split the morning and shattered the pleasant peace of springtime.

Not that the morning had been completely calm, though it had started well enough.

Tate had risen at five, brewed coffee, and fixed a bowl of steaming oatmeal. He knew many folks stopped eating oatmeal in the spring, switching to cold cereals instead, but the sugary stuff didn't stay with him like a large bowl of oatmeal sprinkled with brown sugar and raisins. Which was possibly every ounce as sweet as the store-bought stuff, but it seemed like a more natural breakfast. At least that's what he told himself.

Yes, the day had started out peaceful enough, with time for a second cup of coffee and a few moments spent reading. He was in the sixth chapter of Luke, having started back through the Gospels at the first of the year. He couldn't claim to understand the Scripture any better this time around. He'd been doggedly sticking with the Good Book though, because he knew Peggy would want him to continue reading and studying. But since her death, the words fell flat and meaningless around him.

He might not understand Luke, but he could relate to him a little. The disciple who had been a doctor was the easiest of Christ's followers for him to grapple with. Luke seemed to see things like a common man, like someone who worked out among everyday folk.

He had the feeling Luke would be someone he'd like to sit down with for a cup of coffee. Ask him to clarify a few things. But that wasn't possible, and he'd pushed the questions away and headed outside to tend to the animals.

The morning had immediately gone downhill.

His two new donkeys, which were supposed to act as guards to protect the cattle, had managed to butt their way out of the field he'd put them in for the evening. They'd wanted in with the horses for some reason. And the horses had scattered in with the cattle. Not a big problem, since the cattle were up near the house, and his two mares were grazing near the road. But Tate knew from experience that it was best to keep the animals separate. So he'd set about repairing the fence at the point where the donkeys had broken through.

He was in the middle of the job when the ambulance and police car tore down the road and pulled into the Village.

Tate set the new post into the ground and poured the concrete he'd mixed around it, filling up the hole. The old post had rotted during the winter, which was why the donkeys had been able to push through it. He accepted responsibility for the resulting break in the fence. He should have repaired it sooner, but interior fences weren't usually a priority.

The donkeys aggravated him, which was why he'd put off buying any. But most folks insisted they were a necessary part of life if you were going to raise animals and work a farm. And Tate had recently lost two cows to coyotes. At least it had appeared to him to be coyotes, based on what was left of them. The one sure protection against coyotes, as far as he knew, was donkeys. So he'd purchased them almost a month ago. He didn't particularly like the animals, and so far it seemed all they had done was create havoc and roll on the ground, scratching their backs against the hard soil. Maybe the fact that he hadn't lost any more cattle to coyotes, though, meant they were earning their feed.

The emergency vehicles were another problem altogether.

He supposed the apostle Luke would have been concerned about whatever was happening on the property next door. Maybe he would have hustled over and offered his medical skills, but Tate didn't have any medical skills. He had farming skills. He'd chosen to be a farmer thirty years ago, following a brief stint in the army, which had followed his graduation from college.

He'd chosen farming because he enjoyed the quiet life.

He could have made more money in another profession, but money didn't matter that much to him. Work with results you could see and be proud of did matter. His wife, Peggy, had once said she'd never guessed a man could be so happy as long as he had mud on his boots and calluses on his hands. Peggy had understood him—that was for certain. There wasn't a day that went by when he didn't miss her. Four years had passed, and still his life didn't seem completely whole. He supposed it never would.

The emergency vehicles were out of sight, but their sirens continued to splinter the morning's quiet, as if folks couldn't tell it was an emergency by the pulsing lights alone. He suspected one of the Village guests had managed to fall into the pond or slip on the dewy grass. Those folks should stay in the city. They came from Chicago and Fort Wayne and Indianapolis. They didn't belong in a small town, didn't know how to react when they were in one, and usually caused trouble.

Like this morning.

He realized that was an uncharitable thought, but the Village had a way of bringing out the worst in him.

Tate braced the fence post with a board he wedged into the ground, giving it a little added support until the concrete had time to set up properly. Then he picked up the bucket that held the remaining concrete. As long as he was mending fences, he might as well walk the line and see what else had managed to work its way loose. He'd checked the exterior fence line when the snows had melted, but with the addition of the two new donkeys, he might have to increase his patrolling to a monthly chore.

The blaring sirens fell quiet, and Tate stopped and stared over toward the Village. He could think of two reasons that could have happened. Either it wasn't an emergency—the place had been known for false alarms—or someone had died.

He knew most of the emergency personnel. He had grown up with the older ones, and his two sons had grown up with the younger ones. It was standard procedure to cut the sirens if someone died. Almost seemed like a way of respecting the dead.

Tate was glad that for the moment, peace and quiet had returned to his corner of Middlebury. He found himself whistling as he turned his back on the Village and continued walking down the fence line.

Amber watched in disbelief as the paramedics loaded Ethan's body on a gurney and wheeled it down the sidewalk past each of her shops. Within moments they had settled him into the back of the ambulance, slapped the doors shut, and driven the emergency vehicle out of the parking area.

How could this have happened?

Thoughts circled so quickly in her mind that she almost felt dizzy—prayers for Ethan's family, concern for Hannah, and an ever-growing list of things that would need to be done.

A small crowd of guests had assembled and seemed uncertain what to do now that the drama was over.

"Thank you for your concern, folks." Amber's hands were shaking, but she clasped them around her tablet and pushed on. "We're sorry for any inconvenience. There will be free coffee in the restaurant for everyone. We hope you enjoy the rest of your stay here at the Village."

Turning away from the group, she called the restaurant on her cell phone and alerted them that coffee would be complimentary for the rest of the day. They didn't offer Ethan's strong brew, but it would have to do until she thought of a way to reopen the shop.

"Can I talk to you, Amber?" Gordon Avery touched her arm as he slipped his notepad back into his shirt pocket.

She sometimes wondered how he managed to carry so much on his six-foot frame. Buckled to his belt were the tools of his trade—his holstered service weapon, pepper spray, a Taser, flashlight, phone, knife, baton, and handcuffs. He seemed prepared for anything. His black hair, which didn't have a speck of gray, was trimmed neatly. And unlike the cartoon police officers she'd seen on late-night television when her nieces came to visit, he was physically fit. His age was the same as hers, nearly forty-five, so the fitness part was an achievement.

Or maybe things were different for men.

A few lines fanned out from his brown eyes. The wrinkles spread when he squinted at her, holding his hand up to shield his eyes from the morning sun. "Maybe we should go somewhere private."

"Sure. Yes, of course."

Amber turned to Hannah, who was still standing outside the quilt shop. The young girl, in her early twenties if Amber remembered correctly, looked lost. She was approximately Amber's height and build—in a word, petite. Her chestnut brown hair was braided and covered with the traditional white *kapp*. A dark purple-colored apron covered her dress, which was lilac. Her eyes glistened behind her glasses, and she stood there waiting as if she were cemented to the concrete walk.

"Hannah, I'm going to step away and speak with Officer Avery. You can go back into your shop now, unless you'd rather go home."

"*Nein*. I want to stay and work." The girl continued to run her fingers up and down her *kapp* strings.

She had calmed down considerably since the

initial phone call. Amber was tempted to insist she take off the rest of the day, but possibly the girl was right. Possibly working would help to restore her day to a normal footing.

Hannah was completely opposite the young girl Amber had been. Hannah was quiet, serious, and an excellent worker. When Amber was her age, she'd been a bit too loud, much too energetic, and completely clueless when it came to handling life's ups and downs. When she'd first been employed at the Village as an assistant manager, she'd been good at juggling the various duties, but it had taken her years to learn to do so calmly.

Hannah's life experiences were no doubt different as well. Amber didn't have any idea how to comfort her or even if she needed to do so. She had met and supervised a lot of Amish employees over the years. In her mind, they probably handled matters of life and death more calmly than most. At the moment though, Hannah didn't look exactly composed. Her eyes were wide, her face pale, and her hands constantly worried the *kapp* strings. Still, Amber needed someone in the quilt shop until Carol arrived, and if Hannah was offering—

"Excellent. I'll check back with you later today."

Hannah nodded once and turned to enter the quilt shop. A few customers followed her inside. Perhaps things would return to normal faster than

Amber had anticipated. Already crews were working to board up the window on Ethan's shop until the broken glass could be replaced.

"How about over there?" Amber indicated a wooden bench farther down the walk that circled the pond. "I could use the walk and a few minutes away from . . . everyone."

"The bench is fine." Gordon reached out to cup her elbow, then pulled back his hand.

They walked in silence. The sight of trees budding, ducks on the water, and gardeners tending the flower beds helped to calm Amber's nerves. She didn't know what she'd expected to see when she arrived at Ethan's shop, but it had never occurred to her that he would actually be dead.

They sat on the bench, spring sunshine falling around them, and didn't speak for a moment. Gordon was good about that—good about giving her time when she needed it.

"Will there be an investigation?"

"No need. Nothing appeared out of the ordinary."

Ordinary?

One of her oldest workers, one of her most faithful employees, had died within an hour of arriving at work. She folded her hands together, pushed down her frustration, and turned to the sergeant for the Middlebury Police Department. "Explain it to me."

"Gray arrived at work, probably around six thirty according to the parking attendant who saw him pull into the lot. It looks like he was about to make his first pot of coffee when someone pelted the window with shots from a BB gun."

"You're sure it was—"

"Yes. We found the round shot—steel BBs. They were coated with copper, which is standard. Three of them were on the floor of the shop."

"And that's what killed him?"

"No. BBs might leave a bruise if the shooter is close enough, but they're not fatal. And through glass? It would be startling, not dangerous. The BBs couldn't have killed him."

"Then how did he die?"

"Heart attack. We don't know whether he was aware of a heart condition. Looks like the BB shots startled him, he clutched his chest, and died before he could call for help."

Amber's hand went to her throat. "How terrible."

She closed her eyes and prayed again that Ethan had found peace in his last few moments, and that his family's faith would sustain them during this time.

The song of a bird in a nearby tree brought her back to the present, to the bench, and to Gordon waiting patiently beside her.

"Why would someone want to shoot at his window? Why harass him?"

"My best guess is that it's a simple act of

vandalism. We don't know that their intent was to harm him. It's doubtful anyone knew about his heart condition. Did you?"

"No."

"Possibly he didn't either." Gordon paused, glanced around, and then continued. "Ethan wasn't the most pleasant man in town. He had a reputation for running off kids, right?"

"Well, yes, but—"

"If I remember correctly, he even reported them to us more than once."

Amber smiled for the first time in over an hour. "I finally convinced him to call me before he called the police. I assured him I'd take care of any pranksters. But this, this isn't a practical joke. This killed someone."

"No. A heart attack killed him. The paramedics confirmed as much, and my best guess is an autopsy would too, though I imagine his family will pass on that. Autopsies are nasty things, and I certainly wouldn't recommend it in this case."

"So you think—you're sure—he died from natural causes, a heart attack?"

"I'm as sure as I can be. The three shots were directed at the bottom left of the front plate glass window. It would have been obvious from the lights on inside that Ethan was standing behind the counter to the right."

"They weren't aiming at him."

"No, and there's no other indication of foul

play. If someone were robbing him, they would have taken the cash in the drawer."

"What about the muddy footprints I saw?"

"All accounted for. We checked the size and the tread. All prints matched Hannah's. She got her shoes muddy when she stepped into the flower bed."

Amber blew out a sigh of relief and allowed the muscles in her shoulders to relax. It was bad to have an employee die, especially at work. But at least it was from natural causes. Everyone died sometime, and Ethan had died doing what he seemed to love best—brewing his rich, dark blend of coffee. He loved coffee and he positively doted on his old truck.

Gordon was right. Certainly there was no need for an autopsy or an investigation. She didn't want any of the kind of legal mess they'd been having in Shipshewana the last few years. The place seemed to have a murder every six months, though at least they'd all been solved. She suppressed a shudder and turned back to Gordon.

"Anything else?"

"If you'd like, you can file a vandalism report to help with the cost to replace the broken glass."

Amber shook her head so hard that her shoulder-length hair fell forward, obscuring her view. She tucked it behind her ears and explained, "More trouble than it's worth, thank you. We have money in the budget for repairs."

"I thought that would be your response."

They sat for another few moments while Amber opened her tablet and made a few notes.

"Any more questions?"

"No. Thank you for taking the time to sit with me. You could have merely emailed me a report." She reached out and placed her hand on his arm. "I appreciate it, Gordon."

They stood and turned back toward the shops. Her to-do list had grown in the last hour, so she might as well hop to it.

She thought by the look in his eyes and the hesitation before he said good-bye that Gordon would ask her to dinner. He didn't. He seemed to know intuitively that she would say no, that she would need time to herself.

Gordon was like that.

Some days he understood her better than she understood herself.

⇥ *Three* ⇤

Hannah was relieved that they had a steady stream of customers in the quilt shop all morning. Working helped to push her mind away from what had happened next door.

She enjoyed cutting fabric, helping customers choose from among their sewing kits, and selling quilts sewn by women in her community. At times she was certain she'd been born to work in a quilt shop. Whether she was sewing something for display or helping a customer, she felt completely at ease.

Within the first hour she sold a Log Cabin quilt that Fanny Bontrager had stitched. Hannah knew for a fact that the Bontragers could use that money. Her boss, Carol, paid the women what they had earned on the last day of the month, so Fanny would receive a nice check at the end of the following week. Hannah would be sure to mention the sale to Fanny when she saw her at church on Sunday.

Sunday was six days away.

It seemed like an eternity.

Pulling off her glasses, she brushed them clean with the hem of her apron. Maybe she should stop by and talk to the bishop on her way home. She was having trouble banishing the image of poor old Ethan from her mind. Her stomach started tumbling whenever she remembered how he'd looked—surprised and cold and older. How could one look older after they were dead?

How could that have been *Gotte's wille*? He died alone. He died at work! From the expression on his face, he'd suffered his last few minutes.

Talking to her bishop would be a good idea.

Carol had arrived after Hannah had gone back inside and Ethan's body was already gone. When Hannah told her what had happened, she had pursed her lips in a straight line and crossed her arms, as if she needed to hug herself. She seemed upset but not surprised to hear such tragic news. Hannah wanted to ask her if she'd known that Ethan had a heart condition. After all, they'd both worked for the Village for years, and she'd seen them talking together on more than one occasion. She had no chance to question her though, because customers started spilling in and they stayed busy up through her lunch break.

"Go on out and have your lunch," Carol had said as soon as the hands on the clock tagged eleven thirty.

"But—"

"No buts. You've been here four hours, and a difficult four hours it's been. Go outside. The sunshine will do you good."

Hannah didn't argue. She knew from experience that disagreeing with Carol was as productive as arguing with her own mother. Instead, she went into the back stockroom, removed her lunch bag from the small refrigerator, and headed outside. She started out the door, then ducked back inside to check her image in the mirror that hung on the wall in the bathroom. There was no telling whom she would run into, and she didn't want to look all out of sorts, though she still felt that way. Tucking a few wayward strands of hair back into her *kapp*, she leaned close to the mirror and studied her face. Her complexion was deathly pale. Maybe she would stop on the way home and purchase a little makeup. Maybe it wouldn't be such a sin to try a touch of blush and powder. She'd read that cosmetics contained sunscreen now, which would make the decision more practical and less about her appearance.

She walked across the bridge that spanned the creek on the east side of the property. It was an old-fashioned covered bridge painted red, and never failed to make her smile. Hannah admitted that Carol was right. It did feel better to be outside. The temperature had risen into the sixties, as promised. The sun was shining brightly. *Englisch* children were tossing pieces of bread at the ducks. Life continued around the Village, the same as any other day.

She sat under the kousa dogwood tree and opened her lunch bag. She'd sewn the bag last week, using leftover scraps of fabric. It was reinforced with batting on the bottom and had a drawstring on the top. Hannah loved the patchwork of colors—flowered calico prints, a light purple, blue, yellow, and green. Her mother had frowned at the calico fabric. She still insisted on sewing with only solid colors, which was old-fashioned and not required by their *Ordnung*. Hannah liked the calico print. Carol had also liked it. She'd immediately suggested that Hannah make more and sell them in the shop.

But even her new lunch bag could only distract

her for a moment. She stared out across the creek and back toward the pond, back toward Ethan's shop. How could she eat? Looking at the food made her nauseated. When she'd packed the hard-boiled egg, sliced ham, cheese, and apple the night before, the entire thing had sounded delicious. But she hadn't known then that during her first hour at work she'd be finding a dead body.

"Are you going to eat that or stare at it?" Jesse Miller plopped down beside her on the grass. His blue eyes sparkled mischievously as he pulled her lunch bag toward him and peered inside. "Looks *gut*."

Hannah's hands went to her glasses. She adjusted them and then attempted a smile. "*Ya*, I suppose, but I don't feel much like eating. You take it."

Jesse grinned up at her, his light brown hair—nearly blond if you looked at him in a certain light—framing his face. She hadn't seen him on Sunday, since this wasn't their week to have church service. She admitted to herself that she'd missed him. He was dressed in traditional Amish clothing, which included dark pants, black suspenders, a blue work shirt, and a straw hat. When he took off his hat and placed it on the ground between them, Hannah noticed that his mother had cut his hair. She must have done it over the weekend, because it was shorter than it had been when she'd seen him Friday. His ears practically poked out from the sides of his head. Instead of looking silly, he looked more handsome. Why was that? What was it about Jesse Miller that caused her heart to skip a beat now and again?

"I heard Ethan Gray was gasping for breath when you found him. That he told you a secret."

"*Nein*. He wasn't gasping. The medical people, they said he'd been dead for nearly an hour."

"That so?" Jesse reached for a cube of cheese from her lunch and popped it into his mouth.

"And so of course he didn't tell me a secret. What secret could old Ethan have? All he did was work at the *kaffi* shop and then go home and work on that old truck of his."

"Truck's a beauty. I wonder who will get it."

Hannah slapped his arm.

"What?"

"The man isn't even in the grave yet."

"I meant no disrespect. It's a natural thing to wonder."

Hannah rolled her eyes and stared down the creek bed at some children who were attempting to fish in the gently running water. She could have told them their odds of success were better over at the pond, but they seemed to be enjoying themselves even though they weren't catching anything.

"Are you sure you don't want any of this food?"

"*Nein*." Hannah pushed the lunch bag closer to him. "Didn't you bring anything?"

"Sure. I ate it already." He pulled out the slice of ham, folded it in quarters, and waved it at her. When she shook her head, the ham disappeared into his mouth same as the cheese.

"*Danki*," Jesse said. He lay back in the grass, tilting his hat over his eyes to block out the sun.

"Doesn't it bother you?" Hannah lay back and stared up at the dogwood tree.

"Doesn't what bother me?"

"Having someone die. Right here on the property."

Jesse took his time answering. She thought he might have fallen asleep in the April sunshine, but then he rolled over toward her and looked her in the eye. Whenever he did that, her stomach jumped and her hands began to sweat. Did that mean something? Did it mean she should agree to go to the singing with him, if he asked again?

"Everyone has to die somewhere." His voice grew quieter, more serious. "Every life reaches a natural end, as Joseph reminded us at the last service."

"I know he did, and I do listen to the words of our bishop. It's only that he's so young—not much older than my *onkel*. Do you think he understands as much as Hans did?"

Jesse raised up on one elbow and studied her. "Hans was a *gut* bishop. His moving away was

51

understandable, since he wanted to live with his children in Ohio. But we will miss him."

"He's the only bishop I've ever had."

"Change can be difficult, but don't doubt that Joseph was chosen by God and that he will lead us well."

"*Ya.*" Hannah hesitated, and then she added, "When did you become so wise?"

"Must be the extra lunch." Jesse lay back down and repositioned his hat over his eyes. "I suppose Ethan would have been happy to die at work, or maybe in the classic Ford he loved so much."

Hannah squirreled up her nose. "That old truck? I never understood why he cared so much for it."

"Huh. Must be a man thing. The truck is a work of art."

"Jesse Miller, you sound like an *Englischer.*"

Instead of being offended, Jesse grinned at her from beneath the brim of his hat. "Didn't say I wanted one. I'm happy with my team."

"Sam and Sadie are just about the most beautiful horses I've ever seen."

Jesse nodded in agreement, but he added, "Still, I wouldn't mind driving Ethan's truck."

Hannah didn't know what to say to that, so she stared up at the dogwood tree instead. Finally she asked, "How well did you know him?"

"Occasionally we'd leave work at the same time. We talked about his truck. Once he asked me about my horses, asked if I was satisfied getting around without a combustible engine."

"A what?"

"A car."

"What did you say?"

"I told him that I wasn't worried about the price of gas, only the cost of feed. I also reminded him that since we grow our own feed, the cost isn't much of a problem."

Hannah thought about that a minute. She sat up and pulled the drawstring on her lunch bag, which still held the hard-boiled egg, apple, and some of the cheese. "I never talked to him much. Now and then to say good morning. I'd watch his place for him once in a while, but he left instructions written out for me instead of explaining things himself. He didn't seem like a happy man."

"How so?"

"Several times he'd be out front, sweeping his walk even though you guys on the grounds crew take care of that. Most of the time he'd be muttering about kids and how disrespectful they are."

"Maybe that's what got him killed."

Jesse stood when she did. She thought he might attempt to hold hands with her as they headed back to the Quilting Bee, but he didn't. They did walk close enough that their shoulders were touching.

"Nothing got him killed. He died of natural

causes. Heart attack, that's what the paramedics said."

"*Ya*, but rumor is that whoever did it, whoever peppered his window with BBs—that person knew about his heart condition."

"They couldn't have known."

"That's not what I heard. I heard that several things had happened in the last week, things that were making him anxious. The old guy was probably on edge wondering what would happen next. When the BBs came sailing through, his heart finally gave out."

Hannah stopped on the path that circled the pond. They were in sight of A Simple Blend. She could see the plywood board that had been placed over the window. Her back to the pond, she stared up into Jesse's eyes.

"Who would do that? Why would they do that?"

"It's a mystery for sure, but since it was a BB rifle—" Jesse stopped midsentence and waved to someone across the pond. "I have to go. Harvey doesn't abide anyone taking over thirty minutes for lunch."

"But—"

"I'll catch up with you later." Jesse reached for her hand and squeezed it once, then he began whistling as he hurried around the pond toward Harvey Jones.

Hannah had spoken to the man twice in the

two years she'd worked at the Village. He was the supervisor of the grounds crew, and he seemed even more strict than her boss.

She walked slowly back to the quilt shop.

It was natural for everyone to talk after what had happened, but she thought they had it all wrong. They had to have it wrong. Ethan had died of natural causes. His old heart had given out, and he'd died. As she walked into the shop, she convinced herself that there was nothing more to it.

Amber didn't make it back to her office until three in the afternoon. She practically groaned as she sank into her chair. Though she was used to the rigors of running a complex the size of a small community, some days wore her out more than others. Today was one of those days.

There was a small stack of phone messages on her desk. Elizabeth had placed them there in order of importance. Her mail, opened and neatly stacked, sat in the tray on her desk. All she needed was a hot cup of tea. That would be enough to help her push through the last few hours of her day.

Elizabeth appeared at her door, holding a steaming mug. Her usual smile was missing, and her round face with gentle wrinkles was somber, worried even. Amber admired the woman for both her professionalism and her appearance. Her gray hair was cut in a short, contemporary style, falling a little below her ears. Hazel eyes behind half reading glasses seemed to take in everything. She was stout, wise, and grandmotherly.

She was exactly what Amber needed in an office assistant. They'd been together for ten years.

"You are an angel."

"Hardly, but I figured you could use this after the day you've had."

"First Ethan, then a squirrel loose in the east wing of the inn, toilet overflow in the west, and pie emergencies in the restaurant."

Elizabeth raised an eyebrow as Amber gestured toward the chair in front of her desk. "What could constitute a pie emergency?"

"Apparently the girl who makes piecrusts was out. The bakery manager consulted the list of unassigned employees and grabbed a boy who was floating between positions today."

"Sounds like the right thing to do."

"Except Seth, the boy she chose, had no idea how to make or roll out a piecrust. He's only sixteen and is still working through his ninety-day trial period. Seth pretended he knew what he was doing in the kitchen because he was worried he might lose his job if he didn't."

Elizabeth removed her glasses, cleaned them on the hem of her blouse, and then allowed them to hang from the designer chain around her neck. "So how did the piecrust fare?"

"Worse than the ones I tried to make when I was—"

"Turning forty. You were turning forty and decided it was time you learned to bake."

They shared a smile. That and the memory of her baking fiasco did more to ease her stress headache than two aspirins could have done.

"So how did you handle it?"

"I moved Seth to clearing tables and brought in one of the girls from the dining room to work on piecrusts."

"You'd think Georgia would have thought of that."

"Georgia follows the procedures book by the letter. And the procedure when short an employee is to . . ." She waved her hand.

"Pull someone from the Unassigned List."

"Exactly."

After taking another sip of tea and setting the mug down on a coaster, Amber didn't hesitate to change gears and talk with Elizabeth about Ethan. She trusted her assistant with everything and anything.

"Gordon called and told me he was attempting to notify Ethan's family, but he hasn't been able to reach anyone."

Elizabeth nodded. "He called here too. Wanted to know what was in his file as far as next of kin."

"And?"

"A sister somewhere in the area, and a wife here."

"Any children?"

"I suppose it's possible, but he never spoke of any. Given his age, they would be grown with kids of their own."

Amber picked up the tea and inhaled the scent of cinnamon. "If he had children or grand-children, you'd think he would be showing pictures of them to folks."

"From what I can gather, Ethan didn't socialize much with other employees."

Amber sipped her tea and stared past Elizabeth to the wall of her office facing her desk. She'd painted it a nice warm brown, and she had one thing displayed there—an Amish quilt given to her last Christmas by several of the women who worked at the Village. They'd worked on it together. They called it a Friendship Star quilt. The yellow stars were set against a blue back-ground and bordered with brown, red, and green.

Usually when she looked at the quilt, her mind would relax. Today it wasn't helping. There was something she was trying to remember. It had happened a few days ago, and it was relevant to the discussion about Ethan. Whatever it was hovered at the very corner of her consciousness. Each time she almost grasped what it was, it would disappear.

"Anything else I can do?" Elizabeth stood and

repositioned her reading glasses on the edge of her nose. When she peeped over the top of them, she looked exactly like Amber's fourth-grade teacher.

"No. I plan to work through this paperwork and then leave by—" Amber felt like slapping her forehead. She'd been so focused on trying to remember the lost thing that she had forgotten what she still needed to do.

"Think of something?"

Amber set down her tea and turned to her computer. "I forgot all about finding someone to take Ethan's place. We need to open the coffee shop back up tomorrow. It's one of the reasons visitors stay here . . . they can still buy their espresso while they're experiencing the simple life."

"Anyone on the Unassigned List who can do it?"

"I doubt it. At least not right away." Amber continued to scan through her personnel files. She was remembering something she'd seen on a time sheet. "They could be trained, but—"

"But not in time for tomorrow's caffeine needs." Elizabeth sat back down. "I could call the temp agency in town. See if they have anyone. Though the last time we called it didn't work out so well. We asked for a girl who could care for the indoor plants, and they sent us someone allergic to all forms of vegetation."

"Wait . . . I've got it!" Amber clicked off her computer and hopped up from her desk chair. "We'll use the person who has been filling in for Ethan when he needed to step away from the shop for a moment. I knew I'd seen it on her time sheet."

Grabbing her tablet and keys, she rushed out of the office, calling behind her, "Thank you for the tea."

If she hurried, she might reach the quilt shop before Hannah left.

Her timing couldn't have been better. Hannah was walking away from the quilt shop, headed toward the parking area. She carried a cloth lunch bag by its drawstring, and she barely glanced around at all. In fact, she looked as if her best friend had died.

Ethan was not her best friend, but he had died, and Amber realized that Hannah probably hadn't fully digested all that had happened yet. In her experience, it was when you stopped being busy that emotions caught up with you.

"Hannah, would you mind if we talked a minute?"

"Here?" Hannah stopped walking, pushed up on her glasses, and glanced around.

"How about the bench over there by the bakery?"

"*Ya*. Okay." Hannah looked uncomfortable.

Amber wanted to put her at ease. Perhaps if they talked about something completely unrelated to Ethan's death . . .

"Are those new glasses? I don't remember seeing them on you before."

Hannah smiled shyly as she sat down and once again pushed up on the brown, blue-flecked frames. "They are. I bought them last week."

"Well, they complement the shape of your face very well."

Now Hannah was beaming, but she didn't agree or disagree. After glancing around, she said, "I think my new glasses are not what you wanted to talk about."

"True." Amber sighed. "Honestly, I need your help."

"My help?"

"Yes. Someone needs to open A Simple Blend tomorrow, and since you've worked there before—"

"I've barely worked there at all! Only to fill in when Ethan had a doctor's appointment, which wasn't very often."

"Still, you know more about the shop than anyone else does, and you're good with customers. Carol's said that about you often."

"She has?"

"Yes. I know she will hate to lose you, but even if it's only temporary it would help me a lot."

"Oh."

"And your hours can remain the same. It's no problem if we adjust the hours the coffee shop is open. I know people will understand."

"They will?"

"Certainly." Amber reached across and covered Hannah's hands with her own. "I would be indebted to you for this, Hannah. If you would agree to give it a try, I would be very appreciative."

"*Ya.* All right." She didn't look certain at all, but maybe she'd feel more confident after she'd had a few hours to think about it.

"And I'll come by to check on you, see if you need anything. Or maybe we can just chat." Even as Amber said that last part, she realized how ridiculous it must sound. There was at least twenty years' difference between their ages. What would they chat about? But circumstances had bound them together, and the storms of life could make for strange friendships.

They said their good-byes, and Hannah continued on her way home. As Amber watched, she walked all the way to the shed, probably to retrieve a bicycle. Amber breathed a sigh of relief. Clouds were rapidly building, and it looked as if it would storm soon, but at least one thing had gone right on this day. She'd found a replacement for Ethan Gray.

⇠ *Four* ⇢

Tate adjusted his ball cap as he scanned the threatening sky.

The storm was building in the north, and it promised to be a real soaker.

He was accustomed to Indiana weather; after all, he had been born and raised in Middlebury. But the storm he was watching had moved in especially quick. The weather forecast had shown a mere 20 percent chance of rain. Much had improved in the area of weather prediction, but nature was still able to throw an occasional curveball.

The horses were in their stalls. He'd brought the few cattle he still had into the barn. Probably it wasn't worth his time for him to continue to keep cattle on the place, but a farm didn't seem like a farm without a cow or two.

He latched the barn door shut as the wind gained strength. Rain would be next, and he supposed his fields and crops could use it.

What was he forgetting?

His truck was under the carport in case the storm packed hail.

A bray broke through the sound of the wind, followed by another—this one lower pitched.

The donkeys.

He'd forgotten the donkeys.

The same ones that had caused him to spend his morning on fence repair.

They were at the far side of the field, the south side. He backtracked to the barn, hurried inside, and found the two halters he'd purchased along with the donkeys. As he trudged toward them, he could see they were standing in the very northwest corner of his pasture. On the west side of that fence was the Village, an undeveloped portion of the complex. On the north side the fence separated his property from the Pumpkinvine Trail.

What mess had those two created now?

The storm continued to approach from the north. As he studied the sky, he could see that darkness would fall early. Best to get the donkeys in before they became frightened and broke something else he would have to repair.

He'd bought standard-sized donkeys—two females that were nearly fifty inches measuring from the shoulder. Both had reddish-brown hair and long ears. The one with a white streak between her ears seemed to cause the most trouble. No doubt his granddaughter would insist on naming them. Camille had turned six over the Christmas holidays, and she had strong opinions about most things.

Tate smiled at the thought of his granddaughter. She loved to visit on holidays, and having the chatterbox around lightened his mood.

Unlike the donkeys, which seemed to have a knack for souring his disposition.

As he neared them, he saw that they were tossing their heads. He had no trouble hearing their braying even over the wind. Were they frightened by the storm?

"Whoa, girl." He slipped the halter over the first and then turned to the second—the one with the white marking. She moved out of his reach. "Whoa. Easy now."

She was standing against the fence, head down and eyes studying him with distrust. Tate reached out for her, and she jerked away.

He lowered his voice, aiming for confident but calm. "Easy. Easy now. That's it." She settled slightly at his touch. As he was slipping on the halter, he happened to look over her back, past the fence, and see the Pumpkinvine Trail.

What he spied there kicked his pulse up a notch.

He moved to the left so he could read the large, sloppy red letters splayed across the concrete trail. Anger mixed with concern, and concern won. He pulled out his phone and called Amber Wright.

Amber had just sat down to an omelet when her phone rang. The display said the caller was Tate Bowman. The man hadn't spoken to her in over a year, and then it had been to complain about guests crossing over his pasture fence. They'd only wanted to take a close-up photo of a new-born calf, but you would think they intended to steal him blind by his reaction.

"Hello."

"Amber, this is Tate."

She could hear the wind blowing against the cell phone he was using. Why would he be outside when the storm was about to unleash its fury?

"I'm at the southwest corner of my property. There's something here you're going to want to see."

"Now?"

"Yes, now."

"But—" She stared down at her plate. It was the first time she'd cooked at home in a week, and she wasn't going to enjoy even one bite?

"Now. And bring a camera." Tate clicked off without any further explanation.

Amber stood, eyed her dinner once more, and paused long enough to scoop up one forkful of her omelet. It tasted delicious—exactly the right amount of salt, pepper, garlic, ham, and cheese stirred into the egg mixture. Sighing, she pushed her phone into her back jeans pocket, moved toward her front door, and grabbed the rain poncho hanging on the coatrack. She could drive to his place, but it would take longer to go around by the road versus cutting across the Village's back acre and walking straight to the pasture.

She had no trouble finding Tate. The Village

shared the one fence line with the man. They'd had a few incidents over the years—nothing that couldn't be handled with cooperation. Unfortunately Tate had become more vocal about his distaste for the Village since his wife had died. Perhaps Peggy had softened him up somewhat, smoothed off the rough edges. Since he had become a widower—was it four years ago?—his personality and expressions increasingly resembled those of the stubborn donkeys she saw him standing beside.

Tate Bowman, struggling to handle two donkeys.

The sight almost made her laugh.

Tate wasn't a small man. He towered well above her five feet four inches, and though he had to be on the other side of fifty, he was still all sinewy muscle like many of the farmers in the area. He'd apparently taken to shaving his head, so she couldn't tell how much of his black hair had turned gray. Not that it mattered to her.

The man was as unfriendly as a disgruntled guest, which she only had to deal with occasionally. On the other hand, Tate was her neighbor.

"Problem with the donkeys?" She reached over the fence to pet the donkey nearest her, a beautiful reddish-brown jenny with a white patch between her long ears.

"The donkeys aren't why I called you."

Amber looked at him then. She forgot about her dinner waiting in the house and the rain that had begun to fall in fat drops. She looked at him and saw something on his face that alarmed her. There was a warning in his dark brown eyes that she couldn't quite place. What could be so serious? And why the expression of grim concern? For the Village or for her? The thought embarrassed her and she laughed uncomfortably.

"You seem to be having trouble with these two." She nodded at the lead ropes he was holding in his hands. One donkey was standing at the very edge of her rope, apparently refusing to budge. The other, the one with the white patch, was cornered in between the two fences.

"I am, but I called you because of the trail." He nodded to an area behind her, pointed at what she hadn't seen when she walked up.

Someone had painted large ugly letters on the concrete path with a dark red paint. At least it looked like paint. As she stepped closer, the rain picked up, and the letters began to smear. The running red paint resembled blood, and the words— the words sent a river of worry through her heart.

She closed her eyes and breathed a prayer for patience.

Who would do this?

And why?

"Either it's not paint or it's fresh. Dried paint wouldn't run that way."

"You didn't see anything?" Amber turned back toward him. "Or anyone?"

"No. I came out to gather the donkeys . . ." Tate glanced up at the sky at the exact moment the bottom fell out of the clouds and rain began to drench them.

Amber pulled out her phone long enough to take two pictures, then she stuffed it back into her jeans pocket, under the poncho, safe from the rain.

Tate had begun pulling on the donkeys, who were plainly not going to move for him.

Without knowing why she was doing it, Amber climbed over the fence and took the lead rope for the donkey she'd petted.

She leaned her head close to the donkey's and stroked her again between the eyes. "Good girl. Let's walk. Good girl."

Walking in front of the donkey, but not pulling, she intended to lead the way. Sometimes donkeys needed to know it was safe to go forward, but Tate's donkey still refused to move.

Amber walked back, the rain now pelting down so hard she could see Tate, the two donkeys, and nothing else. "Good girl. That's it." She moved so that the donkey's head was in front of her and she could place a hand on her side. A tremor passed under her hand, and the donkey turned to eye her once. Then she began moving toward the barn.

"Good girl. Walk on. That's it."

They passed Tate at a fast clip, but it didn't

matter. Once her donkey had set off across the pasture, Tate's donkey had seen that it was safe to do so. Either that or she didn't want to be left alone in the pouring rain.

Within a few minutes, they were walking in through the large front door of the barn.

"I have no idea what I was thinking when I bought these animals. I imagined they'd be the same as horses, but they're not. They're unreasonable and impossible to train." As Tate grumbled, he began putting fresh hay into the donkeys' feed buckets. He walked out of their stall and proceeded to fasten its doors.

"Wait." Amber removed her rain poncho and stepped forward. Picking up a brush that was hanging on a hook on the wall, she began to brush one of the donkeys as the jenny ate her feed.

"I'm wetter than that donkey is. Do you actually think I'm going to stand in here and—"

"You'd do it for your horse."

Tate snapped his mouth shut, sighed heavily, and picked up the other brush. It occurred to Amber that he was a good-looking man. It was unfortunate that all her contact with him was over disputes. In another life, they might have been friends, possibly even more than friends. The thought both amused and embarrassed her.

For several minutes the only sounds were brushes against hide and rain on the roof. How long had it been since Amber stood in a barn and took care of any animal? Probably since her grand-parents had been alive. The memory sent a rush of warmth through her. They had lived farther south but still in Indiana. She'd loved those summers more than anything she could remember from her childhood. Perhaps they were the reason she'd decided to return to Indiana after college.

"I'd still be out there in the rain with them if you hadn't convinced her to start moving. How did you know what to do?" Tate stood facing her, the two donkeys between them, but he didn't look at her when he spoke. Instead, he focused intently on the donkey he was brushing.

"We have a couple of jennies at the Village, not that I work with them much. But my granddad raised and trained donkeys, and I loved helping him."

Tate nodded as if he understood. "My parents and grandparents had cattle. It's why I have them, even though it doesn't make sense money-wise."

"These seem like good donkeys, only a little unsettled. How long have you had them?"

"Three weeks or so."

"What have you named them?" Amber moved to the other side of her donkey and continued brushing her.

"I haven't."

She jerked her head around and stared at him. "Nearly a month and you haven't named them?"

Tate's expression changed to irritation, a look

she was more used to seeing on his face. "I never named my sheep. I don't name my cows. Why would I name my donkeys?"

"Well, you name your horses, and donkeys are more like horses than they are like sheep or cows. Donkeys are very affectionate animals, and they need interaction with people or they become depressed."

"Depressed?" Tate shook his head. "I'm not sure I buy that one. I think they're just an ill-natured lot."

Amber wanted to point out that was one thing he had in common with them, but she decided to keep that observation to herself. "Many people don't understand donkeys. It's important that you give them a name. Donkeys can easily live between twenty-five and thirty-five years."

Tate groaned.

"Donkeys are fine animals, Tate." She suddenly remembered her pastor's sermon from the previous Sunday about recognizing when God was working in your life. "They're even in the Bible."

When he looked at her skeptically, she added, "Balaam's donkey. Give it a read sometime. It's in the book of Numbers, but I don't remember where."

She had stopped brushing and the donkey nudged her hand.

"I'd name this one Trixie." Amber rubbed the

white patch between the donkey's ears. "She's a beautiful animal."

"Trixie, huh?" Tate placed his brush back on the hook on the wall. "And what about this one?"

Amber walked over to his animal. Now there were only a few feet between her and Tate, and suddenly it felt very cozy in the stall, almost intimate.

"Velvet. Her color reminds me of velvet chocolate cake."

"I think Vixen would be more appropriate for her, or maybe Viper." Tate took the brush from her, and for a brief second their hands touched. Something deep inside Amber fluttered and a warm flush crept up her neck.

What was wrong with her?

Maybe she'd caught a cold out in the rain.

Maybe she needed to accept Gordon's next offer for a date, because she could not be imagining anything between her and Tate. The thought was ludicrous! He was a grandpa! She'd never even had kids. No, they were total opposites.

"Come on," he said roughly. "I'll drive you home."

Amber wanted to argue that she could walk, but then Tate opened the barn door and she saw the intensity of the storm outside. Rain pounded the ground so hard that the drops splashed back up again. She could barely see Tate's house though it was only a few yards away.

She wouldn't be walking.

How bad could a short car ride with her neighbor be?

She'd thank him for the lift and hurry back into her cozy house, where she could be dry, alone, and satisfied once again.

⇥ *Five* ⇤

When Hannah reached home, the bishop was there, sitting in the kitchen with her parents.

"Joseph came by to speak with you, Hannah. To offer to pray with you after what happened . . . at the Village today."

Hannah slid into a seat at the end of the table. She wasn't surprised that her parents already knew about Ethan's death. Word would have spread quickly, through both the *Englisch* and Amish communities.

She wasn't sure she was ready to pray about Ethan yet. She didn't even know how to put into words all the things weighing down her heart.

Joseph smiled at her and pushed a plate of cookies her direction. Though he was young, already his hair was disappearing from the top of his head. His beard was full though—a dark brown with only a hint of gray, and his eyes were kind. "Your *mamm*, she's a *gut* cook, *ya*?"

"She is." Hannah didn't want one of the oatmeal

cookies, but she took one so she wouldn't appear rude. Breaking off a little piece, she popped it into her mouth. The sugar and raisins reminded her of when she was a child, when things made sense.

"Perhaps you should begin by telling us what happened this morning." Her *dat* stroked his beard. "We were worried when we heard, but your *mamm* said you would have come home if you'd needed to do so."

"There was no need for me to leave work." Hannah stared down at the cookie, and then she told them all that had happened, from the moment she'd arrived, through finding Ethan's body, and even answering the police officer's questions.

"I thank *Gotte* you were safe, Hannah." Her mother stood and fetched the coffeepot, then refilled Joseph's cup. She poured a glass of water from the pitcher that always sat on the counter and set it in front of Hannah.

"*Ya*, I was safe, but poor Ethan . . ." The tears started then, the ones she'd been holding back all day.

Joseph moved beside her. He opened the black Bible he often carried with him, and he moved through the Scripture, pointing out the places where God tells his people not to fear. He worked his way from Psalms into the New Testament. The message was the same. God would take care of them. There was no need to be afraid.

Closing the Bible, he said, "Let's pray."

So they did—her mother and father, the bishop, and Hannah. At first she didn't know what to pray. Her mind was blank. But then she remembered Ethan and prayed for his soul, prayed for his family, and even prayed for his coworkers and herself. By the time the bishop stood, she was starting to feel grounded again.

Joseph was young, as she'd reminded Jesse, but he was a good leader. Hannah no longer felt as if the world around her was fragile, and she didn't worry if she'd be able to sleep later that night. The words *fear not* echoed through her mind and her heart.

Two hours later, Hannah held her baby sister while her mother worked on repairing her brother's pants. Ben, Noah, and Dan were all out in the barn. The storm had caught them by surprise, and they'd claimed to have more work to do after dinner. Hannah suspected it was their way of avoiding dishes. At nineteen, sixteen, and fifteen, they all thought they were too old for women's work. Occasionally her mother, Eunice, made sure they understood kitchen work was for whoever had the time to do it.

Tonight hadn't been one of those times.

Her father had agreed with the three boys that they had more work to do, nodding in his somber way, and all four of them had trooped out through the rain to the barn.

Hannah had washed all the dishes herself while her mother had given Mattie a bath. Afterward, she'd joined her mother in the sitting room, and Mattie had crawled up into her lap. Hannah breathed in the sweet smells of her little sister, shampoo and powder and baby. Mattie was growing sleepy, which was the only reason she'd settled on Hannah's lap. She had her thumb plopped in her mouth. They were both watching Eunice mend clothes, the needle moving back and forth through the material with mesmerizing speed. It was almost enough to settle the worries troubling Hannah's mind.

"Are you sure Mattie will be your last *boppli*?"

"*Ya*, I think so." Eunice leaned forward and added, "Forty-two is old to be birthing babies."

"You're not old." Hannah combed her fingers through Mattie's curly brown hair.

"Maybe not, but I started over twenty years ago. Three boys and two girls are quite the blessing! Some days I wonder how the *gut* Lord thought I could keep up with five children, though I realize many families have more."

"You keep up fine!" As Hannah studied her mom, she realized that she did look tired. Gray had started creeping into her brown hair, but that was normal. Amish women didn't dye their hair like so many of the *Englisch*. They didn't try to hide the effects of time. Yes, Eunice was gray and she looked tired, but in every other way her mom seemed the same. She was the same height as Hannah, five foot four, but quite a bit rounder. Moms were supposed to be rounder. Weren't they?

"You do make a *gut* point. I shouldn't take that new job because I'm needed here."

"*Nein*. Your hours would be the same. Isn't that what Amber said?"

"Yes."

"And I expect you'd be receiving tips like the girls in the restaurant. The extra money would be *gut* for you to put back."

"But, *Mamm*, I'm not a barista."

"A what?"

"Person who makes *kaffi*—at least that's what the tip cup says. *Barista tips*. Not that I saw much money in it. I believe Ethan was too grumpy with the customers. They wanted the *kaffi* but didn't feel a need to tip him for it."

"Each person can do their best and no more. I suppose Ethan was as pleasant as he knew how to be."

"But I'm not a *kaffi* maker. I'm a quilter. That's what I enjoy doing—putting together pieces of a quilt as if they were part of a puzzle."

"And now you can put together customers' drinks like a puzzle. I'm sure you'll do fine." Eunice held up the pair of pants she was mending and studied them in the soft light of the gas lantern. "I won't be able to repair these again.

Noah has torn them so often the fabric is becoming ragged."

"He still runs around like a *kind*. Didn't he tear those chasing after a wild turkey?"

"Yes, he did." Eunice set aside the pants and picked up a shirt that needed the seam under the arm mended. "I am pretty sure I recall you acting like a child when you were sixteen."

"That was a long time ago. I can't remember."

When her mother paused to stare at her with raised eyebrows, Hannah started laughing.

"You've forgotten how you used to spend every spare hour down at our pond? And you always came back muddy or with clothes that needed mending."

Mattie reached up and tried to snag Hannah's glasses. When Hannah pulled away, Mattie put the middle three fingers of her left hand on Hannah's lips. Her sister's right thumb remained firmly planted in her own mouth.

"Tell me what is bothering you most about changing jobs."

"I will miss the quilt shop."

"And I'm sure Carol will miss you, but you'll be right next door. At night you can still sew your projects to sell in the shop. There's something else you're worried about. What is it?"

"He died in there, *Mamm*. Ethan died in his shop just this morning, and I'm supposed to be making *kaffi* in the same spot tomorrow?"

Eunice completed mending the seam before she answered. "Death is a natural part of life, Hannah. The Bible tells us as much."

"I know, but—"

"People die in all manner of ways and all sorts of places. It doesn't scar a place. It marks a place with special memories because it's where a soul left this world and entered the next."

"I'm not comfortable being near Ethan's departure point."

Eunice smiled, stored her sewing, and pulled out a pair of knitting needles. It seemed her mother's hands were never still. She placed a ball of pink yarn where it would unravel easily and set to work on the sweater she was making for Mattie.

"Sometimes *Gotte* has a way of putting us in situations where we're uncomfortable. Though you're uneasy about this new assignment, you can trust *Gotte*. And you can trust your boss. Amber Wright is very thoughtful in the way she runs the Village, and she has always been a fair boss to you. She must think you'd do a *gut* job there."

"I suppose."

Silence settled over them. Hannah could tell by Mattie's breathing that she had fallen asleep. She should move her to the room they shared, but holding her was comforting.

"I've reminded you often that we named you Hannah because it means 'grace.' "

"*Ya*. I know it does, but—"

"And every night I pray *Gotte's* grace on you, on all my *kinner*. He will see you through any changes at your job, *dochder*."

"I know he will."

"You don't need to worry about whether it's permanent or concern yourself with what happened to Ethan. *Gotte* already knows all those things."

"Sure, but, *Mamm*—"

"You need to do *gut* work each day, and always be kind to those you meet." The needles and yarn blurred as her mother continued to knit the sweater.

Hannah fiddled with her glasses. She wanted to argue with her mother, wanted to tell her about Jesse's theory that Ethan's death wasn't merely caused by a heart attack. And what of the strange way Carol had looked at her when Hannah had first told her about Ethan. Carol had hidden her distress well enough and soon enough that the customers hadn't noticed, but Hannah had.

Hannah knew her employer very well.

What was that look of concern about?

When they'd spoken of it later, she had clutched the bolt of sky-blue fabric so tightly her knuckles had turned white.

Still, her mother's words rang true.

Gotte would provide the answers, if he wanted them to know. Of course, Hannah thought, he must also have given her a curious nature for a reason.

It was with those discordant thoughts that she stood and carried her sister upstairs.

Perhaps the next day would be better. She couldn't imagine how it could be worse.

"Will you look at the pictures with me? See if there are any clues as to who did this or why or what it means?" Amber peered up at Tate with such a beseeching look, he found himself nodding in agreement.

They were standing in his mudroom.

Tate had planned on grabbing a raincoat, hopping in the truck, and delivering her to her house. The raincoat wasn't going to do much good though. He was already soaked through and through.

Amber pulled the phone out of her jeans pocket and tapped the icon of the first photo from the Pumpkinvine Trail. It enlarged, but not much. He stepped closer and then shook his head. "Can't tell much from this. The picture is too small."

"I can load it on my computer at home. When you drive me over, you could come inside for a minute. It won't take long."

Tate stared at her in disbelief. They'd barely had a civil conversation between them the whole time she'd lived next door, unless you counted the last few minutes in the barn. What had come over her?

"It's only that the incident occurred on the border of our properties, and we should probably decide together whether to involve Gor—whether to involve the police."

Rolling his shoulders to relax the muscles that were tensed there, Tate stared out the window at the steady rain. He did not want to become involved with this woman or the Village. He wanted to go and rest in his recliner and watch a little television. Glancing back at Amber, he saw that she had been peering up at him as she adjusted her rain poncho.

"But I understand if you're too busy."

"No. I suppose I'm not." He ran his hand from the top to the back of his head. "Let me change clothes first. I'll be quick."

He hurried up the stairs and into his bedroom. The house was ridiculously large for one person, but on holidays it was full with the boys, their wives, and Camille. He expected that over the years he'd have even more grandchildren. At least that was what he and Peggy always said to each other whenever they questioned living in the big farmhouse. Many of the couples their age had sold their farms and bought homes with little or no yards. But the thought of living in such a place made Tate restless and annoyed.

He liked his home, even though it was too empty, too quiet, and too filled with memories of the way things were. He considered the positive side as he toweled off and began changing clothes. The boys came home no more than three times a year, but when they did there was plenty of room for everyone. Pulling off his wet socks and shoes, he shook his head at the absurd turn his thoughts had taken. He could never sell the farm anyway. It had been in his family for three generations.

He quickly changed into dry clothes—shoes, jeans, and a T-shirt. Should have been a quick thing to do, but the first two shirts he tried on looked ridiculous. One was stained and the other had holes in it. Walking to his closet, he pulled a golf shirt off a hanger. He rarely golfed, but the kids insisted on updating his wardrobe. Checking himself in the mirror, he decided he was presentable.

Not that he cared how he looked for Amber Wright.

As he walked down the stairs, he admitted to himself that she wasn't as bad as he had remembered. Maybe she'd softened up a little over the years, or perhaps he'd become less critical.

The thought caused him to remember the Scripture he'd read that morning. Something about judging others. Had he been doing that?

"Ready?" He'd left her in the kitchen. When he walked back in, she was studying the collection of pictures on his refrigerator.

"Are these all your family?"

"Yeah. Every time they send me a photo, I move the others closer together and stick the new one under a magnet."

"At this rate, you might need another refrigerator."

Tate nodded, realizing she was right. "I should take down the old ones, but I can't quite talk myself into doing it. They make me smile, especially the ones of the boys when they were younger. You probably met my boys."

"Sure. Collin is the oldest, right? Star running back."

Tate was surprised she remembered. "Yes. This picture is of him, his wife, and their daughter."

Amber stepped closer to study the photo as if she couldn't quite believe what she was seeing. "How did he get old enough to marry and have a child?"

Tate laughed. The sound was strange even to his ears. "Time doesn't stand still, does it?"

"It seems impossible that they are adults."

"Alan married last year, though I expect they will wait awhile to have children. He's finishing up his master's degree in business and she's a nurse."

Turning to glance up at him, Amber smiled—a real, genuine smile. "I know you are proud."

Her expression turned serious, and she added, "I want to say I'm very sorry about your wife. I came to the visitation, but I'm sure you don't remember."

Something in his chest tightened. Did just the mention of that time still have the ability to hurt him? "There aren't many details about the funeral itself that I remember. Sometimes it seems all of it happened to someone else, but the grief . . . I can recall that well enough."

An awkward silence filled the room. Tate became aware of the clock ticking on the wall, the rain falling outside, and the scent of Amber's perfume—a light floral scent that was also a little powdery.

"I guess we should go." He offered her an umbrella, but she waved him away.

"I have a rain poncho on, though that won't help my jeans or shoes. Sorry about dripping water on your floor."

He shrugged, and she added, "Dashing to the truck won't make me any wetter."

But they didn't have to dash. The truck was pulled up under the carport, and long ago he'd built a covered walkway between the mudroom and where they parked. Peggy had said she was tired of being trapped in the truck, waiting for a wayward shower to pass. She'd had a way of convincing him to do things—not whining but thanking him for it before he'd even begun.

They drove to Amber's house without talking. The only sounds were the rain beating a rhythm on the roof and the radio set low in Tate's old truck. Something by George Strait. He couldn't make out what, and he didn't want to turn it up.

Tate had lived next to the Village all his life, though when he was growing up it was hardly more than a small inn with a café attached to the side. Over the years it had grown until now it was a sprawling complex, like a scar across the fields. He didn't much abide development. Folks could go to the city for that. He bit back the complaint that came to mind. Hadn't worked before, and it wouldn't work now.

"Progress marches on," Peggy would say, a smile playing across her lips. She understood why he hated seeing the fields plowed and replaced with more buildings. She understood, but she was always reminding him not to struggle against things he couldn't change.

He'd never been inside the *Dawdy Haus* where Amber lived, though he'd stood at his window often enough and watched the light in her window. It was on the far side of his property and he could just make it out most evenings—like a sort of beacon assuring him he wasn't completely alone.

Following her up the *Dawdy Haus* porch steps, he had to admire the way she'd left the original style. He was also surprised she hadn't added on to it over the years. Even for a single person, it seemed small—or cozy depending on how you thought of such things.

"Would you like some hot tea or coffee?" She placed her rain poncho on the coatrack near the front door and her wet shoes on a mat. Since he had changed his shoes, his were still fairly dry.

"No. Thank you. I should probably take a look and get back."

"Sure. It will only take me a minute to turn on my computer."

Her clothes had actually remained somewhat dry except for the bottom of her jeans, which were soaked as she'd said, wet from the knees down. Her hair was beginning to curl all over her head. She probably had no idea that the curly look was good on her, or she wouldn't wear it so straight every day. Tate wasn't going to tell her. It was none of his business how she wore her hair.

She'd walked to a small computer desk in the corner of the dining room. The one thing on it was a laptop. He'd never seen a work area so tidy.

A single plate was sitting on the table—the meal uneaten. So that was what he'd interrupted.

"Eggs for dinner?"

"Too often. It's about all I can cook." She clicked away on the computer, opening an Internet browser and her e-mail.

Tate felt something brush up against his legs. He moved to the left, bumped into Amber, and then saw the cat. Jumping back to the right, he managed to avoid stepping on it.

"Does he do that on purpose?"

"Leo? Yeah. It's his way of saying hello."

"Tripping me?"

"No. Winding through your legs. Think of it as a handshake."

Tate didn't want a handshake from a cat. He didn't trust cats. They had a way of staring at you in an arrogant, I-know-something-you-don't manner.

He decided to ignore the cat and focus on the screen.

When Amber double-clicked on the picture and expanded it to full size, he let out a long, low whistle. He'd seen it well enough from his field, but displayed on the computer the message appeared even more sinister.

It struck him as a sad commentary on their community, that such a thing should happen in their midst. And beneath that sense of disappointment was a nervous worry that tonight was only the beginning.

⇐ Six ⇒

Amber stared at the screen, unable to comprehend the how and why of what she was looking at. The graffiti had been written with red paint, the letters shaped in all caps and spaced haphazardly as if someone was in a hurry. Or maybe they merely wanted to cover the entire width of the concrete path.

BEWARE. IRON BREAKS AND SMASHES EVERYTHING.

Amber frowned at the screen.

"Looks worse than it did in person. What could it possibly mean?"

She felt more puzzled than concerned. She wasn't exactly rattled by what this person had done, but she was puzzled and, under that, a little angry.

Tate leaned closer to the monitor. "The 'beware' is easy enough to understand."

"Beware what?"

"Well, the arrow points toward the Village." Tate pulled a chair over from the dining room table and sat down beside her.

"So are they warning the people already at the Village to beware, or are they warning prospective guests to beware the Village? Neither makes sense."

"Maybe they're warning the employees."

Now Amber turned and studied him. Finally she cleared her throat and asked, "Have you heard about Ethan? Ethan Gray?"

"I know Ethan. Not well, but I know him."

"He died this morning, at work."

Tate had been leaning forward to study the screen, but now he sat back against the chair and stared at her. "Today? At the Village?"

Amber filled him in on the day's events, and

then she added, "The police are sure it was a heart attack."

"And yet you had vandalism this morning—the breaking of Ethan's glass—followed by this."

"Yes, but—"

"I'm not much of a believer in coincidences."

"How could the two possibly be connected?"

Tate didn't answer her question. Instead he pointed out the obvious. "Whoever did this placed it at the Village property line for a reason."

"And they knew where the property line was." Amber frowned at the screen, more irritated by it with each passing moment.

"Do you think there are similar warnings at the other end of the trail?"

"I doubt it. Someone would have seen it and notified Larry, who would have called me right away." Amber moved her cursor over the screen, tracing the red letters. " 'Iron breaks and smashes everything.' What in the world could that mean? And why was it written in red?"

Tate frowned as he tried to make some sense of it, but he only shook his head instead of answering her. Leo had hopped up on the desk and sat staring at them, paws tucked under him and large green eyes revealing no interest in what was on the computer screen.

Should they be concerned?

"Maybe it was a prank," Tate said. "Kids. You

know as well as I do that we have our share of hoodlums in this town."

"I wouldn't call them hoodlums. We were young once . . . right?" She smiled, remembering the soap her senior class had placed into the fountain located in the center of the town square in South Bend. Each student involved had been caught. They'd been forced to help drain and clean the bubbles out, plus write a report covering the harmful effects of soapy water on birds. What a sight it had been though, like some giant bubble bath gone wild.

"Maybe we were. But I never would have done that. My dad would have tanned my hide."

Amber tapped her fingers against the desk. "My parents were strict as well."

She picked up a pencil and pulled a pad toward her. "So we have two possibilities for motive—a prank or something darker."

"Darker as in a warning."

Her pencil hovered over what she had written, and then she added his words.

"Why at your property line?" Amber drew question marks in the margin.

"Lucky, I guess. It certainly isn't the first time someone connected to the Village caused damage on my property."

Amber set down the pencil. "It's been better, right? Nothing in the last year. And we paid for the last fence that was damaged and the—"

"I know you did." Tate raised his hand to stop her, like a school crossing guard. "I shouldn't have brought it up, at least not that way."

She started to apologize again, but he shook his head.

"I'm sorry if I sounded bitter," he said. "What I was trying to say is that in a small town, or in the country, what happens to one person often affects their neighbor."

"Good point." She clicked off the e-mail and stood. Tate stood as well.

Then she followed her instincts and reached out and touched his arm. He flinched slightly, but he didn't step away.

"After living here for twenty-two years, I understand how much you care about the area. I do apologize for causing you trouble again."

"Not your fault," he mumbled.

They crossed her living room, which suddenly seemed tiny to her when compared to his home. The room was barely large enough to hold her recliner, small couch, and bookcase. "Do you think I should share this with the police?"

"Not on my account, but if you'd feel more comfortable doing so—"

"No." She ran her hand over her hair, and instantly became conscious of what the rain had done to her styling. "Say, you could have mentioned that I look like Shirley Temple."

A smile twitched his lips, but Tate didn't give in

to it. He told her to call if she needed anything else, and she promised to let him know if they found out who had done the vandalism.

Standing on her front porch, watching the taillights of his truck as he drove away in the rain, Amber realized she'd enjoyed the evening. Not what they'd dealt with, of course, but the fact that they had spent the better part of the evening together. As she tossed her cold dinner into the trash and set about making a mug of hot tea, she thought of how Tate had looked, dripping wet, standing in his mudroom.

He probably had no idea that he was still an attractive man, that a woman might want to pursue a relationship with him. Was he ready to come out from under the cloud of grief he'd lived with since Peggy had died? Was there room in his heart to care for someone new?

She couldn't say, and it didn't matter to her anyway since she wasn't looking for a relationship. It was nice to know that she had a friend instead of an enemy on the other side of her pasture fence. That thought brought some peace to the most hectic day she'd had in quite some time.

The rest of the evening passed quietly. A long shower warmed her, and she still had time to enjoy her favorite chair and the book she was nearly done with. Leo curled on the back of her recliner, his purring harmonizing nicely with the last few minutes of rain that pattered softly against her roof. Within an hour her eyes grew heavy, and she placed her bookmark in her book—a mere twenty pages from the end, but she couldn't stay awake any longer.

Leo tiptoed behind her, following her first to the bathroom to watch her brush her teeth and then hopping onto the corner of the bed. He looked like a golden sun drop on the dark blue Amish quilt that was made in an Old Country Tulip pattern. Red tulips were appliquéd to a black background. The first row of border was a dark blue, and the outer border was a warm pink. The quilt soothed her in a way she would have had a hard time explaining. Sliding beneath the sheets, she turned out the lights and nearly groaned when her head met the pillow.

Sleep claimed her, and soon she was dreaming of running through a storm, running from someone or something. Tate was holding her hand, and he gripped it so firmly she knew that he wouldn't let go. She knew, even though they were being pursued, that she was safe.

A thunderclap startled her out of her dream, but then she realized that the rain had stopped. There was no thunder, not even a whisper of wind outside her window. So what was the sound she'd heard?

She reached for her cell phone, unplugged it

from the charger on her nightstand, and shrugged into her robe. Perhaps she had imagined the noise. Leo padded out of the room in front of her. He headed straight for the front window and jumped up onto the sill. Moonlight was shining in through the window, and Amber could barely make out her cat's silhouette. Then he turned to look at her, and she wondered if a cat could act like a guard dog.

Clutching her phone just in case—in case of what, she didn't know—she moved next to him and peered out into the night. At first she didn't notice the lump on her front porch. Leo became agitated, pacing back and forth on the windowsill and pushing against her hand, which was braced on the pane of glass. She tried to calm him, but he jumped down, his paws thudding against the floor and causing her heart to jump into an erratic rhythm. He walked to the front door and sat, waiting. Amber didn't hesitate. Her cat never asked to go out at night, but she knew from his posture that he was expecting her to let him outside.

When she had opened the inside door and caught a good look through the storm door at what had been left on her doorstep, her knees went weak, shaking like Jell-O. She grasped the door frame and closed her eyes, breathing deeply. Checking the porch again, she convinced herself she wasn't still dreaming. What she saw—

bloodied and thrown onto her porch—was worse, much worse, than the nightmare she'd been having.

Pushing Leo back into the room with her foot, she closed the inside door and locked it. Then she dialed 9-1-1.

⇒ Seven ⇐

Hannah arrived at the Village thirty minutes earlier than usual the next morning. She wanted to have time to look over the instructions folder at A Simple Blend. The folder only held a few sheets, but they were better than nothing. Ethan had created it when she first began to fill in for him, which only happened once every few weeks. He would have an appointment in the morning, and his *kaffi* shop didn't close until noon. His hours had been seven to noon—not bad hours, come to think of it.

Amber had suggested that she leave the shop open until two. By the time she spent an hour cleaning up, that would give her a full eight hours of work since she was arriving at seven. The one catch had been finding someone to stand in for Hannah so she could take a short break in the morning and a lunch break. Amber assured her she'd take care of that issue very soon. Until then, Hannah had permission to eat on the job or hang up the "Back Soon" sign if she had to step out to the restroom.

Hannah wasn't worried about the long hours without a break, though she understood *Englisch* laws required Amber to give her those moments away from the shop. She trusted Amber would work out the details. She was worried about how to make the different types of *kaffi* folks were accustomed to. The times she had filled in for Ethan, everything was already made and she only had to wait on customers and take their money— something she was accustomed to doing in the quilt shop.

She gazed at her old shop longingly as she passed it, even slowed down to stare at the spring window display. Pushing up her glasses, she stepped close to the window and stared inside. Quilting was what she loved. Making *kaffi*? She didn't even drink *kaffi*.

Squaring her shoulders, she moved past the quilt shop and unlocked the door to A Simple Blend, using the key Amber had given her. The place had been completely cleaned since she had gone home the day before. She was relieved to smell the Pine-Sol someone had used when mopping the floor. Her muddy footprints were gone, and the spilled coffee beans had been swept up. The counters sparkled and the front glass panel had been replaced.

There was no indication at all that a tragedy

had taken place within the store. One would never know from glancing around the small shop that Ethan Gray had died there barely twenty-four hours ago.

A shiver traveled down Hannah's spine, but she ignored it as she locked the door behind her, flipped on the lights, and opened the drawer near the cash register in search of Ethan's instructions folder.

The folder was gone.

In its place was a binder. She pulled it out from the drawer and set it on the countertop. On the cover, someone had placed a label that read "Barista Instructions." Opening the binder, she was surprised to see a typed index and headings for every question she could possibly have. The first section was a single page titled "How to Open the Shop."

When had Ethan done this?

Why had he done it?

Hannah didn't have any answers, but she was certain that wouldn't stop the questions from circling in her mind. She'd have to puzzle over it later. She began by dumping fresh beans into the espresso machine, and then she started the three different pots of *kaffi*—regular, bold, and decaffeinated. The rich aroma of fresh *kaffi* filled the shop as she pulled the pastry items from the day before out of their case. None of them had been sold because Ethan had died before the shop had opened. Still, the binder said she was to pull out everything left over from the day before and set it aside. The binder also said fresh pastries would be delivered by—

The knock on the shop's back door caused her to jump and nearly fall off the stool she was perched on. She walked slowly through the back of the shop, past the stockroom and the tiny office, to the rear door.

"Who is it?"

"Pastry delivery."

What if it wasn't? What if it was the person who had shot out Ethan's front window? What if they'd come back to attack her?

Hannah peeked through the peephole in the door.

An old man with a rather large belly and short wiry gray hair waited, holding a tray full of food.

She opened the door.

"I wondered if anyone would be here. I'm Karl."

"Hannah."

"Didn't take long to replace Ethan." Karl scowled at her as if she had been responsible for Ethan's sudden death. "Are you going to let me in or not? Maybe you want me to take this stuff back to the truck."

"*Nein.* Please, come in."

Hannah stepped to the side as Karl trudged through the shop. There was no other word for the way he walked. He reminded her of one of her father's work horses as it pulled the plow down a

100

row in the field. Instead, Karl plodded down the hall.

No taller than she was, Karl looked old, overweight, and gloomy. He certainly seemed unhappy, based on the scowl he maintained as he unloaded the fresh goods and tossed the day-old items into several large paper bags. The bags had been stamped on the side with the words "Food Pantry."

Amber tried not to stare, but there wasn't much she could do as he finished with his work. The area behind the counter was small, and he had trouble maneuvering. She would guess that his weight was a good forty pounds over what it should be. Perhaps he snacked on the goods he delivered.

As to being old though, he wasn't as elderly as he had appeared when she had first peeked through the peephole. He handled the large tray of items he brought in as if it weighed nothing, and the muscles in his arms bulged when he hoisted it back onto his shoulder, now filled with the bag of sweets for the community pantry. At least Hannah assumed that's where the items were headed.

"So you . . . you know about Ethan?"

"I heard. Didn't take you long to snatch his job."

"Oh, it wasn't like that at all. Amber—"

"Seems you could have at least waited until his body was in the ground."

"Yes, but—"

"I understand you people don't pause for death, but there are certain boundaries. We call it respect."

Hannah took a step back. "Everyone here will miss Ethan, but I believe he would have wanted the shop opened today."

Karl grunted and shoved past her, making his way back through the shop. Hannah followed to lock the door behind him. There was no use inviting trouble, and although they didn't lock their doors at home, she was determined to be extra careful in the hours before the Village came to life.

When Karl turned on her suddenly, she had to jump backward to keep from bumping into him.

"Ethan told me what you people were doing. Don't think that you can get away with it!"

He was out the door before Hannah completely understood what he'd said. He thought she was responsible for Ethan's death? Or did he think it was a plot several of the employees had thought up together? Which was ridiculous. It had been a heart attack, plain and simple.

She would have explained that to him, but he flung the tray into the back of his truck and climbed into the driver's seat. Before she could say a word, he sped away.

Amber was finishing the paperwork on her desk when Elizabeth stepped into her office.

Her eyes were crinkled in concern. She'd already popped in once to offer to fetch her breakfast and extra coffee. It was only ten in the morning, and twice she had suggested Amber take off early.

Amber was certain the entire Village already knew about the incident at her home during the night. The police had finished collecting evidence by the time she left for work, and they had given her permission to clean up. She'd called a cleaning crew to the *Dawdy Haus* as soon as she'd arrived at the office. And she told Elizabeth all about it.

Elizabeth would never mention what happened to any employee, but the word would definitely be out anyway. Everyone would know about the sinister message left on her porch, and everyone would have a theory as to what was going on. They were a close community. She understood that nothing remained a secret for long, and everything was everyone's business. Or at least they thought it was.

"Gordon would like to see you."

"He's here?"

"Yes. He said it's about the incident at your house."

"All right. Show him in."

Elizabeth hesitated for a fraction of a second, then nodded and walked back out of the office.

Gordon ambled into the room and dropped into

the chair across from her desk. He looked fresh and full of energy in spite of the hours he'd spent at her house. He looked exactly the opposite of how she felt. Had he even had time to go back home and sleep?

"How are you doing?"

"Fine. I guess." She adjusted her outgoing mail that was already neatly stacked. "I don't know. I'm still a little shocked that so much has happened in, what? Twenty-four hours?"

Gordon nodded. "There's still no evidence that either the vandalism on the trail or at your home is connected to Ethan's death."

"But there was destruction at his shop as well —the busted window."

"True. But in the two most recent instances, the perp left a message."

Amber sighed and closed her eyes.

The Village was supposed to be a peaceful, tranquil spot to visit. This was turning into a nightmare.

Gordon cleared his throat. "We received preliminary results from the . . . package left on your porch."

"And?"

"It was from the local butcher, soaked in red soda to appear more gruesome."

"Certainly worked. I thought a calf had been butchered on my front porch. I wouldn't be surprised if the grounds crew has to repaint the front of my house, and even then it could take several coats to cover the graffiti."

Gordon pulled two photos from his shirt pocket and placed them on her desk. One was of her front porch at three that morning. The other was of the message left on the trail the night before. She had forwarded him the pictures from her camera after he'd shown up at her home when she'd placed the 9-1-1 call.

"Same writing." She picked up the photos and studied them, though touching them made her skin crawl.

"Yes."

" 'A rock was cut out, but not by human hands.' " Amber stared at the photo of the words smeared onto the front wall of her house. She didn't know what offended her more, the words, the slabs of meat on the porch, or the fact that someone had been on her porch long enough to do such a thing—while she slept.

"Both the message written on the trail and the one on your porch are from the book of Daniel."

Amber tore her gaze from the photos. She forced herself to look at Gordon, though what he was saying made no sense.

"Daniel?"

"Old Testament prophet."

"I know who Daniel was." The answer came out snippier than she intended. "How did you figure that out?"

"Internet search. Jasmine is very talented with a computer."

Amber had met the newest addition to the Middlebury Police Department once. She was young and beautiful, with ebony skin and boundless energy. It made her feel older and even more tired to think about Jasmine, so she pushed away that part of what Gordon said and focused on the one clue they had.

"Why would someone scrawl Old Testament verses near and on Village property?"

"It's a good question. One thing is certain. With these two incidents happening so close together . . ."

He paused, and Amber knew he was preparing to chastise her again for not calling immediately when she'd seen the damage done to the trail. Their eyes met, and Gordon shrugged.

"The two incidents occurred a few hours apart, so whoever is doing it is feeling pressure. Something has caused him—or her—to act rashly and impatiently. I'd expect another event soon. I have officers rotating onto the property in four-hour shifts."

"Including Cherry and Jasmine?"

"Yes. Do you have a problem with that?"

"Well no, but it's like asking children to look after the zoo once the animals are out. They're more likely to be eaten by a lion than provide any real help."

"That's not fair and you know it."

"I don't know it."

"Look. Officers will rotate in and out. They're not in uniform, but you won't have any problem recognizing them."

Indeed she wouldn't. Their local department had seventeen officers, including Gordon, Jasmine, Cherry, and the reserve deputies. Amber knew them all, not from official business as much as that they liked to stop by and eat at the restaurant.

"Are you sure that's necessary?"

Gordon stared at her for a moment, and suddenly she did see the exhaustion he was feeling. He hid it well in his posture and demeanor, but she could read it in his eyes. He had wanted to put an officer on her front porch the night before, but she'd refused.

He nodded brusquely. "I'm sure," he said as he stood to go.

Amber realized there was a tension between them, one that wasn't normally there, but she couldn't figure out what it was about. Probably because of the headache she had and the exhaustion seeping through her bones. Maybe it wasn't even important.

"All right. If you think it's that serious."

"I think this is the work of punks, and I plan to catch them."

"How?"

"With each incident we gather more evidence,

and they stand a greater chance of slipping up. It's not a matter of if we'll catch them. We will and when we do—"

Gordon's phone beeped. He pulled it out of his pocket and thumbed through a text.

He stuffed the phone back into his pocket.

"We've located Ethan's wife. She was out of town, but now she's back in Middlebury."

"Oh my goodness. Does she know he's dead?"

"Yes. We went by her house several times, but no one was ever home. So we left a message on her cell phone asking her to call the station. Brookstone took the call and explained about Ethan."

Amber had a curious relationship with Cherry Brookstone. She'd been with the Middlebury Police Department for a few years, was in her midtwenties, thin and fit, with long red hair and green eyes. Things had always been awkward between Cherry and Amber, perhaps because they'd both dated Gordon. How could Gordon date someone twenty years younger than he was? The idea struck her as ludicrous. But there was more to her distrust of Cherry. The officer seemed young and immature—too quick to think she knew the answers when she hadn't even asked the right questions.

"That poor woman."

"I'm headed out there now to see if she has any questions."

When Amber picked up her keys and her tablet, Gordon put a hand on top of hers.

"Where are you going?"

"With you."

He stepped back. "No, you're not."

"Yes, I am."

"Amber, I don't think—"

"He was my employee, Gordon. He died on my property, and I have a box of personal things—"

"What kind of things?"

"A photo that was on his desk, a personal mug he'd brought from home . . . what difference does it make? I need to give these items to his wife. Not to mention the truck—"

"Don't worry about the truck, and I can take the box with me."

"I'm going." Amber couldn't have said why it was so important to her, but it was. She needed to go to Ethan's home, offer her condolences, and close this chapter in the history of Village events. It was the right thing to do.

Gordon's mouth was set in a straight line, his forehead wrinkled in a frown. She wanted to reach out and smooth it away. She wanted this to be over.

"I'll wait for you out front then." He turned and left before she could think of anything to say.

Elizabeth fetched the box of Ethan's personal items from beneath her desk. As Amber made her way downstairs, she found herself thinking of

Tate Bowman and his two donkeys. She had never wanted to be a farmer, but suddenly the thought was appealing. A few hours in a barn would be perfect. She could spend the time brushing down Trixie and Velvet. The names still made her smile.

She didn't head to Tate's barn.

Instead, she finished making her way down the stairs, out the front door, and into her new little red Ford Focus. She'd do her duty, see Ethan's widow, and try to set things right. As she followed Gordon off the property, she glanced over toward Tate's farm. Hopefully he was having a better day than she was.

⇥ *Eight* ⇤

Tate's tractor had stopped running the week before. He'd spent the last hour trying to squash his frustration by working on the old engine. He wasn't having success on either front. The frustration had formed a knot across his shoulders. The tractor repair had turned into a fiasco. He had managed to get the engine to start, but then he'd broken a different part, which forced him back into town, this time to the Tractor Supply store.

Fortunately, they had what he needed, and he was soon at the register checking out.

"Say, I hear there's been a lot of action out by your place." Since there were no other customers in line, Bryan Nordman took his time ringing up Tate's purchase.

Bryan was in his midtwenties and had a man's body but a teenager's attitude. He was close to six feet, wore his dark hair too long, and was growing something on his chin. The boy could stand to see a barber. What irked Tate the most was the kid's arrogance. Bryan knew everything about everything, or at least he thought he did. Every time Tate had come into the store, the boy had voiced a strong opinion about something—usually something he didn't know anything about. Bryan was a young man who didn't realize he still had much to learn.

"The Village is keeping our local cops busy." Bryan punched a key, and Tate's total appeared on the register display.

"I suppose you could say that."

"You were right to complain about them. A death and two instances of vandalism . . ."

Tate winced. He did not want to be pulled into another discussion about all that had occurred at the Village in the last twenty-four hours.

Just thinking of the Village, recent events, and Amber Wright caused the vein in his left temple to throb. After he'd left her house the night before, it had taken him more than an hour to convince himself that she was safe and that the graffiti on the trail was done by a couple of teenage punks. Then this morning he'd gone into town for gas for the tractor—the same tractor that wasn't running. It was there he'd heard about what had happened at Amber's place during the night.

Why hadn't she called him?

Why did she insist on handling things alone?

Or maybe she'd had help. Several folks had been happy to share their suspicions about a relationship between her and Gordon Avery, which was another thing he didn't want to think about. It was none of his business whom she dated, but Gordon didn't seem like her type.

Bryan took his time accepting Tate's credit card and charging him for the purchase. The boy moved slower than an old dog on a cold morning. "No one wants that sort of thing going on next to their home. If it had been at my place—"

"Didn't know you had a place. I thought you were still living with your parents."

Bryan must have heard the remark, but he ignored it. "—I would have sat out back with my hunting rifle."

"Didn't know you were a hunter."

"Folks can't trespass at will."

"Technically the trail is public land."

Bryan shook his head as he pulled the tape from the register and handed it to Tate to sign. "If Amber Wright would—"

"Wasn't her fault."

"What?"

"I said, it wasn't her fault."

Bryan bagged the tractor part, stuffing the receipt inside the plastic sack.

"Seems to me she should have—"

"Seems to me you should shut your mouth regarding things you don't know anything about." Tate realized he ought to stop there, but the frustration had been building all morning.

"No problem. I thought since it's practically on your property line you would wish that she had done more to prevent such things."

"Prevent them how? Amber did not ask anyone to leave threatening messages on the trail or drop bloody packages on her porch. All she's done is run a business that happens to employ over five hundred people in this community, including your sister, if I remember right."

Without waiting for Bryan to respond, he snatched his bag off the counter and hustled out of the store. Why couldn't people mind their own business? And what kind of idiot placed the blame for violence on the person who had been violated?

Amber was a hard worker. She at least cared about what kind of job she did, which was more than he could say for Bryan Nordman. Rather than cleaning or shelving items, he'd been leaning against the counter reading a magazine when Tate walked up.

Tate might not have liked the Village expansion, but he had to admit that Amber had done a good job keeping the place in pristine condition and helping the local economy. No doubt she spent more time on the job than she should. He expected it was hard on a single woman.

Suddenly he remembered her uneaten plate of cold eggs the night before and her admission that she rarely cooked. She'd missed her dinner, her night had been shattered by more violence, and still she'd gone into work at her normal time. He knew because he'd been out in the pasture when her little red car had pulled out of her driveway. Usually she walked to work, so he expected she had errands on top of her normal day—a day that had started too early and would probably end too late.

There wasn't much he could do about what was happening at the Village, and he couldn't shorten her work hours, but he did know how to barbecue. He turned left at the light and headed back toward the grocery store.

He could put some ribs on the grill, or maybe a few pieces of chicken. Women seemed to like chicken. He'd cook both in case she didn't like one or the other.

Taking her dinner would be the neighborly thing to do.

Amber sat in Ethan Gray's living room and tried not to stare at his wife. Margaret Gray wore her short black hair perfectly styled. It had so much hair spray in it that Amber was certain it would withstand a small windstorm without dislodging a single strand. Her eyebrows were waxed, her makeup perfect, if a bit heavy, and her nails manicured with a deep red polish. She was a few pounds heavy for her height, which seemed to be about the same as Amber's five foot four. Fortunately for Margaret, the weight was concealed by designer clothes.

In other words, she was the polar opposite of Ethan, who had gray hair, something of a paunchy stomach, and rarely updated his wardrobe. He had always been presentable for work, but it had seemed to Amber that he'd stepped out of 1950-something, wearing the same clothes and hairstyle he probably had then.

Gordon sat beside her on the couch, and Margaret was perched across from them. She sat with ramrod posture in a straight-back chair. The house looked as if it had been furnished by an interior designer, right down to the custom-made, gold-colored drapes. There was no indication of a pet—cat or dog. Considering the snow-white carpet, Amber suspected there never would be. She'd been tempted to remove her shoes before walking into the living room.

"So you're saying the Village isn't at fault." Margaret had sat silently as Gordon had explained again the results of what he'd found the day before.

"At fault?" Amber's voice came out too high and too surprised. She pulled it down a register. "At fault for what, Mrs. Gray?"

"Ethan's death, of course."

Gordon cleared his throat. "As I explained, Ethan died of a heart attack according to the paramedics and the medical examiner who signed his death certificate. If you'd like to have an autopsy performed, then of course that is your right, but one is not being requested by the police department."

"Of course not. If the police department requested it, then you'd have to pay for the procedure." Margaret's red lips formed a straight line, almost as if she was trying to hold back the rest of her words. Her hand fluttered out, and she added, "Two thousand dollars. That's what it would cost. You expect me to pay for that?"

Amber knew Gordon well enough to read his body language. He'd started out polite when they'd walked in, but now the muscles along his back had gone rigid. When she glanced at him, she saw the tic next to his right eye. Oh yeah. Margaret was skating on very thin ice.

"If the department had found any evidence of a sudden, unexpected, violent, or traumatic death, we would have—"

"You don't call that violent?" The words dropped like stones on the white carpet. "He died clutching his chest. That's what you told me, Sergeant Avery."

116

"The medical examiner accessed his medical files and found a well-documented history of heart disease."

"Because of your Village." Margaret's smile reminded Amber of a snake about to bite. "The way you people worked him from sunup to sundown was disgraceful. Add to that the harassment from the local hooligans—"

"Mrs. Gray, if you have suspicions that this was more complicated than a heart attack, I'd appreciate it if you would share them with me. And if you would like an autopsy, then by all means order one."

Ethan's wife stared out the front window. For a fraction of a second, Amber thought she saw grief shadow her features—a trembling in her bottom lip and a softening of her eyes. Perhaps she imagined those things though because when Margaret turned back toward them, her expression had changed back to the same look of disdain she'd worn since they arrived. "The viewing will be tomorrow evening. An autopsy would interfere with that, and I couldn't bear . . . It's hard enough as things are."

"A brief delay for a viewing or funeral generally doesn't interfere with autopsy results. We have a county pathologist who would perform the procedure and work with the funeral director."

"Why are you suddenly pushing this? What are you hiding?"

Gordon sighed. It was so soft, so miniscule, that Amber suspected Margaret didn't notice. He stood, and Amber popped up as well. She certainly didn't want to be left alone in this room with Ethan's bitter widow.

"For the record, Mrs. Gray, I found nothing at the scene of Ethan's death to suggest the need for an autopsy. Should you choose to order one for personal reasons, that is always a family's right. If you have any further questions, feel free to contact me at the number on the card I gave you."

"Oh, I do have questions, Sergeant." She remained seated, piercing them with a cold, hard glare. "Maybe not questions that you're willing to answer. You can trust me when I say I know plenty of people in this town. One way or another, I will get to the bottom of Ethan's death."

Gordon apparently thought it best not to answer that. He thanked her for her time and moved toward the front door. Margaret stood as well, probably to make sure they actually left, since her manners to this point surely didn't dictate seeing them out.

Amber decided she would try one more time. "What would you like me to do about Ethan's truck?"

"I can't think of that right now. I'll call you next week."

"I am sorry for your loss, Mrs. Gray. The Village

will miss Ethan. He was an excellent employee. If there's anything that I can do—"

Margaret sniffed, as if something about Amber smelled offensive to her. "You can see that the life insurance check is delivered in a timely fashion."

Amber's mouth fell open. She quickly snapped it shut and hurried to catch up with Gordon. He was standing in the entryway of the home, studying the mahogany gun case.

"Are all of these yours, Mrs. Gray?"

"They were Ethan's." If anything, her expression became darker. "A complete waste of money, money that I could use now that he has deserted me."

Gordon nodded once and then stepped out into the spring sunshine. Amber practically ran to catch up with him.

When Margaret shut the door firmly behind them, Amber drew in a deep breath of fresh air. How long had they been in there? Hours? Days? She felt as if she should go home and shower.

"I don't know how you do it."

Gordon had followed her to her car and stood next to it, dwarfed it actually, as she fished out her keys and used the fob to unlock the door.

"Part of the job."

When Amber cocked her head, he admitted, "Though few are as bad as that one. I think I prefer a crying widow to one who is hostile."

"But what is she so angry about? She can't

seriously blame the Village or the police department."

"Probably not. She's striking out at anyone who is close to her."

"I'm sure she did love him, but—"

"Who knows if she did or not? We can never completely know the inside of a marriage, can we?"

Amber shrugged, but the thought depressed her.

Suddenly she remembered Tate and the expression of naked grief on his face the night before when he'd talked of his wife's funeral. That had been four years ago, and he still cared for her. Wasn't that the way loss was supposed to be?

She was about to pull away from the curb when she thought of what she wanted to ask Gordon. She placed the car in park, rolled down her window, and motioned him back toward her.

"Why did you ask her about the rifles?"

"Curious."

"Because—"

"Because the one on the right was a commercial air gun."

"A BB gun?"

Gordon nodded and tapped the top of her car.

She pulled away from the house and headed back to work. The sun fell through the trees like a blessing after the storm of the day before. Flowers were beginning to bloom and yards were turning green. Amber registered all the sights, smells, and sounds of spring. She tried to pull a measure of comfort from them.

But as she drove back to the Village, a feeling of dread persisted. She had the nagging suspicion that she would have to deal with Margaret Gray again—and probably soon.

⇥ *Nine* ⇤

Hannah thought she would miss the quilt shop terribly, but she was too busy to think about it. Customers came into the *kaffi* shop blurry-eyed and barely coherent. When she handed them their order, most smiled at her as if she'd given them a piece of gold.

What was with the *kaffi* addiction?

Did it brighten their day that much?

Her parents drank *kaffi*, but it smelled nothing like what she brewed in the shop. What was the difference between the two blends?

Customers kept her busy, as did the employees who happened to be working near the *kaffi* shop and decided to pop in to say hello.

She'd had several unexpected visitors, all nearly as unsettling as Karl had been.

When Amber walked into the shop, she didn't know whether to sigh in relief or worry that her boss was checking up on her.

"Hello, Hannah."

"*Gudemariye*. That is, good morning." Hannah's hand went to her *kapp* to check if she was presentable. The *kapp* had slipped to the back of her head and her hair was spilling out. She wasn't making the best impression! She tugged it forward and pushed her hair back underneath. Maybe she could run to the restroom and re-pin it during her lunch break—if she had a lunch break.

"I wanted to tell you that I checked my e-mail when I arrived back in the parking lot." Amber tapped the small tablet she carried with her everywhere. "Several people have mentioned to the staff how well you're doing."

"Me?"

"They say your sweet attitude is refreshing and a nice start to the day."

Hannah swallowed, slowly looked around to make sure no customers were in the store, and then asked, "Are you sure they meant me?"

Amber's laugh set her nerves at ease. "You're the only young Amish woman we have working in our only coffee shop, so yes—I'm sure it was you."

Perching on one of the stools near the window, she patted the spot next to her. "Take a break. Come and tell me about your day."

So she did.

She admitted that she couldn't figure out how to turn the bean grinder on, and that she'd forgotten to set out the containers of whole milk, low-fat milk, and skim milk. A customer had asked where they were, and she'd run to the back and found them in the larger refrigerator in the storeroom.

"Even with Ethan's binder, it's a lot to remember."

"But you're enjoying yourself?" Amber smiled and sipped on the bottle of water she'd purchased from the shop.

"*Ya*. More than I thought I would. I thought I'd be miserable outside the quilt shop, but there is so much to do that I haven't had time to focus on what I would normally be doing this time of day."

"Wonderful."

"And the customers are so grateful. I've never had anyone call me an angel when I sold them a yard of fabric."

Amber nodded. "You're providing an important service for them. Quilting is a hobby, even a passion for some people. But coffee? Well, some of our guests consider that sustenance."

"Do you think the music is okay? Carol plays it in the quilt shop, so I knew how to turn the system on. I know Ethan never played any, and of course we don't have any in our homes, but the customers seem to enjoy it."

Hannah noticed Amber didn't answer right away. She stared up at the ceiling as if looking for the string orchestra that was playing the hymns. Finally she smiled and patted Hannah on the knee. "The music is a nice touch. Ethan was stubborn about certain things. He thought music would cause customers to loiter."

"Loiter?"

"Hang around. He wanted them to purchase their order and leave. This is more . . . inviting. Now tell me about the binder of instructions he made."

Hannah did, even offering to fetch it so that Amber could see it for herself.

"Yes, thank you."

When she brought it back to the table, Amber spent a few moments paging through it. Finally she closed it and pushed it back across the table toward Hannah. "You say you've never seen it before?"

"*Nein*. The last time I filled in for him was . . . I think it was two weeks ago. He had two sheets of instructions in a folder then."

"Odd. I wonder what would cause him to type up something so comprehensive."

Hannah hesitated a moment. "Maybe he thought he might be called away, you know, unexpectedly."

"Why would he think that?"

Pulling the strings of her prayer *kapp* to the front, Hannah fidgeted with the ends of them. "I don't know, but people have been saying things."

"Things?"

"Yes. My friend Jesse said—" Hannah stopped suddenly. "I wouldn't want to spread gossip."

"It's not gossip if it's said without malice, and it could be that you'd help us solve the mystery of what happened here."

Thinking back to what Jesse had said the day before, Hannah wondered where she should begin. With what he had suggested? Or with what a few of the customers had told her? And what about Carol, who was still acting odd?

At that moment two moms with children in strollers pushed through the door of the shop.

Hannah stood to make her way back behind the counter, but Amber stopped her. "I'll be back when you close and we can talk."

Hannah nodded hesitantly. She didn't want to be caught up in anything to do with Ethan's death, but she was curious. The things she'd heard today hadn't made any sense. Maybe Amber would tell her it all meant nothing. Maybe she was overreacting. Regardless, Amber was her boss, so it didn't seem she had much choice.

Soon she was mixing one frappuccino and one caramel macchiato. Staying busy was good, and the young mothers were courteous, plus they tipped well. Possibly her mother was right. Possibly *Gotte* had a reason for having her work in the *kaffi* shop.

Amber ate lunch in her office. One of her New Year's resolutions was to stop doing that. She stared at the calendar on her desk. April would be gone before she knew it, and she wasn't doing so well on those resolutions. She'd stopped working on office-related stuff after she arrived at home, unless it was an emergency. But her other two resolutions—to actually take a lunch break and to nurture friendships with people her age—those weren't going so well.

The lunch thing seemed hopeless. By the time she realized she was starving, it was well into the afternoon and she didn't have time for a break. Maybe she could aim to take a real lunch one day a week. That would be a start. Tapping on the calendar icon and then the keyboard for her tablet, she scheduled a lunch break for the middle of the next week.

Pitiful.

Almost as bad as the friendship resolution. But she'd had no luck meeting people her age. Most of the people she met were guests, who were here one night and gone the next. The folks who lived in Middlebury all seemed to be paired up, and then she felt like a third wheel.

She flipped through the upcoming days, weeks, and months on her calendar while she munched on a tuna sandwich she'd ordered from the restaurant. Friends, friends, friends. She'd always been a friendly person, but it seemed close friendships were hard to come by. She longed for the kind of friend that you could call in the middle of the night.

An image of Gordon popped into her mind. When she called 9-1-1 after she'd seen the vandalism on her porch, he had arrived all business. His first question had been, "You didn't touch any of this, did you?" She appreciated his dedication to his job, but she wanted a friend who asked about *her* first and the crime scene second.

She immediately thought of Tate but pushed away the idea. He seemed like a nice guy, but they had nothing in common.

Other than maybe donkeys. Envisioning Trixie and Velvet lifted her mood as she finished her sandwich and turned back to her computer. It was amazing how many e-mails she received in a single day, and her goal was to answer each one that day so there was no spillover. But today her mind kept sliding back to Ethan, the Pumpkinvine Trail, and her front porch. Each time she'd push the images and questions away, but soon she'd catch herself staring off into space again.

Ninety minutes later, Elizabeth walked into her office, smiling and carrying two mugs of hot tea and the local newspaper.

"You're assigning Seth to the coffee shop?"

"I am." Amber reached for the tea, murmuring a thank you and gesturing to the chair opposite her desk.

"You're not worried he might . . . mess it up?"

"He's bound to fit in somewhere."

"Georgia called to warn you it was a bad idea. She claims it took them all afternoon to clean up the disaster zone he'd created in the kitchen at the bakery."

"Concern duly noted."

Elizabeth sipped her tea and peered over her glasses at Amber. "I take it you like the kid."

"He was working very hard when I arrived."

"Maybe he should have admitted he didn't know what he was doing."

"Possibly, but I admire his enthusiasm."

"And Hannah?"

"She's a sweet girl, Elizabeth. You should stop by to see her. Already the coffee shop has a completely different atmosphere."

"Ethan was certainly a grim little man. Are you going to his viewing?"

"I suppose. Mrs. Gray mentioned it will be tomorrow night."

"At seven." Elizabeth handed her the newspaper she'd been holding. "Details are at the end of the article."

Amber scanned past Ethan's picture—he was wearing a military uniform and looked impossibly young. She skipped over the details of his birth and family, finally reaching the information at the bottom of the column.

The viewing was to be held at their local funeral home at seven p.m. the next evening. They only had the one place for funerals in Middlebury, so the location wasn't a surprise. Seeing the details of his life there, summed up in one column of newspaper print, hit her like the time she'd walked behind one of her grandfather's donkeys and had been kicked solidly in the stomach.

"We sent flowers?"

"I did it an hour ago."

"Thank you." Amber sat back and studied her assistant. She realized with a start that Elizabeth was her friend. They'd worked together so long and knew each other so well that it had snuck up on her. "The last few days you've been an anchor in my storm."

"It's our storm." Elizabeth smiled as she sipped her tea. "Any idea what this rash of vandalism is all about?"

"No." She shared Gordon's news that the messages left on the trail and at her house were from the Old Testament.

"Maybe we don't need to worry then. If it's a Christian who is doing this, he must have some moral code."

"I seem to recall many passages in the Old Testament described a pretty harsh, violent society. We recently did an Old Testament study at my church. I remember thinking I wouldn't have wanted to live then, especially when the Israelites were at war—which was most of the time."

"This isn't a war."

"You and I don't think it is, but I have a feeling the person who is leaving messages is raising some sort of battle cry."

"Over what?"

Amber stared at the quilt on her wall so long that Elizabeth finally repeated her question. "Battle over what?"

"If we knew that, we might know whom we're dealing with."

Elizabeth started to respond, but the phone in the outer office rang. "Break's over," she chirped. "Business at the Village waits on no man—or creep."

Amber admired Elizabeth's solidness. She didn't rattle easily. Glancing at her watch, she realized it was time to meet with Hannah.

The young girl was certainly a bright spot in her otherwise dismal day.

⇥ Ten ⇤

Hannah happily agreed when Amber suggested they walk outside along the concrete path that led around the pond. She'd been in the store all day. As she'd worked, she'd been too busy to notice the bright sunshine and warming temperatures. Now her workday was over, a few minutes earlier than she'd expected. It hadn't taken long to go through Ethan's checklist for closing, since she'd cleaned all day when she had a free moment.

She took a deep breath of the fresh spring air and locked the door to A Simple Blend. It seemed odd that she was responsible for opening and closing one of the Village shops, but she was.

Amber waited until they were walking away from the shop to speak. "We found someone to give you a lunch break. You can begin training him tomorrow."

"Him?"

"Seth Kauffman."

Hannah stopped in the middle of the walk. "Seth? But . . . Seth has no experience in a coffee shop."

Amber hooked an arm through hers and started them walking again. "That's true. You didn't either, the first time you filled in for Ethan."

"But Seth—" Hannah clamped her mouth shut. She shouldn't say anything ill against someone else, especially someone from her church community. "Wouldn't he be better helping in the barns or on the grounds crew?"

"There are no openings in either of those areas at the moment. Seth fills in there as needed, but he doesn't have a permanent position yet. We'll watch how he does with you and see if he's responsible and a quick learner. I take reports from all the managers our floating employees work for and consider them at their ninety-day review."

"I'm not a manager."

"You are now." Amber suppressed a chuckle, and Hannah realized the look on her face must be quite comical. She shut her mouth—which had gaped open—and tried to act normal. But her heart was racing. Manager? Seriously?

"I'm sure you'll do a fine job of training him, Hannah."

"I'll do my best."

"Which is all I can ask."

A woman passed them, purse over her right shoulder, a tiny dog peeking out of the leather bag. The woman was a bit large, with dark black hair that looked to be a wig. Hannah had no idea why she would choose to wear a wig, unless there was a problem with her own hair. Hannah was distracted by the sight of the dog. She could only see the top of him. His tiny head and ears peeked out of the large purse. She could tell he was wearing a sweater and a jeweled collar. He barked once as they passed him, and the sound made Hannah smile. His voice was as small as his body.

"I didn't know we allow pets here."

"We don't in the rooms, but folks still come here to shop, and they sometimes bring along their pets."

"I've never seen one so small."

"Looked like a Chihuahua." Amber stopped walking and motioned to a bench. "Can we sit here?"

Hannah nodded. She knew this meant it was time for *their talk*. She'd thought a lot about what she should and shouldn't say.

Amber opened up her tablet and tapped a small picture with the word "Notes."

"Miss Wright—"

"Call me Amber, please."

"Amber, I've thought about what you said, and I agree this may not be gossip. However, I'd feel better if I didn't have to tell you the names, unless . . . unless you think it's something very serious."

Amber studied Hannah a moment, and Hannah had the urge to squirm like she had when her mother used to check to see if she was presentable for school or church. She forced herself not to fidget. Instead she sat very still.

"That sounds fair."

Hannah let out the breath she'd been holding.

"As long as you'll trust me if I tell you I do need to know the name of the person."

"*Ya*. I can agree to that."

"Let's start with yesterday. You said people had said things, and I believe you started to mention your friend Jesse."

Hannah had forgotten that she'd already given Jesse's name, not that he had done or said anything that would land him in trouble. She fiddled with her glasses, taking them off and then putting them back on. "We were on our lunch break, across the bridge and over by the spot where the creek runs between the two smaller ponds."

"And you began talking about Ethan?"

Hannah nodded and wet her lips. "First he asked me about the secret Ethan had told me."

"Secret?"

"*Ya.* Jesse had heard that Ethan was still alive when I found him, which he wasn't. He'd heard Ethan told me a secret."

"Strange." Amber typed a note, though Hannah couldn't see exactly what it was.

"I don't know what secret Ethan could have had."

"It's a good question. Let's keep going. What else did Jesse say?"

"Jesse talked about Ethan's truck a little, and I mentioned how he didn't seem like a happy guy. I told Jesse that he used to sweep the walk in front of his shop, muttering about the young people in the area."

"What did Jesse say about that?"

"He said maybe that was what got him killed." Hannah clasped her hands in her lap.

She didn't like thinking about Ethan as she'd found him, but she was glad Amber had picked outside under the shade of the maple tree to have their talk. The spring weather helped to scatter her worries, even as she talked about the events of the last two days. "I explained to him that Ethan wasn't killed, that the medical team said he'd had a heart attack."

"Which is true."

"Jesse didn't seem convinced. He even said there was a rumor . . . a rumor that the person who shot the BBs knew about Ethan's heart condition."

Amber's fingers stilled over the tablet. "Did Jesse tell you who was spreading this rumor?"

Hannah stared down at her hands. *"Nein."*

"It would help—" Amber waited until Hannah looked up at her. "It would help if we knew who first said this. Maybe it would lead us to the ones who did the vandalism here, along the trail, and at my house."

Hannah hadn't heard about the last, though someone who had stopped into the store had mentioned the painted words on the trail. Amber explained what had happened at her home. "Would it help if I spoke with Jesse?"

Hannah shook her head. *"Nein.* He didn't know. Rumors, they are like streams—it's hard to tell exactly where they begin."

"We are sure the vandalism is connected. At both sites the person left verses from the Old Testament."

"I had heard that about the trail, but I thought it might be another rumor."

"No. It's the truth." Amber tucked her hair

behind her ear. "All right. Is that all for yester-day?"

"*Ya*, except for Carol." The last word slipped out before she remembered she wasn't going to give names.

"Carol Jennings?" Amber's eyebrow arched up in surprise.

"She . . . well . . . she didn't seem surprised about Ethan when I first told her. In fact, she seemed almost angry."

"Any idea why that would be her reaction?"

"None. They didn't talk with each other very much that I noticed, even though their shops were next to each other. I suppose he could have done something to upset her. His manners weren't the best."

"It could be." Amber smiled at her. "You're doing great, Hannah. Now tell me about today."

Hannah glanced around and tried to find a sense of peace, a calmness that would help her to continue. This was the portion of the talk she'd been dreading. She did not want to create a problem for anyone. "Three different people stopped by, not to purchase anything but because they wanted to talk, to talk about Ethan."

"Maybe they were actually checking on you, to see how you were doing."

"Could be. They were each on their break, and they came at different times throughout the morning. The first two came when no one was in the shop, and the third one waited until the customers had left before speaking to me."

Amber didn't interrupt. She waited.

"The first one only wanted to tell me that he'd seen Ethan talking to a homeless man. This was in town, near the park. He thought it was odd."

"Were they sure it was Ethan?"

"*Ya.* His truck was parked by the side of the road. There's no other truck in Middlebury quite like Ethan's—or so Jesse claims. Ethan was standing on the sidewalk talking to this homeless man. You probably know the guy I mean."

When Amber shook her head, Hannah described him. "Tall with a beard, and he wears a ragged army coat. He might not be old himself, but it's hard to tell. I see him sometimes when I'm downtown, and once or twice I've passed him on the Pumpkinvine Trail. Some say he sleeps in the park, but others claim he spends nights in a church basement."

"Maybe Ethan stopped to offer this man some help."

Hannah stared at her, and Amber finally admitted, "That doesn't sound at all like Ethan. Does it?"

They both were silent for a moment.

Amber finally typed a few more notes, and then she sat back and studied Hannah. "It seems people around here trust you. You're easy to talk to, you're a good listener, and you were the one to find Ethan. I'm still sure Ethan's death was from natural causes, but I'd like to help the police figure out what's going on with the vandalism."

"Do you think there will be more?"

"I hope and pray not. Until we've figured it out though, I believe you and I make a good team."

Hannah had never thought about being on a team with an *Englischer*. She used to play baseball in the school yard, and they would divide into teams, but those were her friends. Amber was her boss.

"You notice things too. That's an important skill, and I think God put you here exactly when I needed help."

Hannah felt a blush creep up her neck, but she didn't say anything. She didn't know what to say.

Amber refocused on her tablet. "There were two other people who stopped by today?"

"*Ya*. They wanted to tell me that they'd heard an argument . . . loud voices between Ethan and another employee. This happened a little over a week ago, and they wondered if it had anything to do with his dying."

"I need to know who he was arguing with. Did they say?"

Hannah nodded her head in the affirmative but didn't offer a name.

"Your friends are not going to be in trouble for speaking with you, but I do want to ask a few questions of the person he was having a disagreement with."

Hannah nodded again. Finally she closed her eyes and prayed that she wasn't breaking any rules from the *Ordnung*. They were supposed to be set apart. They were supposed to stay out of others' business. But this was different. Wasn't it?

"It was Larry."

"Larry Sharp?" Amber's voice rose in surprise. "Our assistant manager?"

"*Ya*. And it seems that Larry threatened Ethan. Right before he stormed off. Apparently Ethan called him inept and then Larry became furious. He said they would see who had the last word."

⇥ *Eleven* ⇤

Tate didn't ignore his work to cook dinner for Amber Wright, but he did season the chicken and ribs, wrap them in foil, and set them to cook on his smoker. Using the smoker required that he stop by occasionally and add more chips to the wood box, but that wasn't a problem. It was after he'd fixed the tractor that he remembered she'd probably want a vegetable to go with his BBQ, so he hustled inside, found two potatoes in his pantry, and placed them on the smoker as well.

Meat and taters—it would certainly be better than the eggs she had been cooking.

Normally he worked until sunset, but after another two hours in the pasture, he went inside and showered. No use showing up smelling like his animals. Tate didn't actually plan on staying. His idea was to drive over to her house when she came home, deliver the food, and scat. Whenever she drove to work, he usually saw when her little red car made its way back from the Village to the *Dawdy Haus*—not that he stared at her or watched for her. No, it was more that he was usually out on his porch that time of day. Since his home was on a bit of a rise, it was easy to see what was going on around him.

He'd moved out to the porch with a glass of tea and was watching the sun drop over the horizon when she pulled into her drive.

"Might as well walk over," Tate muttered to himself. Seemed a waste of gasoline to fire up the truck just to travel next door. Since the storm had pushed through the night before, the weather was perfect for a stroll.

He put half the chicken, half the ribs, and one of the potatoes into a warming bag Peggy had purchased for church socials. Guilt rubbed up against his conscience—he'd been faithful to read the Bible each day, and he'd made it to the occasional worship service at their church, but he hadn't been to any socials. He'd sort of dropped off the map as far as social activity went.

By the time he reached Amber's house, he was beginning to question his plan. He considered turning back, but then he spied the damage to her porch. One look convinced him he should knock on the door. The graffiti he'd heard about had been scrubbed clean. It had also taken the paint off her wall and the porch floor. Both would need to be sanded and repainted.

What was wrong with people?

Why would someone do such a thing?

He could think of a few answers, and he didn't like any of them.

Tate opened the storm door, knocked, and then he stepped back and waited.

Amber opened the door, surprise covering her face. She looked tired, but she also seemed happy to see him.

"Tate. How are you?"

"Good. I'm good."

"I didn't expect to see you tonight. Is something wrong?"

"No. I thought I'd stop by and bring you dinner." He held up the warming bag full of food.

Amber's expression almost made him laugh. Apparently she could handle vandalism at the Village, stubborn donkeys in the rain, and an attack on her home, but if someone showed her an unexpected kindness, she was stumped.

"That . . . well, that was very nice of you. Come in."

She pulled the inside door open wide, and Tate walked into her home for the second time in twenty-four hours. Strange. They had been neighbors for longer than he could remember but had never taken the time to know each other.

The storm door latched behind him.

The yellow cat stretched, then wound between his feet, brushing against the legs of his pants. He bent to pet it, but at that exact moment it dashed out through the pet flap that had been installed in Amber's storm door.

"Saying hello, right?"

"Yes. And you're lucky you're wearing jeans and not black pants. Leo's hellos tend to leave a furry residue on black pants."

Tate resisted the urge to reach down and rub any feline hair off the lower part of his jeans. He regularly worked with donkeys, horses, and cows. A little cat hair wouldn't hurt him.

"You didn't have to bring dinner. I was about to make—"

"Eggs?"

She blushed prettily and nodded. "How'd you guess?"

"A hunch, since I interrupted your supper last night."

"Not your fault."

"It seemed like a good day to barbecue, and I

thought I'd share it with you. I heard you had a hard night after I left."

"I suppose the entire town knows by now."

"Pretty much."

Amber shrugged. "Truthfully, I didn't get much sleep, and I'm too tired to cook any dinner—even eggs. My plan was to eat an apple and go to bed."

Tate shook his head and patted the bag he'd brought. "There's chicken, ribs, and a baked potato in here."

"Oh my. Let me grab two plates."

"I wasn't . . . what I mean is that I didn't intend to invite myself to eat with you."

Amber peered into the bag. "You thought I could eat all of this?"

"I only brought half of what I cooked."

"It's more than I can eat. I'd love for you to stay."

Tate shifted from foot to foot. What had he done? If he left she'd think he was rude, and if he stayed she'd think he was nosy—or worse—interested.

He'd been raised not to be rude, and he wasn't nosy. He was concerned.

And why would he be interested?

"I didn't bring both of the potatoes."

"I'll split it with you and add a salad. How does that sound?"

Tate didn't understand women at all, but the

look on Amber's face struck him as hopeful. So he nodded and followed her into the kitchen. Together they gathered plates, silverware, napkins, salad, dressing, and drinks. Within five minutes they were sitting at her small table, a feast spread before them.

Amber stopped, glanced at him uncomfortably, and then said, "Do you mind if I pray over our meal?"

"No. Why would I mind?"

Her request didn't actually surprise him, but when she reached for his hand Tate thought he was going to fall off his chair.

"Lord, we'd like to thank you for this meal. Thank you for Tate's kindness to me, and thank you for watching over us and the people at the Village during this trying time. Please be with Ethan's wife tonight. Comfort her, Lord. Amen."

"Amen."

Amber let go of his hand, and Tate looked up at the same moment she did. Briefly their gazes locked, and Tate felt disoriented.

But then she started praising his BBQ and asking how he cooked it. The conversation helped him to forget what he'd been nervous about.

"I've never eaten salad from a bag," he confessed. "This isn't bad."

"It's one of my signature dishes."

"I don't know how working women do it. There's so much to do around a house—with the cooking, cleaning, and washing. Peggy always said she'd like to clone herself."

Suddenly he wondered if he should talk about Peggy. What if it made Amber uncomfortable? What if she thought he was some weepy mourner who couldn't get over his dead wife?

He wasn't weepy, but he was still mourning, and he hadn't moved past his wife's death. The truth hit him with the force of last night's storm.

"Peggy never seemed to mind," Amber said. "I'd see her in the grocery store or at the library and she'd always be smiling."

"She was usually content, unless one of her appliances went out, and then she resembled a lion with its tail caught in a trap."

Amber laughed. "That's my pet name for Leo— Leo the Lion, but mostly he's a lazy house cat."

Sometime during the meal Tate relaxed and stopped worrying about what he was or wasn't saying. He found himself enjoying the dinner conversation with Amber. She had a positive outlook in spite of what had happened the last two days.

After they'd eaten, she insisted on making coffee.

"Decaf," she promised. "And I have pie from the bakery. Do you like chocolate banana cream?"

"Yes, but—"

"I only have the one piece, so we'll have to share."

"An apple and a piece of pie—that was your dinner plan?"

"Guilty."

"You need to take care of yourself, Amber."

When she looked at him in surprise, he added, "The Village needs you."

They walked out onto the front porch with their coffee and single piece of pie, which she had halved. The workers who had cleaned up the mess had moved both of her rocking chairs to one side, and Leo was curled up in one, winking at them in the darkness.

Amber pulled the cat into her lap, stroking it between the ears. The quietness of the evening was occasionally broken by the sound of horses clip-clopping down the road. Tate sipped his coffee and waited. Amber finally sighed, pushed the cat from her lap, and picked up her coffee. Then she proceeded to tell him all that she'd learned since the night before.

She told him about how she'd discovered the vandalism on her porch.

"I wish you had called me. I can be here faster than the police. And you have my number on your cell phone from when I called you last night."

"Let's hope there's no more trouble, but if there is, I'll remember that."

Which was a fraction short of saying she would call him.

She told him about her visit with Ethan's widow.

"I know Margaret, but not well. She and Ethan attended my church years ago. I haven't seen either in a while, but then, you can't exactly call my attendance regular."

Amber seemed to mull that over, and then she told him about Hannah and all the information the girl had gathered.

Tate set his empty coffee cup on the small outdoor table between them and sat forward with his arms resting on his legs. He could feel the muscles in his shoulders growing more taut as Amber spoke.

"I'm going to be honest with you," he said. "Something about this concerns me. At first I thought we were dealing with teenagers, but now I'm not so sure."

"Do you think the vandalism is connected to Ethan's death?"

"It's something we should consider. I think I mentioned last night that I'm not a fan of coincidences. This has all happened in a forty-eight-hour period. Individually, these incidents don't seem like much, but combined they bother me."

"Any other insights?"

He couldn't make out her expression. She had her back to the living room window and the light fell over her like a veil, revealing little. He could tell from her voice that she was taking what he said seriously.

"No. I do think I know the homeless man Hannah described, if it's the same person. His name is Preston, and he's a veteran who served in Afghanistan."

"How do you know that?"

"He was two years older than my son Collin. In high school he was a fair athlete and a good kid."

"What happened?"

"War. Some vets transition back better than others." He thought of telling her more of Preston's story, but it didn't seem relevant.

Amber hesitated, then told him about the tension between Larry and Ethan the night she'd witnessed Ethan peeling out of the parking lot and Larry's strange reaction. "One of Hannah's friends overheard the two of them arguing with one another. It sounded like more than a passing disagreement."

"Any idea what Larry and Ethan could have been arguing about?"

"No. We usually meet when my day is ending and his is beginning. Today he sent me a text that he was held up on the far side of the property and couldn't make it."

"Humph."

"Larry's been very dependable and trustworthy."

"And yet we have another coincidence." Tate shook his head. "It seems to me that this didn't start yesterday morning. Maybe it started last week with Larry, or even before that."

Amber stood and walked to the porch rail. She stared out into the darkness for a moment. When she turned to look at Tate, she was bathed in the light from the window. He could make out her hazel eyes, prominent cheekbones, and full lips. She was a beautiful woman, and it surprised him again that she had never married.

"I want to talk to Larry, but I wonder if I should go snooping into this. Is it my place?"

"Have you talked to Gordon Avery about what you've learned?"

"No . . ." She started to add something else, but stopped herself.

Tate remembered wondering if there was a relationship between the two of them, but surely if there was, Gordon would have been at her house instead of him. He would have been the one sharing the piece of chocolate banana pie. He would have been the one gazing at Amber and feeling his pulse thrum in his ears.

"You have a right to be concerned about things happening on your property. Our police are busy enough that they're not going to pursue something unless they are convinced there's a reason to do so. Maybe you need to find that reason."

"Yes, that makes sense."

Tate helped her carry the cups and plates into the house. He noticed Leo had dashed back inside and was now perched on the back of her living room recliner, his paws tucked under him and his eyes closed. The cat's purrs blended with the night sounds.

"Thank you again for dinner." Amber followed him to the door. "And for staying to eat with me. It . . . well, it helps to have someone to share all of these details with, someone who is a good listener."

"Anytime." The word had barely escaped his mouth when Tate wondered why he had said it. They weren't exactly bosom buddies. "Call me if you hear anyone outside tonight. Promise?"

Amber's smile was all the reward he needed. "I promise."

Tate hadn't thought it would be so dark when he walked home, but he found that it didn't bother him. There was a sliver of moonlight that helped him to see his way, and he'd walked the old road leading up to his place many times. Though he'd never walked it after eating dinner with a beautiful woman living in the *Dawdy Haus*, which went to show each day could bring the unexpected.

The best part was that he'd done his neighborly duty, and now his life could return to normal. But he'd charge his cell phone and set it next to his bed in case Amber needed him.

⇒ *Twelve* ⇐

Hannah was surprised when Jesse joined her on the trail early the next morning. She reached up to check her *kapp*, then straightened her glasses, and finally settled for grasping the handlebars of her bike. Why was she nervous? Why was she worried about how she looked? Jesse had been her friend for years, and there was no reason to be all aflutter around him.

He lived farther from the Village than she did, and he didn't bother driving his buggy or riding his bike. To match his pace, Hannah walked her bike, and they talked as they continued toward the Village.

"How do you like your new job?"

"Better than I thought I would."

"*Ya?* Have you started drinking the stuff you brew?" He gave her a sideways smile, and Hannah's heart tripped a beat. Jesse Miller was too cute for his own good.

"I haven't yet, but my new goal is to try one drink a day until I've sampled them all."

"Oh, you should be a caffeine addict by then."

Hannah swatted at him, but missed when he ducked away. He was cute *and* quick.

"I went to the library last night and looked up some new drinks I might try. My thought was to have a special each day, like we had in the quilt shop."

"*Ya*? Do you need a sidewalk board to put out front? I think we have one in the grounds crew's shed. Ethan never wanted to mess with it."

"I'd love one. *Danki*, Jesse."

"*Gern gschehne.*"

For a moment they didn't speak. She heard the birds chirping as they hopped from tree to tree and, somewhere close, a calf calling out.

Then, slowly, they began talking about Ethan, the theories everyone had, and the recent spate of vandalism. They didn't come up with any new ideas, but for Hannah it was a relief to share her thoughts with someone—someone who worked at the Village and understood all that was happening. They had left the trail and started across the far side of the parking area when Hannah noticed Henry Yoder waving at them. Henry arrived even earlier than she did. He was in his parking attendant hut, but hanging out the window to try to catch their attention.

"Better see what he needs," Jesse said.

"I'll go with you."

"What's up, Henry?" Jesse leaned on the window of Henry's hut.

Hannah tried not to compare the two guys. She'd seen Henry at church and the Sunday evening singings plenty of times, but he was a good five years younger than her. Next to Henry,

Jesse looked like a grown man. How silly. He *was* a grown man, but somehow she hadn't realized it until that moment.

"I just heard from one of the overnight grounds crew. There's a problem at Katie's Mercantile."

"What kind of problem?" Jesse asked.

"Is Katie okay?" Hannah propped her bike against the shed.

"*Ya*, she's not hurt. Just needed an emergency cleanup. Maybe it's nothing. The grounds guy was passing through like you all, but he was on his way home. He didn't seem happy about having to go back in, and he told her he'd have to re–clock in first. I didn't hear much of her side, but I heard enough to know that she sounded kind of upset."

"Cleanup?" Hannah poked her head in through the shed's window to get a look at the clock on the wall. "At seven twenty in the morning?"

"Odd. I know. I guess when she arrived at the shop she found quite a mess."

Hannah clutched Jesse's arm. When he raised his eyes she knew that he was worried about the same thing she was.

"Can I leave my bike here?"

"Sure, but—"

"I'll pick it up for her later, Henry. *Danki*!" Jesse grabbed her hand and they ran across the parking area toward Katie's Mercantile.

"Maybe it has nothing to do with the other events."

153

"I hope not." Hannah's breath came out in little gasps. She'd never been good at running.

"Seems strange though. Seems like it might."

"*Ya.*"

They skidded to a stop in front of Katie's store. Hannah and Jesse slowly walked inside. She couldn't believe what she was seeing. Maybe she wasn't seeing it. Maybe this was a bad dream. At least half of Katie's merchandise had been knocked off shelves and onto the floor.

"Look at this." Jesse knelt and scooped up a handful of something off the floor.

"Birdseed?"

"*Ya.* Quite a lot of it, apparently."

The seed was scattered throughout the store—on shelves, over furniture, and across the floor.

Katie Schmucker rushed out of the back room carrying a broom and dustpan. Hannah knew Katie had recently turned fifty. She had been married once, but now she was a widow. She had never had children. It had always seemed to Hannah that Katie's customers were her children. She was gray-haired, short, and plump. She was also as sweet as shoofly pie.

"What happened, Katie?" Hannah turned in a circle, still unable to believe the disaster she was seeing.

"How I wish I knew. I arrived at work—to this!" Her voice trembled, and Hannah realized with a start that she was about to cry. She'd never seen

Katie cry, and she didn't want to start with this morning.

"Don't worry. We'll help—Jesse and I will."

Jesse took the broom and dustpan from her and started sweeping.

"But you each have your own jobs."

"We're early," Jesse explained. "Together we can clean this up in no time."

Katie nodded, but she didn't look as if she believed him.

Hannah noticed bird droppings all over one shelf. She headed toward the back for a bucket of water and a sponge. When she returned to the main room, Katie was explaining what she'd found.

"You heard them when you came in the back?"

"*Ya*. It was terrible."

"Heard who?" Hannah began scrubbing shelves and replacing merchandise.

"Not who." Katie continued pulling soiled merchandise off the shelves. She'd brought in a box to place those items in, and the box was nearly full. "What."

"What?" Hannah decided it would be better to work following behind Katie, so she stepped back and waited, gazing around the room, and that was when she saw it.

"Animals! Birds and raccoons. I think there was even a possum."

Hannah walked across the room. Windows lined

the top of the south wall. She stopped when she reached the very last one.

"I opened the front door and hooted and hollered. They fled as if a coyote was after them, but a few of the birds went into a panic. I had to chase them out with a broom."

"Hannah, what are you looking at?" Jesse had finished sweeping the aisle of kitchen goods and was making his way down the aisle of lamps, lanterns, and candles.

Katie had stopped talking and joined her. She heard Jesse set down his broom and walk their way.

"Did you leave it open?" Jesse asked.

"*Nein*. How could I? There's no way I could even reach it."

The window was pushed open all the way. A few feathers remained on the latch, and it was obvious from the disarray below it that the animals had used the open window as their entry point.

"Someone opened it." Hannah moved her head left and then right, but she didn't see anything up by the window. It certainly wouldn't have allowed a person to come through. It only opened about two inches.

"And someone scattered this birdseed through-out the store." Katie sounded more amazed than angry. "But who would do that? Why would they do it? And how would they do it?"

Jesse didn't answer, but he looked straight at Hannah. She didn't doubt for a moment that they had the same thought. They'd just been talking about the recent vandalism, and now this!

There was noise near the front door, and all three turned in that direction. The cleaning crew had arrived.

"Thank you both. You've helped a lot, and you calmed me down."

Hannah gave her a hug, and Jesse promised to stop by later to see if there was anything else she needed.

As they hurried away to their respective jobs, Hannah asked, "Thoughts?"

"Same person. Has to be. Whoever did it— well, it's like they're playing pranks."

"Except they aren't very funny."

"Agreed."

Hannah reached out and touched Jesse's arm, pulled him to a stop. "Did you see what was next to the register?"

"I saw bird droppings everywhere."

"*Nein.* That's not what I mean. There was a framed needlepoint sampler, like the ones done by women from our church."

Jesse shrugged.

"It wasn't there before. Katie keeps all the needle-work on an aisle with embroidery yarn, patterns, Aida cloth—stuff like that."

"Why would someone move it?"

"Because of what was stitched on it—"

Jesse smiled, and then he reached forward and

pulled birdseed from her hair. A delicious shiver crept down her arm when he touched her, but she ignored it. "And what was that, Hannah?"

"Daniel 9, verse 10. The words to Daniel 9, verse 10."

"I don't know that one."

"No one knows that one! And no one would stitch those words onto cloth for framing. It's not a verse to encourage—it's more to warn. Why would someone stitch a warning and place it by Katie's register?"

Amber sat at a table near the window inside A Simple Blend. She sipped Hannah's strongest blend of coffee with a shot of espresso added and whipped cream on top. Dread was filling her stomach, making it difficult to enjoy the coffee. This was not the way she had hoped to start her day. Caffeine was a needed dietary supplement for her, but it didn't make her any happier about what she was holding in her other hand. She had positioned a dish towel over the frame, but even with the protection of the dish towel she tried to keep her fingers at the back. The last thing she wanted to do was destroy evidence.

We have not obeyed the LORD our God or kept the laws he gave us. Daniel 9:10.

She and Hannah both stared at the hand-stitched verse.

Hannah's early morning rush had stumbled out,

clutching their cups of caffeine. For the moment they were alone in the shop.

"How is Katie doing? Was she able to open for customers?" Hannah had poured herself a cup of hot tea, which the shop also offered. Ethan's binder explained that she was allowed one free drink per day. When Hannah had showed it to her, Amber had marked out the word "One" and written "Unlimited" over it.

"Katie's doing all right. She thinks the incident was a prank by local teens. She's not angry as much as she is flustered—and still busy cleaning off soiled merchandise. I sent her an extra girl to help in the store today."

"And she didn't mind you taking this?" Hannah nodded at the framed verse but didn't touch it.

"No. She said she'd never seen it before." Amber sighed and placed the framed cross-stitch back into the large paper bag she'd grabbed from the restaurant. It was possible Gordon would be able to get some fingerprints off it.

"I'm glad you called me, Hannah. It was smart of you to notice that it seemed out of place. Does this verse mean anything to you? Our perpetrator seems to have a fascination with the book of Daniel."

"*Nein*. I've read Daniel before—a few verses here and there. Every Amish child is taught about the servants of God, Old Testament and New."

"What are your church services like?"

"They're in German and last about three hours. We have a lot of singing—"

"No musical instruments."

"Correct. There are also two sermons for each church service, Scripture reading, and prayer."

Amber studied her for a moment. "Not so different from our services, except we only have the one sermon and folks grow fidgety if the pastor goes past one hour."

"*Ya*. But we begin early so I believe we both finish up about the same time. We have *Englisch* neighbors, and my younger *bruders* play with their children sometimes—baseball and such."

Amber stared out the window at another perfect spring day. She didn't want to offend Hannah by questioning her, but she needed to ask. "Do you remember a recent sermon on Daniel?"

"*Nein*. I think that our sermons, that is to say the preaching style, is very different from yours. Mostly our pastors stick to the Gospels. Do you think the person doing these things is from the Amish community?"

"I don't know. I honestly haven't a clue what or whom we're dealing with here."

"How did they get into Katie's shop to spread the birdseed? And why? It's such a mean thing to do."

"Katie discovered her spare key to the back door was missing. She kept it on a lanyard hanging on a hook next to her desk. It was there yesterday, because she used it when she couldn't find her own keys. But she put it back when she discovered her keys next to the coffeepot in her break room."

"What does that mean?"

"Someone must have taken it, then come back into her shop after it was closed." Amber tapped the bag with the stitched Scripture inside.

"Or it could have been someone who had a key already."

Amber shook her head. "The only people who have a set of Village keys are Larry and me, so that doesn't make sense. Speaking of Larry, I had a word with him this morning. He claims to never have had a disagreement with Ethan. Could your friend have been mistaken?"

"*Nein*. It was Ethan and Larry. They were sure."

Amber sipped her coffee, then returned to the previous topic. "I think someone must have stolen Katie's key, then put it back after they did their damage. These messages must be a warning of some sort. The person who is doing this is obviously not happy with the Village."

"I don't understand."

"I'm not sure I do either, but it's a good thing you called me directly on my cell. Katie was so stunned, not to mention overwhelmed, that she might have forgotten. Her first thought was a cleanup crew. It helped that I was able to come down and see the vandalism myself."

"And you took a picture of the shop?"

"I did. Now I have all three incidents recorded. Maybe if I look at it often enough, I'll think of something."

"But the police are helping, *ya*?"

"They're trying." Amber stood and gathered her tablet, coffee, the paper bag, and her keys.

"What are you going to do?"

"I think it's time that I call a meeting of managers. In the meantime, if you hear anything new today, give me a ring."

Walking outside, she held her hand up to block the early morning sun. She wanted to walk around the pond, enjoy the day just a little, but instead she turned right and headed back to her office. She checked her e-mail as she walked, and before she'd gone twenty feet, she bumped smack into Gordon Avery.

"Careful." He reached out and put a hand on both of her arms.

"Gordon. I didn't see you." Amber took two steps back and tried to stop the blush that was creeping up her face.

"Apparently."

"Thank you for coming—again."

"Not a problem, but there wasn't much we could do at your most recent crime site. Your cleaning crew did a good job of obliterating any evidence." The words were said in an even tone, so she couldn't tell if he was angry or not. Perhaps he was just doing his job.

"The birds, coons, and possums beat both of us to the crime scene. I don't think you'd have found anything helpful."

"We did dust the window for fingerprints, but came up with nothing. The window didn't open itself, so we'll assume the perp was wearing gloves."

They'd nearly reached the restaurant. She thought about inviting him up to her office, but she didn't want to lose too much of her morning. She was already behind with her to-do list, and the e-mails that needed attention were piling up. So instead of proceeding to her office, she stepped to the side of the door, allowing customers to make their way around them.

"Maybe this will help." She handed him the bag with the verse from Daniel. "It's the strange verse that was left by the front register. Maybe you can find a fingerprint on it. I don't think someone could stitch wearing gloves. It would be awkward."

"It's our best hope. Thank you for not putting it in a plastic bag."

"I did an Internet search for the best way to handle evidence."

"Couldn't you just have left it where it was?" As if he realized how harsh the words had come out, Gordon attempted a smile. It came out more of a grimace. "We'll dust the frame, but the cloth won't yield much."

"I thought the science had improved, that you could retrieve fingerprints from cloth when you used—"

"You might ease up on your Internet searches. Just because something is possible doesn't mean that we have the capability to do it."

"But—"

"A homicide? We'd send it to Indianapolis or Fort Wayne. They might, and I said might, be able to retrieve prints from fabric. It's difficult, time-consuming, and expensive. There's no way I can request it for a case of vandalism where no one was hurt."

There was no arguing with him. She knew Gordon well enough to understand that. And part of what he said made sense, unless this most recent incident was connected to Ethan's death. Another part of her wondered if he even wanted to find the perp, which was a ridiculous thought. Of course he did. It might seem like he was brushing her off, but no doubt she was being too sensitive. Stress often had that effect on her.

She noticed that he again hadn't asked how she was doing, focusing instead on the crime and the evidence. Well, that was his job, and his attitude shouldn't bother her at all.

Though she had to wonder about their relationship. Did they even have one? She had turned him down the last few times he'd asked her out. With a start, she realized she was more comfortable not seeing him on a personal level. He was a nice guy, her age, and single, but beyond that they didn't seem to have much in common. There certainly was no spark.

Or perhaps she was making excuses, like her sister claimed she did every time a possible relationship began to grow serious.

"Did you handle this?" Gordon held the paper bag as if it had a skunk in it.

"With a dish towel, but I tried to only touch the back. I suspect you'll have the best chance of finding prints on the frame." She waited for him to congratulate her on finding a piece of evidence, but he didn't. "I hope it yields something."

Gordon grunted. "I'm going to be honest with you. It seems more and more to me like this is the work of some teen punks. Maybe Amish—on their *rumspringa*. Or *Englischers*—on a wild tear. Either way, there's no actual violence involved and I don't think you have to worry about anyone's safety."

"And Ethan?"

"We both know that was a heart attack. Look, Amber." He tugged on her arm to pull her away from anyone who might overhear. "I understand you might be spooked by this, but my suggestion would be to perhaps hire a couple of security guards to catch these thugs before they do some real property damage."

"We had video security in Katie's shop."

Amber's voice rose defensively. "Someone turned it off."

"Katie can't even remember if she turned it on." Gordon scrubbed a hand over his face, and for a moment she saw the tiredness there. "Talk to your managers. Maybe schedule a half-day training seminar on good security protocols. I've emailed you the name of a firm that does classes. They'll even come here. I'll also send you the names of a few people who are willing to work security."

"That's it?"

"We'll pursue the clues we have." He looked doubtfully at the bag. "And of course we'll come out if you need us. But I can't afford to leave officers here when it seems certain these are kids playing games."

Amber couldn't believe what she was hearing. He was deserting her!

"Check your files. See if you've fired anyone recently. Send me those names, and I'll check them out."

With that final piece of advice, Gordon turned and walked away.

⇥ Thirteen ⇤

Tate pulled into the parking lot of the funeral home. After placing his truck in park, he fidgeted with his tie one last time. He rarely wore them anymore, and it felt as if someone had their hands clamped around his neck.

The funeral home looked no different than it had four years ago when Peggy had died. He'd been to three other visitations since then. He supposed he was at that age, fifty-two, when funerals became a routine part of life. The thought depressed him.

Walking to the front door, he nodded to several people he knew. In spite of Ethan's sour personality, the event seemed well attended. Folks tended to forgive and forget, at least until the body went into the ground—then old grudges usually flared back up.

He signed the guest book and then hesitated. Should he go straight into the room where Ethan was? Or should he wait and socialize a few minutes? You'd think he'd be better at this. It wasn't as if he had been close friends with Ethan, but the man had attended his church. Proper thing to do was show up at the visitation.

"Tate, it's good to see you." His pastor, Mitch Dodson, signed in behind him and then shook his hand.

Mitch was tall, thin, and had receding hair that had managed to stay black in spite of his age.

He had been the pastor of Tate's church since Tate's boys were in high school—probably over ten years now. Tate thought he was a fair man with a good heart. It helped that his sermons were interesting and not fire and brimstone like the guy they'd had before him. Tate understood too well the repercussions of his sin. He went to church to hear about hope, to be encouraged. That was a thing Mitch seemed naturally born to— encouraging others. The thought made Tate feel all the more guilty that he hadn't been attending regularly.

Mitch never called him on it. Like now, he acted as if they'd just spoken last week.

"How's Margaret?" Tate asked.

"Hard to say. I haven't seen her today."

Tate tried to keep his expression neutral, but apparently he didn't do a good job of it.

Mitch chuckled. "No worries. I don't take it personal when a member of my congregation would rather use the staff here at the funeral home."

Mitch studied the room and the group of visitors before he added, "Honestly, I haven't seen much of Ethan and Margaret in the last few years. I'm surprised she called me at all."

Tate didn't know how to respond, so he didn't say anything.

"Have you been in yet?"

"Um, no. I was trying to figure out if I should mingle first."

They stepped into the entry hall, and Mitch craned his neck to look down the hall toward the chapel. "If the line is short, I say we take the plunge."

Tate had forgotten that Mitch was a funny guy. He admired a pastor who could joke at a funeral home. He also knew, firsthand, how compassionate and helpful his pastor could be. Four years ago, Mitch had certainly been a pillar of strength for him.

"Say, Mitch, before we go in, could I ask you something?"

"Sure."

"How do you feel about the book of Daniel?"

"How do I *feel* about it?" Mitch ran his hand over his jaw. "Humph. Children love the story of Daniel in the lions' den, and of course theologically I find the episode fascinating, but the book of Daniel has a dark side as well."

"How so?"

"Daniel 5 contains some grim stuff. Think if you were eating dinner and suddenly a hand began writing an indecipherable message on the wall."

"That's in Daniel?" Tate thought of the blood on Amber's porch.

"It is. Remember, though, that Daniel is a book about God's people in exile, and how they remain faithful to him. The events there assure us of the sovereignty of God, even in difficult circumstances."

Difficult circumstances. Well, they were certainly having those at the moment. "Thanks. That helps."

"No problem. It's not every day someone asks me about an Old Testament prophet. Let me know if you have any other questions."

The viewing was held in the small chapel, perhaps because the traditional viewing room wouldn't have been large enough. A family of four exited the room as Tate and Mitch moved inside.

There was a short line, in the middle aisle. A few folks—family he assumed—were scattered in clusters in both the right and left rows of pews. At the front of the room Ethan's casket was positioned between two giant floral sprays.

The flowers Margaret had chosen were black, gray, and white carnations.

Had black carnations been Ethan's favorite flower? Who even made such a thing?

And what had he expected? Coffee bean plants?

They seemed an odd choice to Tate, but then, he'd only planned one funeral, and he'd chosen daisies because they were Peggy's favorite flower. He supposed one flower was as good as another though, and it wasn't as if Ethan could see the arrangements.

Pulling his eyes away from the flowers, he

stared at the carpet as they shuffled forward in line. Then he heard a voice he knew, glanced up, and saw Amber.

She was ahead of them. She'd stepped to the side to speak to someone sitting in a pew—another family member he supposed. Amber wore a simple black dress and had her chestnut hair piled on top of her head, a few curls escaping at the base of her neck. His pulse accelerated at the sight of her, and his heart flopped like a fish out of water.

Looking at her, in that moment, in that place, he knew.

He knew it was all beginning again for him, and there was no use in fighting it. He took a deep breath, and his palms began to sweat.

Amber Wright.

The woman who had been his next-door neighbor for years.

His mind blanked in confusion, and then he recalled Mitch's words in the foyer. Hadn't the pastor just mentioned God's sovereignty, even in difficult circumstances?

His last four years had been difficult. He certainly never would have chosen to care for someone again. Suddenly he remembered a conversation with Peggy, only a few days before she died. She'd made him promise that he wouldn't shut his heart to life and to love.

How had she known?

And why now?

It seemed that certain things in life were predetermined or fate or God's will. Whatever you wanted to call it, Tate realized suddenly that there was no use struggling against the tide. He realized that he didn't even want to fight what he was feeling.

Everything before that moment was his past, and she was his future.

Even though a week ago he would have laughed at the idea, would have insisted he was too old and that phase of his life was over . . . he now knew the truth.

And as with most things in his life, he faced up to it.

He was falling in love with Amber Wright.

Amber let her eyes wander over the room—a rather gloomy room it seemed to her, but with a respectable number of mourners. She was going down the row, seeing if there was anyone she knew, when she caught Tate Bowman staring at her. At first she wondered if her hair had started tumbling down or maybe she'd worn two different shoes, but then she realized he was looking at *her,* not at her hair or what she was wearing.

Their eyes locked for a brief moment, butterflies pressed against the inside of her stomach, and then it was time for her to move forward and express her condolences to Margaret Gray.

Margaret wore a black suit with a gray linen blouse. Apparently she had dressed to match the unusual display of flowers.

"I wanted to offer my condolences and again tell you how much we'll miss Ethan at the Village."

Margaret's red lips formed a straight line. She stared at Amber for a moment, not blinking, not speaking a word, not even acting as if she'd heard what Amber had said.

Then she leaned forward as if to confide in Amber, and said, "If you're truly sorry, find his killer." The words were delivered in a staged whisper, loud enough for anyone in the room to hear.

Several of the folks standing nearby stopped talking and turned their attention to Amber. She felt a blush creeping up her neck, but managed to keep her voice polite and lowered.

"I'm sure the Middlebury police will contact us both if there's any change in—"

"The police won't listen!" Margaret snarled. "This is your fault. It happened on your property. You are the one who should clean it up."

Amber was stunned into silence.

She didn't notice Tate had moved to her side until he cupped her elbow in his hand and spoke to Margaret.

"I'm sure you don't blame Amber for what happened."

"How are you sure of that?" Margaret looked up and down the two of them. "Oh. I see how it is. Well, I suppose one can't expect a man to stay faithful to a dead wife forever."

Amber sensed Tate's muscles tense. Before he could respond though, a tall, thin man with receding hair stepped up beside them.

"Margaret, perhaps we should step into one of the prayer rooms."

Ethan's widow pulled herself into a rigid, perfect posture. Amber had the sense that she was about to spit venom at this man as well, when they were interrupted by the woman on Margaret's right side.

The woman looked to be a few years younger than Ethan. Her hair was a mixture of gray, brown, and red, as if someone had started with a bottle of dye but been interrupted. It curled all over her head in a tangled fashion. She reached out a hand to touch Margaret's arm, and Amber noticed that her skin was spotted by the sun.

She was heavy, but not in a soft way, and she wore a bright floral dress.

"Is she the one?" The words were delivered like a well-placed arrow.

Margaret jerked away as if the woman's touch had scalded her. She nodded her head once.

"You're an evil, terrible person. You took my brother away—my brother!" She didn't look directly at them and she rocked slightly as she spoke. "Ethan took care of me and now he's gone. He's gone because of you. It's all your fault! I will never see him again, and it's your fault!"

Ethan was right behind her if she wanted to see him; he was lying in the open casket. Amber didn't think it would help to point that out, and she suddenly hoped this woman, Ethan's sister, would not turn around at that moment. She seemed to be spinning out of control.

The woman reached up and twisted a strand of her hair, causing it to poke out even more. Her face turned first angry and then grief-stricken. It was as if she was flipping through emotions, trying to choose the one that fit. Suddenly she began to cry, quietly at first and then with giant sobs that shattered the relative silence of the room. She attempted to put her arms around Margaret, to hug her and draw some consolation. Margaret stepped out of the way, out of the reach of the woman's arms.

A man who had been sitting on the front pew leapt forward and tucked an arm around her, though he struggled under her weight. He pulled her back toward the pew, murmuring, "It's okay, Pat. It's going to be okay."

The woman continued to cry and twist her hair, now oblivious to Amber and the others. "I want Ethan to wake up. Make him wake up."

Amber turned back to Margaret, who had a smirk on her face. "See what you've done? And I won't be responsible for her. Live with that on your conscience, Miss Wright, because Ethan was the one person standing between her and the street."

Margaret turned and stomped out of the room via a back exit. The tall man who seemed to be with Tate hurried after her. Amber stood there, shocked and unable to move.

"Come on," Tate murmured. "Looks like you could use a cup of punch."

He tucked her hand into the crook of his arm and led her down a side aisle. They had moved into the room with refreshments and Tate had snagged two paper cups of raspberry punch before Amber found her voice.

"Who was that?"

"Patricia, Ethan's sister. I haven't seen her in years."

"What . . ." Amber sipped her punch and studied the room. Convinced no one was close enough to hear them, she asked, "What's wrong with her?"

Tate shrugged, as if to say he had no idea.

Before Amber could figure out what question to ask next, the man who had followed Margaret out of the viewing room joined them.

"Amber, this is my pastor, Mitch Dodson."

"Nice to meet you." Instead of looking aghast or exhausted, the pastor offered a small smile and placed his hands in his pants pockets, jingling the change there.

"I am so sorry about what happened in there."

Amber stared down into her punch. "I don't know what I could have said or done to set them both off."

Mitch waved away her concern. "Patricia has been that way since she was a teenager. I only know a few of the details. Ethan wasn't willing to talk about it. I do know that Patricia has an emotional disorder of sorts. As you could tell, she has trouble dealing with her feelings, or even choosing one emotion for that matter."

"It happened years ago, when Patricia was a senior in high school." Tate moved closer and lowered his voice. "She experimented with some drugs—LSD, I think."

"LSD can cause that?" Amber asked. "She's still having effects from when she was a teen? I don't understand."

"I'm no expert. All I know is that she never quite recovered. She's quite intelligent, but has problems socially and emotionally. Ethan, or maybe it was Margaret, shared the details with Peggy once."

"Is that why she does the repetitive—" Amber made a motion that mimicked Patricia's hair pulling.

Tate nodded. "I can assure you it was nothing you did."

"Still, maybe I shouldn't have come. Margaret obviously isn't ready to see me."

Mitch studied her a moment, then said,

"Margaret can be difficult at times. Don't be too hard on yourself."

"She was upset when Gordon and I visited her, but I thought perhaps she'd had time to calm down."

"It seems she holds you responsible, Miss Wright."

"Amber, please."

Mitch picked up two cookies and offered one to her. Amber declined, but Tate accepted it.

"Yes. She does. I suppose because he worked at the Village."

"Margaret feels you should have prevented Ethan's death since you're the manager there."

"I am. How did you know?"

"It's a small town."

"Pastors tend to know most of what is going on." Tate smiled. "Mitch winds up in the middle of many family feuds."

"It's true. I'm thrown into the role of unwitting negotiator more often than one would expect."

"Is that what this is? A family feud?"

Tate and Mitch exchanged a look, indicating they knew more than they were saying at the moment. Mitch raised a hand in greeting to someone on the other side of the room. "It's a pleasure to meet you, Amber. Tate, see you soon."

Then he was gone, speaking to folks as he made his way around the room, and leaving Amber with more questions than she'd had when she arrived.

⇒ *Fourteen* ⇐

Hannah was locking up the coffee shop the next day when Amber appeared at her side.

"How was your day?"

"*Gut*."

"That's wonderful, Hannah. I knew you'd be a natural at this. You're kind and courteous to customers. That's the main ingredient for success."

Hannah wasn't completely convinced, but she nodded politely.

"I was wondering if you had time to chat with me."

"Actually I was headed home. I promised to help my *mamm* with a quilt we've been working on for one of my cousins."

"Oh. Could I give you a ride? That would save you some time."

"That's not necessary."

"But I want to. You've been very gracious to take on these extra responsibilities, and I appreciate it. Plus, I could use a little time away from the office."

Hannah smiled and pushed up her glasses. She'd never imagined Amber as being like the rest of them. She'd just assumed that Amber lived and breathed the Village, but no doubt she had other hobbies as well.

"*Ya*, okay. *Danki*."

"Did you ride your bike today?"

"No, my *bruder* needed it, so I walked."

Hannah had ridden in *Englisch* cars plenty of times, but Amber's was different. It was small and sporty and red. The seats were black leather and much softer than any leather she'd ever touched.

"Nice car," she murmured.

"Do you think so?" Amber pushed a button and started the car, which barely made any noise at all. "I bought it because it gets great gas mileage. I have to admit that it's fun though. I've never owned a red car before."

"We don't have much of this color in our lives."

"That's right. You don't wear red, correct?"

"*Ya*."

"And I think I read that you don't quilt with it." Amber frowned. "Come to think of it, the quilt in my office and the one in my home have red material and they're both Amish-made."

Hannah was surprised that Amber knew those things. What else did she know about Amish life?

"We do quilt with red fabric if we're making something to sell or as a gift for an *Englischer*. It's not that we think it's a bad color or anything, but it's rather—"

"Bold."

"*Ya*. Bold is a *gut* word."

After she'd explained to Amber where she lived,

Hannah sat back and relaxed. The ride was smooth. She thought it was almost as good as a ride in her parents' buggy.

They spoke about the coffee shop and how busy the week had been. Fortunately Amber didn't bring up the subject of Ethan. Hannah was feeling tired and depleted. She did not want to think about, let alone discuss, the death of Ethan Gray.

Amber pulled to a stop in front of Hannah's home. It was only two thirty, so Hannah's brothers were still at work in the fields, but as soon as the car had driven up, Mattie appeared at the screen door.

"Your little sister looks happy to see you."

"That's Mattie." Hannah hesitated for a moment, then added, "Would you like to come inside?"

Amber's smile pretty much said it all. By the time they'd walked up the porch steps, Mattie had run to fetch Hannah's mother.

"What is it, child?" Eunice was bent over the quilting frame and didn't immediately realize that they had company.

"*Mamm*, this is Amber, my boss."

Eunice stowed her sewing needle in the quilt and walked over to say hello.

"It's nice to meet you." Amber didn't offer to shake her hand; instead she stood staring at the Lone Star quilt on the quilt stand. "That is beautiful."

"*Danki*." Eunice offered Amber something to drink.

"No thank you. I gave Hannah a ride home."

"You shouldn't have gone to the trouble."

"*Ya*, I told her that, *Mamm*." Hannah picked up her little sister, sat down, and settled her on her lap. Mattie patted Hannah's face with one hand and sucked her fingers with the other.

"Truthfully, I simply wanted some time away from the office." Amber folded her arms around her middle, as if she were hugging herself.

"I understand. There are days when I make up errands so I can go to town for an hour or so. I suppose wherever you work, it's *gut* to have time away."

"Hannah told me you're making the quilt for her cousin."

"*Ya*. She marries in a few weeks, and we want to have this finished by then."

Hannah set Mattie on the floor near a basket of toys and pulled her chair closer to the quilt. "You've worked on it some already today."

"Only a little while your *schweschder* napped." Eunice turned back to Amber. "Do you quilt?"

"No. I don't. But I'd love to watch for a few minutes, if you don't mind."

"We don't mind at all."

Hannah wondered if that was true. She'd been looking forward to a quiet afternoon at home, sewing and relaxing. Could she do that with her boss watching over her shoulder? But she soon found that Amber wasn't a distraction at all. As her mother and Amber talked, Hannah forgot about any worries at the Village and did what she loved to do—rocking the needle through the layers of the quilt, laying down a neat, tight row of stitches.

"You make that look so easy." Amber leaned forward. "How long have you been quilting?"

"Since I was small. Would you like to try?"

"No! I wouldn't dare. I might make a terrible mess of your quilt."

"You'll only learn by trying," Eunice said. "But if you don't want to work on the quilt, we have some extra pieces of material you could practice on."

Hannah fetched the sample square they'd made before the work on the quilt had begun. "Use this. It was for practice and we never quilted it, only pieced it together."

The next hour was spent making progress on the Lone Star quilt and laughing at Amber's attempts to hand quilt. It had taken her a good ten minutes to thread the needle, then she'd proceeded to stick her finger repeatedly. Each time she yelped, Mattie ran to her side to be sure she was all right. Her stitches were uneven, too large, and in a rather wavy line, but she was a good sport about it. "My sister would be proud I'm even making an attempt."

Hannah had never thought of her having a sister. She'd always been Amber, her boss. She was learning that even bosses had family and doubts and fears. Amber shared some of those as they walked out to her little car an hour later.

"I'm afraid I'm avoiding work because I'm a little overwhelmed at the moment. I feel as if I should be doing something about Ethan, but I don't know what. I was hoping an hour away might clear my mind."

"Today was his funeral. I'm surprised you didn't go."

Amber shrugged. "I attended the viewing last night."

"And?"

"And I only came away with more questions."

Amber stared at Hannah, wondering how much she should share. She had already taken a ninety-minute lunch, and she should be getting back. But something told her that Hannah was a person she could trust. The girl was much older, much more mature, than her years.

"To begin with, Margaret, Ethan's wife, was quite hostile."

"Toward you?"

"Yes."

Hannah didn't answer immediately, instead she walked over to a maple tree that was resplendent in new leaves.

"Perhaps she doesn't know what to do with her sorrow, with her loss, so she struck out at you."

"That's possible, but it felt . . . more personal."

"It's hard to not take such things personally."

"Then there was his sister, Patricia." Amber folded her arms, again hugging herself. It wasn't cold outside, but she suddenly felt as if all the warmth had fled the April afternoon. "Something's not right about Patricia. She's what we used to call . . . special."

Hannah ran her fingers down the strings of her *kapp*. "Special in what way?"

"I wouldn't say that she is learning disabled, but perhaps emotionally disabled. Something's off. There was a real scene at the viewing last night as I tried to speak with Margaret and offer my condolences. I suppose it left me out of sorts."

"Funerals can be difficult—even Amish funerals. We're supposed to accept everything as *Gotte's wille*, and we try to do that." Hannah pulled in a deep breath and let it out slowly. "There are times though when that isn't so easy. At those moments, people sometimes say and do things they regret."

"Maybe you're right. Maybe Ethan's family has regrets they don't know how to deal with. I suppose every family does."

As they walked to Amber's car and she opened the door, they talked again about the recent vandalism at the Village.

"Do you think it could be someone who is

Amish?" Amber asked the question gently. "It's not something I can imagine, but you know your community better than I do."

"I don't know. Ethan certainly had trouble with some of the teenage boys, both Amish and *Englisch*, but I can't think of any Amish I know who are angry enough to do such a thing."

"If the culprit isn't Amish, then they're *Englisch*. I suppose we'll have to depend on Officer Avery to catch them."

"Do you trust him? Officer Avery?"

"Of course. I mean, he seems efficient and he's a good person." For some reason Amber felt the need to defend him—whether to Hannah or to herself, she wasn't sure.

"We try to limit involvement with the authorities."

"Why?"

"My parents say it's best to solve things ourselves, that we know each other, what everyone is capable of, and how to handle it better than any outsider."

"I suppose. I don't know that Gordon Avery is an outsider, though he's never really synced with the community here in Middlebury either. Maybe it's because he's an officer. Perhaps he can do his job better if he maintains a certain distance."

Hannah stood near the porch, waving at Amber as she backed down the lane.

As she made her way toward the Village, she

realized that Hannah was someone she could be friends with. She was certainly a good person to bounce questions off of, and she had a mature perspective on both the Amish and *Englisch* sides of the community. The question was whether or not—together—they could bring anything to the investigation. Could they help Gordon Avery in any way? Or should they sit back and allow the law to do its work?

All were questions that circled in Amber's mind as she found her way back to the Village, hoping and praying they'd seen their last instance of vandalism.

⇥ *Fifteen* ⇤

Hannah was grateful it was Friday. She'd finally found a rhythm in her new job, but the work was more exhausting than she would have expected. Her days off were scheduled for Sunday and Monday. Make it through today, show up early tomorrow, and she'd have two days to rest.

All of the shops were closed on Sunday—everything except the inn and the restaurant. Even the conference center was rarely used on Sundays.

Ethan had kept the shop open on Mondays, though he didn't clock in the hours, and he left earlier than on other days. He had an agreement with Amber in that he shared in a percentage of the profits from his shop. Profits! The idea was something Hannah had never actually considered. She was managing A Simple Blend on a trial basis. If things went well, Amber had said she'd be offered the job permanently. At that point, she, too, would receive a percentage of what the shop earned.

Hannah tried not to focus on that. She knew the extra income would help her family, but she didn't want to count on what was not certain. Best to be grateful for what she had at the moment.

And she had a very good job with two days off a week. Amber never asked Amish employees to work on Sunday. They would have declined, but Hannah knew it was one of the things everyone respected about their manager. She understood and respected their practice of never working on the Sabbath. And Amber had explained to Hannah that Ethan's sales were relatively low on Monday, and there was no need for her to work the extra day. Perhaps after they had adequately trained Seth, he could work on Monday when Hannah was off.

Hannah had taken her lunch bag to a bench on the other side of the pond and enjoyed a snack as she watched the guests amble about. For a moment, she had let all of her worries fall away. Now she strolled back toward the shop, basking in the sunshine of the spring morning, and murmured a prayer that Seth had managed to stay out of trouble.

Then she opened the door to the shop.

Seth stood behind the counter. The gray wool cap he always wore, identical to the type all the Amish boys wore, was tilted at an odd angle. His smock, which he'd had on no more than twenty minutes, was stained with coffee and whipped cream. An *Englisch* customer, a young mother, was waiting on her order. She held on to a little girl's hand. Both the mother and little girl watched Hannah as she hurried to the register.

Hannah noticed coffee beans had spewed from the grinder and were covering the counter.

"How did you make this big of a mess in such a short time?" She kept her voice lowered, but the customer heard her.

"He had an accident with the whipped cream."

"I did." Seth slowly moved his gaze up to the ceiling.

Hannah willed herself not to look, but her eyes crept upward. Whipped cream dotted the ceiling tiles.

"I'm sorry, Hannah. I was shaking the can and I guess my finger hit the trigger by mistake."

Closing her eyes, Hannah counted slowly to three. Then she directed her attention to the customer.

"You're waiting on your order?"

"Yes, I saw your 'New & Tasty' sign outside and thought a raspberry latte sounded wonderful."

"I'll have that right up for you." Hannah turned

to retrieve the raspberry syrup from the counter behind them. "Start cleaning," she hissed to Seth.

"Only half the espresso, please." The customer smiled broadly when Hannah turned back toward her. "I'm trying to cut down on my caffeine consumption."

"*Ya*. Lots of people are." Hannah pulled the single shot of espresso and combined it with one ounce of raspberry. "Did you want to drink this here or—"

"To go. I thought I'd take Belinda outside and let her play."

"The weather is perfect," Hannah agreed. She poured the shot and syrup into one of their to-go cups and then filled the rest of the cup with steamed milk, topping it off with a half inch of foam. She covered the entire thing with a light dusting of red sugar to give it a raspberry look.

After she accepted the woman's money, she reached into the bakery display and pulled out a sugar cookie with bright sprinkles. "I appreciate your waiting for your order, and I'd like to give this to your daughter."

"That's not necessary."

"But I'd like to, if you don't mind."

"Belinda loves cookies."

The little girl with long red hair looked to her mother, waiting for permission.

"I'm sure one won't ruin her appetite for lunch."

When her mother nodded, the girl clapped her

hands and grinned as she accepted the cookie. She was probably a year older than Hannah's sister, Mattie.

The woman walked slowly as the little girl toddled beside her, out of the shop and around the walkway that circled the pond. Hannah wanted to stand and watch the pleasant spring scene. She wanted to follow the woman back outside! Instead she crossed her arms and turned to Seth.

"What were you thinking?"

"I'm sorry, Hannah." Seth held up both hands, palms out.

"I told you no specialty drinks. You're to tell the customers to come back."

"*Ya*, but she sounded so pleased when she read about today's special."

"*Look* at our ceiling."

"I'll grab the ladder I saw in the storeroom." Seth smiled at her impishly.

As much as she wanted to be angry with him, it was difficult. He had arrived on time each day and always worked with such a pleasant attitude, even if he was a walking disaster.

"Hurry. Before it dries." She turned her attention to cleaning up the espresso beans. Had he forgotten to put the lid on the machine again? Shaking her head in wonder, she ran a clean dish towel along the counter, scooping the mess into the trash can.

Seth returned, climbed the ladder, and began wiping the goo from the ceiling. It was good he was so tall, nearly six feet, if Hannah guessed correctly. She never would have been able to reach the mess on the ceiling, but Seth was having no problem.

Another customer came in, this one requesting hot tea. Their tea selection was woefully slim, but she recited what they offered and then began to fill the older woman's order. After the woman had paid, Hannah jotted a quick note on the pad she kept by the register. She'd seen a nice selection of variety teas in the catalog. Ethan had never ordered any of them, but she was in charge now. The thought cheered her even more, helping to ease the stress of Seth's mishap.

Seth returned the ladder to the back room and proceeded to sign out on the time sheet she kept on the wall beside the register. As he took a pen out of the cup near the register, his elbow bumped the stack of Village fliers and sent them cascading across the floor.

"I've got that. Sorry. I'll put them back exactly like you had them."

Hannah pressed a hand against the counter and stared at him. She'd never met someone who was so clumsy.

"Seth."

"Nearly done—" He was kneeling on the floor, gathering the fliers into a stack.

"Listen to me."

"Sure, Hannah. I always listen. You're a *gut* boss, and I want to learn from you."

"Seth."

Finally he was finished restacking the fliers. "Yes?"

"Sit down. I need to talk to you."

His customary smile dropped and his eyes widened. "You're not firing me, are you? Because I need this job."

"Let's sit at the table by the window. Perhaps we'll have an uninterrupted moment."

Seth ducked his head and followed her to the table. He looked for all the world like one of her brother Noah's pups after he'd been caught making a mess of something.

Hannah allowed the peace and the calm of the shop to settle around them. A hymn played softly over the speakers. Sunshine splashed through the window. The air was rich with the smell of coffee. She prayed for wisdom and then began to question Seth.

"Are you always this clumsy?"

"Yes."

"Have you tried to change?"

"I'm real sorry, Hannah—"

"That's not what I asked you. Have you tried to be less of a disaster?" The words sounded harsh even to her ears, but she knew it was time someone had a talk with Seth. Better her than Amber.

The boy didn't look as if he was used to straight talk, especially from a woman.

"Um, what do you mean?"

Hannah tapped her fingers against the tabletop. "Seth, you need to move slower. Before you do something, like shake whipped cream, stop and think what could happen. Point it in the sink if you think it might explode."

"*Ya*, that's a *gut* idea." His words were mumbled to the tabletop.

"Look at me, Seth."

"Are you going to fire me?"

This time she saw real fear in his eyes, and something in her heart twisted.

"I need this job. I'm the oldest. My *mamm* —she is worn completely out with my little *schweschders*."

"You have six?"

"*Ya*. They're smart little girls too."

"What of your *dat*?" Hannah saw the Kauffman family at church. The mother always seemed exhausted, and the father struck her as a bit grim.

"*Dat*'s doing his best. He tried to get on at the factory during the winter, but they weren't hiring. And his crops, they didn't bring in enough last year. He works hard though, and we'll be fine. It's only that I need to help as much as I can."

"So there's a lot of pressure on you."

"*Nein*. I like to work." Seth's smile returned,

then vanished. "You're not firing me, are you, Hannah?"

"No, I am not." When Seth nearly bounded out of his chair, she raised a hand to stop him. "However, I'm going to give you an assignment."

"Assignment? Like at school?"

"Sort of like that." Hannah couldn't help smiling at the look of dismay on his face.

"School wasn't my favorite place," Seth admitted.

"Here's what I want. Every time you have an accident here in the shop or even outside the shop—any accident that is related to your work—I want you to write out one page explaining what happened before, during, and after."

"Write it?"

"I think this will help you to see what's causing the disasters."

"It's not like it happens every day," Seth argued.

"The bakery?"

"Yes, but—"

"Remember when you dumped packets of sugar all over the floor?"

"I cleaned them up."

"You also filled the milk canister with chocolate syrup."

"An honest mistake."

"And today . . ." Hannah waved at the serving area. No need to rehash what had happened today.

"Do I have to write about all those things?"

"Let's stick with what happened today."

Seth sighed, and his familiar smile returned. "Sure, Hannah. If you think it will help."

"It can't hurt."

Seth stood and walked back behind the counter. He slowly and methodically removed his apron, then hung it on the hook behind the counter. He moved as if he suddenly suspected mishaps were stalking him and might appear at any moment.

"Hannah, do you think Ethan also had accidents? Do you think that's why he kept the box of carpenter supplies?"

"Carpenter supplies?"

"*Ya.* I saw them in the back room when I returned the ladder."

"What are you talking about, Seth? Ethan never did any carpentry work that I know of. He swept the walk out front, but that was about it."

"There are brushes, a smock, a can of paint—"

Hannah's pulse jumped, and she heard a strange ringing in her ears. "Seth, is this something you saw?"

"I just said that." Now he was staring at her oddly. "I saw them in the back corner of the supply room. I nearly tripped over the box when I was returning the ladder. Maybe I should write about tripping, even though I didn't. That could have been a disaster, especially if—"

But Hannah wasn't listening. She was already halfway to the supply room as Seth continued talking. If Seth was describing what she feared he was describing, she needed to tell Amber. But first she should check it out. First she should be sure.

She knelt in front of the box of supplies.

The two brushes were stained and dirty, little pebbles meshed into the bristles. A smock was stuffed into the box, but she could see from the way it was folded that it had been ruined by blotches of paint—some along the hem and some higher up, as if the person painting had brushed against the wet paint and then it had run down the smock.

And the can of paint. It had been hastily closed. Whoever had pressed down on the lid hadn't noticed or cared that the paint squirted out and ran down the side of the can. The color was one Hannah had seen before.

She'd seen it in two photographs.

The color was blood red.

⇥ Sixteen ⇤

Friday morning had started out well.

Amber almost relaxed.

Her nerves had been strung tighter than a violin after Wednesday night's confrontation with Patricia. And then Tate was acting strange. He'd followed her home and insisted on walking through the house before he left. She appreciated his concern, but it seemed overly cautious to her.

Thursday hadn't been much better, except for the brief break she took at Hannah's house, learning how to quilt. That still made her smile, but as soon as she was back at the Village, the troubles had kept rolling in—a small plumbing problem, an employee falling into the pond, and a guest smuggling a rabbit into her hotel room. Amber struggled all day, maybe because in the back of her mind she kept thinking about Ethan's funeral. She didn't regret the decision not to attend, given Margaret's attitude toward her. But she still felt as if she hadn't done enough.

Friday she had hoped her day would find a normal rhythm, and it seemed to—at first. Then she'd stepped out of the office, walked down to the restaurant, and purchased a midmorning snack. When she returned, Elizabeth was frowning at a note she was still writing.

"Problem?"

"I'll say." Elizabeth removed her glasses, allowing them to dangle at the bottom of the beaded chain she wore around her neck. "At least you saved me having to write all of it out."

Amber accepted the "While You Were Out" message and motioned Elizabeth into her office.

"She actually called here?"

"Yes, and may I say that Margaret Gray is not a pleasant woman."

"Tell me. I found that out firsthand. First at her home, then at the visitation. Perhaps her surly attitude is her way of grieving."

"Humph." Elizabeth pressed her lips together. "I won't comment on that since my daddy always said if you can't say something nice—"

"Don't say anything at all."

They shared a smile, and Amber dropped the note onto her desk, sinking back into her chair.

"So she wants us to deliver his truck?"

"Yes, to a Patricia Gray. I wrote her address on the back."

"I met Patricia Wednesday night. She seemed . . . different. For some reason I'm not sure she drives. Do you know anything about what happened to her?"

Elizabeth sighed and frowned at her lap. "It was a real tragedy. I understand teens will try things, but when Patricia experimented with drugs she wrecked her life."

"Was it the amount she took? Or was there something wrong with—"

"Don't ask me. It was years ago and my memory isn't that good. Probably you could go online to the newspaper archives and find some details. All I can tell you is that she has times when she's lucid and times when she's not."

"Wednesday night she was not!"

"I'm not surprised. The shock of seeing her brother in the casket might have pushed her back to the unsteady side. Regardless, Margaret insisted the truck be taken care of today. She said it was the least you could do since . . . and I'm quoting, 'she allowed my husband to be murdered while on the Village time clock.' "

Amber stared at the Friendship Star quilt on her wall. She focused on the yellow stars, which so often reminded her of the warm sunshine outside her window. Today the stars blurred with the blue background. Staring at it produced no answers. She wasn't even able to find her usual peaceful frame of mind. Reaching for the sack from the restaurant, she pulled out Elizabeth's piece of cranberry bread and handed it to her. Then she removed her bowl of fruit, which didn't look nearly as appealing as Elizabeth's snack.

Stabbing her fork into a strawberry, she shrugged. "The address isn't so far. It would be easier to deliver the truck than to endure speaking with—"

"You mean arguing with—"

"Margaret."

"I have a couple of hours before our managers' meeting at noon."

Elizabeth left to retrieve the keys to Ethan's truck from her desk drawer, then brought them back to Amber. "He'd left them in the cash register drawer, and Margaret never picked them up."

"I'll take care of it." Amber pocketed the keys

200

and ate a grape, trying to imagine it was a bite of rich yummy bread.

"The security firm said they'd be here at eleven thirty to set up for their presentation. They requested a projector. I've taken care of it. The restaurant is also bringing up boxed lunches for everyone."

"Thank you."

Elizabeth started to leave and the office phone rang. Instead of continuing to the outer office, she reached across Amber's desk and answered the call.

Amber understood by the expression on her face that the news wasn't good. Her response to the caller was a clear indication that their morning had taken another turn for the worse.

"When? How many? She'll be right down."

Forking a piece of pineapple and a grape, Amber stuffed them into her mouth as Elizabeth hung up the phone.

"Front desk of the inn. They have a situation."

"I'm on it."

"Started about ten minutes ago and involves six guests."

Amber grabbed her ring of office keys, her tablet, and her purse. She checked to be sure that Ethan's truck keys were already in her pocket.

"I'll go to the inn first, then head out to Patricia's with the truck."

As she made her way down the stairs and across

the parking lot to the inn, it occurred to her that her tablet wasn't doing a very good job of keeping her life on a calm and even level. Her apps were supposed to render everything manageable. She had always thought that with enough organization and planning, anything was possible. Until recent events, there hadn't been an emergency she couldn't handle as long as she had Wi-Fi access and her daily dose of caffeine.

That wasn't exactly true.

Loneliness had been a problem, but then, technology couldn't solve everything. She'd resisted her sister's suggestions to try online dating sites. Not that she was against them. She even knew two couples who were happily married after meeting online. But she clung to the stubborn belief that God would arrange for her to actually meet the man she was supposed to marry—in person.

An image of Tate flashed into her mind, but she laughed and pushed it away. Nice guy, but not exactly her type. He was kind, considerate, and had certainly sent butterflies scurrying about her stomach the last few times they'd seen one another. Still, he wasn't her type. There was nothing to bat around in her mind, or her heart, because she and Tate were complete opposites.

Walking through the front door of the inn, she saw that three couples were waiting to check in and the two workers behind the desk looked a few shades past exasperated. Martha and Karen, both young Amish women, had managed the front desk for several years. Karen had been hired first, and then she'd suggested her friend Martha apply. Both were excellent employees. They were two of Amber's most dependable workers.

Karen was short, plump, and walked with a slight limp. Martha was tall and thin with almost a boyish figure. If the guests were surprised to see two Amish women checking them in, they didn't show it. In fact, the guests looked amused about something, sharing smiles and even giving a thumbs-up when Amber walked in the door.

Amber greeted the guests, then walked behind the counter and spoke in a lowered voice to the girls. "Karen. Martha. How are you?"

"*Gut*," Karen said.

"Fine," Martha muttered.

It was plain that their answers didn't encompass the entire situation.

"What seems to be the problem?"

"These guests want to check in for the mystery package." Martha shook her head in frustration.

"We explained to them there is no such package, but they insist there is. We didn't know what you would want us to do."

"All of these people—"

"*Ya.*" Martha put her hand on top of her prayer *kapp*. "I've tried to be clear. I even showed them the packages we have listed on the computer."

"They seem to think it's a game." Karen peeked

around Amber at the six waiting customers. "There is no reasoning with them."

"I'll handle it." Amber turned back toward the guests. When she did, the front door of the inn opened, and Tate walked inside. For a moment, she was disoriented, and she had to fight the urge to check her tablet.

Had they set up a meeting?

Why was he here?

Tate smiled, and she held up a finger to let him know she'd seen him and would be with him soon.

He nodded and stood by the door, waiting. Dressed in blue jeans and an Indiana Hoosiers T-shirt, he seemed completely at ease in her inn.

One thing at a time.

She turned back to the customers.

"Karen and Martha told me you were expecting some sort of mystery package?"

The youngest couple gave her another thumbs-up.

The middle-aged couple nodded in agreement.

And the two elderly ladies, who looked like sisters, whispered to one another.

"I'm sorry, but we don't have any package like that."

"It's probably what she's supposed to say," said the young man.

"Part of the mystery is finding the mystery package!" The young woman actually laughed.

"No. It's not part of any deal currently, past, or

future. We don't have anything remotely resembling a mystery package."

"It says here that there's a special rate." The older of the two women—who had to be in her seventies—began thumbing through the screens on her phone.

"And clues!" This from the younger sister, who stepped closer to Amber and confided, "Exactly like an Agatha Christie novel. We do love her books."

"No. You're not listening—" Amber walked around the counter so that she could speak with them more firmly without raising her voice.

The middle-aged man, who was decked out in motorcycle gear, put his thumbs under his belt buckle—Harley Davidson, of course. But when he spoke, he didn't sound like a biker. He sounded rather cultured. Well, shame on her for thinking in stereotypes.

"It's not solved, is it? Because the site says today is the first day. Doesn't seem as if it could be solved."

His wife rolled her eyes and plopped down in a chair. "I told you we should have left earlier."

"What site?" Amber asked.

All three couples stopped talking and stared at her.

"You said, 'The site says today is the first day.' What site?"

"This one." The young woman tapped twice on

her phone's screen and then thrust it into Amber's hands.

When she saw it, her world tilted slightly for a moment. Then she felt Tate's hand on the small of her back—rooting her, grounding her.

"Nice graphics," he murmured.

At the top of the screen were the words "Who Killed Ethan Gray?" Below that was "Amish Artisan Village. Middlebury, Indiana. Mystery Package."

"Looks like a type of geocaching." Tate pointed to a tab that was labeled "Clues."

"How do you know about geocaching?" Amber had the distinct feeling she'd stepped into an alternate world. One that looked like hers but didn't follow the same rules.

"My younger son loves to do it. He drags me along occasionally when he comes home to visit. They even had a club for it at his college."

"You're right." The motorcycle guy rubbed a hand along his jaw. "It is like geocaching. It even gives you coordinates to the first clue."

"And it says that you'll be given additional clues as you go." The elderly woman with the beehive hairdo had become suddenly serious. "Stella and I are very good with clues. We have a real shot to win if you'll let us in our rooms."

Amber closed her eyes and prayed for patience. When she opened them, the six guests were still waiting.

"I can give you our lowest rate." When she named the amount, they all nodded agreeably. "But I don't have a prize for anyone, there is no mystery package, there are no clues, and there hasn't been a murder."

"Ethan's dead, isn't he? Because the site gave the funeral details." The woman in motorcycle gear reached for her own phone, but Amber waved her away.

"Yes, Ethan is dead, but we're not offering a mystery package. There is no mystery! He died of natural causes."

The guests exchanged knowing looks, and Amber understood she was fighting a useless battle. Instead of continuing to argue, she walked around the check-in counter and showed Martha and Karen a special code for a 15 percent discount. "Call me if you need anything else."

She practically pulled Tate out of the reception area.

She needed a little sunshine.

⇥ Seventeen ⇤

Tate followed her out into the perfect spring day.

"Tough morning?"

"You don't know the half of it." Amber sat on a bench outside the inn. Her hair—which seemed more cinnamon than chestnut to him now that they were out in the sunlight—was once again straightened. She wore black slacks and a white, neatly starched blouse. In other words, she looked gorgeous.

"Now tell me what you're doing in the neighborhood."

"I live in this neighborhood."

"Good point, but you've never stopped by before." She looked up at him and smiled, and Tate's palms began to sweat. He'd needed to see her, but now he wasn't so sure he should have stopped by. He felt like a lovesick pup, which was absolutely ridiculous.

"Tate?"

"Oh. Yeah. Sorry. I was thinking about something else." He glanced out across the Village, shading his eyes against the morning sun. "Truthfully, I didn't have a reason. I mean, I can make up one if you'd like me to, but I wanted to see you, is all. I didn't mean to interrupt your workday."

"You're not interrupting me." Amber's voice was soft. Her expression was unreadable. "How did you know to find me at the inn?"

"I called your office. Some lady named Elizabeth said I could come to your office and wait, or walk to the inn where you were likely to be for a few minutes." He looked away, but hadn't he come too far to back down now? "Look, Amber, I feel bad—now that I know you—that

I've been so critical of the Village. I thought I'd stop by and see things for myself, and I did want to see you. I had been to town, and when I drove back by here on my way home, I had an urge to stop. So I did. Probably I should have called first."

"You did fine. I'm glad you were there to help me through the mystery guests." Amber laughed and sat back so that she was leaning against the wall of the inn. Closing her eyes, she murmured, "I think I need a few hours of sleeping in the sun. It's such a nice spring day."

They sat that way for a moment.

Guests walked back and forth on the pavement, ducks settled on the pond, and a light breeze blew through the trees. It was spring in Indiana, one of Tate's favorite times.

Amber groaned and stood up. "I'd love to give you a tour, but I have a truck to deliver."

"A truck?"

"Yes, Ethan's. Margaret wants it delivered to Patricia, and I volunteered to do it."

Amber was facing Tate. Looking past her, he saw an Amish girl hurrying toward them.

"How were you going to get back?"

"Back?"

"After you drop off the truck."

"Oh." Amber shook her head and pulled her purse strap higher up on her shoulder. "I'm off schedule today, and I am not thinking straight. You're right. I'll need to ask one of my employees to follow me over. Fortunately it's not far."

"I could do it." The words were out of Tate's mouth before he'd even stopped to think of what his chore list included back home.

"Why would you do that?"

"Like you said . . . it's a nice spring day."

"All right. I accept your offer of help."

She was fishing the keys out of her pocket when an Amish girl, the girl who had been hurrying, stopped in front of them—red in the face and breathless.

"Hannah, is everything all right?"

Hannah shook her head yes and then no. She fiddled with her *kapp* strings and then glanced from Amber to Tate and back again as if she was uncertain whether she should speak.

"Do you two need a minute?" he asked.

"No. Hannah, this is Tate—my neighbor. He's been helping me out since the vandalism began."

Hannah nodded as if that made perfect sense.

"We found a box. Seth nearly tripped over it in the back storeroom."

"Of the coffee shop?"

"*Ya.*"

Hannah looked flustered. To say she was distressed would have been an understatement. And somehow, Tate knew that the next thing she was about to say would complicate Amber's morning more than it already had been. He also stopped worrying about being in the way. Maybe there were several reasons why he had felt the intense need to see her.

Hannah lowered her voice and stepped closer to Amber. "The box . . . it's full of things."

"What type of things?"

"A stained smock—"

"Stained?"

"Brushes—"

"What kind of brushes?"

"And paint!"

Amber shifted her tablet from her right hand to her left, checked Tate for his reaction, and then asked what they both were thinking. "Red paint?"

"*Ya.*" Hannah began bobbing her head so hard Tate feared her prayer *kapp* would slip off. "*Ya*, it was definitely red."

Fifteen minutes later, Tate was in his truck following Amber, who was driving Ethan's 1969 Ford.

It seemed to him that she looked completely at home in the classic truck, but then, he supposed that spoke more of her personality than of the vehicle. She was probably at home . . . wherever she was planted.

Ha! That thought had come straight from his wife. She was always admonishing the boys, "Bloom where you're planted." By the time they were in high school, they'd learned it did no good complaining to their mother about teachers, coaches, or chores. Her response was consistent throughout their road to adulthood.

Is that why he was so taken with Amber Wright?

Did she remind him of Peggy?

No. It was more that they shared certain personality traits. They both certainly dealt with adversity well. But Peggy was content being a wife and mother, and she was also old-fashioned in a lot of ways. She had suited Tate in the same way the ranch had, and she had become his soul mate. Something a little rare if what he read in the newspapers was true.

The thought caused him to grip the wheel more tightly as he drove east on County Road 16. He and Peggy had been like the two donkeys he owned—identical in many ways. Amber Wright was his polar opposite.

Was he being foolish to consider a relationship with her?

There was a surprising amount of morning traffic, and they managed to get caught behind two different buggies. Still the trip was short. Within ten minutes, they'd turned north toward the lake.

As they pulled into a neighborhood that bordered a small pond, Tate noticed a small discreet sign that read "Grounds of Helping Hands. No solicitations."

Helping Hands?

Amber parked in the driveway of a modest duplex, and Tate parked on the street.

She waved for him to join her, so he got out of his truck and walked up the path to the door.

As Amber raised her hand to knock, they heard a dog yipping from the house next door. They both walked toward the sound and saw a small dog— a Chihuahua mix of some sort. He was standing in a fenced yard, barking with all of his might.

"Something about that dog seems familiar, but I can't think of how. I can't quite catch the image that is lurking at the corner of my mind. Do you know what I mean?"

Tate shook his head in the affirmative but didn't rush her. Then they heard singing coming from the back of the duplex and forgot all about the noisy dog.

"Backyard," he said, and they hustled around to the back.

They found Patricia Gray moving through a row of plants, bent close to them as she walked, and singing at the top of her lungs. Tate could hardly believe he was looking at the same person who'd been by Margaret's side at the viewing. With her facial muscles relaxed and her hair pulled back by a bandanna, she looked ten years younger.

The entire backyard had been dug up and converted into different gardens. Some were planted in raised box beds. Others were directly in the soil where grass had probably once been. A medium-size greenhouse, complete with solar panels on the top and a rainwater recycling system, was toward the back of the property line and positioned with a view of the duplex and the pond. Two of the walls were solid glass. The other two consisted of siding about waist high and glass on the top half. Someone had spent a lot of time in the planning and design of the area. It was small for a yard, but surprisingly large for an individual's garden.

Patricia wore blue-striped overalls and a multi-colored, long-sleeve shirt. Her hair was a wreck of curls, and she paused in her singing to reach up and give it a twist. Then she resumed moving from plant to plant, pouring water from a can on them.

Tate had the sense that she knew she wasn't alone. Everything about her body language—back turned, shoulders pulled back, eyes pointed down at the plants and then up at the sky—indicated she wasn't ready to speak with them yet.

Perhaps it was the plants that surrounded her that were more surprising than Patricia's activity. This wasn't a vegetable garden—Tate would have recognized those plants even at the seedling stage. There were also very few flowers. What was she growing? And why so much of it? Whatever it was, there was a large variety of plants in various stages of spring growth.

"Patricia?" Amber stepped closer. She started to

reach out and put a hand on the woman's shoulder, but apparently changed her mind and stepped back. Plainly, Patricia knew they were there. They were standing three feet in front of her.

The singing had stopped, but not the watering. She still didn't look up. "Why are you here?"

Tate stepped closer to Amber and put his hand at her back. It helped to have some physical contact when he felt she was being threatened, like Wednesday night at Ethan's viewing. He wasn't worried that an older, confused woman could hurt Amber, but he was glad he'd come along.

"I brought you something."

Patricia finally placed the watering can on the ground. "You brought me something?"

Tugging on her hair again, she turned in a circle, taking in a view of her entire garden. Finally she faced Amber and Tate and dropped her gaze to her shoes. "Why would you bring me something?"

"Ethan asked us to," Amber replied.

Tate nodded once.

"I was singing to my plants."

"We could see that. You have a very nice voice." Amber's own voice remained soft.

"Plants don't know what you sound like. They consume the carbon dioxide from my breath, from my singing. That helps them to grow." Patricia fidgeted with the bib of her overalls.

"I didn't know that. Are you done? Can you

walk around to the front of your house? We brought you Ethan's truck."

Tate had been worried that Patricia would freak out at the mention of her brother. So he was relieved when she clasped her hands and smiled. "Nell? The old truck? We call it Nell. I love that truck. It's a 1969 Ford F-100 Ranger."

"That's the one we brought."

"Let's go look!" Patricia led the way back to the front of her house, her garden apparently forgotten.

Tate moved close enough to Amber to whisper, "Something's out of whack here."

"I'd say. Let's give her the keys and scram."

It was a good plan.

It didn't work.

Patricia placed her hand on the hood of the truck, standing there in the sunshine, an expression of complete satisfaction on her face. Then she turned to them and insisted they come inside for a soda. When Amber started listing the reasons she couldn't, the hair tugging resumed with greater intensity.

"Well, maybe for a minute."

"Sure," Tate chimed in.

"We'd love to."

They followed her inside, and Tate had his third surprise of the visit. He'd never have expected to find Patricia having an episode in the dirt behind her home. He had never seen or imagined a garden such as hers. And then there was the inside of the duplex. Patricia's living room and dining room were full to overflowing —floor to ceiling—with books.

What did he know about drugs, bad trips, and long-lasting effects? What had Peggy said to him that winter day years ago? He'd been sitting down to lunch, and she'd said, "Patricia's not stupid. In fact, her IQ is probably higher than yours or mine."

"Mine's not that high sometimes."

"Her problem is handling emotions and relating to others. It's very sad. Ethan is doing his best, but it isn't easy."

That conversation came back with complete clarity as he studied the rows upon rows of books in Patricia's house.

"You have a lot of books." Amber stayed next to the door as Patricia walked into the kitchen.

"I love to read. I read every day. I read in the morning and at lunch. I even read at night before bed." She set three orange sodas on the pass-through bar between the kitchen and living room. They were in glass bottles and ice cold. "We can sit down at my table."

Tate hadn't had an orange soda since he was a kid. He didn't know you could buy them anymore.

"All right, but we can't stay more than a few minutes." Amber picked up their drinks, passed one to Tate, and then they followed Patricia to the small dining area. "Delicious. Is orange your favorite?"

"Maybe. I like sweet drinks, and I like the color orange. My favorite colors are the ones you can find in nature."

Tate and Amber nodded as if that made sense.

"I get to keep the truck?"

"Yes." Amber fished the keys out of her pocket and slid them across the dining room table where they were seated. "Ethan wanted you to have it, and Margaret asked that I bring it out here."

Patricia stared down at her soda and reached up to tweak her hair. Tate could feel a change in her emotional barometer same as he could feel a storm barreling across Middlebury.

"Margaret is not a nice person." Wrinkles creased Patricia's brow, and she added, "People should be nice."

The words were spoken in an eerily calm voice, but then her glance slid over to the nearest stack of books. Almost as if he and Amber weren't in the room, she whispered, "If you're not nice, something bad can happen to you."

A switch had flipped, and the singing woman was gone. Her shoulders hunched, and her brow furrowed. There was something hidden under the words—*something bad can happen to you.* Her eyes became cold, calculating even. Or maybe Tate imagined that.

Taking another big drink of her orange soda, Patricia added, "She doesn't like me."

Tate didn't know what to say to that. Apparently, neither did Amber.

"So you like books?" Patricia asked.

"I do. That's why I read them so much." Amber turned her bottle round and round in her hands. "Do you?"

"Yes."

"What kind do you read?" Tate prayed that reading material would be a safer topic. He needed to get Amber out of Patricia's house before the woman had another angry outburst like the night of the viewing.

"I read all kinds. That's why I have so many. My favorites are about how to make things grow." Suddenly her scowl returned. "I was pouring fertilizer on my plants as I sang. I made it myself. Maybe the mixture I used will help to kill the insects. Since the last rain, the insects have been worse."

"Have you tried insecticide?" Tate asked.

"No. Ethan said not to use poison. He said it was dangerous." A smile played on her face, but the scowl quickly returned. "I put a special ingredient in the fertilizer. If the insects eat it . . ." She slapped her hands together and smiled. "If they eat it they'll die."

"One of the Amish women I work with says to use soapy water." Amber ran her thumb down the side of the soda bottle, wiping off the condensation. "They say it works every time."

Patricia smiled and pulled a book off a nearby shelf. "I've read that before. I forgot, but it might work. I have soap! I can try to make some."

She frowned and squinted her eyes. Her emotions were all over the place. Was she always like this? Or was it worse because of Ethan's death? "I used that last year, used dish soap in a mixture. Sometimes I forget things."

She rubbed at her brow, as if a headache was forming. "I forget some things, but I don't forget important things."

Was she referring to Amber's supposed role in Ethan's death?

Amber either ignored the comment or didn't pick up on the underlying meaning. "The soap would probably work longer and be easier. It works best if you put it in a squirt bottle, if you have one."

"I do."

"Excellent." Amber took another sip of the orange soda and then asked, "Would you mind if I use your bathroom?"

"Sure. It's clean. The lady who cleans for me, Shiloh, she came yesterday. The bathroom's clean."

"All right. I won't be long."

"When she cleans she moves my books. I don't like it when she moves my books. I don't like when people touch my things."

"Who would?" Tate asked.

"That's what I told her. I told her she wouldn't want me coming into her house and moving her books. She said it's the only way to get rid of the dust, but I don't mind a little dust here and there." This was all delivered to a spot on the floor. Shrugging, she stood and turned her back to them, rocking slightly as she studied the books on the nearest shelf.

"Okay. I'll be right back then." Amber leaned down and whispered, "Watch her," and then she hurried from the room.

"First door," Patricia called after her. "Only the first door."

She added in a soft whisper, "Don't open the second door, or you'll be sorry . . ."

She held out the two syllables of the last word, like the ending of a song.

Why had she said that? And what was he going to talk to her about while Amber was gone?

Books. Patricia loved books.

"Which of these are your favorites?" Tate motioned to the stacks of books, hoping Amber wouldn't take too long. He had no idea what to say to the woman.

Patricia's voice softened. "Come and see."

The tenseness that had grown more apparent while they were drinking their sodas vanished. Tate had the disoriented feeling that he was looking again at a completely different person.

She studied the shelf a moment and then walked across the small room to a different shelf of books, one where the titles were at eye-level. She glanced at him, never for more than a second, and said again, "Come and see.

"Herpetology books are the best. Horticulture books are good too." She reached out and caressed a book cover with her fingertips, seemed about to select it, but then she moved on to the next.

Tate again remembered what Peggy had said: "Patricia's not stupid. In fact, her IQ is probably higher than yours or mine."

"Books with herbal remedies are good."

She pulled out a thick volume. When she opened it, Tate saw that the text was quite dense, certainly at a college level, and there were detailed illustrations on each page. There were also notes that someone, perhaps Patricia, had written in the margins.

"Do you know anything about herbs?" She flipped the pages quickly.

"No. Can't say I do."

"They work! They can be used for different reasons, different maladies. You have to be careful though. Some herbs are dangerous. Some can even kill."

⇚ Eighteen ⇛

Amber stared at Tate as he drove his truck, making their way back toward the Village.

"She said that?" Amber's words came out too loud, but she'd had the heebie-jeebies since they'd arrived at Patricia's. She worried her thumbnail and spoke more softly. "You're sure?"

"Word for word—'Some herbs are dangerous. Some can even kill.'" Tate paused, then suggested, "Maybe we should tell Gordon. He might still be at the Village when we get back."

"I had the distinct feeling, last time I spoke with Gordon, that he's tired of handling this case. He's convinced we're dealing with some bored teens. Besides, tell him what? She didn't threaten us."

"And she certainly didn't confess to anything." Tate rubbed his hand along his jaw.

"But something's wrong there." Amber tapped her tablet and typed something on it. "There are too many oddities popping up. I don't like it at all."

"I'll agree with you there. The list you're making on your tablet is getting awfully long." When she gave him a pointed look, he couldn't help grinning and then agreeing with her. "I suppose it wouldn't hurt to speak with the good sergeant. Maybe he can make sense of it. But don't you need to get back to the Village?"

Amber studied her watch. "Yes, I have a meeting, and it starts in thirty minutes."

"I could tell him."

"Do you have time?"

"I do. Though I'll have to be heading back home after that. I have two rambunctious donkeys who can't be left alone for long."

The thought of Trixie and Velvet made Amber smile. Then she remembered what she'd seen at Patricia's, and a shiver tiptoed down her spine.

"Patricia worries me."

"She's an odd one, that's for sure. But being odd isn't a crime." Tate could have been speaking to himself. He kept brushing his hand over the top of his head. Amber could tell that he was worried. It was both endearing and comforting at the same time.

He glanced at her, then refocused on the road. "We don't even know that Ethan was killed, and the thought that his sister might have done it seems far-fetched. Does she even drive? If not, how could she have made it to the Village? Take a taxi to a murder? That might be a first. What would her motive have been? And what was her weapon? He died of a heart attack."

"There is something else." Amber reached out and touched his arm. "Something I saw when I went to the restroom."

"I'm all ears. This is the most mystery we've had in Middlebury since the Amish buggy stopped appearing on rooftops."

"I've seen pictures of that. It was always at Halloween."

"Correct." Tate propped his elbow on the side panel of the door. "It was in the '60s and '70s. I remember clearly, when I was eight years old, seeing it on the top of the old building down on Main Street."

"I wish this were as harmless as a small-town prank." She paused, trying to think of how best to admit she'd nosed around. She couldn't even explain to herself why she'd done it. Perhaps it was the prevalent feeling that something in that house was not right. "Remember when Patricia told me not to open the second door?"

"She said you'd be sorry. I thought it was an odd thing to say at the time, but then, Patricia is a little strange. A mixture of child and adult."

"My assistant, Elizabeth, mentioned Patricia's history. She said it was tragic, but she didn't remember the details."

"Most of us would rather forget things like that. Seeing your son or daughter through the teen years is frightening at times. I spent a few nights at the kitchen table, praying one of our boys would come home safely."

"I can imagine, not that *I* ever broke my curfew or caused my parents any anxiety." The memory of how she had done those things was bittersweet. Both of her parents had died in the last five years, and she missed them terribly.

Amber rolled her window down a little, needing to feel the breeze on her face. "The second door was closed and locked. Who locks the door to a room when they live alone? And the room across the hall from that was like a chemist's play area."

"You snooped?"

"I peeked inside. I suppose I thought I might find more cans of red paint or a BB gun."

"A BB gun was in the corner of the living room. I spotted that right away."

They both fell silent. Tate merged with Middlebury's lunchtime traffic. Amber had too many things circling in her mind. She needed a few minutes to sit in her office, jot it all down, and make some sense of it.

When Tate pulled into a spot in the Village parking lot, Amber let out a groan and nearly slapped herself on the forehead. "I've got it. That dog."

"Dog?"

"The one next door to Patricia's house."

"The yippy dog?"

"Yes! Hannah and I were sitting outside of the coffee shop talking when a woman passed by. She was carrying a dog just like that in her purse."

"And . . ."

"Maybe it was her! Maybe Patricia was here."

Tate drummed his fingers against the steering wheel. "Maybe, but that isn't a crime. And why would she carry her neighbor's dog with her anyway? The more likely scenario is that it was a different dog that you remembered when you heard the noisy beast today."

"I suppose."

He made it around to her side of the truck and opened her door while she was gathering her things. She hopped out of the truck, then looked at him and said softly, "Thank you."

"For opening the door? My momma taught me well."

"Thank you for everything." She stepped closer and peered up into his face. Tate Bowman had the warmest, brownest eyes she'd ever seen. "And the door thing is nice."

"Glad to hear it. Some women are more independently minded."

"About doors?"

"About everything. I wouldn't want to be smacked for treating a woman like a . . . well, like a lady."

"So you were taking a chance?" Amber liked teasing Tate. He looked so surprised when she did. It was the most relaxed she'd felt since her day had begun. Perhaps the drive out in the April sunshine had helped. The thought had no sooner passed through her mind than she remembered the coffee shop, the trail, her front porch, and Katie's shop.

She sighed and turned away slightly. "This is serious and terrible and so unexpected."

"About Ethan?"

Instead of answering, she scanned the property—a property she'd dedicated her life to, at least the last twenty years of her life. "These seventy acres are supposed to be a haven of sorts. A place where people can work and rest in peace, but I'm beginning to wonder . . ."

She stopped before voicing the next thought. It was painful to admit what she was contemplating. When she turned and met his gaze, it seemed from the expression on his face that possibly he understood fully how much she cared about the Village, all the people she employed, and her guests.

"I'm beginning to think it might have been murder. I don't know how, but there are too many coincidences. Too many things out of place. Too many questions."

"You don't have to be afraid." He stepped closer and reached for her hand.

The full impact of what they were discussing hit her, and she nearly dropped her tablet. Was there a murderer loose in Middlebury? One who had a vendetta against the Village?

"I'll check to see if Gordon's still here and tell him about Patricia."

"And I'll go to my meeting—we've contracted

a security firm to come and speak to our managers. Text me what Gordon says?"

"Sure will."

She had the strangest notion that he was about to kiss her before she walked away, but he didn't.

It had probably been her imagination.

But it occurred to her as she hurried toward her office that Tate Bowman would make some lucky woman a very good husband.

Hannah joined the group of managers eating lunch around the conference table. She'd rather have taken her break outside in one of her usual spots at the pond or down by the creek. But the memo had gone out to all managers, and for the moment that included her.

She had walked over to the office with Carol. They'd talked about the quilt shop, the *kaffi* shop, and the weather. When Hannah had brought up Ethan, Carol's lips formed a tight, straight line, and she grew quiet.

Hannah didn't know if that was normal or not. She'd worked with *Englischers* since she'd turned sixteen, and she'd lived beside them always. Still, it was hard to know what was and wasn't unusual for a group of people—especially a group she didn't belong to.

She did know that sometimes death was a difficult thing to accept, even within the Amish community. They were taught to acknowledge *Gotte's wille*, but the hole left from someone's passing hurt. She'd lost a grandparent two years earlier, and she understood this firsthand. Carol and Ethan had worked next to each other for years. Perhaps a friendship had developed, though Hannah found that hard to imagine since Ethan was so unsociable.

She didn't have much time to dwell on friendship and death and dying.

They'd climbed the stairs to the office and entered the conference room, and everyone had turned to stare at her. Hannah knew it wasn't because she was Amish. More than half of the people seated around the large table were from her community. No, the looks weren't because of her prayer *kapp* or her long dress. Each person turned and stared at her because she was young. She understood in an instant. The person nearest her age was still twenty years older.

What right did she have to be here?

What made her think she could do the job they had been doing for years?

Elizabeth fluttered around the room, making sure everyone had a boxed lunch and something to drink. Hannah had taken the first bite of her tuna sandwich when Amber hurried through the doorway. Their eyes met, and she knew—was absolutely certain—that something else had happened.

Something to do with Ethan.

Amber didn't speak of it. Instead, she moved to the middle of one side of the table and took her seat.

"Thank you all for coming. I apologize for my tardiness. Please, finish your meal." Again her eyes sought Hannah's, but then she turned to the Amish man beside her and engaged him in conversation.

Hannah ate slowly and used the time to study the group.

Five were not Amish, seven if you included Amber and Elizabeth. The *Englischers* appeared at ease, though several glanced at their watches occasionally as if they had other places to be. She didn't know Larry, the assistant manager, very well. She'd had no cause to speak with him directly yet. When he came on duty in the late afternoon, she was already gone for the day. Harvey supervised the grounds crew, and Jesse spoke well of him even though he was a demanding boss. Stanley was in charge of the restaurant. He was older, with a large belly and a constant smile.

Only one Amish man had joined them. Norman made wooden toys. Hannah had known him since she was a child. He was quiet, and he always had a twinkle in his eyes as if he was remembering something that amused him.

The *Englisch* women were Carol, manager of the Quilting Bee, and Georgia, who oversaw the bakery staff. Seth had told her a little about Georgia. Plainly, she was someone who intimidated him, but after working with Seth for a few days, she understood the reason for that could lie in Seth's work habits.

The Amish women rounded out the group. Karen managed the inn. Mary ran the Cat's Meow, their yarn shop. Letha made and sold the clothes at Village Fashions, with the help of her sisters. And Katie was in charge of Katie's Mercantile, which was actually named after the owner's aunt. An Amish person didn't normally put his or her name on a marquee. It had seemed like an amusing coincidence when Katie took charge of the shop. Hannah could remember the women teasing her that soon she would start a line of goods with her name plastered on the label. Katie had laughed good-naturedly when the idea was brought up, but she couldn't have known that her shop would be such a hit among the *Englischers*. Sales had increased dramatically since she had taken over the store's management.

Some might think it was a lot of folks to fit in one room, but Hannah was used to church services in people's homes—services that often numbered more than one hundred when children were counted.

No, the number of people didn't bother her.

Her age and the fact that she was sitting in Ethan's place did.

"Please don't rush through your meal. Feel free to continue eating while I explain the purpose of our meeting." Amber pushed away her barely touched salad and stood. "I asked you to meet here today because of what happened on Monday."

"Ethan's dying." Stanley frowned at his plate. The expression looked out of place on him, and Hannah wondered if the two men had been close.

Carol pushed her food away at the mention of Ethan's name. She looked awfully pale to Hannah, who wondered if perhaps she wasn't feeling well.

"Yes, in a way." Amber took a sip from her water bottle and then recapped it. "As you know from the email we sent out, Ethan died from a heart attack. However, we did find evidence of vandalism at his shop that morning."

"The bullet holes?" Harvey placed his hands palms down on the table. "You're talking about his window being cracked by bullets."

"The damage to the window was not caused by bullets. Sergeant Avery assures me it was BB shot that pierced Ethan's window, and BB shots could not have caused Ethan's death. In fact, there was no evidence he had been hit."

"Kids." Georgia practically spat the word.

"Possibly. We don't see many adults with BB guns walking about, but occasionally we've caught teenagers out in the fields—never near the shops. In the past, we've asked them to leave and they've always complied."

"If these . . ." Georgia hesitated, looking first to her right and then her left.

Hannah was sure she was about to say *Amish*, but she didn't.

"If these kids were in school all day, at least until they're eighteen, then we wouldn't have to contend with this sort of thing."

"I disagree." Harvey drummed his fingers against the table. "I've caught some of them myself, Georgia. They're rarely Amish. Most of the time they're *Englisch* kids skipping school. Amish kids may have a BB gun, but it's for hunting small game."

"At this point we have no clues or evidence as to who is responsible for these incidents," Amber interrupted.

"Incidents?" Katie glanced around the table. "There's been more? In addition to Ethan's shop and . . . and . . . and mine?"

Katie's face turned as white as her prayer *kapp*.

Hannah had an urge to reach across the table and pat her hand. Katie was a hard worker, and she had been terribly upset about the chaos in her shop.

Everyone began talking at once.

Amber held up her hand to quiet them.

"On Monday we had the incident at Ethan's shop. Monday evening there was vandalism on my end of the Pumpkinvine Trail, at the property

234

boundary. Wednesday morning, Katie found her shop in complete disarray."

Hannah noticed Amber left out the incident at her house.

Everyone again began talking. Amber raised her voice over theirs, and the individual conversations quickly stopped.

"We do not know if these events are related, but it is worrisome that there have been these three occurrences in less than a week. I spoke with Brad Shipley, who you all know is a member of the family who owns the Village. Brad, as well as Sergeant Avery, feels there is no danger to employees or guests, and that in fact this probably is the mischief of teens. However, Avery suggested that we bring in a security consulting firm, and Mr. Shipley agreed."

"Consulting firm?" Harvey sat back in his chair and folded his arms across his chest.

"Yes. They have assessed our current security measures and suggested ways we can enhance them. Those changes will be made on Monday."

"This Monday?" Larry scowled and peered around the table. "Spring is one of our busiest times of year. The tourist surge is just beginning. Is this necessary?"

"I believe it is, and the sooner we do it the better. The manager of M&S Security has assured me they can complete the work without interrupting the flow of what happens here at the

Village. The guests shouldn't even notice. They'll be out of our way by Monday evening. In addition, they are going to speak with you in a few minutes about safety measures, what to watch for, and how to respond if you see anything untoward."

"I believe I know how to take care of a couple of punks if I see them. No worries there." Harvey shook his head as if the meeting was a complete waste of his time.

Stanley leaned closer to Norman and asked him a question, but Hannah couldn't hear it. She did see Norman shake his head. He'd yet to actually speak in the meeting. Amish men were traditionally quiet, so Hannah wasn't surprised.

"We'll take a five-minute break. At that time, if you'll return to your seats, the presentation by M&S, Middlebury and Shipshewana Security, will begin."

Carol pushed her chair back from the table and rushed out of the room. Perhaps she was sick. Would she want to be alone, or should Hannah follow her and see if she could help? She stood and walked toward the side table, which held sodas and a pitcher of water. Perhaps it would be best to give Carol a few minutes. If her old boss didn't come back soon, she'd go and check on her. She was pouring more water into her glass when Amber clutched the back of her arm and whispered, "I want to see you in my office. We'll have to hurry."

They scooted out of the room, trying to look inconspicuous, but they needn't have worried. Everyone was busy talking, and no one appeared to pay them any attention.

Hannah stopped inside the doorway and studied Amber's office. The desk was picture-perfect neat, like something out of a magazine. An Amish quilt hung on the wall, and the view out the corner window was beautiful. Amber shut the door, again grabbed her arm, and pulled her to a chair sitting opposite her desk.

"What did he say?" Amber perched on the chair next to Hannah's.

"Who?"

"Avery! Sergeant Avery! What did he say about the box of stuff you found?"

"Oh. That." Hannah clasped her hands in her lap. "He didn't actually come to the shop."

"What?" Amber opened her tablet, which she had brought from the meeting, and studied her notes. "This could be it. This could be the key to all that is happening. And he didn't come?"

"He sent Cherry Brookstone."

"She's a child! She wouldn't know what to do if she stumbled over a dead body."

"I was also surprised how young she is." Hannah thought back to the looks she had received in the room down the hall. "I thought you had to be older to be an officer, but perhaps not. Perhaps she is already an officer because of her skills."

Several things about Officer Brookstone had surprised Hannah, but then, she'd had very little interaction with the Middlebury police. As she had told Amber, problems within the Amish community were handled by their bishop—unless it was an extreme matter that put members in danger. Hannah couldn't even remember such an occurrence.

Officer Brookstone had long red hair pulled back in a simple ponytail. She couldn't have been older than twenty-five. Her figure was thin but muscular, unlike most Amish women. They had all sizes, to be sure. But Amish women seemed softer to Hannah. Perhaps it was their clothing. Brookstone wore the full officer uniform. In fact, she practically looked like a man in it. Then there was her name—Cherry. Cherry Brookstone. Who named their child Cherry? And had they done so because of the red hair?

Amber flopped back into her chair, her gaze traveling to the clock on the wall. "We'd better go back."

They walked to the office door, but Amber paused before opening it. "What did Brookstone say?"

"That they'd try to get prints off the items. That we did the right thing to call." Hannah ran her palm across her apron to smooth it out and to calm the fluttery feelings surging through her stomach.

"Anything else?"

"Ya."

Hannah glanced at her boss, unsure if the last part would be welcome news. "She said to tell you Avery will be in contact if he needs anything else. She said he's too busy to deal with vandalism cases and that we should contact her or our security firm with any future problems."

She reached into her pocket, pulled out the officer's business card, and handed it to Amber.

Her boss stared at the words printed there, frowning and muttering something under her breath before accepting the card. Then she straightened her posture, pasted on a smile, and marched back toward the meeting room.

⇥ *Nineteen* ⇤

Tate remained seated as Amber walked to the door and greeted Gordon Avery.

She had called the sergeant midafternoon and left a message on his cell phone. The meeting with the security firm had gone well, and she'd convinced Avery to stop by so they could speak to him directly, not to Cherry Brookstone. Avery had suggested seven o'clock at her house. Something told Tate the good officer had expected, or at least hoped, he would be alone with Amber. The expression on his face of real disappointment was genuine, but he covered it quickly.

Then he crossed the room and shook Tate's hand.

"Didn't expect to see you here."

Tate almost laughed. Avery reminded him of his children, when they would wake up the week before Christmas and realize the grand day hadn't yet arrived.

"Amber asked me to stop by."

"So much has happened so quickly." She opened the storm door again so Leo could saunter in, though he could have pushed through the pet door.

Spoiled, that's what her cat was. Tate found it amusing.

Finally Amber turned toward them. "I didn't want to leave anything out, and Tate has witnessed most of what I've seen."

Avery removed his hat—a ball cap. He'd stopped by his home and changed out of his uniform and into jeans. The thought crossed Tate's mind that perhaps he had considered Amber's request a date, until he'd learned there were three of them. No wonder he had looked so disappointed!

"All right." Avery sat down on the small couch, sighing dramatically.

Tate popped out of the recliner and motioned for Amber to sit in it. He pulled a chair from the dining room and placed it in front of the bookcase. They made an odd sort of triangle. Tate wasn't sure why Amber had wanted him there. Perhaps for moral support. She kept detailed notes of everything on her tablet. He'd seen them. She'd even asked him to read over them when he had arrived at six thirty. Yes, she'd asked him to come thirty minutes before the meeting.

Together they had somehow become a team.

Against what, he had no idea.

"First I want to say that you should not have been offended when I handed this over to Brookstone. She's an excellent addition to our force, and she can take care of whatever you need."

"But, Gordon, you know me. You know the Village. I don't want some new kid on the block showing up in her recently issued uniform. This is serious. Let her take care of monitoring the speed trap on the north side of town."

"That's not fair, and you know it. Cherry's youth doesn't prevent her from doing a good job, and your bad attitude toward her—and Jasmine— isn't helping things."

"I have a bad attitude?"

"You do." Avery waited until Amber shrugged and nodded in agreement. "So let's hear it. Whatcha got?"

"From the beginning?" Amber asked.

"Why not?" Avery sat back and placed his ball cap beside him on the couch. "From the beginning."

Amber picked up her tablet from off the end table, opened it, and began reading. "Hannah found Ethan on Monday morning. The glass was shot through by what you think was a BB gun."

"It was a BB gun."

"That same evening, there was a warning of sorts left at my end of the Village property. 'Iron breaks and smashes everything,' which is from the Old Testament."

"Left in red paint," Tate added. It seemed significant to him. Red was the color of danger, plus it had a gruesome similarity to blood. The choice could not have been accidental.

Avery only nodded. None of this was new to him so far, and Tate could tell that his patience was wearing thin.

"Since then I've learned that Ethan had recently argued with several local boys—"

"Do you know their names?" Avery asked.

"No. Hannah didn't see them. She heard yelling, but when she stepped outside to see what the commotion was, the boys were walking away. Teenaged and dressed in jeans. They could have been Amish or *Englisch*, since some Amish boys do wear jeans."

Avery moved his hand in a circular motion, as if to say *continue*.

"Ethan had also argued with Larry Sharp, my assistant manager. I spoke with Larry. He claims, quite adamantly, that no disagreement took place.

They did discuss work the grounds crew had done around the coffee shop. Larry said he and Ethan disagreed, but it did not grow into an argument. He claims that whoever said he had threatened Ethan was not remembering correctly."

Avery's eyebrow arched. "But you don't believe him?"

"I'm not sure. I saw Ethan race out of here that afternoon. Usually he treated that old truck with kid gloves. He even named it—Nell. Who names their truck?"

Avery shrugged and held out his hands, palms up.

Amber shook her head, causing her hair to bounce and shimmer in the lamplight. "He must have been more than a little upset to blow off steam like that."

"Didn't you say that Ethan did his own grounds work?" Tate asked.

"True. He always swept his own walk, carried his trash to the large Dumpster, and even cleaned his windows." Amber forgot her list for a moment, staring out her front window into the darkness, as if she might find answers there. "It's possible Larry was lying."

"Why?" Avery asked. "Why would he do that? What motive would he have?"

"I don't know. Guilt, maybe. He could have felt guilty about what happened to Ethan, about pushing him over the edge. Or maybe he was embarrassed to admit he'd had an argument with an employee of the Village. It's not exactly professional. It's also not exactly a motive for . . ."

Avery ran his hand up and around the back of his neck. "For what, Amber? Are you still worried this wasn't simply a heart attack caused by a fright?"

Instead of answering him, she blinked twice and then continued reading from her list.

"Hannah reported that Carol had an odd response to Ethan's death. As did the person who delivers supplies to the coffee shop. His name is Karl, and he was very belligerent, according to Hannah. She remembered his parting words exactly"—Amber ran her finger across her tablet—" 'Ethan told me what you people were doing. Don't think that you can get away with it.' "

Tate noticed that Avery had no response to that. He did sit forward and rest his forearms against his thighs. Perhaps they had finally gained his complete attention.

Amber continued. "In fact, the word around town is that Ethan was acting strangely. For someone who didn't interact with others much, he drew a lot of attention the last week of his life."

"Is that it?" Avery allowed his gaze to shift from Amber to Tate and back again.

"No. There's the odd response of his wife, Margaret, plus the BB gun you spotted in her home. The vandalism at Katie's shop, including the cross-stitched warning, the box Hannah found in the back of the coffee shop yesterday, and finally—" She hesitated, glanced at Tate, and then continued. "Finally there's the visit to see Patricia earlier today."

"Patricia?"

"Ethan's sister. His wife called the office and asked that we take his truck out to her."

"You went alone?" Avery's voice took on a sharp edge.

"Actually, I didn't. Tate went with me, so he could drive me back. Would it have been a problem if I'd gone alone?"

Avery ignored the question and asked, "What happened at Patricia's?"

"It was a very . . . odd situation. She vacillated between anger, curiosity, and even happiness that she was receiving the truck. But here's the thing. She also had a BB gun—"

"Many people do."

"And one of the rooms in her duplex is locked."

"How would you know that?"

"I had asked to use her bathroom, and she warned me. She said, 'Don't open the second door, or you'll be sorry.' "

"And you did?" Avery's voice held a note of accusation.

"I tried, but it was locked! Who locks one of their bedroom doors?"

"She actually warned both of us. When we first went into her house, she said, 'People should be nice. If you're not nice, something bad can happen to you.' " Tate crossed his arms tightly as the words and the tone of Patricia's voice came back to him. "At the time I thought it was odd, but then, the entire visit was off. She also said that herbs can be dangerous."

"And there was a room, like a chemist's lab, in her duplex. It was probably a large closet but had been turned into a workroom—complete with a long table, flasks, and even one of those bowls you crush things in."

"A crucible?" Tate asked.

"No. I remember using one of those in high school. This was a—" She opened her left hand, palm up. With her right hand holding an imaginary tool, she made a grinding motion.

"Mortar." Avery scrubbed his hand over his face. "It's called a mortar and pestle."

"Yes. That's what I saw." Amber closed the cover on her tablet and sat forward. "Don't you think all of this adds up to something, something more sinister than a natural heart attack?"

"Like what?" Avery reached down to shoo away Leo, who was attempting to rub against his legs. "What is it you think this is all proof of? Murder?"

"Maybe. Probably. Yes, yes, I am beginning to think Ethan was murdered."

"Beginning to think?"

"Don't look at me that way. You have to

admit everything I've laid out sounds suspicious."

Tate knew in that moment that Avery didn't believe them. He wasn't going to believe them unless they brought him the culprit, holding the murder weapon and babbling a confession.

That was a snap judgment and probably uncalled for. He realized that, but he was feeling protective toward Amber.

"There are different types of murder, and frankly I don't see any of those in this situation." Avery began to tick the items off on the fingers of his left hand. "Intentional murder is what it sounds like, and none of the evidence points to that. If someone had wanted to kill him, they could have used a shotgun or a handgun."

"But—"

"Even a knife or a rope. None of those items were involved in this case."

Amber tried to protest, but Avery plodded on.

"There are also situations where death is a result of the intent to do serious bodily injury— the person was aiming to injure, not kill. This doesn't fit Ethan's situation either. There is no evidence that anyone intended to cause him serious bodily injury when he died."

"Because he seems to have been alone?" Tate asked.

"Yes. There's also killing that results from extreme recklessness, for instance, irresponsible use of a firearm. Nothing like that here."

He'd reached his fourth finger. "And finally, murder committed by an accomplice during the course of other felonies—like robbery. The cash drawer was full, and nothing else seemed to be missing. So this doesn't apply either."

"I don't need a law course, Avery." Amber reached down for Leo and pulled him into her lap.

"Maybe you do, because plainly you're confused about what might have happened. I see no motive from the people you have described. We've found no murder weapon, and most important—Ethan died of natural causes."

"How do you know that? Because of an emergency medical worker's report? There wasn't even an autopsy."

"We've been through that with Ethan's wife. The case doesn't warrant an autopsy."

Amber set Leo on the floor and stood, pacing in the small area between the front door and her chair. "What if it wasn't a heart attack? What if it was something made to look like a heart attack? Someone could have drugged him."

"But all evidence points to the fact that he was alone. And why would anyone do that? What would their motive have been?"

The clock ticked loudly as they all considered Avery's last question.

"What is the situation with Patricia?" Tate tried to find a way to tactfully phrase his question. "She seemed—different. Peggy once told me she had a high IQ and that she never recovered from experimenting with drugs. Do you know anything about that? Is it even possible?"

Avery again ran his hand over the back of his neck.

"What's with the way she pulls on her hair?" Amber's hand went to the top of her head and she mimicked pulling and twisting.

Tate tried not to smile, but Amber's imitation of Patricia was spot on. "We saw a sign when entering her street. It said 'Helping Hands.' "

Avery sighed and sat back. "I can't go into details about residents. I can tell you that Helping Hands is an assisted living facility, or neighborhood, which helps adults with physical, emotional, and mental disabilities to lead independent lives."

Again the room fell silent.

"I pulled up the old newspaper files during our security meeting."

Tate stared at her with his best "You didn't!" expression.

"I've already been through that training, so don't look at me that way. I pulled up the old articles. They said the drug dealer was never caught."

"There are drugs in Middlebury, Amber. Like any town, the best we can do is educate citizens on their danger and try to catch the bad guys. But a new dealer replaces the one we catch every time."

"The article also highlighted the dangers of LSD."

"It's a terrible drug. Fortunately usage has dropped over the years."

"According to a site I found, people who use LSD occasionally manifest long-lasting psychoses, such as schizophrenia or severe depression." She was reading from her tablet again. When she finished, she closed the tablet, rested both hands on top of it, and stared first at Avery and then at Tate.

Avery didn't comment on the article, and Tate didn't know what to say. Finally Amber picked up the conversation.

"What of the other events we've had this week? The warning on the sidewalk, the red paint in the coffee shop, the rumors about Ethan, and all these guests who are showing up for a 'Who Killed Ethan?' special?"

"I did check into the website you forwarded to me." Avery smiled for the first time since he'd arrived. "From what I can tell, they scour newspapers. When they find a death near a tourist destination, a new mystery quest pops up on their website."

"Who owns the website?" Amber asked.

"We're still researching. Even if we found them, the most we could charge them with is false advertising. I looked at the ad closely though, and the wording is a bit ambiguous. Probably we wouldn't be able to prosecute. It's a scam. Folks making a buck—"

"How?" Tate rubbed the top of his head. "I've never understood how these sorts of web scams make money."

"In this case, every time you access a clue, you're charged a couple of bucks. Over time, they could make a fair amount, depending on how many scams they're running."

"Creeps," Amber muttered.

"I agree, but they're not your real problem. You could place a sign at the desk that alerts guests to the scam, or even run a disclaimer on the Village's website. Or you could ignore it and the whole thing will go away within a month. Three to four weeks was the maximum amount of time we could find for any *quests*." He held up his fingers to place the last word in quotation marks. Tate shook his head. "No, your real problem is vandalism. We've discussed that, and I'm pleased that you had M&S Security in to speak with your staff."

"You trust them to assess the security needs and then come up with viable solutions?" Tate knew the name though he'd never had a need for a security firm.

"Yes. Several businesses in town have used them, and they did a very good job." Amber studied Avery. "You still believe it's kids?"

"I do. They could have found a way into Ethan's

shop and left the box of paint supplies. Maybe they were afraid of being caught, especially with the increased attention."

"And the rumors? The arguments and odd behavior?"

"Who's to say what's odd and what's not? You think you knew Ethan. Maybe you didn't." Avery hesitated and then continued. "I'm afraid you're feeling guilty because one of your employees died at work, but that's not your fault."

Tate noticed that Amber stared down at her lap. Her straight brown hair fell forward and obscured her expression.

"As far as the rumors, towns talk. Small towns talk more than most, because something like this is unusual. It doesn't mean that the talk is true, only that folks want to explain what's happening. They want their sense of security back."

Amber nodded, tucked her hair behind her ears, and stood. "I guess we're done then. Thank you for stopping by."

Avery stood, the expression on his face a combination of surprise and relief.

Tate remained seated while Amber walked him out onto the porch. He wasn't spying or eaves-dropping, but the house was small. He couldn't help but see Avery reach out and touch her face. The same way he couldn't help but hear him say, "You know I'm on your side. I'd do anything to protect you, but there's no need for you to worry."

⇒ *Twenty* ⇐

Hannah relaxed on her family's front porch step and watched the stars come out one by one as the afternoon light faded. This might be her favorite time of day, the minutes before evening. The time when life slowed and the day's work was complete.

She could see the field across from their porch, the flight of birds headed for their nests or hunting for insects, the colors in the night sky deepening from blue to black. To her, it felt like *Gotte*'s final blessing upon their day.

"Those stars are quite a sight."

Hannah had been staring up at the sky and hadn't seen Jesse step out onto the path leading up to their home. She hadn't even heard him. She could barely make out the smile on his face from the light that shone through the front window. Her *mamm* was in the sitting room reading to Mattie by the gas lantern. The sound of her voice coming through the window seemed like a lullaby.

"The night sky is nearly as pretty as you are, Hannah Troyer."

Was he teasing her? Was he flirting?

She wasn't sure, but with those words he'd dispelled her worries that she looked like a four-eyed, plain Amish girl. Jesse Miller thought she was pretty. Matter settled.

Hannah thought for a moment about both of the boys who had seemed interested in the last few months. They'd asked her to singings, taken her to town for ice cream, even brought flowers once. But as she looked at Jesse, she realized she was not interested in those boys.

Was she interested in Jesse?

Was he interested in her?

"The night sky is nearly as pretty as you are . . ."

He couldn't be serious. The line sounded like something out of an *Englisch* romance novel. She hadn't read any herself, but several of the girls at work did. They checked them out from the public library and enjoyed reading aloud their favorite portions when they managed to snag a few minutes alone together. Mostly they giggled at the sappiness, so why did Hannah's heart lurch when the words were coming from Jesse rather than off a written page?

"Thinking serious thoughts?"

"*Nein.* Maybe. The past week it seems I've been completely caught up in Ethan's mystery and learning my new job."

"Is that a problem?"

"I haven't made much time for my *freinden* at the Village. We'd sometimes take our breaks together, or during our lunch break we'd occasionally look through the clearance sales in the shops."

Jesse moved closer, enough so that she could smell the scent of his soap. He'd cleaned up after work?

"Tell me what you're doing out this time of night, Jesse."

"Stopped by to bring a message from my *dat* to yours. Something about trading hay for seed."

"Our hay?"

"And our seed."

"*Dat* said the first cutting was *gut*." Hannah scooted over, and Jesse sat down beside her. Their shoulders touched, sending her pulse into a rapid rhythm.

"*Gotte* is *gut*," Jesse murmured. "We've been blessed with the right amount of rain and decent temperatures."

They sat there for a moment, watching more of the stars make their appearance, watching the darkness completely envelop the fields, the yard, and finally the steps at their feet.

"Do you think about going anywhere else? Doing anything other than farming and working at the Village?"

Jesse turned so he could lean against the porch post and study her. "*Nein.*"

"Because of your *bruder*? Because he left?"

"That's part of the reason, I suppose. *Dat* needs me here to help with the crops. What I earn at the Village is useful too."

"But . . ."

"But I'd stay even if Andrew hadn't moved to Chicago." An owl hooted from a nearby tree, its voice merging with the night sounds surrounding them. "I visited him once. Did I ever tell you about it?"

Hannah shook her head no, then realized he might not be able to see her. "I remember you being gone last winter. I didn't know where you went, though."

"Did you miss me, Hannah?" His voice was lowered, as if they were sharing a secret.

She didn't know how to respond to that question. She didn't know if he actually expected an answer, so instead she asked, "What was the city like?"

"What you'd expect—crowded, noisy, and too busy."

"There must be something people like there. Every year we lose one or two of those entering their *rumspringa* to Chicago or Fort Wayne or Indianapolis."

"I can't speak regarding the other places since I haven't been to them and don't plan to if I can help it. Chicago was like something out of a bad dream for me. Though I'll admit the lake was pretty. The park beside it was a place you might want to see." He reached for her hand and twined their fingers together. "For all I know, you'd like the city, Hannah. It just wasn't the place I'm meant to be. I found it hard to take a solid, deep breath, if you know what I mean."

"I do." Hannah laughed, though her palms were sweating and her heart continued to tap an erratic rhythm. Had Jesse come to see her? Surely the message to her father could have waited. "I've only been to South Bend, but I didn't like it very much either. To me, everything smelled funny."

"The exhaust from all those cars is worse than horse manure."

They sat that way for a few minutes, and Hannah returned her gaze to the stars, though her attention was split between Jesse holding her hand, the sounds of her family inside the house, and the night sky.

He scooted closer on the step and whispered, "I believe we're being watched."

She spun around and caught her two youngest brothers with their faces pressed to the window screen. Realizing they'd been caught, Dan and Noah fled, the sound of their footsteps running up the stairs causing Hannah to laugh.

Jesse cleared his throat. "Would you like to go for a walk? We might be able to see the stars better down by the pasture fence."

It wasn't far to the pasture. Probably it would be proper. It wasn't late. Her oldest brother was still in the barn, bedding down the horses.

"Let me check with my *mamm*."

Eunice thought it was a fine idea. She even

insisted on sending warm cookies wrapped in a freshly laundered dishcloth. "Don't be too long," she cautioned. "We'll be up by six in the morning. You have work at the Village, and then we have cleaning and gardening."

Hannah slipped the cookies into the pocket of her apron. The night was cool enough for a sweater, so she grabbed one from the mudroom.

"Hannah has a boyfriend." Dan was back downstairs, sitting at the kitchen table and pretending to read a book about camels. He'd been pestering their father about buying some, since ole Manasses Hochstetler had begun making a good profit on the milk from the four he owned. Dan hadn't convinced anyone it was a wise investment though, or that he was responsible enough to care for them.

"You'll get more out of that book if you hold it right side up, *bruder*." She leaned closer to him as he righted the book. "And spying is wrong!"

"Wasn't spying. Happened to walk by and look out the front window and see you two there, mooning over one another."

Hannah wasn't in the mood to argue, and besides—the warm cookies were in her pocket and Jesse was waiting on the front porch.

They walked to the pasture and leaned over the top rail as they ate the cookies and watched the sliver of moon pop out. Then they stopped by the barn to see Noah's newest pups.

"They're *gut* dogs, Jesse. Beagles are fine hunters, and they train easily." Noah ran his hand over the smallest in the litter. It was plain he thought the dogs were the best to be had in the county.

"I'll think about it, but no promises. My *mamm* has enough mouths to feed."

"Don't wait too long, or this lot will be gone."

Jesse claimed her hand again as they walked back toward the front porch. He stopped at the set of swings her father had hung from the tall maple tree. "These old things still work?"

"Try it and see."

"Remember when we were in the second grade? You begged your *dat* to put them up for us."

"I told him I'd help clean out the horse stalls."

"Which he wouldn't let you do because you were too short—the top of your head didn't even come up to the horse's back."

"You were as short as I was!"

They sat in the swings, side by side. The history of their friendship spread like a warm blanket over them as the night cooled.

Hannah pushed with her feet and pumped lightly with her legs to gain a little motion on the old wooden swing. Then she straightened her arms and leaned back, staring up at the night sky. Ribbons of starlight peeked through the branches of the trees.

The swing slowed, and she sat up, glancing

toward Jesse as she smoothed her apron down over her dress. She couldn't see his expression at all now—only his outline was visible against the two lights coming from her house. When had he grown taller than she was? When had he become a man?

"It's easy to forget the simple things in life," she whispered.

"Like swinging?"

"*Ya*. And old *freinden* and family."

"Are you calling me old?" Jesse laughed and bumped her foot with his. When she didn't respond he added, "Life isn't so complicated as we like to believe, Hannah."

"I suppose." She stood and walked toward the house.

"This situation at the Village still has you worried."

"It does. Amber—" All of the worries from the past week crashed down on her at once. She stood, frozen, halfway between the swings and the front porch.

"Amber what?" Jesse stopped in front of her, placed a hand on each of her arms, and began to rub up and down. "It's okay to tell me, Hannah. Everyone needs someone to speak with, and you know you can trust me."

She wanted to step closer, allow Jesse to enfold her in a hug, but instead she focused on the comfort of his hands warming her arms. "She doesn't believe Ethan's death was unintentional."

"Want to tell me why?"

So she did. She told him everything, even describing the box of paint supplies Seth had stumbled over.

"You knew Ethan as well as anyone." Jesse spoke softly. "What do you think?"

"I've been trying to go back over the last week he was alive. Honestly, I don't think I was paying much attention. Maybe it's my fault. Maybe I should have noticed something."

Jesse touched her face, then leaned forward and kissed her softly on the lips. She wanted the moment to last forever. She wanted to burrow into his arms. Jesse trailed his fingers down her face, caressing her neck, and then stepping away. The sensation left her confused and certain every inch of her skin must be sparkling in the moonlight.

"Don't be blaming yourself for the evilness in this world. You were a help to Ethan, filling in when he needed you."

Hannah tried to focus on what he was saying, but her heart was still dancing to a triple rhythm, and she had to resist the urge to reach up and touch where his fingers had been. Jesse claimed her hand, and they walked back to the porch, back to where they had started.

"I suppose you're right." Hannah made a valiant effort to refocus on their conversation, which actually was the last thing she wanted to talk about. She wanted to talk about that kiss! Had it felt to him like it felt to her? Had it been his first as it had been her first?

"Suppose?" Jesse laughed and bumped her shoulder with his.

"I almost feel as if I owe it to him to figure out what happened. He was sort of my neighbor."

"We're separate though. We're plain."

"*Ya*, we are. And maybe in some places Amish communities remain completely separate. Here in Middlebury though, it seems that *Gotte* has woven our lives together in some areas, especially at work. What if there's a reason for that? What if we're supposed to look out for one another?"

"The police are looking into this—"

"But they think it was a natural event. Amber and I don't." She realized then that she was partnered with Amber in a way she hadn't realized. They were both advocates for Ethan. They were committed to solving this mystery and being a friend to him, even in his death.

Jesse didn't argue with her.

He didn't bring up the countless holes in their logic. Instead, he walked her up the porch steps and said, "Tell me how I can help."

⇒ Twenty-One ⇐

Amber watched the lights of Gordon's car blink and then disappear as he made his way out to the main road. When she could no longer follow his progress, she squared her shoulders and marched back into the house.

Where she stopped short at the sight of Tate holding Leo in his lap.

"When did you become a cat person?"

"Can't say I have, but Leo doesn't know that."

"You like him. I can tell. You were smiling when I walked in."

"Maybe I was smiling at you." Tate's eyes locked on hers, and Amber had to shake her head and look away.

"Don't distract me," she begged. "It's up to us to find Ethan's killer."

"Us?"

"Yes. You're in the thick of this already."

"I won't argue with you." Tate gently set Leo on the floor. "Mainly because this time you're right. It was plain Avery isn't going to be any help."

"Who can blame him? All we have is suspicions and a lot of—"

"Coincidences."

"Exactly." Amber had always been a practical

woman. At the moment though, she was having major problems focusing on her next course of action. Tate had crossed the room and was standing directly in front of her. When he reached up and touched her face, ran a thumb down her jawline, and finally cupped his hand around her cheek, all her thoughts flew out the door and down the lane.

When he kissed her, she was certain the purring sound was coming from her!

It wasn't as if she'd never been kissed.

She'd had boyfriends throughout the years, though there'd been nothing that had lasted past a few dates. Gordon had kissed her several times, but it hadn't been—well, it hadn't been like this. She nearly whimpered when Tate stepped back and stuck his hands in the pockets of his jeans.

"Maybe I should apologize for that, but I can't say that's what I want to do." The grin on his face reminded her of the giant, dopey Labradoodle her sister owned.

"We should talk about the next step." She walked to the dining room and stared at the empty table.

What had she eaten for dinner? She'd had fruit for lunch, but dinner was a blank in her mind.

Or rather her mind was filled with Tate.

When she sensed him behind her, she spun around and added, "Next step regarding Ethan, I mean. Not . . . the kiss, or . . . whatever." A slow, warm blush started creeping up her neck and into her cheeks.

For some reason that amused Tate. He looked away, still smiling, and then motioned to her dining room table. "Have you eaten?"

"I was just trying to remember."

"Which means you probably haven't. Let's fix you something, and while you eat we'll plan our next move."

"Good idea. I have some—"

"Eggs. I know."

"I make a mean omelet. If you're hungry."

"Had a sandwich at home before I came over, but I can always eat."

Working in her small kitchen next to Tate did nothing to calm her nerves. Or maybe *nerves* was the wrong word. She suddenly felt completely and totally alive. Because of one kiss? Maybe her sister was right. It could be that she needed a vacation.

Or maybe she was falling in love with her neighbor.

The thought snuck up on her, and she dropped the spatula she'd been using to fold the omelet onto the floor.

"Got it." Tate picked up the utensil and handed her another spatula from the jar where she kept her cooking gadgets.

The one she'd dropped had been a summer green. This one was turquoise blue.

"Interesting. Mine are all black."

Amber laughed. "You cook?"

"Of course I cook. I brought you some chicken. Remember?"

"I do." She thought of all the food he'd brought, expecting her to eat it, and nearly laughed. "You barbecue."

"Same thing, except you do it outside."

He'd brewed a pot of decaf. Passing her a mug, with a little cream and no sugar—exactly the way she liked it—he turned and studied her. His back was to the counter, and he leaned against it but didn't slouch. He held one of her Charlie Brown coffee mugs, and drops of water glistened on his hands from washing vegetables and slicing them for the omelets.

How could he look so at home in her kitchen?

What was she going to do with Tate Bowman?

"Best turn that omelet." He smiled over the top of the mug as he took another sip. "Want to tell me what you're laughing about?"

"I was thinking that mug is appropriate for you."

He held the mug in front of him, stared at it, and confessed, "I don't get it."

"Charlie Brown? You sort of look . . ." She mimed rubbing her hand over the top of her head.

"Oh. I see. You lump all men without hair together into one barrel."

Now she did laugh out loud, and the sound immediately eased the tension she'd carried all week. Laughing felt as good as an hour-long soak in the tub.

"Actually, I'm not bald, you know."

"I never said you were."

"But you were thinking it." He stepped closer, took her hand in his, and ran it over the top of his head. The sensation disoriented her again, sending goose bumps down her arm. When had she last been this close to a man? The times with Avery . . . well, she'd quickly stepped away, not wanting to encourage his advances.

"See? Hair."

She turned back to the omelet, slipped it from the pan to a plate, and poured in the remaining eggs to make another. "So why do you shave it?"

"Easier."

"You shave your head for convenience?"

"Sure. Actually I don't shave it. I have the barber in town do it."

"How long have you had this . . . style?"

"Since I left the army, which would have been 1982, if you're wondering."

"Did you see any conflict while you served?"

"No, and I'm grateful for that. Those four years gave me a real appreciation for all our service members. I thought I wanted to see the world." He shrugged as he handed her another plate for the second omelet. "It sounded good at the time, but after the end of my commitment I was ready to come home."

"You didn't reenlist."

"Didn't even consider it, and I never thought about living anywhere else other than Middlebury. I came home, and I've been on the farm since."

They carried their plates to the dining room.

Amber thought about what Tate had said as they bowed their heads and prayed silently over the food. She found herself thanking God that he had brought her neighbor back to Middlebury and into her life.

Tate's experience in the military explained a lot. He had a no-nonsense way about him, but he also seemed to appreciate life. She'd read that having your life in jeopardy could do that to you. Military service, even during peace time, could probably change your perspective permanently. Amber realized what she was doing in 1982. A giggle escaped as she popped a forkful of egg into her mouth.

"Tell me you're not still laughing about my hair."

"No. Your hair, or rather your lack of it, is nice. It suits you." She forked another piece of omelet, studied it a moment, and then plopped it into her mouth. The taste was rich and creamy. "I was thinking that in 1982 I was a sophomore in high school. You had already graduated and were serving overseas."

"Does it bother you?" His expression turned

suddenly serious, and he set his fork down on his plate. "Our age difference?"

"Seven years isn't that much of a difference." She sipped her coffee. Were they in a relationship? Is that what Tate was hinting at? "At least it doesn't seem like much now."

Tate resumed eating. "You're right. I wouldn't have wanted my boys dating someone in high school when they were out of college, but I can hardly see how it matters in our case."

"Are we dating?" She blurted the question before she considered whether she should ask it.

Tate cocked his head and studied her. "We're chasing a murderer together. Usually that comes after a formal date. Doesn't it?"

"I don't usually chase murderers."

"So maybe we should—" Whatever he was about to say hung suspended between them as they both turned toward the sound of a knock at the front door.

She set aside her fork and napkin. "I better get that."

Amber noticed as she walked toward the front door that he had stood, as if he needed to be prepared, as if they needed to face whatever came next together.

⇒ Twenty-Two ⇐

Carol Jennings had finally agreed to sit, and she murmured her thanks when Tate brought her a mug of decaffeinated coffee. Amber had always admired the older woman. She wore her brown hair, which was streaked with gray, in a stylish bob, cut a half inch below her jawline. Her clothing was always conservative, clean, and neat. Tonight she wore the same long denim skirt, starched blouse, and sweater she'd had on at the managers' meeting.

Amber couldn't remember her age, probably sixtyish. She did know, without looking at Carol's employee file, that she rarely missed a day of work and had been with the Village for many years. She was what Amber's mom would have called a "no-nonsense type of woman." She worked methodically and efficiently.

At the moment Carol was perched on the edge of Amber's recliner, staring at an envelope she was clutching. Tate and Amber were seated together on the small couch. She'd always thought of the leather and cloth sofa as plenty large enough. Sitting so close to Tate, she was reminded of what her mother would have called it—a loveseat.

"I should have given this to you earlier, at the

meeting this afternoon or as we were leaving." She glanced up and then away. "I didn't know what to do. I almost couldn't believe who it was from. Then I went home and showed it to Stu. He said I shouldn't be in the middle of this. He said to bring it to you."

"Bring me what?" Amber kept her voice low and calm, but her pulse had begun to thrum like the bass drum in a rock band.

Carol held up the envelope, stared at it a moment longer, and then thrust it out toward them.

Tate reached for it and handed it to Amber.

She was glad he was with her.

She was comforted to know that they were a team. What could possibly be in what she could now see was a letter? It was addressed to Carol Jennings. Why did they need to read it? She didn't know if she could handle one more surprise, but she did know with a deep certainty that she didn't want to face it alone.

Given a choice, two were better than one.

Together she knew they could make sense of this bizarre turn of events.

"It came in the mail. Today. I'm sorry I didn't bring it to you immediately, but I . . . I . . . I still couldn't believe it was from him. Maybe it's not." She picked up the coffee mug Tate had set on the table beside her and wrapped her hands around it.

"Read it," she whispered.

The envelope had been opened with a letter opener, one smooth slit across the top. It occurred to Amber that Avery might want to check the envelope and its contents for fingerprints, but then, Avery didn't believe there had been a crime.

Amber pulled out the single sheet of paper. Writing covered both sides. Their heads nearly touching, she and Tate read what was written there together.

April 21

The clock has not yet passed four in the morning. My wife sleeps on the other side of the house, oblivious to my suffering. I tried to speak with her yesterday, but didn't get far. Her preoccupation with remodeling the kitchen kept her from listening.

A kitchen remodel.

As if that matters one bit when your soul is standing at heaven's gate. I'll be pushed across that threshold soon—every fiber of my being knows it. I'm like the song playing on the old radio here beside my desk. Solitary. A cry in the darkness. No one listening. No one who cares.

Perhaps that is fair. I spent my life concerned over the wrong things. One more regret piled upon many.

My wife will be fine—of that I'm sure. But

what will become of Patricia? All she can speak of is the land. Her future weighs heavily on my mind, on my heart.

Carol, I am sorry to pass to you this burden. Preston will post my last letter to you when something happens to me. You were always a kind coworker. Perhaps you will know who to turn to with the final details of my life. Perhaps you can help to find my killer.

"You received this today?" Tate's voice was grave, and Amber was conscious of events taking another turn. The letter she was holding confirmed so much of what they had suspected. It didn't prove anything, she was aware of that. But it did line up precisely with their darkest fears.

"Yes. It came this morning in my regular mail."

"According to the top line, Ethan wrote it the twenty-first. That was the day he died."

Carol didn't answer that, but she nodded in agreement.

"If it was mailed Monday, it shouldn't have taken five days to reach you. Not in a town our size."

"He left off the zip code." Amber turned the envelope over and tapped the address. "Middlebury postmark, so we know he mailed it from here. Date of the postmark is Wednesday.

273

Normally mail across town arrives in one day, but no zip may have caused it to take two."

"But how? It's not possible. He couldn't have mailed it on Wednesday if he died on Monday. This Preston must have mailed it, whoever he is." Carol set down the coffee. She still hadn't taken a drink, but the warmth of holding the beverage seemed to have calmed her. Now she rubbed one hand with the other, her brow lined in confusion. "Unless he stopped by the post office before he came to work on Monday. But why would he, when he could have walked next door and handed it to me? And then there's the postmark date . . ."

"It breaks my heart to read this." Amber ran her finger over the handwritten lines. " 'Standing at heaven's gate . . . A cry in the darkness.' "

A shiver passed over and through her. "He felt so alone, and I didn't even realize."

"*You* didn't?" Carol's voice teetered as she shook her head. "I knew and did nothing. I worked next door to him every day. I saw how withdrawn he had become—withdrawn and exhausted. We even argued over it a few weeks ago, but he wouldn't listen. I should have told someone."

Tate took the letter from Amber's hand. "He says right here . . . 'You were always a kind coworker.' It sounds as if you were the one person Ethan felt he could trust. But what was going on? What did he try to speak with his wife about? And what is this about land and Patricia?"

Amber covered her mouth with the fingers of her right hand. How long ago had that land transaction taken place? She'd need to look at her records . . .

Suddenly she remembered, and another piece of the puzzle fell into place.

Tate knew the moment Amber had begun to make sense of this latest development. Her expression changed from puzzlement to realization to something akin to despair. He also knew she wasn't connecting all the dots, probably because she was upset to hear about Ethan's state of mind.

"What is it?" He reached out and took her hand in his. Her fingers were ice cold. She continued to gaze at the envelope on her lap for another moment before raising her eyes to his.

"Ethan once owned the land across the road. It must be what he was referring to in the letter. What was it he said about Patricia?" She picked up the letter, turned it over, and found the spot she needed with the fingers of her left hand, leaving her right hand tucked in his. " 'All she can speak of is the land.' "

"And you think he's referring to the land across the road from the Village?"

"I do. It's a rather small piece—no more than twenty acres. Ethan came to me at some point, maybe eight or ten years ago. He wanted me to ask the owners of the Village if they'd like to purchase it, which they did. No improvements have been made to it, but our grounds crew keeps the area properly mowed."

"Why would he offer to sell it?"

"He needed the money." Carol again picked up her coffee, turning the mug round and round in her hands. "His wife always wanted a higher standard of living than he could afford. I remember him telling me that once, and then there was Patricia—"

"Who apparently didn't want the land sold." Tate looked from Carol to Amber. "Any idea why she'd care?"

They both shook their heads.

"I'd never even met her until the night at the funeral home." Amber leaned forward. "Carol, do you know anything about Patricia? Anything that might help us?"

"Years ago Ethan made the decision to move her to the duplex, the one supervised by Helping Hands. At first he used his savings to subsidize her rent, but then that money ran out."

"Do you remember how many years ago that happened?"

Now Carol ran her fingers up and down the side of the mug as she stared across the room, out past the front window.

"It was fourteen—no, fifteen years ago. I remember that because my first grandbaby had been born a few weeks earlier. I was over in Goshen, helping with Little Liza. That's what we called her." Carol shook her head, bringing her attention back to the present. "She turned fifteen this year. Stu offered to help with the move, but Ethan insisted he could handle it alone."

"Who turns down moving help?" Tate placed his arm across the back of the couch when Amber stood and began pacing the little room. A restless feeling gnawed at his gut, probably because of the letter, because he could see where it would lead them next.

He knew where to go. The question was—would it be better to wait until morning? Something deep inside whispered "Hurry," and he thrummed his fingers against the back of the couch. What should he do? Amber wouldn't let him go alone. Did he want to take her there, after dark?

If he told her, he wouldn't have any choice. "Was he embarrassed about Patricia? About her . . . disabilities?"

"I don't know if he even understood exactly what was wrong with his sister. After the drug incident that sent her over the edge—I can tell by your expressions that you both know about that —Patricia couldn't keep a job. She also scared the people who lived around her. She'd go off on a tear for no reason . . ."

"Were the police called?" Amber sat forward.

"Sometimes. Often she simply had a tantrum

277

like a small child—hollering and throwing things. Ethan finally moved her to the duplex, and most folks put her from their minds. It's easy to forget what you don't see."

"He was supporting his sister and his wife." Amber stopped mid-pace. "We need to go and see Patricia, or Margaret, or both of them. We need to find out who or what was putting pressure on Ethan. Find the answer to that, and we might find a motive for murder."

"Perhaps the police should go," Carol said.

"We talked to Avery earlier tonight. The police are convinced Ethan's death was simply from natural causes—"

"But with the letter . . ."

"I doubt it would change their minds. Ethan didn't go to the police, even though he was plainly frightened. He wanted someone to know though, and he chose you. He sent you this letter in the hopes we would figure it out."

Amber was moving toward her purse, retrieving her car keys and pocketing her cell. Carol had stood, but waited as if she wasn't sure whether they were done with her.

Tate knew now was the time to speak up, but he hesitated, unsure whether they should attempt this alone or try with Avery one more time. Then he remembered the way Avery had dismissed them, the way he had insisted they have evidence.

"It's only one letter that anyone could have

written." Tate stood, unsure that he wanted to encourage her on this mission.

"I recognize Ethan's handwriting—he wrote it, and I want to know why. Avery will explain it away or say it doesn't prove anything. But I want to know. I need to know." Amber had stopped at the door, and she looked back at him quizzically. "Are you coming with me?"

"Yes." He grabbed both of their jackets off the hook by the door. "I am, but we're not going to see Patricia or Margaret."

"We're not?"

Tate understood that they were moving into the unknown, maybe into danger, but he could no more stop these events than he could stop Amber from stepping out into the night. "Carol, thank you for bringing Amber the letter and for bringing it tonight. Do you need us to follow you home?"

"It isn't that late. I'll be fine. Thank you."

He motioned to Amber's car—the little red Ford that would stand out like a sore thumb. It would have to do. As long as she was driving, he could keep watch out the window.

She started it with a push button. His kids had keyless ignitions as well, but he preferred the solid feel of a key in his hand. Then she placed the transmission into drive and pulled down to the main road.

"If we're not going to see Ethan's wife or sister, where are we going?"

"To find Preston."

The puzzle piece clicked into place. "The homeless man. The man Hannah told me about. The man Ethan was seen talking to."

"And I only know of one Preston in town. Of course, there could be more, but they'd be kids, and I doubt that's whom Ethan was talking about."

Tate gave her directions, and Amber kept her eyes on the road, focusing on the curves and twists until they reached the bottom of the hill. He directed her left and then left again. Finally he motioned for her to pull over on the side of County Road 8, directly across from Krider Garden.

"So, as you told me before, Preston is a veteran."

"He is."

"And he . . . what?" She turned to look at him. He couldn't see her eyes in the darkness, but he could feel her gaze, could imagine her features scrunched trying to figure out this latest turn of events. "He lives here? In the park?"

"Last I heard. During the day he moves around, but at night he tries to find some shelter—a place that will protect him from the weather."

"The mushroom?" Amber's voice rose a notch. "He sleeps under the mushroom sculpture?"

"He did."

"Whoever spotted the two of them was sure it

was Ethan because his truck was at the side of the road near the park, near here."

She glanced left and then right, as if she might be able to spy him in the darkness.

"Why though? Why would Ethan meet with him? I can see why he might be kind to him, to this Preston. The no-begging ordinance the council passed doesn't stop folks from noticing and trying to help." She hesitated, then pushed on. "Helping a homeless person doesn't exactly sound like the Ethan we all knew."

"Maybe he wasn't helping Preston. Maybe Preston was helping him."

⇒ Twenty-Three ⇐

Hannah stayed out on the porch after Jesse headed for home, walking off into the darkness, whistling a tune they had recently sung at church.

She hadn't known she was going to ask for his help, probably would have never dared to. When he offered though, she realized what she wanted to do, what she needed to do. Was it the right thing? She couldn't be sure. She couldn't even think what part of the *Ordnung* would apply.

Finally she stood, stretched, and walked into the house. She stopped suddenly when she noticed her mother sitting in the corner rocker, a fire in the hearth because it was colder inside the house than outside.

"Practically used up all the gas in this lantern waiting for you to come in."

"*Mamm*, you didn't have to wait for me. I'm not a *kind*."

"You're practically grown. Aren't you?" From anyone else the words would have sounded like a scolding, but Eunice glanced over the top of her reading glasses and smiled. She seldom wore the glasses, but did mainly when she was reading a recipe or sewing. She turned her attention back to the quilt top on her lap, pulling the needle through the seam she was making to connect the dark blue material to the white.

"Still working on Mattie's new quilt?"

"*Ya*. She's ready for a regular-sized bed, asks me every night when I tuck her in. Your *dat* promised to go next week and pick up the extra bed Fanny Bontrager has. It's fortunate you heard she had one for sale. With most of her children grown and moving off to different parts of the state, she doesn't think she'll need it. I want to have the quilt done by the time he brings it home."

Hannah sat in front of her mother's chair, sat on the floor so that she did feel like a child, and studied her mother as she finished sewing the border around the quilt. It was a twin-size nine patch, and she'd filled the squares with appliqués of Sunbonnet Sue in different-colored dresses.

"What will you do with the crib?"

Eunice didn't even hesitate. "Someone will be needing it eventually. We'll store it in the barn."

"Ben is nineteen with no girl in sight, and I certainly won't need it anytime soon."

"Uh-huh."

"It's not like Jesse and I are courting, and even if we were . . . courting isn't marrying."

"True."

"But I suppose it would be foolish to give it away."

"It would."

Hannah was unsure whether her mother was teasing her. She stood and removed her prayer *kapp*. She loved pulling the pins from her hair, running her hands through it, relaxing completely. "Think I'll grab another cookie. Want some?"

"I put back a few in the bread box. Otherwise your *bruders* would have eaten every one."

"Jesse appreciated the ones you sent home with him." Her head was in the icebox as she called out from the kitchen. She rummaged around and came away with the milk.

"Oatmeal and raisins seem to please everyone, plus it's a *gut* way to sneak a little fruit into their diet."

She placed the cookies on a plate, the plate and glasses of milk on a tray, and carried it all into the sitting room. "Where is *Dat*?"

"Bed already. This time of year, he's practically asleep before the sun bids good night."

"Farming's hard work." Hannah bit into the cookie and almost moaned. She was a good cook, but no one she knew could bake like her *mamm*. The flavors reminded her of childhood and winter nights and standing on a stool to help mix ingredients into the batter.

Eunice set aside her quilting and reached for one of the cookies. "If you weren't courting out under the stars, what were you and Jesse doing?"

So she told her—about their walk, sitting in the swings, and the kiss. They both reached for another cookie, and she confessed her worries about Ethan and what she had in mind to do, the thing that Jesse said he would help with.

"Is it wrong, *Mamm*? To involve myself?"

"Do you feel it's wrong?"

"*Nein*. I feel it's right, but I can't always trust my emotions about work or Jesse. Sometimes he feels like my old *freind* from school. Other times he seems like a person I hardly know."

"That will work itself out. No need to worry yourself about it."

"And what of Ethan? Should I be helping Amber? What would the *Ordnung* say?"

"Perhaps you are confused about what the *Ordnung* is. It's not a special book that holds all of the answers we seek. The word *Ordnung* means order and discipline, and this is what it gives to our lives."

"I've heard you speak of it since I was small. Every time I'd ask you why, you'd say, 'Because of the *Ordnung*, because it is the plain way.' "

"An answer that caused wrinkles on your brow even when you were a child."

"Since I joined the church last winter, I find myself wondering, questioning, whether the things I do are right or wrong." Hannah finished her cookie. She was again sitting on the floor, and she drew her knees up under her dress and circled her arms around them.

"It's normal to question such things. It's a sign that you are maturing."

"I don't feel mature. I feel confused."

"Think of the *Ordnung* as a set of rules. Your teacher had rules at school, *ya*?"

"She did." Hannah laughed. "If there had been no rules, it would have been chaos. Forty children in a one-room schoolhouse can be a lot to handle."

"It is the same with the *Ordnung*, but it applies everywhere, not just within the walls of a schoolroom. The rules about how we dress, what technology we use, and how we interact with one another . . . they help us to live better Christian lives. But always remember that the heart of all we do is based in the Scriptures."

"Last time I checked, the Bible didn't say anything about solving mysteries or catching a murderer."

"*Nein*. And it's not your place to do so. The *Englisch* police will tend to that if it needs to be done."

"What about—"

"Hannah, you must promise me. If you even think you are near such a dangerous person, you will come away. Together we will go to the bishop, who will accompany us to the police."

"I don't plan on stepping into *Dat*'s field and running into Ethan's killer!"

"I should hope not." Eunice stood and attended to the fire, then returned to her chair. She didn't pick up her sewing. Instead, she rocked and studied her daughter. "Why is it you feel so strongly about helping Amber?"

"We are *freinden*, *Mamm*. I know that sounds odd, but it's true."

"One can never guess who will or won't become important in their life."

"A month ago I would never have expected to find myself running the *kaffi* shop, supervising Seth, and speaking with Amber on a daily basis. A month ago, my life made sense."

"And now?"

"Now I feel as if I should do something. The entire thing reminds me of the jigsaw puzzles we work on in the employee lunchroom during the rainy days. It's as if I can see the piece that is missing, but from the back side. I don't know what the picture will look like yet."

"And this thing you will do with Jesse, going to see Minerva, you think it will reveal the picture to you."

"*Ya.* I do."

"Then you have my blessing, Hannah. After we finish cleaning tomorrow, you and Jesse may go and visit her. We'll make an extra pie for you to take. Minerva doesn't bake much anymore, since she's alone now."

"That would be *gut.*"

"Promise me that you will be careful, and that you will remember your baptism in Christ and your commitment to the church. Always, even when completing puzzles, conduct yourself in a plain way."

Hannah finally smiled. She couldn't help it. Her mother's face was so serious, so grave. "I can do that. You don't have to look so worried."

"It's normal to worry. It's what a mother does." Eunice stood and darkened the gas lantern, then made sure the fire had safely died out. There was enough light coming through the window—from the moon and the stars—to make their way across the room, into the entryway, and up the stairs. She looped her arm through Hannah's before adding, "You'll know what that's like one day. And then you'll remember this old woman's fussing and you'll understand."

"You're not old!"

"I'm not young."

"Which means you are as you're supposed to be."

"I'm glad you think so." She kissed Hannah on the forehead and said good night.

Hannah made her way into her room, preparing for bed quietly so as not to wake Mattie. It wasn't until she had snuggled under the sheets and blankets and quilt that she realized her mother hadn't questioned why Minerva—why the answer might be brought to light by the woman who tended a garden of herbs.

The idea had come to Hannah as she'd walked with Jesse. If Ethan's death wasn't natural, then it was murder. But it was murder made to look natural.

Had someone poisoned Ethan?

And if they'd used herbs, was the person *Englisch* or Amish?

It was with that final troubling thought that she tumbled into a deep and dreamless sleep.

⇐ Twenty-Four ⇒

Amber and Tate walked quietly toward the giant mushroom. Amber hadn't been there in years. Why didn't she take the time to walk this portion of the path? The gardens were a special place. Small lights had been placed at intervals along the footpath, but they provided barely enough

288

light to keep one from walking off into the trees by mistake. In the near darkness, she couldn't see the flowers that had been planted, but she could smell them.

It was the heady, sweet smell of spring.

They stopped near the mushroom sculpture.

There was no sign of Preston. Had he heard them coming and skedaddled? Or had he moved on to a different spot?

Tate used a small flashlight on his keychain to scan the area. He focused its beam on the bench. Pushed underneath it, into the far corner, were a green backpack and a folded tarp.

"At least we know he's staying here." Tate toggled off the light.

"So what do we do?"

"We wait."

Tate sat on the bench, and Amber joined him.

She didn't say a word. Her mind was locked up with the endless possibilities of what they might find.

"Do you know the history of Krider's?"

"Who?"

"Krider's." Tate bumped her shoulder with his. "That's who this garden is named after."

"Oh. Yeah, I remember reading something about that."

"There's a plaque." He pointed to the right in the darkness. "Over there."

"They were some sort of wholesale nursery?"

"One of Middlebury's largest. Their business lasted nearly one hundred years. Closed in 1990. Real shame too, as they employed quite a few folks."

"So why the gardens?"

"Vernon Krider designed the gardens for the Chicago World Fair. That was in the thirties. This is a miniature replica of that. Right down to the giant toadstool in front of you."

"I thought it was a mushroom."

Tate's laughter surprised her. How was he able to stay so relaxed? She felt wound tight sitting beside him, but it was tempting—oh, so tempting—to allow his mood to be contagious.

"They're the same thing. Some folks say toadstools are the poisonous kind, but basically they're the same thing."

Poisonous mushrooms? She'd forgotten that so many things could be dangerous, so many things you passed in your everyday comings and goings. Somehow she had started taking life for granted, but the last week had wakened her.

The sound of feet on the pathway pulled her back to the present.

A man stepped into the clearing. Amber could see no more than the outline of him by the glow of the path lighting.

He was medium height, and he apparently didn't trust them.

He stepped closer, and she understood he was

concerned about his bedroll. His body turned ever so slightly toward the far end of their bench and then back toward Tate and Amber. She realized that Tate had purposely chosen the opposite side of the bench for them to sit on.

Had he been worried they might spook Preston away?

Did they appear threatening to him?

"Preston."

"Tate."

Neither man moved, and Preston seemed to be making a choice. Stay? Or run?

"Wondered if you might have a minute to talk with us."

"You a cop now?"

"I'm not."

"Talk about what?"

"Ethan Gray."

Preston reached up and tugged his wool camo-colored cap farther over his ears. "I figured someone would come about that eventually. Never did feel good about any of it."

"What do you mean—"

Tate's hand on her arm quieted her. "I could use a cup of coffee."

Preston ran his thumbs under the straps of his backpack.

"And maybe some pie."

Even in the dim lighting, Amber could see the way his body relaxed. "Pie would be good."

She tried to study him, without being obvious about it, as they walked to a diner a block down the road. Preston had a scruffy beard, and he wore an old army jacket that matched the cap. The black straps of his green backpack were fitted over the jacket.

After the waitress had brought coffee and taken their orders for pie, Amber looked to Tate. He nodded, and she pulled out the letter—the one Carol had allowed them to keep.

"Preston, my name is Amber. I manage the Village. Do you know where that is?"

"Sure."

"Ethan Gray worked for me there, and we're trying to figure out what happened to him, what exactly he was doing in the last few weeks. Did you know Ethan?"

Preston shrugged as he stirred cream and sugar into his coffee. "How well does one person know another? We would have spoken to each other if we'd passed on the street. That was the extent of it. I was surprised when he came looking for me."

Now that they were in the light, she could see that he was cleaner than she'd expected. But then, what did she know about being homeless? What did she know about how he lived or why he chose to live that way?

"Have you heard he recently died?"

"I didn't know it when I mailed that letter. It

was the following day when I read about his death in the paper."

Amber's pulse ratcheted up a notch. She set the letter on the table and wiped her palms on her pants. "Did you read it?"

"Not at first. Not when he gave it to me. That seemed like an invasion of his . . . I don't know, his personal things. Everyone needs privacy. You know?"

"Yes, I do."

"I never did feel right about what he asked me to do, about taking money for it."

The waitress returned, and Amber spent an agonizing moment waiting for her to dole out the pie and refill their coffee mugs. Finally she left them alone, or as alone as you could be in a small-town diner on a Friday night.

"What did Ethan ask you to do?" Tate sipped his coffee and waited.

Preston didn't answer immediately. He focused on the plate in front of him, swallowing half of the chocolate pie in two bites. "Hold on to what he gave me. Said he'd pay me twenty bucks a week. All I had to do was hold on to it, and if he didn't show, put it in the mail."

"If he didn't show?"

"Yes. He knew where to find me, down in the park, and he'd come by every day after work." He finished the pie and slugged it down with the rest of his coffee.

Tate signaled the waitress to once again refill their mugs. "When did this start?"

"Is this Friday?"

"Yes."

"Two weeks ago this coming Monday was the first time I spoke with him. A crew always comes to do the garden work on Mondays, and I stay out of their way. When I go back, the place always smells of cut grass." He watched Amber, though he was answering Tate's question. "It was on Monday. I'm sure."

Amber glanced at Tate, who shrugged and pushed his pie toward Preston.

"That's yours." Preston didn't touch the second piece of pie, though he eyeballed the dessert with a hint of a smile.

"I'm not as hungry as I thought I was. You eat it."

Preston didn't hesitate long. He dug into the apple with the same gusto he'd used on the chocolate. The food seemed to relax him, or maybe he'd decided they could be trusted.

Finally he pushed back the plate and studied them both, and that was when Amber realized she had completely misjudged this man. It was a thought that was immediately followed by embarrassment that she had presumed to judge him at all.

Tate was relieved by what he was seeing across the table, even while he was troubled by what he was hearing.

Preston Johnstone looked better than he had in years. His eyes were clear, he was clean, and he wasn't fidgeting—scratching or jumpy. Whatever difficulties Preston had faced when exiting the US Army, he had found a way to overcome them. Or perhaps he'd had help. The last conversation they'd had played through Tate's mind. Had it been two years ago?

Preston was still living on the streets, but he had come a far, far distance from where he'd been the last time Tate had seen him. Since then it had been an occasional wave from his truck when he'd passed him on the street. Should he have done more? Could he have done more? The questions circled in his mind as he listened to the boy—the man—who had graduated from Middlebury High School two years ahead of his own son.

Tate cleared his throat and wrapped his hands around his coffee mug. "Carol Jennings brought us this letter a few hours ago. We had suspected that something was going on with Ethan, that his death might not have been unintentional."

He noticed Preston didn't even blink at that, so he pushed on. "We want to be clear. The Middlebury police believe the cause of death was a heart attack, plain and simple."

"But there are other . . . factors." Amber stuck her fork into her peach pie. "This letter for instance, and the way he had been acting the days and weeks before his death."

She set down the fork, as if reconsidering Ethan's circumstances had caused her to lose her appetite.

Tate eyed the remaining portion of pie. "Are you going to eat that?"

"I don't think so."

Tate pulled it toward himself and forked a big chunk of peaches and piecrust and sugar into his mouth. *Heavenly.*

"Thought you weren't hungry." Preston almost smiled.

"Can't let good pie go to waste. You want some of it?"

Preston shook his head and stared down into his coffee. "Ethan was acting differently. As I said, I hadn't spoken with him in a couple years. I'd see him sometimes, and he'd nod like most folks. But he didn't seem to know what to say."

"That changed? Almost two weeks ago?"

"Yeah. He showed up—on Monday—and asked if I could do something for him. He asked if he could trust me. I thought that was a funny question. Why wouldn't he be able to trust me? And why did he need to?" Preston sipped his coffee, which had cooled. He didn't seem to notice. "There's something else that might help you. He looked strung out to me."

"Strung out?" Amber leaned forward. "Drunk?"

"No. I've never seen anyone that hyper from alcohol, though I suppose it's possible. Alcohol is a depressant. It might have caused him to react differently, sluggishly even, but not agitated and restless."

"Drugs?" Tate asked around the last bite of pie.

"Maybe. I couldn't say, and I don't mean to speak ill of him. It was something I noticed, and it bothered me at the time. He would pace back and forth, couldn't look me in the eye as he spoke, and was constantly fidgeting with his clothing, almost like it was bothering him. It was plain he wasn't sleeping much—eyes were bloodshot, and he'd scan the area constantly. Strung out is the best way I know to describe it."

Silence enveloped the café when someone in the back dropped a plate. The sound of its shattering on the floor carried throughout the restaurant. The hush was followed by a smattering of applause, and then the low hum of chatter resumed.

"So what did he ask you to do, exactly?" Amber stared at Preston with those beautiful hazel eyes, and Tate knew the man wouldn't be able to resist her. Who could?

"He said he needed someone to keep something for him."

"A letter?"

"Yes, and he offered to pay me twenty dollars a week, as I said. I told him there was no need. It's nothing off my back to hold on to somebody's mail, but he insisted. Said this was important—

vitally important. Those were his exact words. He didn't give it to me that first day. It was like he was checking me out. But he came back each night and on . . ." He hesitated, staring again out the window. "On Thursday he did give me a letter."

Amber ran her fingers over the address penned on the front of the envelope. "So you agreed to keep it?"

"Sure. Ethan gave me the first week's money up front, said he'd pay on Mondays, but he might bring a letter by every day. I didn't expect that to happen. None of it made sense to me. But he did start showing up daily to talk a little, and then he'd leave. He did pay me another twenty. I don't mind admitting I could use the money. It's hard to find work, especially in the winter, and especially . . . given my circumstances."

"He came back to see you again this past Monday? The day he died?"

"I know. It's strange, right? He looked even worse than the week before, and he showed up early in the morning. The times before he came in the evening, like you did."

"But the day he died he came before work." Tate was beginning to visualize the sequence of events.

"It was still dark. I knew it was him though, before I even saw him. Hard to mask the sound of that old truck."

"And?" Amber was practically leaning across the table.

"And he was a mess, completely reamed out. I tried to help, offered to go with him to a hospital, or wherever he needed to go. But he refused."

"Refused? Why didn't you make him?" Amber's hands came out, waving as she spoke.

Preston didn't answer right away. He sat calmly and quietly. Somehow Tate knew what his next words would be. They were words he had said to the boy when he'd initially returned to Middlebury, when it was first obvious that he wasn't adjusting.

"Can't force anyone to do anything. Not really." Preston was staring at him now. "A good friend told me that once. You can offer, and you can pray, but you can't force."

Silence settled once again over their table.

Tate fiddled with the fork, scraping it across the crumbs on his plate.

Amber sat back, looking deflated—and maybe a little embarrassed.

Preston had turned his attention to the scene outside the window—a few folks walking by, the soft glow of streetlights, and beyond that the pitch-black night.

Finally he scrubbed a hand across his face and finished his story. "When he didn't show up after work on Monday, I thought maybe the morning visit was all I'd get. Then he didn't show by Tuesday late, and I knew something had happened. Wednesday morning I opened the letter and read it. Some things it seemed to explain, but mostly I found more questions. So I did what I promised. I resealed the letter and mailed it."

When Amber pulled out her wallet, Tate stayed her hand. "I got it." He dropped a bill on the table, one that would cover the pie, the coffee, and the tip, and then he stood up.

Reaching across the table, he shook Preston's hand. "Thank you, Preston. You've been a lot of help, and I want you to know I'm still praying for you."

"I know you are."

"If there's anything I can do—"

Preston waved away the offer. "I'm good. Much better than I've been in a long time."

Amber murmured her thanks, then reached down to pick up the letter Ethan had written, the one Preston had mailed and Carol had brought to them.

They had turned to go when Preston spoke up again. "What should I do with the rest?"

"The rest?" As they turned back, Amber glanced from the letter in her hand to Preston to Tate. "What rest?"

"The rest of the letters from Ethan."

⋙ Twenty-Five ⋘

Preston pulled the stack of letters from his pack as Amber and Tate sat back down. "I only mailed the one, per Ethan's instructions. At that point he was acting pretty paranoid. He'd show up and give me a new letter that was *the* letter. He didn't seem to realize he was building up quite a stash of them. I wasn't sure what I was supposed to do with the rest. Seemed wrong to toss them in the trash."

At Preston's words, Amber's heart had felt as if it stopped, but now it began to thump against her rib cage again—a steady, urgent beat. She accepted the letters from Preston and stared at them. There were six in all, seven if you counted the one they'd already read. Preston had stacked the six neatly and bound them with a rubber band. He explained that the letter on top was the first one, the one Ethan had brought to him that evening two weeks ago.

Tate motioned the waitress over, handed her the money he had put on the table and the check, and asked for more coffee.

"Sure thing, hon. Everything all right here?"

"Yeah, we're good. We're going to be a little longer. Hate to hold up your booth, but we'll leave a tip big enough to cover another party."

"No problem. You all take as long as you want." She topped off their coffees, picked up the dirty dishes, and left.

Amber heard the conversation between Tate and the waitress, and she felt Preston's eyes on her, gauging her reaction. But she could only stare at the letters. Was the answer on the pieces of paper she held? Would they learn the identity of Ethan's killer?

They began with the first one.

April 10

A grown man putting pen to paper because he has no friends is a pitiful thing indeed. Yet here I am. Can't say that it ever bothered me much before. Life was always too busy with work and family to give friendship much thought.

Now it seems to be on my mind often.

So what has changed?

Don't know that I'm able to explain that, not even to myself.

These are the things I know—

There is no one I can talk to, no one I can trust with my suspicions.

It's important that I leave a trail that some-one can follow, in case the worst happens.

Someone—may the Lord help me because I don't know who—but someone wants me dead.

April 12

I remain convinced I'm being watched . . . watched and possibly followed.

Not that I've seen anyone. No. Whoever would harm me is crafty. But a man knows. When he's spent the entirety of his life alone, working in the same place, married to the same woman, and living in the same house . . . a man can tell.

Small things like a pen left out on my desk in the stockroom, my accounts ledger put back in the drawer the wrong way, the echo of footsteps when I'm certain that I'm alone.

So why don't I go to the police?

Because I have no proof.

I mentioned my suspicions to Karl. I've known that man for years. He delivers pastries to my shop every morning. He looked concerned, but what could he do?

I need proof, and I will find it. I promise that I will.

April 14

Lost my temper this evening with my boss, though I'm loath to call that man by such a name.

Larry's a poor excuse for a supervisor— arrogant and inept. My mistake might have been in telling him so. The fury in his face provoked my own.

At the time, it almost seemed like he was baiting me, trying to push me over some proverbial edge.

And I took it out on Nell. I've always treated that truck with complete respect, but not this evening.

I slammed the door.

Ground the gears.

Pushed the engine as fast as I dared.

Tore out of the Village as if the demons of hell were chasing me.

Somehow, it seemed they were.

April 15

I am more anxious than I've been at any other time in my life.

I'm tempted to go and see the doctor again, but he told me his opinion a year ago. My heart isn't as young as it used to be. I need to work less, relax more, and ease up on the stress. Watch what I eat and drink. I'm old, yes. But more than time can take its toll on a heart. What about the futility of a life spent unwisely? I'm consumed by fear and my shattered dreams.

If I told him what's happening, he'd probably prescribe more medicine, which I wouldn't take. How can I know if it's been switched out by whoever wants me dead? I found a message in the coffee shop drawer today. It said, "Daniel 5:25–26." The message was typed, so there's no sense in taking it to the police.

When I looked it up, I read about the fall of a kingdom. But I have no kingdom. So what does my attacker want?

I found myself flipping through the Bible, reading words of God's love I had forgotten. For a brief time—less than an hour—I was able to rest.

April 17

I've found someone to leave my letters with. Someone I can depend on, though I wouldn't go so far as to call him a friend. He is a patriot, in spite of how he looks, and a patriot is someone you can trust with your most prized possession—which would be this pitiful stack of letters, I suppose. A month ago I would have said Nell was my most precious thing, but a truck is of no use if you're dead.

Am I a good judge of character? I like to think so. If someone is reading these letters, then I have chosen my confidant well.

I remain convinced that someone means me harm. Whoever that is has increased the pressure—following me in the dark, listening in on my phone, reading my mail, even tampering with my food.

Yes, tampering with my food! Yesterday I left my lunch for a brief moment, came back, and it had been moved. Instead of eating it, I set it out for the old tomcat that burrows in the bushes at the back of the shop. He sniffed it once and walked away.

Maybe I should have taken it to the police. Had it analyzed. But how do I know the police aren't in on this? And what does the person torturing me want?

April 19
Today someone stole my key to A Simple Blend. I have a backup, but what does it mean?

Do they plan to attack me at work?
Will they wait until I walk to my truck?

What is it they want? Retribution? I fully realize I'm not the most social of souls, but would that cause one man to kill another? Maybe it's a sick sort of entertainment.

Perhaps they want to rob me, but then why the cloak-and-dagger tactics? I tremble, even while I write, as if I'm a character in a spy novel. Not one of those happily-ever-after stories either.

I'm afraid to eat, though I keep pushing the coffee down. It's decaffeinated like the doc insisted, but the smell and warmth help me stay awake. Sleep has been difficult. I stay awake at night—puzzling, worrying, and watching. I'll see Preston again tonight. I've given him instructions, what to do if I don't show. And he's given me his word.

Amber finished the last letter and handed it to Tate. He had been reading them and passing them to Preston. She excused herself to use the ladies' room, and by the time she had returned, the letters were back in a stack, bound once again by the rubber band Preston had originally put around them.

"Thoughts?" Tate sighed and pushed his coffee cup away.

Preston drummed his fingers against the table. "It doesn't actually explain anything, though it does raise more questions."

Amber stared at the letters, and suddenly she felt so tired she wanted to cross her arms on the table, place her head down on her arms, and sleep.

"Do you mind if we take these?" Tate was up and pulling on his jacket.

"They're not mine."

"We're going to head home, get some rest, and maybe tomorrow it will make more sense. Can we come back to see you if we have more questions?"

"Sure. I might be gone during the day, but I'm always back at the same spot in the evenings. No one has run me off yet."

Tate seemed about to say something, but instead

he handed Amber her wrap and helped her shrug into it. Ten minutes later they'd walked back to the gardens, Preston had disappeared into the darkness, and they were driving back toward the Village.

Amber wanted to talk about those letters, the ones that were tucked safely into her handbag. She wanted to go over each one, line by line. She wanted answers.

When she admitted as much to Tate, he disagreed. "Not tonight. We're both too tired to make much sense of it."

"Should we take them to Avery?"

Tate stared out the car window, considered what she was suggesting, and then shook his head no. "Avery's a good cop, Amber. Don't think other-wise."

"I didn't say he wasn't."

"No. But it's easy to believe he dropped the ball on this one. I don't think he has. He did what had to be done, what should have been done, and it revealed nothing."

"So what do we do with the letters? What do they tell us?"

"I'm not sure. Maybe they simply speak to Ethan's state of mind the final few days. Maybe more."

She'd pulled up in front of her house and turned off the car with her little push button. Neither of them moved. Amber was too tired, and she expected Tate felt the same. Truthfully, it was nice to simply sit in the darkness, Tate beside her, and allow the questions in her mind to stop whirling for a few moments.

Gradually she became aware of a few cars passing out on the main road, a night bird singing from a nearby bush, and someone's cow calling out.

With a sigh, she opened the car door.

A little luck and she'd be able to make it inside before she crashed.

Tate followed her up the porch steps and waited for her to unlock the door, but declined when she invited him in. He did lean forward and kiss her gently on the lips. Without another word, he turned, walked to his truck, and drove away.

⇐ Twenty-Six ⇒

Hannah and Jesse did not go to see Minerva on Saturday.

Jesse's youngest sister, Teresa, fell off a fence rail and broke her leg. It wasn't a bad break, only a fracture, but he ended up driving his mom and sister into town to see the doctor.

Hannah learned all this from Jesse's oldest sister, Susan, who was sixteen and worked at the furniture store on Main Street. She actually worked in the small coffee shop in the back of the store. They sold coffee, deli sandwiches, and a variety of pastries. Since she worked in the downtown area, she accessed the trail at a different point than the Village, and she passed Hannah's house on the way to and from work.

"Jesse tells me you are coming up with new drinks. Want to share?" Susan had blonde hair the color of new wheat. She also had the prettiest blue eyes and the sweetest smile, with a smattering of freckles across her cheeks. She was a bit on the heavy side, but probably she would grow out of that in the next few years— though working in a shop full of sweets apparently wasn't helping.

"Will your boss allow you to order some different syrups?"

"*Ya*. I asked him about it today."

"*Gut*. Then I'll give you some of the recipes I found, if you'll promise not to steal my customers."

"Steal them? They drink *kaffi* at your place, then mosey into town and drink more *kaffi* at mine. I'm not sure we could fill them up if we had a *kaffi* trough running the length of Main Street."

"You're right, though I'm also noticing an increased interest in different decaffeinated blends. You might want to stock up on some of those."

They were in the kitchen, examining the spiral notebook Hannah used to write her recipes in. A soft rain was falling outside. Hannah had been working since sunrise, first filling orders at the Village—though Amber had suggested she shorten the hours for the first Saturday. Then she had come home, grabbed a quick lunch, and begun cleaning and cooking. She was grateful to rest a few moments and visit with Susan.

"Where did you find all of these? This toffee latte sounds yummy."

"Praline, chocolate, and caramel syrup. What's not to like?" Hannah pushed up on her glasses and walked over to the counter. She poured two glasses of lemonade and carried them back to the table. "I found some of the recipes in books at the library, and some in magazines. Keep your eyes open. You'll start noticing recipes in all sorts of places."

"I'll keep a notebook too, and we can swap!"

"*Wunderbaar.* Also, after you try a new recipe or blend, make a note in your book as to how the customers liked it. You think you'll remember, but it all starts blurring together for me."

"Same here."

"Now tell me about Teresa."

Susan sipped at the lemonade. When Hannah offered cookies, Susan waved them away, but not before a look of pure longing had covered her face. Hannah placed a dishcloth over the plate and set it back on the counter so she wouldn't be tempted.

"Teresa was climbing on the fence, you know

311

the one—it separates our west field from the goat pasture."

"It's an old wooden thing."

"Right. *Mamm* had told her more than once not to climb on it. *Dat*'s been meaning to replace the boards, but somehow that always gets put off for another day. Since it's an interior fence, it doesn't matter so much. This morning she was out there again."

"In the rain?"

"*Ya.* Supposedly she was checking on the goats. It hadn't started raining in earnest yet, but I'm sure the boards were slightly wet. We think that's why she slipped. We heard her scream from inside the house. If there's one thing my *schweschder* can do it's let out a holler. She told us she was trying to walk across the top rail of the fence."

"I can picture Teresa doing that. She's like a butterfly the way she flutters about."

"A slow-learning butterfly. It hasn't been a week since she tore a scrape down the entire length of her arm."

"Doing what?"

"Climbing down from the tall maple in our backyard."

They shared a smile. Younger siblings were always into some sort of trouble, or so it seemed to Hannah. "What about her leg? You're sure she's all right? What did the doc say?"

"*Ya*, she'll be fine. Jesse stopped by the store on his way back home. *Mamm* wanted me to pick up some groceries, and he left the list. Doc said it's a minor fracture, but he does want to put her in a cast. With my little *schweschder*'s energy, one of those black boots that go up your leg probably wouldn't slow her down much."

"Did he put the cast on today?" Eunice had walked into the kitchen as Susan was explaining the situation.

"*Nein*. Jesse says he has to wait until the swelling goes down. They'll go back on Monday for the cast."

"Poor thing. I'll send one of these pies. I'm sure your *mamm* hasn't had time to cook."

"You don't have to do that."

"I want to. Besides, Hannah had planned to take it to Minerva, but now she won't be able to."

"I could drive our buggy over," Hannah protested.

"Your *bruder* Noah is using it to pick up supplies from the feed store. By the time he gets back, it will be too late."

"Noah is in town? I was hoping to see him." When Hannah and Eunice smiled at one another, Susan blushed a deep red. "Not see him exactly. That's not what I meant. I was wanting to talk to him about the puppies. You know, in case my *dat* decides we can have one."

"I can show you the pups," Hannah offered.

"Maybe another time. I need to get these groceries home."

Hannah walked through the sitting room and to the front door. When they reached the porch, Susan pulled a rain poncho from her bag and put it on over her dress.

"Nice look."

"*Ya*, it's a crazy color." Susan stared down at the bright orange plastic. "My boss gave it to me when the rain started this morning. I told him I'd be fine, but he didn't want me riding the bike home without some sort of covering to keep me dry. Like everyone else, he's worried about the flu. Said he doesn't want to lose his barista to a bug."

"It's a funny word, isn't it? Barista. All the magazines use it."

"I suppose. I'd rather not wear this crazy thing, but since I told him I would, I'll suffer through."

"Certainly anyone on the trail will be able to see you. Are you sure you don't want to wait until the rain has completely stopped? Noah could drive you when he gets back."

"It's not far, and the rain is letting up now." Susan started down the steps, then turned and said, "You'll tell Noah I stopped by, won't you?"

"Sure. If you want."

Susan's only answer was a smile. She set Eunice's pie, wrapped in two plastic bags, in the basket fastened to the front of her bike. It barely fit next to the small sack of groceries. Then she climbed on her bike and pedaled off down the lane to the Pumpkinvine Trail.

Hannah watched her, curious about the visit. When she walked back into the house, she went in search of her mother and found her attempting to measure Mattie for a new dress.

"Hold still or I can't pin this right." Eunice attempted to stab a pin through the hem as Mattie twirled first left, then right.

"Mattie, let's play statue."

Her sister stuck her thumb in her mouth and scrunched her nose.

"Can you be a statue? Like the ones in the park? Can you be perfectly still?"

"*Ya.*" Mattie nodded as she jumped from foot to foot.

"Statues can't jump, sweetie. Stand up straight and tall, like this." When Hannah imitated a statue, Mattie did the same.

"*Gut* idea. She's like trying to measure a calf—all legs and energy."

"*Mamm*, do you think Susan likes Noah?"

"*Ya.* Seems she does."

"But they're barely sixteen! They're too young for that."

"I didn't say they were marrying, did I? They're not too young to be curious about such things."

"I suppose, but—"

"No supposing. It's as natural as rain falling

315

from the sky." Eunice finished pinning the green material she was using for Mattie's dress. "That's *gut*, love. You can stop being a statue now."

Mattie laughed and resumed hopping from foot to foot, little bits of her curly hair escaping from her *kapp* with each hop.

"I don't know." Hannah bent down and kissed the top of Mattie's head as her sister wound her arms around her legs. "Seems to me the world has gone crazy."

"*Nein*. It's simply that spring is in the air."

Hannah wondered if spring explained the way her pulse raced every time she was around Jesse. Was that why she sometimes felt like she had the flu? Would it pass after a few days or weeks?

"Too bad I couldn't see Minerva today."

"*Gotte* knows what he's doing, Hannah. Don't be questioning the rain or your *bruder*'s work or even Jesse helping his family."

"I wasn't," she mumbled.

"Minerva will be at our church meeting tomorrow. Perhaps you'll have a chance to talk with her after the luncheon."

And indeed it did seem that *Gotte* knew what he was doing. Barely an hour had passed when a small red car pulled down their lane. Amber and Tate stepped out into the damp afternoon. The rain had stopped, but thunderclouds loomed on the horizon. Hannah guessed they'd have another downpour before long.

She invited them inside, though at that point the sound of her siblings in the house was a small roar of feet on the stairs, folks vying for the bathroom to clean up, and her mother in the kitchen preparing dinner. Noah had even brought in one of the puppies and been caught on the way up to his room. They heard several barks, followed by a discussion between him and his father. They could hear every word outside. It was plain Noah was losing the discussion.

"The porch is fine," Amber assured her. "Can you spare a moment?"

"*Ya.*"

"We have something we'd like to show you." Amber pulled a bundle of letters from her handbag. "They're from Ethan. He wrote them."

Amber and Tate sat quietly and rocked while Hannah read through the letters.

"Who gave you these?"

"Preston. Preston Johnstone." Tate hesitated, then added, "He's homeless. Maybe you've seen him around town. A little taller than I am. Late twenties. He has a beard and wears a green army jacket."

"The homeless man Ethan was talking to."

"Yes. It seems Preston is the person your friend mentioned." Amber went on to explain about the letters and why Preston had them.

"It's so sad that Ethan was frightened and alone when we were all around him. Maybe there's something we could have done, something we should have done."

"Don't go blaming yourself, Hannah. He could have reached out to us, but for some reason he chose not to."

"It sounds as if someone had taken his shop key. Maybe that's how the paint supplies ended up in the back room."

"I agree, and I had the locks changed today."

The panic clawing at Hannah's throat backed down. Certainly, she didn't want to think of someone having the key to the *kaffi* shop. They could sneak in and be waiting for her when she arrived at work. The thought sent goose bumps across her arms.

She thumbed back through the letters. "And the night he was arguing with Larry? The night you saw him drive away in a hurry . . . he mentions that too?"

"It seems so. Tate and I have been studying the letters, trying to come up with any angles that might explain what happened, but we wanted your opinion. You knew him as well as anyone."

"What he says about the tomcat. That's true. He hunkers down out back and will eat practically anything." She found the letter and read the line that was bothering her. " 'He sniffed it once and walked away.' "

Hannah stared again at the letters.

"The rest he could have been imagining, but that seemed odd to us as well."

"That tom's appetite is never satisfied. A bag broke on me Thursday as I was taking it to the trash out back. Some *kaffi* grounds spilled out, and before I could get it cleaned up, he had his whiskers in it. We all try to bring him a few scraps, poor little beast, but he never seems full."

"I've heard that if food is tainted, an animal can tell." Tate rubbed his thumb across the arm of the chair—oak that had been worn to a shine over the years.

"Tainted or poisoned?" The words slipped from Hannah before she had a chance to think, but the look on Amber's face told her she wasn't alone in her suspicions.

"If it wasn't a heart attack, and it seems no one here believes it was, then it had to be something else." She pushed up on her glasses and continued when no one interrupted. She explained her logic, the same reasoning she had shared with Jesse the night before. "If his cause of death was something else and there was no sign of a confrontation, it would seem we could guess what it was, or at least narrow down possible causes."

"There are many ways to kill folks without a traditional weapon. A blow to the head, strangulation, electrocution, suffocation—" Amber stopped abruptly and crossed her arms. "What? Why are you both looking at me that way?"

"Your list." Hannah licked her lips. "It's terrible."

"I found it online."

"That can't look good on your search history." Tate reached out and patted her hand. "I'll vouch for you if the government comes knocking on your door."

"But all of those things require someone to be in the room with the victim." Hannah closed her eyes and again envisioned a puzzle with a few crucial pieces missing. When she opened them, Tate and Amber were staring at her. "I don't see it. The one possibility that makes sense to me is poison."

⇒ Twenty-Seven ⇐

Tate did not agree with Amber's plan. "It could be dangerous."

"How? She's one woman."

"One woman with big issues."

"We drive by. We look. Maybe we stop and go in."

"Big issues that we don't understand."

"If we go in, it'll be for a minute, no more."

"Issues that could be volatile."

"And only if the door is unlocked or maybe a window is open."

They both stopped talking and peered out through the car's windshield at the gathering storm. Though it was still more than an hour before sunset, the sky was nearly as dark as night.

"I doubt a window will be open." Tate adjusted the seat belt so that it choked him a little less. "And Patricia might not even be the person we're looking for."

"Or she could be the very person we're looking for. She could be Ethan's murderer."

"Maybe, but it's difficult to imagine a sister killing a brother."

"Eighty percent of murder victims are killed by acquaintances or members of their own family."

"You need to turn off the computer."

Amber smiled as if he had paid her a compliment. They were nearly at the lake now. He could see the small cluster of houses up ahead. The neighborhood looked ominous with the storm building above it.

"We still don't know how she could have done it without being in the room."

"That's why we need to snoop around."

"We could be trespassing for nothing."

"I'll admit that, but you said you finished all the work at your place this morning. It's this or play Scrabble back home."

He liked how she assumed they'd spend the rest of the day, now almost evening, together. "We might find something we don't know how to deal with."

"And if we do, we'll call Avery."

"Do I have your word on that?"

"Absolutely. I won't even argue."

"That would be a pleasant turn of events." He thought he'd muttered his sarcasm too softly for her to hear, but she slapped his arm and grinned. Yeah, she'd heard. And he was sunk. He was obviously in love with this woman, which explained why he was willing to follow her on a who-done-it mystery tour.

"The truck is gone." Amber drove by Patricia's house slowly.

They both craned their necks, looking for evidence as to whether Patricia might be gone as well.

"I think she's out in the truck."

"Maybe. Or maybe she sold it, and this very moment she is sitting at home in the dark waiting for someone to break into her house."

Amber made a U-turn at the end of the road, smiling as she checked the rearview mirror. "I like that you contradict me on every point. That way I'm assured we've thought this through."

He started to answer, then clamped his mouth shut.

Whatever he said, she would turn into support.

She passed the house and parked two doors down. Pulling out her phone, she scrolled through her contacts until she'd found his number. Then she pushed Talk.

"Why are you calling me?"

"Now you call me. This way, we just have to push Talk and it will immediately ring one another. In case we get separated."

"We are not getting separated." But he called her number all the same. A last-resort plan never hurt.

"You take the front. I'll take the back."

"Uh-uh. We go together."

"Are you kidding me? We have maybe three minutes before the bottom of this storm falls out."

"Fine. *I'll* take the back." He strode off toward the gardens behind Patricia's duplex before Amber could argue.

Their initial plan had been that Amber would keep Patricia talking at the front door while he snooped around the gardens. He didn't know what he was looking for, but Amber had decided pictures might be all they'd need. So he moved through her plants, carefully walking along the path that was covered with gravel so as not to leave footprints, and he snapped photos of anything over an inch tall.

He jumped in spite of himself when Amber touched his arm. "No answer from the front, and all the lights are off."

"Good. I'm nearly done. We can get out of here." He was speaking to thin air. She'd already moved to the back porch and was jiggling the door.

"It's locked!"

"Really? How could she lock her door? You'd think she wanted to keep strangers out of her home."

"We're hardly strangers."

"We aren't friends."

"Can you break in?"

"What?"

"With a credit card or something. I want to see what is in that room that looked like a lab." She was now moving from window to window in search of one that wasn't locked.

"You're acting like a starving dog with a bone," he muttered.

"I heard that."

"Leave those windows alone."

"I need to get inside."

"That's breaking and entering!"

"Not if we don't break anything."

Knowing he was going to regret it, he pulled a credit card from his wallet and jimmied the lock.

"Where'd you learn to do that?"

"Don't ask."

"The army?"

"Hardly."

She moved to pass him, but he reached out and snagged her arm. "Better take your shoes off or you're going to leave a trail."

Amber hesitated, but in the end her curiosity won.

She removed her shoes, leaving them on the back porch. Tate did the same. It now felt as if he was moving through a bad dream. Being near Amber, the smell of rain in her hair, her hand on his arm—it was all heavenly. But lurking over that was an impression of danger and regret and foolishness. Like in a nightmare, he was powerless to stop her as she crept toward what she had begun to call "the lab" since they'd left Hannah's. Had the young Amish girl brought up the idea of poison only a few minutes ago? It felt as if they'd been discussing it for months.

He stood at the front window in the dining room, where he'd stood with Patricia a few days earlier, and watched the street. The smell of books permeated the room. He glanced at the table and saw a big fat volume, a blue hardback with gold lettering titled *A Field Guide to Venomous Animals and Poisonous Plants.*

Which seemed to him like an odd reading choice. If she had killed Ethan, and he wasn't ready to admit that, she wouldn't need to keep studying poisonous plants.

Unless she was planning another murder.

Thunder rumbled across the sky as fat drops of rain began to hit the pavement.

"We should go. It's starting to—"

Amber's screech caused his heart to slam

against his chest. He sprinted down the hall. In his stocking feet he nearly slid into her, but he was beside her in less time than it took to ask what was wrong.

"There's something on the other side of this door."

"I thought you were going to the lab."

"But this is the door that's locked. I rattled it, and something hit up against it from the other side."

"Maybe you imagined that."

"Try it yourself."

Tate could hear the rain hammering against the roof, falling in sheets now. Wiping his palms on his jeans, he reached forward, grasped the door handle with both hands, and gave it a good hard shake.

Nothing happened.

He shrugged and turned back toward the front of the house.

And that was when, from the other side, something bumped against the bottom of the door.

"What *was* that?" Amber's eyes were opened so wide they were comical—or would have been if it weren't for the thing that had thudded against the door. His mind flipped through a dozen possibilities of what could make that sound, but he came up with nothing that seemed remotely feasible.

"Do you think it's a person?" Amber had stepped back from the door.

"No. A person would call out."

"What then?"

"I don't know, but Patricia could be back anytime. Take some photos of the other room and let's go."

He returned to his lookout spot at the front of the house. The rain was falling so hard he could barely make out Amber's car parked two doors down. The sky had darkened to a deep night, and a few lights had come on in neighboring houses.

Amber joined him at the window, thumbing through the images on her phone. "I think we can go." Her voice sounded at once triumphant and filled with sorrow. Apparently she'd found what she was looking for, and it wasn't a cause of celebration.

He turned to speak to her, took his eyes off the street for less than a second, and they were bathed in the headlights of a truck pulling into the driveway.

⇐ Twenty-Eight ⇒

Amber was sure she was having a panic attack.

How had she managed to put them in this situation?

How had she managed to put them in danger?

She was a manager of an Amish facility—a place that represented peace and quiet and the simple life. She should not be running from a murderer.

And she was convinced now that Patricia had killed Ethan. How, she wasn't quite sure, but the woman had done it. There was no doubt in her mind.

Maybe a jury would rule reasonable doubt, based on what they'd found so far, but Avery's team could come in and collect all the evidence they needed for a solid case. All she wanted now was to be home, dry and safe and falling in love with Tate Bowman.

Was she falling in love with Tate?

She peeked up at him as they crouched under the roof overhang at the corner of the house.

He held the index finger of his right hand against his lips, banging his shoes against his chest in the process. His left hand firmly grasped hers.

They'd grabbed their shoes as they ran from the house, Tate pulling the back door shut as they heard Patricia's key open the front door. There had only been time to snatch up their shoes and run, so now they stood in their socks with the rain drenching their clothes.

What were they waiting for?

Then she heard it, Patricia stomping through the house, toward the back door. Tate held up three fingers, then two, and finally one. As Patricia stepped out on the back porch, they sprinted around the corner of the house, past Ethan's truck, and to Amber's little red car.

She started the car with one hand and slipped her seat belt on with the other.

"Go, go, go, go. I think I see her coming."

Amber didn't have to be told twice. She sped away from the curb as if their lives depended on it.

The rain was now a wall of water. She could barely make out the road. She slowed as she approached the stop sign, carefully looking left, right, and then left again. The last thing she needed at this point was a fender bender half a block from Patricia's house.

As she turned left toward the main road, toward home and safety, the beam of her headlights swept in an arc. When she saw Patricia standing on the side of the road, standing and staring at them, she almost stopped.

"No, no, no. Keep going!"

So instead of the brake, she hit the gas, spraying the puddles of rain and obscuring their view, hiding them in a veil of water from Patricia's gaze.

"How did she catch up with us?"

"She must have run to the intersection while we were getting in the car. A bigger question is how did she know which direction we were headed?"

Amber made it to the main road, turned right, and drove another half mile before pulling over into the fluorescent glare of a gas station's lights.

Tate had been talking her through the escape, watching left, right, and behind them while she focused on the road. Now they sat in the little car, the windshield wipers still thump, thump, thumping as silence enveloped them.

"Pull up to a gas pump."

"I don't need—"

"The middle one. It will keep us dry."

So she did, and she'd no sooner killed the engine than Tate was out of the car, around the front, opening her door, and pulling her into his arms.

That was when she began shaking.

He rubbed her back, wrapped his arms around her, and pressed his lips to her hair. She was drenched! Her clothes stuck to her skin like an old Band-Aid. Her hair dripped rivulets of water onto her shoulders, and her stocking feet were cold and wet.

"It's okay. We're safe."

"She—"

"She didn't follow. We're fine."

"Do you think she saw us?" Amber raised her eyes to his, knowing he would tell her the truth.

"I'm not sure. Probably not. Unless she knows what kind of car you drive, and there are plenty of small red cars, I don't think she'd know it was us."

"Okay. You're right." Amber believed him.

Patricia hadn't seen them. She'd seen someone fleeing her house and she'd followed on foot. But she couldn't have seen them in the rain.

"Let's walk inside and get you a cup of coffee."

"We should go."

"You're shaking, and she's not following us. She couldn't have known which way we went or where we'd stop. Let's get the coffee."

They put on their shoes, but still she felt ridiculous walk-ing into the small store, dripping a trail of water. The coffee tasted terrible, nowhere near as good as what Hannah brewed, but a few swallows and the chill coursing through her veins fled. Tate had purchased coffee for himself as well as a package of small chocolate donuts. She ate two, figuring the fear had used up all of her calories.

They sat in the car, the heater turned to high, and watched the storm subside. For a few moments neither spoke.

Finally she set her coffee in the cup holder and started the engine.

"Want me to drive?"

"No. I'm good now. Lost a year of my life when I saw her on the side of the road, but I'm good now."

"Where are we headed?"

"Home! Don't you think? We can look at the pictures we took, call Avery, and figure out our next step."

Tate reached across, ran his hand up and under her hair, massaged the muscles in her neck that had cramped into a solid fist. How did he know?

"Sounds good, but let's go to my house."

"Yours?" She felt like a cat that was being stroked in the one unreachable spot. She probably would have driven to Chicago so long as he kept massaging.

"Mine."

"Okay." They were driving into Middlebury proper now. The rain had nearly stopped, and Saturday night traffic was picking up. "Why yours?"

"Because the temperature has dropped." He leaned forward and studied her dash display. "According to that it's forty-one outside. Cool enough for a blaze in the fireplace."

"Do you have coffee?"

"I can rustle some up, though some hot decaffeinated tea might be a better choice. I feel keyed up enough without trumping it with more coffee."

She turned onto their road, passed her house, and pulled into his driveway. How was it that they had been neighbors for so many years? Been neighbors and hadn't even known each other?

Tate again caught her hand as they walked toward his front door.

"I should have stopped at my place, at least long enough to find some dry clothes."

"You can wear something of mine."

"The last time I was here I was soaking wet. This is getting to be a habit, and now you want me to wear your clothes?"

"Sure. What are you saying? That I'm too big?"

A smile tugged at the corner of her mouth. "I didn't say that . . ."

"You wait and see. I'll find something warm and dry, and while you change I'll start that fire."

It didn't take long to change into a pair of his gray sweats, cinched tight at the waist and rolled up at the ankles. He'd also handed her an old Northridge Raider sweatshirt that nearly reached her knees.

"This is yours?" The arms extended a good two inches past her hands.

"It is. Bought plenty of athletic shirts while the boys were in school." He handed her a mug of hot tea. He had changed, too, and was wearing an outfit similar to hers, except his Northridge shirt was black while hers was green.

"Chamomile?" She brought the tea to her lips and inhaled deeply.

"Lipton."

Amber tried not to laugh as she sat on the couch. Why would a single man have chamomile tea? She was lucky he hadn't given her cowboy coffee.

"If you'd rather, I can make some hot choco-late." He took a sip and waited. There wasn't a trace of worry on his face. In fact, he looked almost content.

Was he that easily satisfied? Hot chocolate and a roaring fire. Two things she could grow used to—three if you included the man waiting on her answer.

"I don't need any more sugar, thank you."

"We both need food. I ordered pizza while you were changing. Should be here in another fifteen minutes."

"Let's look at the pictures, before the food gets here."

She sat close to him on the couch, suddenly self-conscious. Her hair was beginning to dry into a curled mess, and her feet were bare though he'd offered her socks. She propped her feet beside his, on the coffee table, and pretended to be offended when he laughed at her toenails that were painted a warm pink.

He opened his phone and began thumbing through the pictures. When he reached the photos of the garden, he slowed down as they both bent closer to the small screen. "See anything you recognize?"

"No. Then again I wouldn't know hemlock if it was growing outside my kitchen window."

"What made you think of hemlock?"

"Read it in an Agatha Christie novel."

Tate seemed unsure how to answer that and opted instead to thumb through the rest of his pictures.

When he was finished, Amber stared into what remained of her tea.

"Finding any answers in that mug?"

"None."

Though what they were contemplating was serious, Amber was learning that Tate's perspective helped her to push away the emotions and think about things objectively. "We'll need to hear from Hannah before we know any more. If she can give me a few leads, some potentially poisonous plants that are commonly grown around here—or that she knows can be grown in greenhouses even if they aren't—I can look them up on the Internet and try to match them to your pictures. Hannah said her friend is a local expert."

"Why not go straight to an Internet search?"

"I could, but the list of toxic plants is rather large, I suspect."

Tate stood, moved to the fire, and added another log.

"I wish we could have seen the inside of her greenhouse. There might be more answers there."

"Possibly."

She was surprised at how comfortable she felt in his living room, how comfortable she felt in his life. Could a relationship between two people change so quickly? But then, the last few days hadn't exactly been normal.

"So what did you find in 'the lab'?" He sat down, even closer than before so that their shoulders were actually touching. His proximity helped the nausea that was tumbling through her stomach. Looking at the first picture was enough to make her wish she hadn't drunk the tea.

"I can't quite read what the label says."

Using two fingers, she expanded the picture of some jars on her phone.

The image adjusted, and the words were crystal clear—"Ethan's sugar sub." Next to that was a jar that said "Ethan's salt."

Tate ran his hand up and over the top of his head. Finally he moved so that he was sitting sideways on the couch and looking directly into her eyes.

"So you think this is proof enough? Those two bottles?"

"It makes sense. Doesn't it? She was putting something poisonous in his food or his drinks and passing it off as sugar and salt."

To give him credit, he didn't laugh at her, and he didn't argue with her. Instead he said, "Perhaps it's time we handed this back to Avery."

"So you're convinced?"

"I didn't say that. Ethan didn't die at Patricia's. He died at the Village. If it was a fast poison, he would have died at her place. If it was a slow-acting poison . . . I don't see how he would have eaten enough meals with her for this to work. After all, he had a job and a wife. How many times a week did he go out there? How are you envisioning this?"

"I don't know."

"It could be that we're at the end of what we can do, of what we should do. We're not professional investigators, and if she is guilty, this could become dangerous."

Amber crossed then uncrossed her legs. One part of her was relieved. Seeing Patricia standing in the rain had scared the curiosity out of her. She was ready to put the entire case back in the Middlebury PD's court. But another part of her, the stubborn part, still wanted answers.

She pulled up Avery's number and punched Talk.

No answer. It went straight over to messages.

"That's not like him."

"What?" Tate had answered the door, paid the pizza delivery guy, and returned to the living room with a large box.

Amber's stomach grumbled at the smell of warm yeasty crust and pepperoni.

She stared down at her phone and dialed 9-1-1 for the Middlebury PD.

"Please state your emergency."

"It's not an—"

"If this is not an emergency, please call the following number."

She grabbed a pen from the coffee table and wrote the number on the outside of the pizza box.

"Problem?" Tate walked back into the room

with two plates, two bottles of water, and a roll of paper towels.

Amber held up her hand in a "just a minute" gesture.

"Middlebury PD, this is Officer Brookstone."

Cherry Brookstone! The young officer with green eyes and red hair that probably didn't frizz into a halo. The woman rubbed her the wrong way. It was all Amber could do not to disconnect.

"I was looking for Gordon."

"Who's speaking?"

"Amber Wright."

There was a pause on the other end of the line. "Sergeant Avery isn't available at this time. Can I help you?"

"I'd rather speak with Gordon."

"Again, ma'am, he's not available, but I'm sure I can address any—"

"Where is he, Cherry?" She pictured the officer—young, fit, and arrogant. Even beautiful. She didn't mind admitting it, but she was not going to let a twenty-five-year-old rookie stand in her way now.

"I can't—"

"Where is he?"

There was a sigh on the other end of the line, very unprofessional phone etiquette in Amber's opinion. "He's on a fishing trip. No cell service before Monday. Said he'd check in if he could."

"I am going to call back and leave a message on his cell. If you talk to him, you tell him to call me."

"I'm sure I can help you."

"I'm sure you can't."

"How about you give me a try?"

Tate watched her, one eyebrow cocked higher than the other. The pizza was still calling her name. She'd rather be burrowed into Tate's couch, eating pizza, than dealing with this woman.

"We found Ethan's murderer."

"Not that again."

"Listen to me, Cherry. We have letters that Ethan wrote, and we have some photos that you should see."

"Do the letters explicitly state that someone had threatened him?"

"No, they—"

"And the photos, were they obtained legally?"

"Well, that depends—"

"You need to let this go."

"I'll do no such thing." Amber's temper rose to the top and bubbled over. "How can you refuse to even look at what we've found?"

"Because you're not a police officer. You're not even a licensed investigator. You're an employer who feels guilty because an employee died on your property. If there was any substance to your allegations, which according to Sergeant Avery there is *not,* we would be happy to pursue any leads you could provide. Now if that's all, I need to get back to real police work."

She didn't hang up on Amber immediately. Perhaps she was waiting for a retort. Perhaps she had misgivings, in spite of her adamant response. Amber might never know. By the time she finished counting to five, the phone was emitting a dial tone.

"Did she hang up on you?"

"Not exactly, but close enough." She plopped onto the couch and accepted the piece of pizza Tate offered. "Why would Gordon leave in the middle of our investigation? Leave and not even tell me?"

They chewed in silence, some of the tension melting away as the fire crackled and her stomach filled with more than worry. By the time she was halfway through her second slice, she'd decided what she needed to do.

She picked up her phone and dialed Gordon's personal number. It occurred to her that perhaps she should walk into the other room, considering what she needed to say, but Tate was a big part of her life at the moment. He'd been willing to risk going up against Patricia. He'd taken care of her, though she was perfectly capable of taking care of herself.

He cared.

Gordon's phone rang once and then shot over to his message box.

340

"Gordon, this is Amber. Tate and I have been digging some more, and we have a few additional leads we want to share with you. Please call me. And, Gordon, I'm sorry things didn't work out between us—not like you wanted. But I know you're a good friend, and I believe you're a good cop. Please, when you have cell service, call me so we can talk about Ethan's murder."

⇒ Twenty-Nine ⇐

Hannah sat on the hard wooden bench and attempted to focus on what their minister was saying. Something about the peace of Christ.

She stared down at her Bible.

It was opened to Colossians, another letter from Paul.

She ran her finger down the page, first on the German side, then on the *Englisch* side. Some days she read the old German text quite well, but today she was off her mark. She'd wakened during the middle of the night, worried about Amber and poisons and her job. She'd wakened and been unable to go back to sleep.

Let the peace of Christ rule in your hearts . . .

That was it! That's what Amon Birkey had referenced before he began his sermon. It was the second sermon of the morning. Hannah honestly couldn't remember a thing about the first, though she did recall singing the *Loblied* when they had begun the service. She also remembered kneeling and praying.

But the sermons? Nothing. Her mind was a blank slate.

What was wrong with her?

Why was she so distracted?

Mattie sat beside her, swinging her feet and clutching a pencil she had been using on a tablet their mother brought to help the youngest in the family through Sunday services.

Feeling Hannah's eyes on her, Mattie gazed up at her sister. Then she yawned once and snuggled in close.

Let the peace of Christ rule in your hearts, since as members of one body you were called to peace.

That was why she hadn't been able to sleep well. She hadn't felt any of the peace described in Paul's letter. Instead she'd spent all night troubled and worried and anxious.

Let the peace of Christ rule in your hearts . . . Amon was talking about the choices they made, choices to embrace peace or chaos.

Her life was certainly chaotic at the moment. But how could it be helped? She hadn't asked for Ethan to die. She certainly hadn't asked to be the one to find him, but somehow she was caught up in searching for clues. That had felt like the right thing to do a few days ago, but now she wasn't so sure. How many more sleepless nights could she endure?

Before she could answer any of those questions, they were once again kneeling and praying, then standing and singing. She went through the motions even while her mind struggled with the Scripture they had read.

When the service dismissed, Mattie stood on the bench and threw her arms around Hannah's neck. "Up, Hannah."

"You can walk!"

"Up!" Mattie put one hand on each side of Hannah's face and squeezed. "Up!"

"Stubborn, aren't you?"

"She gets that honest." Eunice gathered up her Bible and the wrap she'd worn while walking between their buggy and Amon's shop.

Usually they held church in someone's home, but occasionally it worked out better to have the service in a member's place of business. Amon had a large bay on the south side of his shop where buggies were in different stages of repair. During church services, he would move the buggies to the sides of the giant room, all in a line, so that it looked as if they were about to go out visiting— one after the other.

"Well, she didn't get her stubbornness from me."

"Don't be so sure. Some things are inherited.

Other things are learned. Mattie looks up to you and wants to imitate everything about you—from the color of your dress to the mood you're in."

"Are you saying I'm moody today, *Mamm*?"

"I'm saying to remember there are often little eyes on you." And then Eunice was gone, joining the other ladies who were setting out casseroles, plates of sliced ham, large bowls of chicken salad, fresh breads, and desserts.

Hannah hugged Mattie and then placed her on the ground. When Mattie began to whine, Hannah caught her little hand and tugged her toward the large bay doors. They'd been opened when the service was over, and sunlight poured into the area where they'd worshiped. "Let's go out and play. Some of your *freinden* will be here."

Mattie's mood improved at the word *play*. She began to skip to the door, which was when Hannah looked up and saw Jesse standing there waiting for her.

They walked out into the late morning sunshine. The fields and grass appeared to be quite muddy, but the parking area was relatively dry. Most of the children were gathered there—some playing games, others chasing one another, and the oldest of them talking in small groups.

"You looked kind of worried in there, Hannah-Bell."

Hannah stopped dead in her tracks. Jesse hadn't called her that nickname in years.

"Something wrong?" He reached for Mattie's other hand and continued walking toward the group of small kids.

Instead of answering, Hannah asked how his sister was doing.

"*Gut.* As you can see, she's not too happy about having to slow down."

Teresa was sitting on the front steps of the shop's porch, which wrapped away from the bay doors, around the front and down one side of the building. She wore a giant black shoe that extended up to her knee. Even from a distance, Hannah could see she was pouting.

"Perhaps it's hurting her today."

"Maybe. Or maybe she wants to play tag but is afraid my parents will see. They gave her a long talking-to last night, reminded her she needed to act like a girl and not like a young colt."

"I imagine that went over well."

"Not exactly." They had walked to the middle of what was becoming a playground. Mattie spied a giant yellow ball and went running off to claim it. "So what gives? I could see you were miserable from my side of the room."

"It was that obvious?"

Jesse nodded and waited for her to answer. But how could she answer? How could she explain this uneasiness that upset her stomach and stole her sleep?

"Life was easier when I was twenty-one."

"Is that so?"

"It is, and you can stop laughing at me, Jesse Miller."

"Didn't laugh."

"But you wanted to."

"I'll admit to that."

Somehow his mood helped to brighten hers, or perhaps it was being outside after the dark storm of the day before.

"All Amon's talk of peace, it made me *narrisch*. If I could buy peace at the general store, I'd happily do so."

"Peace is something within, not without. Can't put it in a shopping cart."

"Now you sound like Amon! And when did you become so wise?"

Jesse ran his hand down his jaw, pausing to rub his fingers over a small cut. Had he nicked himself shaving? *When did Jesse become a man?* she wondered again. He'd always been her best friend. The changes in him, in them, were confusing.

"I believe it was a week ago last Tuesday. Yes, that was the day I put aside foolishness and became wise."

"Wasn't it *this* week you fell in the pond at the Village?"

"Yes, but—"

"Doesn't sound wise to me."

"I was trying to step out of the way of one of

our new guests, a mystery guest. Didn't realize I was so near the edge until it was too late. The guest thought the pond might contain a clue and asked if I'd mind swimming around for him while I was there."

"A likely story."

"A true story."

"Which brings us back to my point—we don't work at a very peaceful place. We did, but now we don't!"

Jesse reached for her hand, and they walked over to where Mattie had sat down on the concrete. Fortunately it had dried in the morning sun. Someone had given her a piece of sidewalk chalk, and she was attempting to draw on the pavement.

"The things at the Village, they will be resolved or they won't. I know you want to help Amber, and that's *gut*. But it's not your responsibility how things turn out."

The tense bundle of nerves in Hannah's stomach relaxed. Was that what she'd been doing? Claiming responsibility for something she couldn't control?

"*Gotte* will watch out for your *freind*."

"*Danki*, Jesse. I suppose I was making myself too important, as if *Gotte* couldn't work things out without my help."

"He did all right before we were born. He'll do fine long after we're gone."

Hannah couldn't help laughing. Sometimes Jesse sounded like a boy still in school. Two Sundays ago he'd played ball with the younger boys, hollering out and racing into the woods when her brother Noah had hit one past the outfielders. Other times he sounded more like her dad, all serious and knowledgeable.

She turned to say as much to him, and that was when she noticed he was looking past her, looking toward the front porch.

"Minerva has walked out to sit in one of the rockers. Now might be a good time for us to go speak to her."

She liked the way he bent down and scooped up Mattie, who began laughing. She liked the way he'd said *us,* as if he were in this with her come thick or thin. But mostly she liked the way her anxiety evaporated. Regardless of what they learned from Minerva, she realized *Gotte* was still in control.

As they approached the porch, Hannah peered at Minerva. It had been quite a while since she'd done more than say a polite hello to the woman. Their paths didn't cross very often.

Minerva's skin was as wrinkled as the raisins Mattie loved to eat. Her *kapp* was pinned precisely, set on her head to reveal a very small portion of her snow-white hair. She had combed her hair in the same manner for so long that her center part resembled a plowed row. It flashed through Hannah's mind that Minerva reminded her of Mattie when her sister was a baby with wrinkled skin and a bare whisper of hair.

Jesse's sister Teresa was happy to have more company on the porch where she'd apparently been warned to stay. She immediately set to playing with Mattie.

"Sit. Both of you." Minerva tapped the porch floor with her cane. "Hannah, your *mamm* mentioned you might like to have a word with me."

That surprised Hannah, but she sat as instructed on the steps in front of Minerva. Jesse sat beside her, and they both turned to face the elderly woman—how old was she? Hannah remembered she was a great-grandmother and a widow, but other than that she only knew that if anyone had questions about herbs, they went to Minerva.

The woman's garden was legendary.

She'd even had visits from both Indiana University and Notre Dame—folks who were writing research papers about Amish ways and the value of herbal remedies. Hannah's *dat* had showed her the article in the *Budget* a year or so ago.

"What would you like to know? There has to be a reason two youngsters *in lieb* would spend time with this old woman."

"Oh, we're not—" Hannah's face flushed a deep red. She could actually feel the heat.

Jesse nudged her with his foot, a smile playing on his lips.

"Are your questions about the herbs?"

"Yes, they are." Hannah sat up a bit straighter and smoothed out the dark blue apron that covered her pale blue dress. She'd rehearsed how to say this a dozen times since she'd first thought of asking for Minerva's help. "You heard about Ethan? Ethan Gray?"

"*Ya*. His life was complete. No one knows when that day will be, but *Gotte* knows. Praise be to his holy name."

"Yes, well, we think Ethan's day may have been rushed."

"Do not doubt *Gotte*'s reach." Minerva set her chair to rocking, even as she hummed one of the morning's hymns.

Hannah didn't know how to answer that. This conversation was not going as she'd envisioned it.

"Hannah wanted to ask you about herbs . . . plants someone might have used in a harmful way."

"So you think he was killed?" Minerva's eyes fixed on Hannah. Her gaze was clear and bright, and Hannah was suddenly embarrassed that she had doubted the woman's clarity merely because of her age.

"Possibly. The police say it was natural—a heart attack—but we're not so sure."

Minerva continued rocking. She didn't answer immediately. When she did, her voice was soft but strong. "See those birds? The ones past where the children are playing? They are searching for worms, brought up by the rain. The other birds, the ones in the bushes, they eat from the seeds of the plants and from the flowers. It's rare that you will see the two flocks together because their needs are different."

"Are you telling me I shouldn't be helping Amber? She's my boss and I promised—"

"I know who she is. I'm not telling you what to do or not to do. The story is meant to point out the natural way of things."

Jesse reached out and touched Hannah's arm, then he tilted his head toward the children who had stopped playing. Older sisters and brothers were gathering them up and scooting them inside. The meal was about to begin.

"Do you know of any herb that someone might use for poison? Something that could cause a heart attack or look like a heart attack?"

"Many things may be used in a dark way, even natural things. The list of everyday plants might surprise you. Buckeye, coral bean, vetch, western yew, as well as cedar and locoweed."

"Are all of those available here?"

"*Nein*. But nearly anything can be grown in any climate now, with the use of greenhouses and such."

Jesse pulled a pen and piece of paper from his pocket. How had he thought to bring that? Hannah had assumed the list would be short and she could remember the plants. Minerva still wasn't done.

"The blueberries from our Virginia creeper are poisonous, as is the more traditional hemlock. Death camas look like a plain onion but don't have the odor, and they are quite deadly. Foxglove and wild iris, buttercup and jimsonweed. These are the plants that come to mind. There are more, but I'd need to review my notes."

"I had no idea there were so many!"

"*Ya.* Nature is a dangerous place. Always you must be sure before consuming something you find growing. This is one reason we are a community, to share knowledge and lend a hand. When I'm gone, one of my *grandkinner* will take up where I have stopped."

Hannah wasn't comfortable with the thought of more death. The longer she sat with Minerva, the healthier she looked! Why was she talking about dying?

The idea of moving from this life to the next didn't seem to bother Minerva one bit. She must have noticed Hannah's discomfort, for she reached out and patted her hand. "Don't look so surprised. Death is a natural part of life."

"Not this kind. Not poison."

"True, but we all have an appointed day to face our Savior."

Hannah stared at Jesse's list. How would they begin? There were so many . . .

Jesse tapped the page with his pen. "Would any of these cause a heart attack, Minerva? If given in sufficient amounts?"

"Foxglove can affect the heart as well as one's vision and state of mind. Hemlock looks much like parsley and has been used for evil purposes throughout man's time on this earth. It contains chemicals that are quite toxic."

"Any others?"

"That have the power to stop a heart? Many flowering plants—oleander, lily of the valley, peonies, rhododendron. Possibly the most dangerous of all plants are castor beans. They can be purchased at practically any nursery."

"Could . . . could they be given to someone without their knowing?"

"Certainly. Dried and crushed they can be hidden in most foods."

Hannah didn't know what to say. Her head was spinning. Her mind was dashing back and forth between the list of poisons and the way Ethan had looked when she'd found him. Her stomach suddenly turned, and she was certain she wouldn't be eating, though Minerva was now standing and moving across the porch toward the yard, toward their luncheon.

"*Danki* for helping us." Jesse stepped closer so that Minerva could lean on him as she made her way down the porch steps.

"Of course." Minerva had reached the bottom

of the steps and turned to gaze directly into Hannah's eyes. "Often a death is just that—the end of one's completed life. I've seen many people struggle with that truth, because they weren't ready to be without their loved one."

"Can't tell that anyone is grieving for Ethan."

"Then perhaps their faith wasn't strong enough. We all must accept how temporary this life is, which is sometimes a painful idea."

Hannah blinked. Why did she suddenly find herself fighting the urge to cry? Why was this all so hard?

"Other times, evil methods are at work." She leaned closer until her wizened old eyes were a mere inch from Hannah's, reached out her hand, and placed it on top of Hannah's. Lowering her voice, she said, "Be careful. Poisons do not have to come from a garden. One can purchase them off a store shelf."

She straightened and smiled broadly, revealing what had to be a nice set of dentures. "I will pray that *Gotte* will guide your path."

And then she was gone, hobbling back to the bay area of Amon's shop.

Hannah was left standing beside Jesse, with their sisters playing behind them and a beehive of questions swirling in her mind.

⇥ *Thirty* ⇤

Tate's Sunday morning found a new rhythm, one he hadn't known in quite some time.

The moment he opened his eyes, he knew he'd go to church. He'd been remiss the last few years, and it was time to turn that around. The service had gone well too. For once he didn't feel on the outside of things. Several old friends greeted him and seemed genuine when they said they were glad to see him. Nice people, and he was a little ashamed that he'd felt so isolated after Peggy died. His church had been there to support him. But for some reason he'd pulled away, until now.

The music included two of his favorite hymns. He didn't actually sing them; Tate wasn't one to belt out a song even if he was alone. But he did follow along, reading the words in the hymnal, even humming occasionally.

The service had progressed quickly, and he found himself appreciating Pastor Mitch's sermon on spring, the renewal of life, the resurrection of Christ, and their hope in him. Together they read Scripture from Psalms—a book Tate wasn't terribly familiar with. Perhaps he would try reading that during his morning time the next week.

As he was leaving, he stood in line to shake the pastor's hand.

Mitch leaned forward and asked, "Can you wait a moment until I'm done here? I'd like to speak with you."

Which is how Tate found himself standing to the side, watching the old and young pass by the pastor and out the door to enjoy their day of rest.

"Let me grab my things and I'll walk with you to our cars." Mitch popped into the church office, returning with a to-go coffee mug and a set of keys. "The wife hates when I leave these mugs here. We have three or four, and they'll all be stacked up in my office."

"Don't you have coffee here?"

"Sure, but I need some for the drive over." Mitch laughed at himself, then grew serious. "I wanted to talk to you about those verses from the Old Testament. The ones you asked me about at Ethan's viewing."

They pushed out the church door into the spring sunshine.

"From the book of Daniel."

"Those. I read about the vandalism at the Village. The newspaper mentioned there had been graffiti sprayed on both the Pumpkinvine Trail and Amber's porch."

"Yes . . ." Tate had read yesterday's article the evening before, after Amber left. He was wondering if she'd seen it.

"The report also mentioned that what was left on her house was Scripture."

"It was."

"Also from the book of Daniel?"

"Yes."

They'd reached the pastor's sedan. The day was sunny, bright, and warm. Tate welcomed the change in weather after the storm of the night before.

"And you saw what was painted on the trail?"

"Sure. I found it and alerted Amber. It was on the border of our properties."

"A quotation from Daniel?"

"Yes." Tate wasn't sure how much he wanted to share with Mitch, how much the man even needed to know. He had an entire flock to look after. Their problems weren't something he needed to be involved in any more than necessary. "Amber found both of the Scriptures. They don't make much sense to us, but they were both from the Old Testament, from the book of Daniel."

Tate hesitated as he thought about the letters from Ethan they'd read. He'd mentioned finding a slip of paper at the coffee shop. "There's more. Someone may have left a note for Ethan with verses from Daniel, and then there's the odd cross-stitch found in one of the Village shops. It also referenced Daniel."

Mitch's eyes crinkled as he stared off into the distance. Finally he turned to Tate. "Promise me you two will be very careful."

"Of course."

"The Scripture was given to us to teach and to uplift. To provide a path to God. Occasionally a person fixates on a certain portion, a portion that many of us would consider narrative history—such as the book of Daniel. It is a record of Daniel's experience in exile, in the court of Babylon. We can see God's sovereignty over kings, in this case Nebuchadnezzar."

Tate jingled the change in his pocket, unsure where Mitch was headed.

"In addition to the historical aspects, there are spiritual lessons to be found within this portion of the Scripture—God's faithfulness to his people and his omnipotence."

"But . . ."

"But when someone fixates on one portion versus the Scripture as a whole, confusion sets in. They pick and choose certain words and use them to justify almost any action."

Tate hesitated, then asked, "Even murder?"

"Especially murder."

"I was afraid you'd say that."

"If there's anything you need, anything I can do—"

"I'll let you know. In the meantime, pray that the person who is responsible is caught soon. The vandalism is disruptive, and the longer it continues, the more dangerous work is for Amber."

Tate's phone vibrated, and he pulled it from his

shirt pocket. He read the text once, then again. It made no sense.

"I need to go, Mitch."

"Call if I can do anything." Mitch added, "And go in grace."

Tate thanked him as he trotted toward his truck. He would need grace along with a giant dose of restraint if the message on his phone was true.

Amber had enjoyed the early morning worship service at her church, especially the praise portion. She had a special place in her heart for music. She'd taken to making playlists on her tablet, filled with music from church, from the radio, and even songs she'd grown up hearing. During the morning's service, she'd been particularly moved by a young girl's solo, accompanied by an acoustic guitar and keyboard. The old hymn "Showers of Blessings," played with a new syncopated rhythm, had soothed her soul.

She had many blessings in her life, and the words the young girl sang helped to remind her of them. She had a good job, a sister who was closer than any friend, faithful employees like Hannah, and she had Tate.

The last thought jumped into her mind unbidden.

But as she bowed her head for prayer, she knew it was true—Tate was a blessing. Not just because he helped her when others hesitated. She liked being around someone she was comfortable with. Someone who occasionally told her how pretty she looked, kissed her when she least expected it, and made sure she ate when she'd probably forget.

As the pastor ended their prayer time, Amber was comforted by those thoughts, by those truths.

Then Pastor Ann stood and began to preach.

She always spoke in a soothing, encouraging voice, but today the Scripture she'd chosen did not soothe or encourage Amber. Instead it started her mind to spinning.

Their reading came from 2 Samuel, the eleventh chapter. King David had fallen in love with Bathsheba, but she was a married woman. This didn't stop David from lying with her, and Bathsheba became pregnant with the king's child. So David sent Uriah, Bathsheba's husband, into the heart of battle. The king arranged to have his lover's spouse, a man serving in his own army, killed.

Pastor Ann went on to speak of David, a man with weaknesses, a man who had sinned, but ultimately a man after God's own heart.

The entire thing disturbed Amber. Why couldn't the Bible be clearer? Good people should be good, and bad people should be bad. David's story seemed to suggest otherwise. It spoke more of the nature of God and how his capacity for forgiveness was unlimited.

As she drove home, she thought of the sermon and Ethan and Patricia. Her mind relaxed completely as she passed a field with ewes grazing beside newborn lambs. The sight was so natural, so right, that for a moment she forgot to worry. And that was when she thought of the one person whom she had allowed to slip from her mind. The one person who might hold the answers they needed.

⇥ Thirty-One ⇤

Amber had been driving back toward the Village, toward home. When she realized the piece of the puzzle she'd overlooked, she moved to the center turning lane, waited for oncoming traffic to pass, and made a U-turn.

Fortunately she remembered where Margaret lived, or she thought she did. When she reached the neighborhood, she turned the wrong way— left instead of right. It took another five minutes to straighten herself out. By the time she pulled up in front of Margaret's home, her stomach was growling. Lunch would have to wait. She was close to solving the identity of Ethan's murderer. She could feel it as surely as she could feel spring in the air.

Grabbing her phone from off the front seat, she saw that she'd missed a call from Tate. It must have come in while she was walking from the church to her car. Sometimes she didn't hear the phone's ring in her purse, but the car always alerted her. In fact, she'd finally figured out how to sync her phone, and she could now talk hands-free.

She didn't have time to talk hands-free. She didn't have time to talk at all! Instead, she dropped the phone into her purse and hurried up the walk to Margaret's home.

What if Ethan's wife refused to let her in?

What if she didn't even answer the door?

Amber breathed a silent prayer for intervention, for direction, and for wisdom. Then she pushed the doorbell.

Margaret Gray answered the door, but she barely resembled the woman Amber had met so recently. Her hair was a mess—sprouting in every direction. She wore what looked like Ethan's old warm-ups, and she had not bothered to apply makeup—or take off yesterday's for that matter. Dark smudges puddled beneath her eyes where her mascara had smeared. When she raised her fingers to press them against her lips, Amber saw that her polish was chipped and two of her nails were broken.

How could one person change so much in such a short amount of time?

Had grief finally caught up with her?

Or had guilt?

"What do you want?" A week ago the words would have been a snarl, but now Margaret's voice trembled and cracked.

"I wanted to speak with you. May I come in?"

Margaret stared at her blankly for the space of a heartbeat, then shrugged and turned away from the door.

Amber glanced to her left and her right, as if someone might be waiting in the bushes. Finally she hurried through the front entryway to catch up with Ethan's widow. Margaret didn't stop at the living room, but they passed it as they moved through the hall that ran the length of the house. On the floor boxes of old photos lay open, their contents spilled out in haphazard disarray. Take-out containers covered the end table, and empty cans of diet drinks filled a trash can. On the floor was a copy of their local paper.

Unable to resist, Amber walked into the room. She picked up a few of the pictures: Ethan and Margaret marrying, standing in front of the house as they removed a "For Sale" sign with "Sold" over it, kissing under a sprig of mistletoe. She returned the pictures to the container they'd fallen from and picked up the newspaper. The front story was about the recent vandalism at the Village, but below the fold on the right-hand side was a picture of Ethan and an article about his death.

Amber dropped the paper back on the floor and retraced her steps. She could hear Margaret at the back of the house, slamming cabinets hard enough to rattle the dishes. Amber entered the kitchen and immediately thought of the remodel Ethan had mentioned in his letter. A new sitting area had been added on to one side, but it still lacked paint and flooring. A skylight sat on the floor in the corner, waiting to be installed. One of the counters was missing its top.

The chaos was a surprise, but Amber had little time to dwell on it. Margaret was searching in the pantry, and soon the sound of her sobs filled the room. Amber rushed over and flipped on the light in the large closet.

Margaret stood with her elbows propped on one of the shelves, her hands covering her face.

"What is it? What's wrong?"

"I can't . . . find the coffee!"

Amber didn't know whether to laugh or be alarmed. She'd expected a confession of some sort, maybe a tearful declaration of how much she missed her husband. Instead Margaret was falling apart over her need for caffeine.

"It's there." Amber reached past her and picked up the package of gourmet blend.

Margaret wiped her nose on her sleeve, plucked the package from Amber's hand, and shuffled over to the coffeepot. However, she couldn't manage that either. First she forgot the filter, pouring the grounds directly into the coffeepot's canister. When she realized her mistake, she tried to dump the grounds into the trash, but instead spilled them on the floor.

"I'll do that. You sit down."

She didn't even argue, and that said more to her condition than anything else. Instead she sat at the table in the room with no flooring, with only the concrete slab showing. She sat and picked at her red fingernail polish. Amber cleaned the coffeemaker, added a filter, new grounds, and water, then turned on the machine. While she waited for the coffee to brew, she found a broom and dustpan and swept up Margaret's mess.

"Have you eaten anything?"

"Eaten?" Margaret stared at her as if she were someone she'd never met.

"When was your last meal?"

Margaret looked around the room, staring at the walls in search of answers. Finally she shrugged and lay her head down on the table.

So Amber went back into the pantry. A quick search produced granola bars, raisin bread, and single-serving cans of peaches. It wasn't the healthiest of meals, but it would do. She placed all of the items on a plate and carried it to the table. Then she went back to the cabinet and retrieved two coffee mugs.

She poured the steaming coffee into each and carried both mugs over to the table. "Do you take sugar or cream?"

"Both." Margaret seemed to have revived at the

sight of food. She carefully unwrapped a granola bar but seemed confused as to what to do with it.

Amber opened the cabinet over the coffeepot, then the one to the left, and finally the one to the right. When she did, she almost let out a scream.

Her heart pounded so loud she felt as if someone had stuck cotton into her ears so that she could hear nothing else. Everything froze in that moment, everything except the boom, boom, boom of her pulse.

The cabinet was full of spices and such, including coffee creamer and a canister of sugar. But that wasn't what she picked up with her trembling hand. Instead, she pulled out two small glass jars filled with a white substance. One was a shaker jar, like you'd use for seasonings. The other had a spout on top. She set both on the counter in front of her. The first said "Ethan's salt" and the second "Ethan's sugar sub."

Was she looking at the murder weapons?

Were they filled with poison?

Wiping her sweating palms on her skirt, she picked them up again, carried both over to the table, and set them in front of Margaret.

"I don't want those."

Amber noticed she had eaten half of the granola bar.

"What are they? Why do you have them? What's in these jars?"

Margaret seemed about to answer. She didn't.

Instead she reached for her coffee, took one sip, grimaced, and looked around in confusion. Amber jumped up and retrieved the creamer, sugar, and a spoon.

After she'd doctored her coffee, Margaret picked up the shaker with the label "Ethan's salt." She ran her finger over the label as tears rolled down her cheeks.

She was going to confess!

Should Amber call Tate?

Did her phone have a recording app?

Should she call 9-1-1?

"I killed him." Margaret set the shaker down, brushed at her tears, and cradled her coffee mug in both hands.

Amber licked her lips, now afraid to touch her own coffee. No one knew she was there! Margaret might have poisoned all the food in the house. Perhaps that was why she was acting so strangely. Had she taken her own diabolical mixture?

"You killed him?"

"If I had paid attention, maybe I would have noticed how ill he was. I was a terrible wife."

"Why? Why were you a terrible wife?"

"Because I never listened! I never had time for him, never made time, and now he's gone." She abruptly changed directions. "How could he leave me alone? How could he be so selfish?"

"Margaret, tell me about these jars. Are they from Patricia?"

"Yes."

"Why?"

Margaret closed her eyes, and the next question slipped from Amber before she could consider whether she should ask.

"Were you poisoning him? Did you and Patricia kill Ethan?"

The question was like cold water splashed into Margaret's face. She drew herself into perfect posture and ran her right hand through her tangled hair. "What did you ask me?"

"What is in these bottles, Margaret? Why did I see the same thing at Patricia's house? What is it?"

Margaret seemed about to argue, or maybe order her to leave, but then she deflated—literally slumped into her chair. "It's his stuff."

"Stuff?"

"The salt—it was supposed to be a special kind of seasoning. Like a salt substitute."

"Had he been told to reduce his salt?"

"Yes. That and caffeine. He had borderline hypertension, and then more recently a weakening of his heart muscle. The doctor said with medication and by adjusting his diet, he should be fine."

"So he gave up caffeine?"

"And salt. Patricia was always good at chemistry, and she told him her mixture would be better than anything he could buy at the store. She also gave him some kind of sugar blend that was supposed to help keep his weight down, not that he had a weight problem."

"So you both have been using it?"

"No." Margaret picked up the half-eaten granola bar, looked at it as if she'd never seen it before, and then returned it to the plate. "No. Ethan did, but I didn't want anything from that woman. I refused to touch it."

"There were problems between you and Patricia."

"We fought."

"Recently?"

"Years ago." She stared into her coffee and tried another sip. Slowly her attention came back to the room, to the present, and to the questions Amber was asking. "From the first I suppose, maybe even before Ethan and I were married. But it grew worse, more bitter, in the last ten years."

"What did you argue about?"

"Everything."

"There must have been something in particular."

"She used him. She pretended to be sick but she wasn't."

Amber thought back to the night of Ethan's viewing. Patricia had been sobbing and crying out for her brother. She'd been inconsolable. Had that been an act? Amber didn't think so. But neither did the woman she'd seen that night jibe with the woman who lived in the duplex on the lake.

"Ethan couldn't see it, but I knew. I tried to tell

him." She rubbed the fingers of one hand with the other, and suddenly Amber saw her for what she was.

A woman who had grown old.

A person who had dwelled on the things that were wrong in her life.

Someone filled with bitterness and regret.

But was she a killer?

"Ethan wouldn't listen. He thought I was jealous—of *her*. He thought I was incapable of feeling sympathy, but that's not true." She raised her eyes to Amber, misery etching deep lines on her face. "I hated her, but I shouldn't have drawn away from him. Now I'm . . . now I'm alone."

Amber waited a moment, unsure how to respond.

Margaret pushed the jars toward her. "You take them. I have no use for them."

"What was the sugar for?"

"She would blend white sugar with brown sugar. He used it in everything—his coffee, his cereal, even in his oatmeal."

"Did he take it to work with him?"

"He didn't have to. She always made sure he had extra bags of the stuff."

Instead of picking up the jars, Amber walked across the kitchen, pulled off two paper towels, and found a drawer with brown paper sacks. Avery had been upset with the way she'd handled the framed picture, but she couldn't leave the jars there. Whatever was in them needed to be analyzed.

She picked up the jars using the paper towels. Their fingerprints were already on them, but maybe Avery could still find a trace of Patricia's. Maybe he could build a case from it.

As she placed each one into a bag, she studied the powdery mix inside. The blend was not pure white as you'd expect salt and sugar to be. The salt had flecks of herbs in it . . . or something more sinister. The sugar was brown and white, as Margaret had explained.

She didn't know what was in the concoctions—not yet—but somehow she was going to find out. After making sure Margaret called someone to come and stay with her—the woman was a mess—Amber hurried out to her car.

Margaret's grief could be an act. She could have been the one to blend together ingredients for a lethal potion and give it to Ethan.

Or it could have been Patricia.

How would they ever know? How would they prove anything?

She'd take the jars home and show them to Tate. Together they would decide if it was time to turn all they had over to the Middlebury Police Department.

⇐ Thirty-Two ⇒

Hannah sat beside Jesse in the buggy. Was she actually riding alone with him? Were they courting? "I'm sorry my *bruders* were staring at us when we left the house earlier."

"I have siblings too, Hannah. I know how they can tease, but they mean no harm by it."

"Maybe."

"Does it embarrass you?"

"My *bruders* staring?"

"Our riding together, to the singing."

"Technically we're riding *from* the singing."

Jesse winked at her and pulled down on his hat. He had winked at her! What did that mean?

"You spoke with Amber? About the things Minerva told us?"

"I walked down to the phone shack this afternoon, but she didn't answer her phone. I left a message." Hannah folded her hands in her lap. Jesse had offered a blanket, but she liked the cool spring air. The day had been warm, and now, with evening approaching, the temperatures were once again dropping. It all reminded her that soon she'd be wearing sandals and lighter dresses. Soon she wouldn't need the wrap draped around her shoulders. The days passed so quickly. The month was flying by like one of the

Englisch planes overhead—in sight and then gone.

"Do you think it was wrong of us to leave the singing early?"

"Wrong in what way?"

"Our parents don't know where we're going. They think we're still at Amon's."

"*Ya*. We didn't lie to them though, and we are adults now. I suppose they also snuck away while they were courting."

"Jesse!" Hannah's squeal came out louder than she intended. She fought to lower her voice. "Do you mean to say that we're—"

"We can be. If you want." He pulled his attention away from his gelding, reached over, and squeezed her hand.

When he did, sparks shot up her arm.

"I don't know what I want," she answered truthfully. "Everyone says all these changes are natural, but they feel awfully strange to me."

Instead of being offended, Jesse laughed. "So you're still thinking on it."

"I suppose."

"Fair enough."

That was one thing she appreciated about Jesse. He didn't push, but he also was up-front about his feelings. When had this happened? Less than a week ago she'd been celebrating her birthday. She remembered walking to work, relieved that the two boys who were interested in courting her had both left to help with spring harvests at their *gross daddis*' farms. Somehow, while they were gone, Jesse had slipped in under her defenses.

"What is it you're looking for in your shop?"

"Something that I saw, or I think I saw. Now I can't remember. Maybe I dreamed it or made it up with all this talk of poison." The sun had set, leaving behind a kaleidoscope of color—reds, pinks, even purples. She had trouble focusing on the possibility of danger.

"But you need it tonight?"

"*Ya*. I think I do. Or rather Amber might need it."

"We'll fetch it then. And maybe we can stop by the restaurant and treat ourselves to ice cream while we're there."

"Ice cream sounds *gut*."

Ten minutes later they were parking at the Village.

The grounds were usually quiet on Sunday evening, but even from the parking lot they could see an unusual amount of commotion.

Hannah pulled her shawl more tightly around her shoulders. "Wonder what's going on."

"Let's cut through the inn and ask."

As they passed into the employee side door using their pass key, a couple standing nearby spotted them.

"Say, they're Amish. Maybe they have a clue."

Jesse pushed Hannah through the door and closed it firmly behind them.

"More mystery people?" Hannah peeked back out through the glass of the door.

"Sounded like it."

"I wonder how long it will take them to figure out that there *is* no mystery."

"Actually there is, but it's not the kind of game they're expecting. Does Amber have any idea who is responsible for the false advertising?"

"*Nein*, but she explained the people who want to play the game receive messages on their phones."

"I've seen the text messaging. Don't stare at me that way, Hannah. You know many of the young people in our group have phones."

"Well, yes, but—"

"And many have text messaging on them."

"Do you?"

"*Nein*. I'm saving my money for more important things."

A ripple of pleasure passed through her for a moment. Then they came around the corner in view of the front desk and saw the chaos.

The two employees working—Jake and Beverly —were not Amish. Hannah knew that Amber insisted on scheduling *Englisch* employees for Sundays. She really did go out of her way to respect their traditions. Beverly had explained to her once that her church had services on Saturday evening, so she was free to work on Sunday. And as far as Hannah knew, Jake didn't attend church anywhere.

Beverly was probably in her midtwenties, with long black hair and a slender figure. Jake also had long hair, which he kept pulled back, and was younger. He'd been on the job less than a month.

"What's going on?" Jesse slipped behind the desk, pulling Hannah along with him.

"These mystery guests, that's what." Jake shook his head in disgust. "They're making us crazy. And they won't go to bed!"

"It's hardly time for sleeping." Hannah glanced at the wall clock. It wasn't even six in the evening. Still, Jake was correct. The room was shockingly full of people milling about, and the noise level was quite loud.

"You have no idea what today has been like." Beverly answered the phone, muttered something into it, and hung up rather abruptly. "They found their way into the storage area and the barn. Someone left the door unlatched, and animals that were supposed to be in the barn escaped."

Jake grabbed a bottle of water and gulped half of it. "Animals that were supposed to be pastured went in the barn—made a real mess. Some of these people have been going through the stock in the restaurant store, looking for clues. They're even digging in the gardens. It's complete madness. No matter how we tell them there's no mystery, they insist there is."

"One person showed me their phone," Beverly said. "They type in what we say, and if it's any of a half dozen phrases—such as 'There is no mystery'—then they receive five points. Five points! It makes no sense."

Jesse put his fingers into his mouth and let out an attention-getting whistle.

The room quieted instantly.

"Most Amish folk I know spend Sunday afternoons and evenings outdoors."

That was all he said, but it was enough. There was a pause as his words sank in, and then a stampede for the door.

Beverly stared around the empty lobby and then turned on Jesse. "Why did you say that? What in the world does it even mean?"

"Figured it might help you two out if the room was clear. Enjoy your quiet."

He laced his fingers with Hannah's and pulled her down the hall, out another side entry.

"Where are we going now?"

"To your shop! That's where you wanted to go, right?"

"*Ya*. Sure. Do you think we can get in without a crowd following us?"

"If we keep to the shadows and cut between buildings. Do you have your key to the shop?"

"I do."

"Let's give it a try then."

One person, a middle-aged man who kept holding his phone up to the sky, tried to follow them, but Jesse lost him when they ducked into an alcove between the maintenance shed and the quilt shop. From there, getting into the back of the *kaffi* shop was easy.

"Better keep the lights off, or we'll have a rush of mystery guests with us."

Hannah reached into her purse and pulled out a small flashlight.

"You came prepared."

"It's something *Mamm* gave me last Christmas. Fits on a keychain, but the only key I have is for work." They'd entered through the back of the shop. She led Jesse down the hall and into the storage room. They paused in the doorway. She was suddenly glad Jesse was with her. Being at the shop when it was closed in the evening was a bit creepy.

She slowly crossed the room to the corner where Ethan's desk sat.

"Tell me again why you had to see this tonight?"

"So I could sleep. I barely slept at all last night, and then this afternoon I kept remembering something in here that didn't belong. Something that was off." She played her flashlight over the desk, then up and over the shelves that lined the wall.

She was slowly moving from left to right, along the second shelf, when she backed up. "That's it. The box."

"Got it."

Hannah would have needed a ladder. Jesse

barely had to stretch. He started to hand it to her, but she motioned to the desk.

"Looks like a shoe box."

"We don't keep supplies in old shoe boxes."

"Pretty old."

"Hold this."

Jesse positioned the light on the box as Hannah opened it.

"Huh. Ethan must have used it as a keepsake sort of thing."

"Look at this picture."

Jesse stepped next to her with the light, close enough that their shoulders were touching and their heads were nearly together. "Is that Ethan? As a boy?"

"*Ya*. But who are the girls?"

"Flip it over."

"Over?"

"Look on the back. *Englischers* often write on the back of pictures, especially old ones like this, with a white trim around them. I think they call it a Polaroid."

"How do you know that?"

"I listen to the old folks as they sit on their benches outside."

Written on the back were three words—*Ethan, Patricia, Priscilla.*

"These must be his *schweschders*."

"I heard he only had the one."

There were other things in the box. A football

program from high school. A handmade birthday card signed by Patricia and Priscilla.

Hannah pulled something small out of the corner. "A rock?"

"That's not a rock. It's an arrowhead."

"Arrowhead?" Hannah turned it over in her hand.

"From the Native Americans. You've heard of arrowheads."

"I had trouble paying attention during history. It was always right after lunch when I was sleepiest."

Beneath it all was a single sheet of paper, folded in thirds. The writing was very old. Even studying it closely, Hannah couldn't make out all the words.

Ethan,
   You are a man now. You are the head of this (smudged).
   What happened to (smudged) was not your (smudged).
   Take care of your (smudged).
   It's all I ask.
                     Your loving pop,
                     (signature smudged)

"Do you think . . . do you think his other sister died?"

"Maybe, but look at the date on this letter. Over forty years ago. He couldn't have been much over our age when this letter was written."

Amber suddenly wasn't so glad to have found

the box. She'd seen it there one day when she'd been taking an inventory of supplies. It had looked out of place, and now she knew why. This sort of thing should be at home. Why had he brought it to work?

"Look at this." Jesse pulled out a yellowed newspaper clipping with a date on it. Though it was older than the letter, it was easier to read since it had been printed.

"She fell through the ice."

"He saw it." Jesse ran his finger down the single column. "Tried to save her, apparently."

"And Patricia was watching."

They put everything back into the box. "I want to take this over to Amber's. Maybe . . . maybe it will make sense when added to everything else she knows."

Jesse played the light over the desk.

Everything seemed in order.

Everything seemed as she'd left it.

Except for—

She reached forward and pulled the single sheet of yellow paper from the back of the box.

"Looks like something from a phone book."

"It is. He must have ripped it out and brought it back here."

"What's on it?"

Hannah raised her eyes to his, understanding finally dawning. "Lawyers. Divorce lawyers."

Her pulse began to race, and she suddenly

worried that Ethan's widow might pop out of the shadows and demand the evidence back. "This is it. Don't you see?"

"*Nein.*"

"Ethan was going to divorce his wife. She must have found out, and that's why he was keeping things here. She must have found out and decided to kill him before he had the chance to leave her. She poisoned him!"

"Slow down. *Englischers* don't kill one another over divorce. I suppose it's a difficult time, but I've heard women say things like 'Now I can start over.' Or 'We'll both be happier.' They sound sad and at the same time sincere, maybe even hopeful."

"You heard women say this?"

"*Ya.*"

"You're beginning to sound like an eaves-dropper," she teased.

"*Nein*, but they don't seem to notice I'm there. It's as if I become part of the shrubbery when I'm working on the landscaping. They talk away on their phones or to their *freinden* or family."

"And what do the men say?"

"Couldn't tell you. I guess the women come here to get over it. The men, I don't know where they go. Fishing maybe."

"You could be right, but this time something went wrong. This time someone ended up dead."

"Don't you think you're jumping to conclu-sions?"

"It makes sense, Jesse. Amber said Ethan's wife was terribly angry, that she wasn't grieving at all. Now we know she was mad because he was going to leave her. Maybe he would have left her without any money. Margaret was mad, and she decided to strike first."

⇚ Thirty-Three ⇛

Tate was surprised he could eat.

He was so tired, he thought he might fall asleep at Amber's table.

They'd both had a terrible day. The message he'd received had been from the police department, informing him there was livestock on the road near his home. Someone had opened all of his gates. He knew he hadn't left them open. One gate? Possibly. All four? Not a chance.

He'd spent the majority of the day rounding up both donkeys, which had followed the cattle across the road to an open pasture. Fortunately only one of the horses had wandered. Still, the recovery effort took all afternoon. When he'd spied Preston walking by, he'd asked if the man could help. Tate didn't know what he had expected, but he hadn't expected Preston to be a hardworking, capable ranch hand.

He glanced up at Amber, and his weariness slipped away. "You didn't have to order dinner for me."

"I owe you! After risking your life at Patricia's home? Free dinners on the house for a week."

"Can't remember the last time I ate in the Village's restaurant. Great chicken and dumplings."

"Now you see why I'm a bad cook. It's too tempting to call and ask them to bring something over."

"Tell me about your day."

"I will, but first I want to hear more about how you coaxed Trixie and Velvet home."

"You would have been proud of me. Let's leave it at that."

"So you're more patient with them?"

"Being impatient with a donkey is a futile exercise."

Amber smiled, but he could tell she was distracted. Something was worrying her. He reached across the table and covered her hand with his. "Tell me about your day. I see something's bothering you."

"I didn't want to ruin your dinner."

"No worries. I'm finished." He pushed the almost-empty plate away. He'd consumed the chicken, dumplings, salad, and fresh bread, and given a few minutes, he could probably eat a piece of pie.

"My day was nearly as bad as yours." She went on to describe the chaos at the Village. "I don't know what we're going to do about these mystery guest people. I've always wanted to maintain a full inn in the off-season, but they're not our normal type of customer."

"Can't hardly kick them out."

"Can't let them keep running over my staff either. And the way they're trampling around the property—searching in staff-only areas, bothering my employees, making a general nuisance of themselves. I'm going to have to do something."

"Someone is provoking them." Tate spun his dinner knife on the table—once, twice, three times. "I'll be glad when Avery's back in town."

"Still no word from him, and when I stopped by the police department, he hadn't checked in with them either."

For a moment the night quieted, highlighting the sound of her wall clock ticking and Leo's purrs. He was curled up on the rug at their feet, oblivious to the conversation going on around him.

"You went by the police department?"

Amber squirmed in her chair. She also looked everywhere but at him.

"Amber?"

"Yes?"

"What aren't you telling me?"

Drumming her fingers on the table, she hesitated but then plunged in. "I had to go by there. I had new evidence, from Margaret."

"Margaret Gray?"

"Yes. I went to see her after church, and—"

"You went to see Margaret alone? For all we know she's the one who killed Ethan."

"Oh, I don't think so, Tate. You should have seen her. She's a devastated woman."

"That could have been an act."

"Maybe, but I doubt it. Anyway, I wasn't in any danger. I think I can defend myself against one sixtysomething widow."

Tate leaned forward, elbows on the table, head in his hands, and rubbed at his temples.

"I'm giving you a headache?"

"This situation is giving me a headache. I'm ready for it to be resolved."

"I was making her coffee, and I found two jars labeled like the ones at Patricia's house. I think it's how Patricia poisoned him. I was going to bring them home and discuss it with you, but then I received the call from the Village about the problem with the mystery guests, not to mention your text saying you wouldn't be able to meet for lunch. It seemed wiser to take the jars by the police and drop them off with Cherry."

"First sensible thing you've said," he muttered. "But how do you know Margaret wasn't in on it?"

"I don't."

Silence once again fell between them. Tate studied Amber, the lamplight on her face, the way she pulled in her top lip when she was thinking, even her hands on the table. He needed to tell her how he felt. Then she'd understand why he worried.

"There's something else." She scooted her chair closer to his, opened the cover on her tablet, and pulled up photos. "Here's one of the pictures you took. You emailed them to me. Remember?"

"Sure. They're the pictures from Patricia's garden."

"Yes. You can tell this plant is more developed than the others. I think she must have grown it in the greenhouse and then transplanted it outside."

"Possibly."

"And here is what I found on the Internet."

"Why did you think to look for foxglove?"

She told him about Hannah's message, explaining what Minerva had said, detailing the list of poisonous plants easily grown in local gardens or possibly in greenhouses.

"And you checked them all out?"

"No. I checked out the first few she listed. As soon as I saw this one with the pink flowers, I knew I'd seen it before. I'd seen it here." She touched the tablet, and the picture Tate had taken once again filled the screen.

"Same plant, but it could be a coincidence."

"You don't believe in coincidences."

"Not as a rule."

"And today? The chaos you had to deal with combined with what has been going on at the Village? I think—"

"You think we're close and that Patricia is trying to stop us."

"Yes. I do."

"And Margaret?"

"What would her motive have been? As Ethan's wife, she would have received any life insurance or monies they shared."

Tate leaned back in his chair and studied her.

"What?"

"You've worked hard on this. And I think you've come to some realistic conclusions. But Avery is going to need a motive, a reason for Patricia to kill her own brother."

"That I haven't been able to figure out. We know from the letters that she was upset about his sale of the land. And we know that he was scraping the bottom of his savings." She stopped for a moment. "Who told us that?"

"Carol, from the quilt shop. She said Ethan's savings had run out."

"Maybe Patricia was afraid she was going to have to move."

"What's the advantage though? How is she better off with him dead?"

Leo stretched and wound first through Tate's legs and then through Amber's.

"It's possible that Patricia's line of reasoning might not make any sense. That she's not completely aware of what she was doing or why she was doing it."

"She had to be pretty aware to grind up a plant and slip it in his coffee."

"True."

"You're right that she seems emotionally and possibly mentally unstable." Tate remembered running from Patricia's home, and how afraid he had been for Amber. If something were to happen to her now when he'd so recently realized his feelings for her—

"What are you thinking about?"

Tate sat forward in his chair, pulled Amber's hands into his lap, and jumped into the topic that mattered most to him. "I'm thinking about how much you mean to me. How devastated I'd be if anything happened to you."

Amber began to interrupt him, but he leaned forward and kissed her softly on the lips. "I'm thinking about how much I love you."

If his kiss had settled her, his words caused her to rocket out of the chair.

"What did you just say?"

"I said I love you."

"Why?"

"Why do I love you?"

"Why would you say that? We've only known each other, what? A week?"

"We've known each other for years."

Amber stared at him a moment and then began stacking dishes together. Finally she dropped them back onto the table.

"I'm not ready for this."

"Not ready for what?"

"To discuss . . ."—her hands waved back and forth, up and down—"*this!* Us. I thought I might be ready, but I'm not."

"You thought you might be. So you do have feelings for me."

"Of course I do." She shook her head, causing her hair to tumble forward. "But we almost have her. We almost have the person who killed Ethan. I need to focus on that."

"Sometimes being close to death allows you to appreciate life." He stood in front of her and put a hand on each of her shoulders, but he didn't kiss her again. The panic in her eyes tore at his heart. What was she so afraid of? How had she been hurt before? Or was she so used to being alone that she was terrified by the thought of depending on someone else?

"Do you love me, Amber?"

"Yes. Maybe. I don't know." Tears pooled in her eyes, and he regretted bringing up the subject. Perhaps he should have waited. He couldn't pull it back though. He couldn't unsay the words that had risen from his heart.

"I'm a patient guy. You don't have to know right now. And you're right. We were basically strangers to one another until a week ago. This all started when you rescued my donkeys."

She smiled at the mention of Trixie and Velvet.

Tate walked across the room and picked up his jacket. They'd spent nearly every evening together. Perhaps she needed time alone. Maybe she needed to rest.

"If there's one thing I've learned through Peggy's death and my time as a widower, it's that life is short."

"I know that," she whispered. Then she added, "And I know the answer is to trust one another, and trust whatever God is doing here. I do care for you, Tate. I may even love you. I might be frightened because this is all so sudden. A girl needs time to think."

"Take all the time you want." When she didn't answer, he added, "You look tired. Promise me you'll get some rest?"

"Sure. I'm going to clean these up and go straight to bed."

"I could help."

She shook her head. "Some time alone would be good."

He moved next to her, squeezed her hand, and didn't let go until she smiled, albeit shakily. "If you need me, I'm right next door."

He walked out into the night, not relieved exactly. He'd rather she had jumped into his arms and proclaimed her love with certainty. But he was satisfied that he'd said what was on his heart.

He'd said what needed to be said.

Now all that remained was to wait.

⇒ *Thirty-Four* ⇐

Amber went to her bathroom, splashed water on her face, and ran her fingers through her hair. Had Tate said he loved her? Was all of this happening, or was she dreaming?

She walked back into the dining room. Best clean up the mess. Once she hit the bed, she didn't plan to stand back up for eight hours. Though she questioned whether she'd be able to sleep in spite of her exhaustion. So many questions were buzzing through her mind that she felt like she'd consumed an entire pot of coffee.

Did she love Tate?

Did they know each other well enough to even talk about their feelings?

She carried their glasses to the kitchen, and that was when she heard her front door open, heard someone step inside. Tate must have forgotten something.

But when she walked back into her dining room, her heart stopped.

Patricia stepped closer. Amber fought the scream clawing at her throat. She needed to remain calm. She wanted to look directly at Patricia Gray, to talk with her and try to persuade her to stop this madness.

But she couldn't take her eyes off the enormous snake that was draped around Patricia's shoulders like a shawl. Amber knew very little about snakes. She'd had a paralyzing fear of them since she was a child, but she was fairly sure that Patricia had brought a boa constrictor into her home.

What else could be so large?

"Charlie's fascinating, isn't he?"

Amber pulled her gaze away from the snake long enough to see the smile spreading across Patricia's face. Yes, she was going with a diagnosis of flat-out crazy. For the briefest second, sympathy surged through her fear, but then Patricia lowered the boa to the floor. It slid across the tile toward her.

"Don't run," Patricia whispered. "Charlie loves a game of chase."

Amber stood so still she felt as if she'd turned to stone. Maybe Charlie would pass her by and slide out the back door in search of a more appetizing dinner.

"I wish you could have seen him when he was a baby. He hit six feet by the time he was two years old. Unfortunately, it seems he has stopped growing. A shame, as I have heard that many red-tailed boas can easily grow to ten feet and fifty pounds. My Charlie seems to have stopped just under seven feet, but still I love him."

Patricia pulled out one of the dining room chairs

and sat down. Her voice sounded surprisingly normal, almost devoid of emotion, as if she'd locked all she was feeling inside.

"What do you want?" Amber's throat was suddenly so dry that the words came out scratchy and little more than a murmur.

Charlie had moved in a straight line, toward her, and was now starting to coil around her feet. Amber wanted to scream. She wanted to run, but she feared that would cause the snake to attack. Perhaps she should remain still and attempt to talk some sense into Patricia.

Or she could die of fright.

"What do I want? I think you know the answer to that. I want what's mine. What my brother gave away to you."

"That acreage was sold to the Village."

"Call your little scheme whatever you want. I want it back." Patricia's expression never lost its congenial smile.

Charlie had continued coiling around her legs. Perhaps he was simply curious. Did snakes have a sense of curiosity, like a cat? Amber's heart thumped in triple rhythm. Was this what a heart attack felt like? Was this how most snake victims died? From fear?

"There's something about Charlie you should know." Patricia leaned for-ward. "He hasn't eaten."

She sat back, relaxed and apparently enjoying herself. "I usually feed him every seven to ten days, but I decided to wait this week. I wanted to have your attention."

Amber felt her entire body go cold.

"Why, you look as if you've seen a ghost. No need to worry about Charlie, dear. Unless you've eaten recently." Patricia reached out and tapped one of the dinner dishes left on the table—dinner for two. The plates still held the remains of the chicken, dumplings, salad with bacon and cheese, fresh bread—all that she'd shared with Tate a few minutes ago. "Ah . . . I see you've barely finished dinner. Well then, Charlie might smell the chicken on you and become . . . interested."

She paused, and Amber knew Patricia was waiting for her to look up. There was no doubt this woman had planned out her every move, had probably waited until after Tate left but before Amber had cleaned up the dishes. Her eyes were the one thing she felt safe moving. She was still wearing her khaki slacks and dark blue blouse from church that morning. The snake was now brushing against the material of her pants. He was still coiled loosely but had worked his way above her knees.

Most of his body remained on the floor, but she was beginning to feel the weight of him. What would happen if she stumbled, if she fell over onto the floor?

She had to find a way to survive this. She did not want to be suffocated by a snake in her own dining room. "What do you want me to do, Patricia?"

"I'd love to see you close the Village, since it sucked the life out of poor Ethan."

"You killed Ethan."

"Of course I didn't."

"You hired the boys to shoot at his window—"

Patricia clapped her hands, which startled Charlie. Amber still didn't dare to look down at the snake, but she felt it tense, then resume its long, slow crawl up her body.

"They did a wonderful job! I wanted to pay them double, but I don't think that would be teaching them a good work ethic."

"You knew about Ethan's heart condition."

Patricia ran her palm across the top of Amber's table. "Ah, yes. Ethan always did have problems of the heart."

"We know you put foxglove into the sugar and salt you gave him."

"You figured that out? You should receive a grade of A+, Amber Wright."

"You killed him."

"Of course I didn't. At first I ground up caffeine pills and put it in with his sugar, but it wasn't working fast enough. Ethan had found me another place to live, a less expensive place, a home where I'd be looked after. Do I look like the kind of person who needs a house parent?" Rather than aggravated, Patricia seemed amused. She waved away Amber's accusation and explained, "I kept the caffeine in there even though it worked too slowly. At that point he was addicted and didn't even know it. I didn't kill my brother. The caffeine did, and the foxglove—a lovely plant—and the terrible fright from those boys, and his heart condition."

"I can't give you that land back. I work there. I don't own the place."

"I thought you might say that. So instead I'll take money. Poor Ethan was always saying he couldn't give me money, but I think you can. Tell me the combination to the safe in your office."

Amber wasn't going to die for money. At the same time, if Patricia had what she wanted, she might decide to let Charlie have a surprise dinner. Praying for wisdom, she tried to think of a way to stall the woman in front of her.

"Did you go into Katie's shop?"

"Yes. I thought you had recognized me when I passed you with my neighbor's little pooch in my bag. Wasn't that fun? You and that little Amish girl stared at the dog and ignored me completely. Snatching her key so I could go back later and open the window was child's play. Once I'd spread bird-seed throughout the shop, it was only a matter of minutes until all manner of critters came inside."

"Why—"

"Because I could! And I wanted to hurt your precious Village. Do you realize how much time

Ethan spent there? Whenever I asked him to take me somewhere, he said he couldn't because of work. Always work! You think your little group of stores and tourists, the little kingdom you've built, is strong and secure. But it's not! Iron breaks and smashes everything, and I will break you."

"Daniel." The word nearly stuck in Amber's throat. "Those words are from Daniel."

"Handy book. Don't you think? I love to read about battles, and I plan to win this one. Now tell me the combination for your safe."

Amber rattled off a string of numbers. She couldn't imagine how Patricia knew about the safe. Perhaps she had only guessed.

"Very good. I shouldn't have any trouble finding it since there's just the one quilt hanging on your office wall, and we both know the safe is behind that quilt." Patricia stood and patted her pockets. All of her moves were slow and methodical. Possibly she was taking some narcotic that delayed each response. Or it could be that she was aware any sudden move would attract Charlie's attention.

How loyal were snakes to their owners?

Hadn't she seen on the Internet that one had recently eaten its owner?

Amber closed her eyes.

"Keys?"

"Promise me you will take this animal with you, and I'll tell you where the keys are."

"Of course."

Her eyes flicked toward the living room, toward the table near the front door.

"You and I have a lot in common." Patricia moved into the living room and pocketed the keys. "We both have small homes. We both are smart women, and we both live alone."

"The snake?"

"Oh. I'll come back for him after I make sure that combination you gave me is correct. Just hold perfectly still and I think you'll be fine. Charlie has never eaten a person before." Her laughter was soft, controlled. "Of course there's always a first time."

Then she stepped out onto the porch, into the gathering darkness, leaving Amber alone with Charlie, with no alternatives, and paralyzed by her fear.

Tate had backed his pickup truck into the carport. He sat watching Amber's place.

He'd seen the headlights pulling into her place. The vehicle arrived at the same time he'd cut his engine. So he sat there, waiting and wondering. What if it was someone she didn't want to see? What if it was someone who wanted to hurt her?

The person had left not long after arriving.

So he should relax.

But he didn't.

Instead he checked his phone display again. No missed messages. No calls.

Why would she call him? He'd just left there.

Watching her house, he felt his adrenaline begin to pump as his anxiety increased. Something wasn't right, but he couldn't put his finger on what.

"Trust." That's what she'd said to him as he had poured out his heart, revealed his love for her. "The answer is trust."

But who or what was he supposed to trust?

Her? That was easy enough.

God? Sure. Okay. In spite of what had happened with Peggy, he was ready to trust God again.

Himself? That was harder.

But maybe it was time, and if he trusted himself, then he listened to that small voice. He stopped pushing it away, ignoring it, or drowning it out with the television. He listened.

Whether it was paranoia or instinct or God's Holy Spirit prompting him, urging him forward, he couldn't say. But he was going to trust.

So he started his truck, and he drove back down to her place.

Amber didn't come to the door when he pulled up. The storm door was closed, but the inside door was open. He was able to see through that into her home. All he could make out was the right portion of her dining room table, which still held the remains of their dinner together.

She had said that she was going to clean up the dishes and then go to bed early. He'd offered to help, and she had refused, saying she'd like some time alone.

But the dishes were still on the table.

And she was plainly not in bed since the lights were still on.

So where was she?

Tate got out of the truck and quietly pushed the door shut.

Something was not right here, and the last thing he wanted to do was spook anyone.

Leo sat on the front porch, near the door but not in front of it. The top half of the storm door was glass, and the bottom half was metal. Cut into the metal was a pet door, but Leo had not gone through it. Why was he waiting?

When Tate climbed the steps of the porch, Leo arched his back and hissed. But he didn't back away.

"Easy, boy. You know me."

He raised his hand to knock on the door, and that was when he saw her.

He saw her, and his heart stopped beating.

Amber was standing in the space between the kitchen and the dining room, and she had a boa constrictor wrapped around her. Eyes bigger than half dollars, she stared at him, pleading for help and warning—all in one long, terrified look.

The boa was an adult and had wrapped around her torso.

Tate breathed a prayer for her safety, for his own wisdom, and for deliverance.

Then he carefully, quietly opened the door.

Leo crept in behind him, stopping on the inside of the door as it swished shut.

How had this happened?

Where had the boa come from?

And how had it managed to wrap itself around Amber?

The questions piled up in his mind like debris in a river. He pushed them aside and walked slowly toward her.

"It's going to be okay," he said.

Amber only blinked.

There was no doubt in his mind that the snake was a boa constrictor. The pattern on its scales consisted of jagged lines, diamonds, and circles. It was a brownish color, with red markings prominent toward its tail. And most important, it looked to be over six feet long.

"I'm going to pick up the bottom half of its body. When I do, it should uncoil." He kept his voice low and calm. The last thing he wanted to do was frighten the animal. He also didn't want the boa to squeeze. "Amber, you're going to be okay."

She blinked again. The fear was so evident in her face that he wanted to put his arms around her. But first he needed to remove the snake.

"Trust me?"

Her nod was barely perceptible.

He stepped closer and reached for the bottom two feet of the animal. He placed both hands firmly under its coils, supporting its weight, the part that had not yet tightened around Amber—though how she could remain standing with it hanging on to her he couldn't begin to guess. He guessed the boa weighed between thirty and forty pounds.

Now that he was closer, he saw that sweat was beading down her face.

"I've got him. Now I'm going to slowly unwind." If what he was doing worked, the snake would shift its weight to him at the same time it disengaged from Amber.

He began to walk around her, and the snake slowly began to unwrap, slithering and sliding down her torso, then her legs. Tate lowered the end of the snake to the floor, and that was when Leo hissed.

The snake responded immediately, its head moving toward the cat.

Leo dashed through the pet door out into the night, and the snake moved in a straight line after it.

The last thing they needed was a loose boa constrictor on Village property. Tate reached for the item closest to him, a glass of water, and threw it at the farthest corner of the living room, where it shattered against the wall.

The snake stopped, changed directions, and then moved toward the water and broken glass before disappearing beneath the couch.

He turned back to Amber as she sank to the ground.

"Not here." He scooped her up into his arms and headed out the back door.

Kissing her once, he placed her in the porch swing. "I'll be back. I need to close the front door before that boa goes after your cat."

⇒ *Thirty-Five* ⇐

Tate wasn't keen on circling back around the house in the dark.

The boa could have gone out the pet door when he took Amber out the back, but it was unlikely. In all probability, the snake had wound itself into the coils of the couch. He prayed that was the case. They needed to resolve this situation tonight, and the snake complicated things.

He stumbled to a stop when two yellow eyes blinked at him in the dark, then he realized it was Leo.

"Glad you made it, buddy."

Leo blinked again, then walked over and rubbed against his legs.

"Best stay here." Tate reached down to scratch between the feline's ears, then he continued around to the front porch.

Since the cat was fine, probably the boa was in the house. He climbed the porch steps slowly and peered through the glass in the storm door, searching for any sign of the boa. He didn't think the snake would strike, but there was no use in acting rashly. His heart thumped in a quick, steady pattern, and he had to wipe his palms on his pants.

Slow and steady would do the job.

The room appeared clear, so the boa was probably still under the couch. Opening the storm door as quietly as possible, he reached for the doorknob of the inside door to pull it shut. When he'd nearly closed the door, there was a distinct rustling under the couch. Not moving an inch closer, he waited, and there was the flick of the snake's lower scales, peeking out of the back of the couch. He pulled the door shut. His heart rate slowed a fraction. One emergency dealt with, one to go.

Certainly the boa could find a way out of the house, but if Tate remembered correctly, they preferred to hide rather than chase things. Their power—and danger—was in their ability to strike.

And why hadn't it struck Amber? Or crushed her?

What would he have done if it had? If he hadn't returned to check on her, when would he have heard that she'd died less than a mile from his home?

His heart ached, and he had to reach up and rub at his chest. The doc had given him a clean bill of health not three months ago, so it must be fear.

Fear of losing Amber.

Fear of caring again and being hurt.

Fear of trusting God.

Tate made his way back around the house. With the light from the kitchen window, he was able to see that Amber remained precisely where he'd left her—in the swing. He couldn't make out her expression in the darkness. Sitting next to her, he pulled her into his arms, kissed her hair, and breathed in the scent of her.

"The boa's locked in your house. You can relax." She trembled against him. No doubt she was in shock. Who wouldn't be?

"You gave me quite the scare there."

"S–s–sorry."

"It isn't every day a man sees his girlfriend in the embrace of a boa."

"How . . ." Her teeth chattered, but she pushed the words out. He waited while she found her equilibrium. "How did you know . . . what to . . ."

She gave up trying to speak and burrowed into the circle of his arms. His heart was pattering faster once again, but he realized it was a strong, good, healthy beat. It was the new beat of his life, of his future, and he could get used to it.

"National Geographic," he explained. "With some Animal Planet thrown in."

She nodded against his chest.

"How did you know not to move, Amber?"

"I did . . . didn't. I was too frightened . . . and, and Patricia warned me to stay perfectly still."

"In this case, your fear might have saved your life." Even as he spoke the words, Tate knew in his heart that he didn't believe them. He rubbed her arms and whispered, "God saved your life, Amber, and I'll be on my knees tonight thanking him for that."

She pulled away from him then, enough to stare up at him in the darkness. He could feel her gaze, the same way he could feel a pull toward her that was tangible. It was physical and emotional, and it was stronger than the pull of the moon on the tide.

Knowing it was the right thing to do, he kissed her.

Had he ever felt this way before?

Had he believed he could feel this way again?

It was as if all the ice he'd carefully packed around his heart had melted. It was as if he was experiencing life for the very first time.

When the kiss ended, when Amber pulled away, she seemed steadier. But the first words out of her mouth weren't what he expected.

"Patricia. It was . . ." She pulled in a deep breath, then blew it out slowly. "It was Patricia Gray, and she said she'd be coming back."

"Good. I'll be at the front door waiting for her."

Amber reached for his hands, squeezed them with her own, adding urgency to her words. "She's at the Village, and there's no telling what she'll do. Tate, she isn't right."

She reached up and touched his neck, ran her hand down the front of his shirt. The physical contact seemed to calm her, and when she spoke again, Tate realized she was recovering quickly from the night's trauma. No surprise there. He'd known she was a strong woman.

"Remember when we visited her, and we realized something was off? She seems eccentric, but she's not. She's completely disconnected from this reality."

Tate stood and pulled Amber to her feet.

"Do you know where she is, what part of the Village?"

"Yes. She went to my office to try to get into the safe."

He grasped her hand in his, and they walked around to the front of the house, both moving automatically to his truck. Amber was halfway in the truck when she started to back out.

"Where are you going?" Tate reached over to stop her.

"Leo. I have to make sure—"

"I saw him near the side of the house earlier. He's fine. He won't go far, will he?"

Amber shook her head once, got in, buckled her

seat belt, and they took off down the road. It might have been quicker to walk, but Tate wanted the truck in case they had to follow Patricia somewhere.

"Here's my phone." He fished it out of his pocket. "Call the police department and tell them there's a robbery in progress at the Village. Ask them to meet us in front of the restaurant building. Also tell them we need an animal control unit at your place, and let them know what they're dealing with. The boa is curled under your couch."

Hannah and Jesse were on their way back into the inn and conference center, the largest building on the Village property, when the fire alarm went off.

The pulsing blare of the alarm and the blinding red lights nearly knocked Hannah over.

She moved closer to Jesse and shouted, "What now?"

"Fire alarm, but I don't see any—"

He was cut off by a flood of guests exiting their rooms. The two employees working the front desk were calmly directing everyone to the parking lot.

Hannah and Jesse stood frozen in the middle of the doorway as the sea of guests poured around them.

Hannah recognized one of the guests. He had been in her shop the last two mornings. He stopped next to them and hollered, "Is this part of the mystery game?"

Hannah shook her head no. There was no mystery game, but the more they told folks that, the more insistent they were that they had found another clue.

"Could be real." Hannah could barely hear her own voice, though she was shouting. "Better head out."

The guest shrugged. Still staring at his phone's screen, he stumbled out into the evening.

Jesse tugged on her hand and pointed to the back corridor, which wound through the meeting rooms. They jogged through the hall and out the back door.

Outside the siren was still loud, but Hannah at least could think over it.

"Why are we leaving?"

"Because I think this is a decoy."

Hannah nodded.

"*Ya*. Like the letter said, the ones you told me about."

"By Ethan?"

"He said something like 'I'm being stalked—' "

" 'By the master of illusion.' I remember."

Jesse's expression was so certain, so determined, and even a little excited, that Hannah found herself believing him.

"So why a fire alarm?"

"Everyone comes over here, and the person

410

causing the ruckus is free to snoop around somewhere else. We're going to the somewhere else."

They'd walked around the corner of the building and now stood staring at the crowd. The scream of a fire engine pierced the night. Guests were also leaving the restaurant and the bakery and walking over to the inn to see what the commotion was about.

"The office," Hannah murmured. It made sense, and when she closed her eyes, she could see the events of the last few weeks falling into place. Like the quilts she sewed, the pattern was beginning to make sense. Like the specialty drinks she sold, all of the ingredients combined to make the perfect brew. "Someone is in the office."

Jesse held tight to her hand as they worked their way through the crowd and into the restaurant building.

A few workers remained, but the scene struck Hannah as bizarre. Half-eaten meals at deserted tables, waitresses holding trays of food ready to be delivered. There was no one sitting at the tables. It reminded Hannah of a game of statue, the game she had practiced with Mattie, where they would freeze until someone said "Go."

"What's going on out there?" Seth hustled across the room to meet them.

"You're not supposed to be working."

"I'm not—not exactly. I skipped the singing

and came over to pick up one of their chocolate silk pies for my *mamm*. I've extra money from the tips I made at your shop. *Mamm* is feeling a bit low, and I thought it would cheer her up." He wore traditional Amish clothing—dark pants, blue shirt, suspenders, and his wool cap, and it occurred to Hannah that he was going to make a good worker there at the Village. "Is there a fire?"

"Not that we saw, but you should get the other employees out in case there is a real emergency." Jesse pulled Hannah down the hall, toward the stairway that led upstairs to the offices.

"Where are you going?"

"To check something out." Hannah looked back over her shoulder. "If you see Amber, tell her we went to her office."

"But—"

"Hurry, Seth!"

Jesse opened the door leading to the staircase and stopped. Hannah turned toward him to ask what they were waiting for, but Jesse clamped a hand over her mouth.

"Quietly," he whispered in her ear. "I see a light."

They crept up the stairs, rounded the corner, and heard voices arguing.

"She gave you the wrong combination." This from a man.

"Try it again." The woman's voice sounded like she was irritated.

"I've done it twice."

"I said try it again."

They had tiptoed to Amber's office and were standing outside the room, waiting beside Elizabeth's desk. There was a small circle of light from the beam of a flashlight someone was holding in Amber's office. The strobing, pulsing light from the fire truck outside also peeked through the window. Hannah glanced over at Elizabeth's desk, at the pictures of grandchildren and one large dog. Life was supposed to be like that—work and family. How had they ended up in the middle of this chaos?

"Patricia, I told you it's not working."

She recognized the male voice now. It was Larry. She mouthed the name to Jesse, and he nodded in agreement.

"Then we'll just have to use this." The woman sounded unperturbed, maybe even amused.

"What is that? What are you doing?"

"It's a small explosive device. No worries. It should blow the front off this little safe."

"Are you crazy?"

In lieu of an answer, Hannah heard something smash, and then someone fell to the floor.

She didn't realize she was still holding Jesse's hand, clutching it actually, until he covered her hand with his and removed the one she'd squeezed any circulation out of.

"Who's crazy now?" The woman didn't even

attempt to lower her voice. "Trauma to the head can cause that. Best to be careful."

"Larry's down," Jesse whispered. He had nearly jumped out of his suspenders when the body crashed to the floor. Scanning the room, he finally turned to stare at Hannah, his eyes wide and his breathing shallow.

He somehow managed to keep his voice down, but Hannah wondered if the woman could hear their hearts beating. Hers was hammering loudly enough to be heard out in the parking lot.

"Do you think anyone else is in there?" Jesse asked.

Hannah didn't need to know. Patricia was in there, and that was bad news enough. They stood there in the dark, side by side, standing perfectly still and waiting. Suddenly there was a hiss and the smell of sulphur.

Patricia had lit a match.

Pushing Elizabeth's chair out of the way, she tugged on Jesse's hand, pulling him down under Elizabeth's desk, urging him into the safety of the only cover the room provided.

They huddled under the desk, and Jesse snagged the wheels of the chair and hauled it back into place, completely hiding them from view.

Seconds later there was a flash of light, followed by an explosion and the sound of Patricia's laughter.

⇒ Thirty-Six ⇐

Amber and Tate had intended to wait near the front door of the restaurant, where she'd told Cherry to meet them. But then Seth ran out of the building, face red, sweat staining his shirt, and pulling in big breaths. He explained that Hannah and Jesse had gone upstairs and that they might need "backup."

Amber wanted to laugh at the *Englisch* lingo coming from Seth, but this wasn't a funny situation. It bothered her that the Amish teens working for her found themselves involved with a crazy lady like Patricia. Their innocence was important to her, and she felt as if she'd let them down.

There was no time to beat herself up about it now.

Tate told Seth he had to stay outside to wait for Officer Brookstone.

Amber added, "Repeat everything you told us. Warn her that we're upstairs and that Hannah and Jesse are too."

Seth nodded once, and Tate and Amber hurried inside and down the empty corridor. They had tiptoed halfway up the stairs when they heard the sound of an explosion.

Their eyes met for a moment. Amber's heart

felt lodged in her throat, and then they both began running to the top of the stairs, no longer trying to mask the sound of their approach.

As she rounded the corner of Elizabeth's desk, Amber hesitated. She could make out a body on the floor of her office, and Patricia reaching her hand into the wall safe. It was all too much. She stormed into the room.

"You blew it open?" Amber stopped once she was inside her office. She was so angry and her pulse was racing so fast that she was actually seeing Patricia through a red haze. "Are you crazy?"

Something flashed in Patricia's eyes, something dark and sinister. Recovering quickly, she smiled and explained, "I wouldn't have needed the explosive if you'd given me the correct combination."

Tate had knelt at Larry's side and was checking his pulse. "Larry seems okay, but he's unconscious and has a huge lump on the back of his head."

"What did you do to Larry?"

"Poor Larry didn't really have the heart to pull this off. He was wavering, and I can't stand wavering." She tweaked her hair, an impulsive gesture that she couldn't resist though her voice sounded completely calm. "Larry wasn't careful enough. Working late at night can be dangerous."

"So he's in on this with you? He's your

accomplice in this foolish scheme?" Amber was no longer afraid, now that Charlie the boa constrictor wasn't on the scene. She was furious, and she saw no need to hide it.

"Larry?" Patricia flicked a hand toward the still body on the floor. "Not a good partner, if you know what I mean. I had to cut him loose."

"Looks like you beaned him with a flashlight."

"You see it your way. I see it mine." Patricia stretched her arms over her head, as if the entire evening had put a kink in her back. Shaking off the fatigue, she returned her attention to the safe.

"Step away, Patricia." Amber felt bold and confident. Tate was standing beside her now, and she knew Patricia was no match for the two of them.

"Or what?" Patricia swung around to face them. When Amber saw what was in her hand, her stomach lurched.

"Scared of guns too? You are a fussy little thing." Patricia's eyes flicked up and toward Tate. "I brought this with me as a backup plan. In case Charlie failed me. I wish you could have seen her with Charlie. I thought she was going to faint dead away before he had a chance to have any fun at all. I would have liked to have that on video, but I had to scoot."

"As you can see, we found a way around your snake." Tate kept his voice calm, soft almost.

Amber wondered how he was able to control

his emotions. She wanted to stomp across the room and slap this woman who had caused such havoc in her life.

When Tate stepped toward Patricia, she raised the small handgun and thumbed off the safety.

"I wouldn't." Her voice remained pleasant. "My brother made sure I had a firearm and knew how to use it. He wanted me to be able to protect myself. Remember, 'Iron breaks . . .' "

"Is that what you were talking about? Guns are made of steel, not iron." Amber thought her head was going to burst wide open.

How did you reason with someone who wasn't anchored in reality?

A small voice told her to tread carefully. After all, this crazy woman had a gun pointed at her, a presumably loaded gun. But the last few days had taken their strain, and her patience had reached a breaking point.

"This gun is quite deadly, my dear Amber. You need to remember that iron—"

" 'Iron breaks and smashes everything.' Yes, I remember your first message on the Pumpkinvine Trail."

"Excellent! I admire folks with a good memory." Patricia actually smiled. "I'll tell you a secret. That's one of my favorite verses."

"Because it talks about iron? You think it gives you permission to carry that gun and—"

"It speaks of breaking and smashing!" Patricia's

face contorted in anger. "I will break and smash you and this Village. Maybe not tonight. Maybe not this time. Certainly not with this small amount of money you hid."

She rattled the money bag she'd removed from the safe. "Feels like a pitiful amount."

"It's tomorrow's deposit, Patricia. Nothing more."

"Certainly not worth going to jail over." Tate maintained his distance and kept his voice free of emotion. "Put the money and the gun down. You can walk away."

Patricia's laughter broke out in stark contrast to her anger seconds before. "I like your spunk! Are you two—oh, I guess you are a couple. I can tell by the way he wants to protect you, Amber. Too bad."

She directed her next words to Tate, wriggling her eyebrows as she spoke. "I think you're kind of cute, and you'd make a better partner than Larry ever did."

Tate shook his head. "No thanks."

"Not interested? Well, too bad." She kicked a duffel bag across the floor toward him. " 'A rock was cut out, but not by human hands.' I suppose this is all predestined, or something."

"Stop quoting Daniel!" Amber's adrenaline had been pumping for too long. She suddenly felt exhausted. "Daniel loved God. Who do you love? Yourself. That's all—not even your brother."

Patricia looked as if she might argue, but then she shrugged and said, "I loved Ethan. I'm going to miss him, but I needed him out of my way so that I could retrieve what you owe me. He never understood that you stole what was ours. Now get out the plastic ties, cutie-pie."

Tate glanced once at Amber, mouthed, *Humor her,* and bent to unzip the bag.

"It would have been easier if you'd allowed Charlie to nibble on you." Patricia stared at her with a what-can-I-do-with-you look. "Charlie has never killed anyone! No, you had to be difficult. Turn one of those chairs around so you are facing me and have a seat. Your man-friend is going to fasten your hands behind your back. I don't have all night. Sit!"

"Why would I do that?"

"Because you have not obeyed the Lord our God or kept the laws he gave us."

Amber had to fight the desire to stomp her foot. "Patricia, God's Word is not a weapon. It doesn't justify what you're doing."

"How could you possibly understand?" Patricia pulled back the hammer of the gun. "I'm in a hurry, and you two have already taken more of my time than I had to give. My little diversion next door isn't going to last forever."

She made encouraging remarks as Tate bound Amber's hands behind her.

"One last chance, cutie-pie. Come with me?"

Tate again shook his head. Patricia shrugged her shoulders, then sighed as if she was terribly disappointed.

"All right. Now, obviously I can't tie you up while I hold this gun, and I can't put the gun down because you're not trustworthy."

"Sounds as if you have a problem." Tate set his feet as if he were preparing to charge her.

"Do you think so? I could always shoot you."

Amber stared at her, unbelieving, as Patricia gripped the gun in both hands and pointed it at Tate. From the corner of her eye, Amber saw a shadow in the outer office. She prayed someone would come, someone who could help them. She prayed for God's deliverance.

And then, like the deluge of a storm that had been building for hours, everything happened at once.

The shadow flew across the room, aiming for Patricia.

Amber rocked her chair to the left and crashed to the floor.

Patricia pulled the trigger as Gordon tackled her from behind.

And Tate fell to the right, blood splattering from his arm.

Tate felt the bullet graze his right shoulder. Amazing how a person didn't forget certain things. Even though it had been over thirty years since he'd served in the military, and been shot in a training accident, he instantly remembered the searing heat, the surprise, and the pain.

He also realized that his arm would be stiffening up. He needed to help Amber while he was still able.

He forced himself into a sitting position and noticed the room had filled up with people.

An Amish couple had rushed in after Gordon. The girl was Hannah. And the young man with her? Must be Jesse who Amber had spoken about.

"Are you all right?" They both rushed to where Amber lay and helped to right her chair.

Gordon was busy handcuffing Patricia. "Is everyone okay?"

"Yes." Amber's answer was shaky.

Tate nodded as he stood and clamped a hand over his shoulder, trying to staunch the flow of blood.

Hannah and Jesse murmured their replies, though they both looked like a pair of deer caught in the headlights of Tate's truck.

Patricia was spouting nonsense about her constitutional right to steal what was hers.

Larry had nothing to say since he was still unconscious.

Gordon gave the group a quick once-over, assured Tate he'd have a medic up quickly, and ushered Patricia out of the office.

It took Tate three strides to reach the drawer of Amber's desk. Opening it, he wasn't at all surprised to see that everything was lined up and neatly placed within partitions. The scissors were to the left.

He cut the bind holding her wrists behind her back, the bind he had placed, and cupped her face in his hand. "Are you okay?"

"Yes, but—"

"You're bleeding." The young man rushed back out to Elizabeth's desk and returned with a quilted coffee coaster. "Elizabeth won't mind. She can buy another in the shop. Go ahead. Use it."

Tate thanked him and pressed the cotton against his arm.

"I'm Jesse, by the way. And this is—"

"Hannah. I know. Nice to meet you, Jesse."

They could hear Gordon reading the Miranda Rights to Patricia. He must have called downstairs first because a fireman and medic entered the room.

"There's no fire here," Amber said to the fireman.

"Still have to check it out, miss. Anytime there's an explosion we have to follow procedures."

The medic moved toward Tate, but he waved him away. "See to Larry first. He's been out for several minutes."

Amber was up and rifling through her lower desk drawer. She produced a first aid kit and told him to sit. "She shot you. I can't believe she actually shot you."

Tate saw the look of amusement exchanged between Hannah and Jesse.

"Is she always bossy like this?"

"Maybe a little." Hannah laughed when Amber paused to send her a look of disbelief.

Amber shook her head at the ribbing. She focused instead on finding a roll of gauze in the first aid kit and began wrapping it around Tate's arm, leaving the pressure bandage—the coffee coaster—in place.

He appreciated her effort but figured it was needless. The medic would see him next, and either bandage him up there or send him on to the hospital. Tate sensed, though, that Amber needed to be doing something, and she seemed calmer as she tended to his wound. When Patricia's gun had gone off, the fear in Amber's eyes had nearly torn his heart in two. If it calmed her to wrap his arm with gauze, he'd gladly sit still and allow her to do so.

"Is it necessary to put the gauze all the way to his elbow?" Hannah asked.

"He resembles one of your *Englisch* mummies at Halloween," Jesse chimed in. "I believe he's safe from bleeding any more—ever."

"I thought we were a team," Amber said, standing back to study her attempt at first aid.

"*Ya*, we are a team. That's why Jesse and I were

here to begin with." Hannah explained about the things they'd found in the old shoe box—the picture of Ethan and his two sisters and the letter from his dad. She described how it had led them to Amber's office.

"So you were hiding under the desk? We never even saw you." Tate stood and slipped an arm—his good arm—around Amber.

"We did see—and hear—you." Jesse stepped to the left so he could watch the medic who continued to work on Larry. "Is he going to be okay?"

The medic never paused to look at them, though he did glance at Gordon, who was walking into the room.

The two spoke for a moment as Gordon asked basic questions about Larry's condition and then phoned his status in to the police station. Finally he turned his attention to them.

"Why are you here?" Amber asked. "I thought you were fishing. I kept leaving you messages—"

"And I started back when I heard the first one. I reached the office as your call came in about needing animal control." He shook his head, as if he couldn't believe the mess she'd made. "It looks like Larry will be fine, though when he wakes up, he's going to have a gigantic headache."

"And a new place to live. He is going to jail. Right?" Amber tapped her finger against her bottom lip. "I still can't believe he betrayed me. He swore to my face that he had no major issues with Ethan, and all this time he was working with Patricia to kill him."

"I'm sure he thought he had good reasons. Most criminals do, and many are able to fool the people they're closest to—including family and coworkers." Gordon checked his phone and then slipped it back into his shirt pocket. "Once the hospital releases him, he'll be at our jail until his transfer to county, where he will probably await his trial. Any idea how involved he was? Do you know if he was in this from the beginning?"

Amber shook her head, and Tate could sense the energy draining from her. She'd been through a lot in one night. A tremor started down his right arm as he realized how close he'd come to losing her.

Gordon was still focused on Larry. "I imagine he'll be eager to talk when he learns we have Patricia Gray under arrest."

"How did you know where to find us?" Tate asked.

"A young man downstairs told me that you were all in the office area—"

"That would be Seth," Hannah murmured.

"And then these two showed up." Gordon pointed at Hannah and Jesse. "They came flying down the stairs, claiming Patricia had a gun and was going to use it."

"Thank you, Gordon." Amber stumbled over her words, then pushed forward. "I doubted you. Thought . . . I'm not sure what I thought. Things have been strained between us, and maybe that's my fault. Tate assured me you were a good cop, and I should have trusted his word—trusted you."

"Apology accepted." Gordon touched her shoulder, then shook hands with Tate. "But you should be thanking these two. They thought logically and quickly while in a dangerous situation."

"As soon as we saw the gun, we knew we couldn't keep hiding under the desk and waiting for help to arrive. We knew we had to do something." Hannah blushed when Jesse stepped closer and slipped his hand over hers.

"Plus it was cramped under there." Jesse stepped back when Hannah took a swipe at him.

Tate realized he was looking at young love, though they didn't seem to know it yet. He remembered being that age and having feelings he didn't understand. It was an exciting time, but also a difficult one. Looking at Amber, he realized he liked his current age a lot better—this time around he understood his feelings and how important it was to cherish them. Young love was good, at least for a time. But what he saw in Amber's eyes? He wouldn't trade that for anything in the world.

≈ *Thirty-Seven* ≈

A week later, Hannah worked out in the afternoon sunshine, helping her mother in the garden. Eunice was using the hoe to break the sod around the rows of vegetables they had planted—vegetables that were flourishing in the Indiana spring. Hannah followed behind her, pulling up weeds and dropping them in the pail her little sister, Mattie, carried. Every once in a while, Mattie would plop down in the dirt and upend the pail.

Which might have irritated Hannah a week ago, but it didn't any longer. Instead she was grateful to have the day to spend with her family, to still be alive so she might see her sister grow, and for simple things like working in a garden.

What if Patricia had killed someone with that gun?

What if she had turned the gun on Jesse and Hannah as they hid under Elizabeth's desk? An image of Jesse's smiling face passed through her mind. If he had been hurt, or worse, killed, would she have been able to accept it as *Gotte's wille*? The thought of what they had been through together caused sweat to slip down Hannah's back, though the afternoon wasn't all that warm.

All of those incidents from last week had changed her.

Now when she awoke in the morning, she found herself appreciating the blessing of life, even when her day off included weeding the vegetable garden.

So she laughed with Mattie and then squatted beside her to help put the weeds back into the pail.

Her mother paused, leaning on the hoe, and studied her. "So everything is *gut*, *ya*? Things at the Village have settled down."

"They have. Amber's interviewing people for the assistant manager position, and the vandalism has stopped, but . . ."

"But what, *dochder*?"

Hannah stood and pushed up on her glasses. She also pushed her hair back into her *kapp*, then bent to retrieve more of the weeds Mattie had dumped in the dirt. "Those mystery guests still arrive every day, especially on the weekends. It's easy to trip over them because they're always searching for clues in bushes, behind buildings, and even in the *kaffi* shop."

"I suppose they'll grow tired of the game eventually. Until they do, perhaps you should create a new drink for them."

"Like a mystery coffee?"

"*Ya*. You'll probably sell twice as many." Eunice put her hand at the small of her back and rubbed. "I'm glad you are happy in your new job."

"As you said I'd be, *Mamm*. How did you know?"

"I've known you a long time." Eunice resumed hoeing, though she stayed close enough that they could continue talking. "You're pretty much happy wherever you are planted, sort of like these tomato plants. As long as they receive a little sun, some water, and a bit of care . . . they thrive."

"Hmm. I suddenly feel like someone might shake salt on me and take a bite."

Mattie heard the word *bite* and decided it was time to eat. She threw herself against Hannah's legs, tugging on her apron and insisting, "Mattie snack. Mattie snack, Hannah."

Fortunately Hannah had an apple in her pocket that she'd remembered to carry out for her sister. Mattie said, "*Danki*," then skipped ahead to stand next to her mother. She showed her the apple before plopping on the ground and taking a bite. Juice dribbled down her chin and she laughed.

"Little things make her happy," Hannah said.

"Same with us, if we let them."

"Oh, I'm happy." Hannah had returned all the weeds to the pail and was now working on the plant next to where her mother stood. "I'm happy I'm alive after seeing that gun in Patricia Gray's hand."

"Violence is a terrible thing."

"And I'm glad that Amber and I are *freinden*. I never expected to have an *Englisch* friend, especially one who was my boss."

"*Gotte* provides." They'd reached the end of the row, so Eunice set the hoe aside and sat on the ground under the shade of the ash tree. Mattie crawled up into her mother's lap, and Hannah sat beside them. "Never think because someone is different that *Gotte* can't pull you close together."

"But we're supposed to be . . . separate. It confuses me sometimes."

"*Ya*, I know what you mean. But Christ commands us to offer our friendship freely and always to minister to others."

"I know."

"We are separate because of the way we worship and the way we live, because we have committed ourselves to following the *Ordnung*, as you did when you joined the church."

"Amber attends a church in town."

"And we will not be judging her where her beliefs are different than ours."

"*Nein.*"

"It isn't as complicated as we sometimes wish to make it." Eunice reached out and patted her hand. "When you are confused, *Gotte* will show you the way."

Hannah didn't answer for a moment, not sure if she wanted to reveal all that was on her heart. Then she remembered Patricia and the gun and that life could suddenly be cut short. Why would she want to hide things she was feeling when life was so uncertain?

"Sometimes I'm confused about Jesse," she confessed.

"He is a *gut freind* too."

"Yes, but now that he's asked to take me to singings, I don't know how to act around him."

"You've had other boys take you to singings before, even on buggy rides for picnics."

"*Ya*, but those times it was like going out to play with other students at the school yard." Hannah stared into the afternoon sun. "I didn't feel differently about them."

"But you feel differently about Jesse?"

"I do." She turned to her mother, relieved that she understood. "I don't know if it's love. I don't even know what that kind of love is. But I do know that my hands start sweating and occasionally I trip over nothing at all, and when we're together, I sometimes can't think of a thing to say. Other times I'm with him, I can't seem to stop talking."

"Those things are normal." Eunice set Mattie on her feet and then pushed herself to a standing position. She still hadn't lost any of the weight from when she was pregnant with Mattie, but Hannah thought her mother was beautiful. She was exactly as she should be.

"If this is all so normal, why do I feel strange? And who wants to go around feeling as if they're going to throw up at any moment? What fun is that?"

Eunice laughed and slipped her arm around Hannah's waist as they made their way back to the front porch, Mattie running in front of them. "Falling in love can be like catching the flu—sometimes. Not always, but sometimes."

"Do you think I'm in love?"

"I couldn't say. Do you?"

Hannah shrugged. She didn't know. It was part of what caused her to hesitate each morning before she hopped out of bed. There was so much about herself she didn't understand.

"Don't worry, Hannah." Eunice placed her hands on both sides of Hannah's face and pressed her forehead to her daughter's. Her next words were more like a prayer than words of advice. "*Gotte* will direct you. He loves you."

"*Ya, Mamm.* I know."

Her mother's words seeped into Hannah's heart and calmed the troubled places. It wasn't as if she had to make any decisions about Jesse right away. All she'd promised to do was sit by him in the buggy. As she climbed the porch steps with her mother and sister she vowed to even stop worrying about whether he would kiss her again.

Boys were a mystery, rather like the drink her mother had suggested she make for the *Englisch* guests.

Which reminded her, she had a book upstairs full of recipes. Perhaps she'd show them to Jesse, and together they could come up with something "New & Tasty" for the guests to enjoy.

⤖ Thirty-Eight ⤕

Amber stared out at the setting sun. There were probably thirty minutes left until darkness, and she wanted to sit still and let the sun dry her hair. Since the incident with Patricia, she had learned the importance of savoring each day.

Leo sat beside her on the porch, paws tucked under him, eyes closed, napping in the last of the day's light.

She'd spoken to Tate three times in the last week, but each time had been on the telephone, and a short conversation at that. Why did it bother her so much that he hadn't stopped by, that they hadn't shared dinner together? He still emailed her each morning, checking to see how she was doing. And he had mentioned that there were several things that needed his attention.

For two days he'd even gone out of town on some family matter.

Still.

A woman liked to see the guy she was in love with.

And she was in love with Tate Bowman. She'd realized that when Patricia had shot him, when his life had flashed before her eyes.

So why hadn't he been to visit?

And should she walk up the road to his place?

While she tried to make up her mind, a delivery truck turned off the main road and trundled toward her house. As it drew closer, she saw that it was their local florist, which was odd. A cheer-you-up delivery wasn't due from her sister for another five months. She sent them twice a year, as predictably as the arrival of spring and fall.

The delivery guy hopped out as she stepped into the yard. He retrieved a bouquet from the back of the truck, handed her the dozen pink roses, and then said, "Sign here, please." The smile on his face made her wonder if he'd read the card, but she didn't call him on it. She scribbled her signa-ture, thanked him, and walked back toward the porch.

The pink roses were wrapped in silvery tissue paper. There was no vase, which was a little odd.

She sat on the top step of her porch and placed the flowers across her knees. They were beautiful, reminding her of summer days and dreams she thought she had abandoned.

God had been faithful to hand her those dreams, to hand her *the desires of her heart*. At least it seemed so. That had been her hope and prayer this last week.

She fingered the card but didn't open it.

Somehow she wasn't ready to read whatever was written there—the roses, the card, and the words were either a beginning or an end, and she was afraid to find out which.

So instead she let her mind drift back over her afternoon. She'd already had dinner—a salad with turkey, which she'd put together herself. It wasn't cooking, but it was a start. She hadn't looked at her tablet since she'd arrived home from work, opting instead to spend her time on the flower beds bordering the west side of her house. The grounds people normally took care of that, and they'd be surprised to see that the weeds had been plucked.

But puttering in the sun had felt good. It had felt right.

As she had knelt in the grass and worked her small rake through the sod, the anxiety from the day had drained away from her. The shower she'd had afterward had done more than remove the dirt from her time gardening—it had also washed away most of the worries that tried to crowd into her mind. She'd pulled on a pair of work-out pants and an old T-shirt and gone to sit on the front porch, not bothering to put on makeup or dry her hair.

Which was when the delivery truck had driven up.

She stared at the card, and somehow she knew that it did indeed represent another turn in her life.

Closing her eyes, she whispered a brief prayer. "Please, Lord, don't let these be break-up flowers."

Selfish? Perhaps, but she was learning that God

cared about her dreams. All she had known of romantic love was how it disappointed, how it could hurt, leave you bereft, and how difficult it was to overcome all those feelings. She barely recognized the glimmer of hope now pumping through her veins.

She pulled the card from the bouquet and opened it. Leo chose that moment to show an interest in what she was holding. He sniffed the flowers and repeatedly bumped his head against her hand, making it difficult to read the words on the card.

Three words, but they had the power to change her world.

Then she heard footsteps. She closed her eyes, unwilling to hope that it was him. She clutched the bouquet, looked up, and saw Tate walking toward her. He'd had a "haircut" since she'd seen him last. He wore jeans and a tan denim shirt, and he was carrying a vase. She looked down, ran her fingers over the flowers in her lap, then raised her eyes to his.

"I thought you might need one of these."

"I have vases," she whispered.

"Yes, I've seen those." His words were teasing, but his expression was serious. "I thought I'd start a new tradition with this one."

The vase was simple, elegant, and even from where she sat she could see that it was crystal. He'd bought her a dozen roses and a crystal vase.

He had timed his visit just right, appearing as the delivery truck scooted on down the main road.

Now he waited at the bottom step, studying her and holding the vase as if he was unsure she'd accept it.

"Is there room on your shelf for one more vase, Amber? Is there room in your heart for me?"

Instead of answering him, she put the flowers down next to her, stood, and walked into his arms.

Tate's laughter was like rain on Amber's soul.

When his lips found hers, she didn't hesitate. They kissed as if it had been a month rather than a week since they'd seen each other. When he snuggled her neck, she ran her hand up and over his head, feeling the stubble where he'd recently had it shaved, then back down to his shoulders.

Tate Bowman was solid—physically, emotionally, and spiritually.

"Get my card?"

Amber nodded, trying to blink away her tears.

Tate led her back up onto the porch steps.

They both sat on the top step, and he pulled her hand into his and kissed it, sending a shower of shivers up her arm and into her heart. "Take this," he murmured, placing the vase in her hands.

And that was when she saw he had brought her more than a crystal vase and a dozen pink roses. She peered down into the vase and saw a small box. Her heart beat a tango, and she blinked back tears.

Slowly, she upended the vase, and the ring box fell into her hand. As she opened it, the last of the day's rays fell on the diamond, causing it to sparkle and shine.

She glanced up when Tate moved away from her and dropped to one knee on her top porch step. Then she couldn't stop the tears from brimming over.

"It's not young love, but it's true love, Amber. God has blessed us with another chance, another path, and I would be honored if you'd share that path with me. Will you marry me, Amber?"

She tried to answer, but didn't trust her voice. Her emotions were holding together by a slender ribbon, and she didn't want to ruin the moment by blubbering in his arms.

"If you need more time—"

"I don't."

She picked up the card, held it in one hand and the box with the ring in her other. Her gaze fell to his note, written under the printed word "From": "Your true love."

"Want to share your answer?" Now he was teasing. She supposed she'd have to get used to that.

"Yes. My answer is yes!"

He stood in time to catch her as she threw herself into his arms, nearly knocking him off the step. Tate's arms went around her. He kissed her lips softly and ran his fingers through her hair.

Amber knew in that moment that her dreams had come true. She felt God's favor as surely as she felt Tate's heart beat in his chest where she snuggled against him. And though she didn't think she deserved all that she'd been given, in her heart she said a prayer of thanksgiving.

They sat on the porch steps until darkness fell completely around them, more comforting than a handmade quilt. She moved closer into the circle of Tate's arms. Leo lay next to them, his yellow eyes and rumbling purr indicating his approval. The stars came out, a stellar display of God's provision, especially designed for them—or so it seemed to Amber.

Tate explained that he had gone to visit both of his sons. He didn't need their approval, but he wanted their blessings.

"And they're okay . . . with us?"

Tate ran his fingers through her curly hair. "They can't wait to meet you. The first week of summer they'll both be home."

"With Camille?"

"Yup. My granddaughter is eager to meet the lady who named my donkeys."

Amber stared down at their hands in the darkness. She couldn't see where her fingers and his were intertwined, but she could feel their connection. And she knew that she could put her trust in him, the same as she put her hand in his, the same as she put her trust in the Lord. Tate was a blessing God had given her. One she had been afraid to ask for, but God had sent nonetheless.

When she started crying, he pulled her even closer to him, kissed the top of her head, and waited for her pent-up emotions to work their way out.

Finally she felt clean from the stress of the last week. Her heart and her life felt as if they had been turned about, tossed upside down, and finally scoured clean by the fury of a spring rain.

Wiping her face on his shirt, she laughed through her tears. "I love the ring, but I didn't need another vase."

"Oh, yes, you did. Those crazy vases are fine for your sister's flowers, but my flowers can always go in this crystal vase."

"You mean I'm going to get more flowers?"

"Does Leo like to chase after the birds?"

The answer to that seemed to be yes. Amber thought about Tate regularly bringing her bouquets, and she felt as if she'd stepped into a romance novel.

"Want some hot tea?"

"I thought you'd never ask."

They walked into the house. Tate stopped when he saw her living room. He seemed especially interested in the new loveseat positioned in the corner.

"Nice," he said, running his hand over the tan-colored leather.

"I donated the old one to the Salvation Army."

"Because—"

"Because I thought of Charlie every time I walked into this room. It wasn't worth the cost to keep it. I'd have needed therapy to overcome my aversion to snakes."

Tate stared down at his feet, but Amber saw the grin he was trying to hide.

"I know you are not laughing at me, Tate Bowman."

"No, ma'am."

"Because if we're to marry, you're going to need to find a place for my new couch in your house."

He walked slowly back across the room to where she waited. His eyes on her sent a delicious warmth all the way to her toes. His look was a combination of love, devotion, and amusement.

"We'll find a place for the couch. Did I tell you that I saw the animal control director on my way out of town?"

"You didn't." She started to protest when he drew her back into his arms. She was supposed to be making tea.

"They found a nice spot for Charlie at a zoo in Fort Wayne."

"I'm so happy to hear it, especially the Fort Wayne part."

He kissed her softly. "I love you, Amber Wright."

"And I love you." She could have stood in his arms forever, but then she realized her crying had made her thirsty. So they moved to the kitchen, and she set a kettle of water on the stove as he pulled out two mugs.

A few weeks ago, she had stood in her kitchen trying to convince herself that she was too old to find love, that it was too late for God to satisfy her dream of marriage, that she would never have children of her own.

She and Tate might have found each other late in life, but they had found each other. God willing, they had many days and nights left to share together.

Two donkeys, a small herd of cows, one yellow cat, plus Tate's children and grandchild.

She was going to be a grandmother!

And all of it might not have happened if it hadn't been for Patricia Gray, her plan to reclaim lost property, and the chaos she wrought. God had turned that destruction into a blessing.

Which seemed to her to be the biggest miracle of all.

⇜ Epilogue ⇝

August

Hannah and Amber stepped out of the summer heat and into the air-conditioned foyer of Happy Hearts Therapeutic Center. Hannah was holding an afghan she had crocheted. Amber carried an armful of magazines.

"Jesse heard that Larry found a job at the downtown hardware store." Hannah still didn't like to think that someone who had been a supervisor to her had been instrumental in a murder plot, but the more she thought about it, she found she wasn't actually surprised. There had been small indications that Larry was troubled—the strange expressions, rumors of his temper, even missed meetings toward the end. His behavior had definitely become more erratic as he'd been drawn into Patricia's web.

"That's true." Amber signed in for both of them at the front desk, and the receptionist told them they could proceed to Patricia's room. "He received a lengthy probation—ten years."

"Because he knew of what Patricia planned to do?"

"He suspected, and he did nothing to stop her. He also admitted to provoking Ethan into arguments, trying to push him into quitting his job. It's not clear how that would have helped Larry or Patricia, but then, her methods didn't always make sense."

"And he was involved in the robbery."

"Yes. The judge wasn't convinced he would have gone through with it, only that he was willing to help Patricia. Since Larry pleaded guilty, his sentence was lighter than it might have been."

"And he has to stay in the area." Hannah reached for the strings of her prayer *kapp*, ran the fingers of her right hand down the entire length. Was Larry still a threat?

"Yes. He must report in with a guidance counselor and his parole officer." Amber reached out and squeezed her hand. "There's no need to worry about him."

"You're not worried that he's still a danger to us? Or to the Village?"

"No. Gordon was able to trace Larry's Internet activity and found that he had huge online gambling debts. I think Larry was caught up in Patricia's scheme, hoping he would get some money out of it, and possibly he was harboring resentment that he hadn't been promoted to general manager instead of me."

"That's what made him so desperate—gambling debts."

"His gambling addiction was apparently severe.

Which was one of the reasons he started the mystery guest sites. He was pulling in a nice chunk of change from that side job. The gambling though, it's what undid him."

Hannah had trouble imagining how anyone could place bets on a computer and then owe that computer thousands of dollars. It was something she'd rather not know more about.

"Ethan knew something was wrong. There were the letters and also the new binder he made with instructions for the shop."

"Yes, he suspected, but he couldn't prove any of it."

They stopped at the doorway of Patricia's room. The room was small, neat, and clean, with sunshine streaming through the window. The only person there was an orderly putting fresh sheets on the bed.

The young man with hair pulled back with a rubber band turned and smiled. "Miss Gray is in the garden."

They thanked him and turned back the way they had come, down the hall and to the outside area.

"Why did she do it?"

"No one really knows. Patricia's drug use started when her sister, Priscilla, died. She's been unstable since that time."

"How long will she have to stay here?" The facility was nicer than Hannah had imagined. She was suddenly glad she'd asked to tag along. Perhaps seeing Patricia and where she was to live for the foreseeable future would help to squelch some of her nightmares.

The bad dreams plagued her at least twice a week. In the dream she was always hiding in the darkness, shaking and unable to scream. Though she knew Amber could be hurt, she couldn't stop the shot that rang out or the red blood that seeped across the carpet.

"A judge will reevaluate her case every six months."

They pushed out into the atrium, where a large garden area was divided into sections—flowers, herbs, native plants, and a small fish pond.

Patricia was working in the herb garden, which didn't surprise Hannah at all. Perhaps the work was therapeutic. Perhaps it would allow Patricia to find a legitimate way to use her talents of growing, drying, and mixing things.

When she looked up and saw them, Patricia waved.

Hannah was reminded of what her bishop had said to her when she'd spoken to him of her dreams. "Our mind has a way of working out our fears, but God—he has a way of making us a new creature if we let him."

Patricia had no family now that Ethan was gone. Margaret had moved, declaring she hoped never to set eyes on her sister-in-law again. At least that was what Hannah had heard through the Village grapevine.

Amber and Hannah had spoken about that at length. After praying and talking to their families —she suspected Tate and Amber's wedding would be soon—they had both decided to be Patricia's family. That was their plan. They would pray for her, visit, and take small gifts.

Perhaps like the herbs growing around her, Patricia would find health, a measure of peace, and God's grace.

⪧ *Acknowledgments* ⪦

This book is dedicated to Kristy Kreymer. I held her in my arms the day she came home from the hospital, and twenty-six years later I was in the room when her daughter was born. Ours is a friendship that has lasted a lifetime, and that is a precious thing indeed. Although she has a full-time job, she works as my assistant in the evenings. Her help is invaluable.

I'd also like to thank my new friends in Middlebury—both Amish and *Englisch*. You were a joy to visit, very welcoming, and kindly offered information about your lovely town. A special thank you to Jeffrey Miller, operations manager of Das Dutchman Essenhaus.

Thank you to Donna and Dorsey, my pre-readers. I also appreciate the work of my agent, Mary Sue Seymour, and my editors, Becky Philpott and Sue Brower. My husband deserves a special thanks. His patience as I submerge myself in the writing process continues to amaze me.

I enjoyed this return visit to northern Indiana. If you're in the area, I encourage you to stop by Middlebury, Goshen, Nappanee, Elkhart, and Shipshewana. Visit the local shops, enjoy the beautiful countryside, and by all means take a walk along the Pumpkinvine Nature Trail.

And finally . . . *always giving thanks to God the Father for everything, in the name of our Lord Jesus Christ* (Ephesians 5:20).

Blessings,
Vannetta

8. In chapter thirty-four Tate realizes the time has come to trust God again, and to trust the things that God puts on his heart. Describe a time you've had trouble trusting the Lord. Then describe a time when you did place your trust in him.

9. By the end of the story, Hannah is no longer irritated by the small things her sister, Mattie, does. After all she has been through, Hannah realizes the value of life and the importance of her family. Discuss a time when you were especially grateful for your family.

10. Hannah's mother tells her, "*Gotte* will direct you. He loves you." In the end, that's all we really need to know—that God does love us. How has God shown his love to you, and how has he been directing you?

⊰ Discussion Questions ⊱

1. In chapter two we learn that Tate is reading through the gospel of Luke, but the words don't seem to make any sense to him. Later, when he hears the ambulance rushing toward the Village, he understands that his reaction is not charitable. How can we be more Christ-like, even when we don't feel like it?

2. Chapter five finds Hannah talking to her mother about Ethan's death. Eunice reminds her that death "marks a place with special memories because it's where a soul left this world and entered the next." Sometimes people are uncomfortable with death. What can we do to make such times easier for each other?

3. Amber's heart desires friendship. In chapter nine she wrestles with this. "She'd always been a friendly person, but it seemed close friendships were hard to come by." Do you agree that close friendships are rare? How can we have more meaningful relationships with those we see on a day-to-day basis?

4. In chapter eighteen we learn one of Amber's main worries. She considers the Village to be

a mission, "a haven of sorts. A place where people can work and rest in peace." But it had become a place of possible danger. How important are such places for all of us? Name one that you've been to in the last year, and express how it served to revive you mentally, spiritually, and emotionally.

5. In chapter twenty-four we meet Preston Johnstone, who is a veteran. Preston is homeless and living in a city park, but it's obvious from the things he says to Tate that he is on the mend. Often our veterans do have trouble transitioning back to civilian life, though their difficulties aren't always as obvious as Preston's. List ways we can help these memers of our community who have served in the military.

6. When Hannah attends church, she is convicted about "the peace of Christ." She hasn't *felt* peaceful. Can you relate? What does "the peace of Christ" mean to you, and how can it help with daily trials?

7. In chapter thirty Amber hears a sermon about King David. She's disturbed by this picure of David, this imperfect picture. Why do you think the Bible includes the experiences of flawed individuals? What can we learn from these portions of Scripture?